PRAISE FOR *MURDERLAND*

"A black, comic, highly suspenseful literary thriller of the mob and conspiracy-theory myths that permeate American pop culture. *MurderLand* is a hugely entertaining look at the dark side of the American dream, particularly through the author's invention of MurderLand—a landmark tourist trap of murder-related memorabilia set in the center of the old, tacky, Coney Island-like entertainment district overlooking Niagara Falls. Definitely one of the best books I've read in a long time. You'll never see the picturesque innocent honeymoon capital of the world again in the same way after reading this unique, gritty literary tour de force which is both wacky and profound."

JAMES DUBRO, PAST PRESIDENT, CRIME WRITERS OF CANADA; AUTHOR OF MOB RULE: INSIDE THE CANADIAN MAFIA, DRAGONS OF CRIME, AND OTHER TRUE CRIME BESTSELLERS; DERRICK MURDOCH AWARD WINNER AND TWO-TIME ARTHUR ELLIS AWARD NOMINEE

"Think of *MurderLand* as Joseph Heller, Elmore Leonard, and Carl Hiaasen meeting up in Niagara Falls at an episode of the *Antiques Roadshow* gone wrong. Glazner's antihero, Harry Holiday, is a fascinating train wreck. Glazner may well have written the crime novel equivalent of *Catch 22*. An absolute treat from beginning to end."

AL ABRAMSON, THREE-TIMES CHAIR OF BOUCHERCON, THE WORLD'S LEADING ANNUAL INTERNATIONAL CONFERENCE OF CRIME FICTION

"Beautiful, lean writing; rich, original characters, and the fresh and unusual location of *MurderLand* made me think of John Berendt's novel, *Midnight in the Garden of Good and Evil*. I loved it."

JOHN BECK, ACTOR (PAT GARRETT AND BILLY THE KID, SLEEPER, ROLLERBALL, DALLAS)

"I loved *MurderLand*. It is an original, gripping, and funny as hell story. More twists than a snake on drugs. I liked its weird characters and connection to JFK's assassination. What makes Harry Holiday totally believable and memorable is that he is refreshingly irreverent and politically incorrect. This is *noir* writing at its best. A masterpiece of edgy, smart literature."

CHRISTOPHER G. MOORE, SHAMUS AND GERMAN CRITICS' AWARD WINNER, AUTHOR OF THE VINCENT CALVINO SERIES

"Joseph Mark Glazner has produced a relentlessly intense ride full of hairpin turns that make *MurderLand* a compulsion from the first page. Inverting all the usual narrative touch points of the sleuthing thriller, he gives us a new kind of lead character in a deliciously rendered subterranean world. Meticulously researched and incisive, *MurderLand* casts disturbing shadows across its characters, their turbulent world, and America itself."

SALEM ALATON, JOURNALIST AND *LITERARY REVIEW OF CANADA* REVIEWER

"Love him. Hate him. Love him. Hate him. Just when you think you've made up your mind about Harry Holiday, hero of *MurderLand*, he spins you around with another exceedingly good or bad deed. It makes for a thoroughly involving, interesting and entertaining read from start to finish."

PHIL HAYNES, FOUNDER AND CREATIVE DIRECTOR,
JOE HILL COMMUNICATIONS, TORONTO

"A wonderful, contemporary walk on the wild side with edgy, unpredictable characters, dark, penetrating insight and humor, and set in a part of Niagara Falls that the tourists never see. In its own unique way, *MurderLand* is put together with as much care, brilliance, and originality as such classics as *The Confederacy of the Dunces* [John Kennedy Toole] and *Slaughterhouse-Five* [Kurt Vonnegut]."

BRUCE BEERY, ARCHITECT/DESIGNER, CENTRAL COAST, CALIFORNIA

"*MurderLand* grabs you by the throat and will not put you down until you've read the last page. I loved it. Each time I tried to stop reading, a new twist kept me going. Joseph Mark Glazner's research into the history of American gangland crime, the Kennedy assassination, and murder-related memorabilia is staggering, and he integrates it seamlessly into a riveting plot that draws you gradually into darker and darker places. But the darkest, most devilish aspect of *MurderLand* is its main character, Harry Holiday. He makes you wish desperately that a young Humphrey Bogart were still with us, because you can't imagine another actor capable of capturing Harry's combination of offensive hard-boiled amorality and tender engaging commitment. The chill of finding yourself cheering for this character you're sure you should despise is one of the special charms of this thriller."

HELAINE GOLANN, PHD, PSYCHOLOGIST, BOSTON

"Totally captivating. Awesome. A literary gem of the highest quality. I loved it."

LARISSA COVATO, PH.D, ENGLISH, TORONTO

"If the Coen brothers wrote books, they would have written *MurderLand*. It is fresh, wild, and wonderfully inventive."

CYNTHIA COULTER, INTERNATIONAL BUSINESS CONSULTANT, LOS ANGELES

"In *MurderLand*, Joseph Mark Glazner peels back the glitzy façade of a flashy tourist town and plunges us into the ugliness beneath, providing the perfect backdrop for this uniquely twisted coming of age story, full of sex, drugs, and deadly secrets."

COLEEN STEELE, MYSTERY AND SUSPENSE WRITER AND TWO-TIME ARTHUR ELLIS AWARD NOMINEE, BOWMANVILLE, ONTARIO

"I sat down with a cup of coffee on Friday afternoon, intending to read a few pages of *MurderLand*. When I looked up, I was already a third of the way through and couldn't stop. I stayed up all night to finish it. Wonky, compelling characters set against one of the greatest natural wonders of the world. A great, great read and terrific fun from a master storyteller."

BILL KURCHAK, BUSINESS EXECUTIVE AND TV PRODUCER, VANCOUVER

"I loved it. Politically incorrect, bold, sexy, provocative, fast paced, and funny with a parade of intriguing and original characters and a story that unfolds on a dozen levels at once. What more could you ask for in a first-rate thriller?"

TOM LEVIN, LAWYER AND CORPORATE CONSULTANT, LOS ANGELES

"Thoroughly enjoyable. Escapist literature at its best."

DWIGHT GOLANN, LAW PROFESSOR, BOSTON

"A hard boiled and exciting page turner with characters that came out from the shadows long enough to make *MurderLand* one of those dark pearls, which kept me totally on the edge of my seat. The historical references woven into the story added to the fun. Kudos!"

DANIEL KRAMON, PH.D., PSYCHOLOGIST, LOS ANGELES

"I just loved it. The off-the-wall characters, a haunting, memorable setting, and a roguish, yet delightfully charming protagonist completely captured my imagination."

JILL FITZGERALD, BOOK REVIEWER, MONTREAL

MurderLand

A crime novel

Joseph Mark Glazner

Published by Joseph Mark Glazner
Toronto, Ontario, Canada
Email: glaznerbooks@sympatico.ca

Front and Back Cover Design by Joseph Mark Glazner
Front cover photo, Niagara Falls, December 2003, © Joseph Mark Glazner
Back cover photo, © Joanie Shirriff, 2017, used with permission
Formatting and Interior Design by Woven Red Author Services, www.WovenRed.ca

MurderLand /Joseph Mark Glazner—First Edition
ISBN ebook: 978-1-7750058-4-1
ISBN print book: 978-1-7750058-5-8

For Joanie Shirriff with all my love.

CHAPTER 1

MONDAY

I TWISTED TO ONE SIDE, hoping to deflect Joey Angelo's punches to my stomach and chest.

"Straighten him out, Pinkie," Joey told his partner in crime. Pinkie the Lizard was holding me from behind in a full nelson. He yanked me straight again so Joey could resume slugging me.

Joey hadn't even worked up a sweat. Pinkie was another matter. I could hear the three-hundred-pound thug grunting in my ear, trying to see how close he could get to breaking my arms without actually breaking them.

"I'm sorry about this," Joey said between punches, not sounding very sorry.

Years ago, Joey Angelo and I briefly went to high school together.

Before he dropped out—embarrassed to be seventeen and still a freshman—Joey had shown me how to hot-wire a car and trip a door lock with a credit card. I'd shown him how to sneak into the country club without looking suspicious so we could steal cases of beer from the banquet hall.

That was then, this is now, I thought, wondering how many more punches I could take before I passed out.

"Hit the fucker in the face, Joey," Pinkie insisted. Pinkie the Lizard, another long-ago dropout from my high school, got his name from a childhood disease that left him with flakey, reptilian skin the color of bubble gum. "Split his lips open so we can get out of here and go eat."

No doubt, Joey could have split my head open if he wanted to. Before going to work for my bookie, Frankie Argyll, Joey had briefly been in and out of the fight game as a featherweight. His downfall was that he could punch but he couldn't take a punch. He'd been knocked out cold in his first and only professional bout.

"Just hold him straight, Pinkie." Joey sounded annoyed.

Pinkie gave my arms an upward jerk that sent a new jolt of pain to my brain.

"Argh," I cried in spite of my best efforts to deny them the satisfaction of knowing just how much I was hurting.

Joey lifted his eyebrows. "Attaboy, Harry. Show me the pain. Then, I can tell Frankie I did my job." Thunk-thunk-thunk. He threw a few more blows at my gut and ribs.

Eager to please Joey, Pinkie yanked hard on my arms again.

I forced myself to remain silent. I wasn't much of a brawler, but I had an unusually high tolerance for pain.

"You're lucky, Harry. I'd be busting your legs or knocking your teeth out right now if Frankie didn't like you," Joey said.

"Frankie knows I'm good for the money."

Frankie Argyll had been lending me money for years. He had been my father's bookie forever. I had every intention of making good on my debts. Somehow.

"You owe thirty-five grand, Harry. Frankie says you're out of control."

"Bullshit. I'm not out of control," I said, knowing full well I was.

Joey stopped punching and instead slapped me a couple of times across my face with the back of his small, gloved hand.

I suppressed the urge to kick him in the balls. With Pinkie behind me, ready to pull my arms out, my odds of surviving weren't good.

Besides, the idiots are only doing their jobs, I told myself just before Joey took a couple of quick shots at my stomach, knocking the wind out of me.

"See if he can stand on his own," Joey told Pinkie.

When Pinkie let go, I tried to stay on my feet to show them how tough I was.

In spite of my best efforts, my legs gave way under me. As I crashed to the ground, gasping for air, I heard a crunch from my pocket where I kept my phone.

"Good boy," Joey said, stepping back to admire his work. "Now, remember, Harry. Pay up by the end of the day, or we gotta do this all over again. Frankie told me to tell you: 'No more extensions.'"

"Yeah, fucker. Pay up," Pinkie grunted. He kicked me in the rear as he waddled by.

"Kiss my butt, Pinkie," I wheezed.

If I could have lifted a finger, I would have flipped him the bird.

No doubt if he was quicker, he would have taken another swipe at me, but Joey grabbed his arm and pulled him down the driveway.

For the next five minutes, I just lay there in the parking lot of Murder-Land, staring over the roof of the museum at the clouds drifting overhead, west to east, while I choked down the thought of killing someone. I didn't regard myself as a violent person, but lately, the list of people I wanted to see dead had been growing.

It was late February. Niagara Falls had been experiencing a week of cooler than normal weather. Even with the sun out in the middle of the day, the temperature rarely rose above freezing.

Look on the bright side, I told myself. The brisk weather had its advantages. The cold air felt soothing on my face. My down coat and heavy sweater had absorbed some of Joey's punches, and my driving gloves had saved my hands when I fell. No bones seemed to be broken anywhere although my ribs hurt like hell when I took a deep breath.

I thought help might be on its way when an elderly couple entered the parking lot from the driveway. They stopped, silently stared, and then made a wide berth around me to get to their car, which was the only other vehicle in the lot besides my father's old, powder-blue Lincoln Continental—mine now. Unfortunately, Dad's Jaguar had been totaled when he'd been run off the road and nearly killed.

"Did you enjoy the museum?" I mumbled.

The elderly couple quickly got into their car, pretending they hadn't heard me.

Bottom feeders, I thought. They probably hadn't been to the museum. They'd just found a free place to park so they could spend their old age pensions on the nickel slots at the casino down the street.

I began to cough from the exhaust when the bottom feeders started their car. It took me another ten minutes after they drove off to stagger to my feet. I checked my phone. It was smashed beyond repair. I hobbled through the rear door of the museum and down the hallway toward the ticket counter in front, looking for my assistant, Gina Polly.

The ticket counter and front door were unattended. Again.

Anyone could have walked in for free.

I should have been pissed, but who was I kidding? In the six months since I'd been forced to take control of the business, MurderLand had been drowning in red ink. In the darkest days of the off-season, the museum, which once owned the world's largest collection of murder and gangland-related artifacts, was like a morgue.

I dragged myself into my father's office. It was mine now, but I'd been too busy trying to save the business to worry about changing the décor.

I eased myself into the padded swivel chair behind my desk with almost as much effort as it had taken me to get to my feet in the parking lot.

I wheeled the chair to the TV surveillance monitor that used to sit at the security guard's station before I'd downsized the security staff. I zeroed in on the staff lounge. Gina was there, gawking at herself in a hand mirror, trying to make sense of her tangled blond and pink dreadlocks. What a mess.

Life can be messy I reminded myself as I let my head fall back on the headrest for a few seconds. The office was a daily reminder of the old glory days of my family's business. The walls were filled with framed, black-and-white, celebrity photos; giant, multicolored posters; and my father's and grandfather's hunting trophies. The celebrity photos were of Mae West, Jean Harlow, Marilyn Monroe, Joe DiMaggio, and dozens of others—all with my late grandfather or father in the photos and inscribed to them. The large, gaudy, polychrome posters had once been displayed out front like carnival broadsides, steering the tourists into a sideshow. Niagara Falls enjoyed the reputation of being the most visited natural wonder in North America with more than twelve million tourists a year from every corner of the globe. Despite being the Honeymoon Capital of the World, families with kids were the mainstay of the tourist industry. Kids wanted thrills and freak shows, not natural wonders. The Clifton Hill tourist district overlooking the Rainbow Bridge was kitsch central— the place where the tourists flocked in droves in the summer to buy cotton candy, ice cream, T-shirts, supposedly genuine Canadian souvenirs made in China, and tickets to crazy, lowbrow exhibits like ours.

In the past, MurderLand had proudly competed head-on with the very best Clifton Hill tourist traps that fed people like me. The posters hanging on our walls depicted some of the treasures that used to lure the curious to MurderLand by the busload. At one time, we had on display some of the most famous icons of past crimes—a Browning Automatic Rifle owned by Clyde Barrow of Bonnie and Clyde fame; a tooth from the step-mother that Lizzie Borden had axed to death; underpants from one of the Boston strangler's victims; a Remington 10 pump-action 12 gauge trench shotgun that Al Capone carried with him in his golf bag on the golf course; a prison outfit that Teamsters boss, Jimmy Hoffa, wore when he did time at Lewiston for jury tampering and fraud; the barber chair in which Murder Incorporated's high executioner, Albert Anastasia, was shot to death; and the Sing Sing electric chair that was used to execute seven of Murder, Inc.'s most notorious hoods, including Louis "Lepke" Buchalter, the highest-ranking crime boss ever to fry. The electric chair was so popular in the old days that my grandfather and father hired a full-time staff photographer to snap pictures of the kids sitting in it—MurderLand's answer to the department store Santa Claus.

Due to a run of bad luck, I had been forced to sell most of these treasures to help keep the museum afloat. Even that wasn't enough. If it wasn't for my luck at sports betting and the casinos most of the time, MurderLand would have already folded instead of just dying a slow death.

After six months under my management the museum had been reduced to exhibiting cheap reproductions of weapons and artifacts, scale models of famous murders, photo displays, and tableaus with costumed mannequins of famous murderers and their victims—the most popular of which remained an exhibit on the second floor depicting the assassination of President John F. Kennedy. The trouble was that we were no longer drawing the kids. Most of our recent customers were seniors or cheapskates looking for the most budget-friendly exhibits in town.

"You can rest assured no one will ever sell you, Old Smokey," I said to the stuffed grizzly bear beside my father's desk. The bear stood on all fours as if getting ready to charge. Its large glass eyes and ferocious jaws appeared at eye level to anyone sitting in the chair on the other side of my desk. My father shot Old Smokey as well as half of the moose, mountain lions, fox, big horns, and elk whose heads graced the office walls. My grandfather shot the rest.

Visiting the office as a child, the grizzly had always been a favorite of mine. I would stand on a chair, climb on its back, and pretend the bear and I were charging the bad guys. The bear became even more important to me when I found out that its nose could be pulled off, revealing a large secret cavity in its head. As a preteen, I used the nook to hide candy bars I'd jimmied from the museum's vending machines. More recently, the cavity had become the repository for my recreational drugs.

In addition to weed, I was a fan of Soma, the latest, all-natural, mood-altering drug circulating on the street. Its name was a tribute to a euphoric drug in Aldous Huxley's dystopian novel *Brave New World*. Soma's greatest appeal was that it produced a sense of well-being without turning you into a zombie, and at the same time, it boosted your energy without making you aggressive. It came from lichen discovered by some health guru in the Canadian Arctic. Old potheads called Soma the new marijuana because it could be smoked or ingested like cannabis. Some called it the new coke because it also could be chopped up and inhaled like cocaine for instant results. It was expensive, semi-legal, hard to get, and, so far, impossible to detect in humans.

I was in the process of reaching for the pharmaceuticals, hoping to take the edge off my bruises, when Pilot came shuffling in.

Felix "Pilot" Pringle had been working for MurderLand since my grandfather founded the museum in the 1940s.

"You all right?" he asked. In the few surviving photographs from the early days of the museum, Pilot looked old even as a young man. Then as now, he had the same skinny frame and concave chest. A few tufts of wispy, prematurely white hair hung from the sides of his otherwise bald head. Thin lips, sunken cheeks, and watery, gray eyes gave him a ghoulish look. A master of odd jobs, one of his skills that fascinated me as a child was taxidermy. Over the years he had stuffed all the hunting trophies in my granddad's and dad's collections and carried out all of the taxidermy and preservation projects at MurderLand.

"I'm fine." I managed a weak smile.

"You look like shit."

For many years, Pilot had not only managed MurderLand but was my grandfather's and father's chauffer on business trips. Back in the old days before my father sold the Cessna, Pilot had also been my father's and grandfather's pilot, flying them around Canada and the US to hunt game and chase new acquisitions for the museum.

"Any customers while I was gone?" I'd taken the morning off to try to win enough at the craps tables to repay Frankie.

"The place has been dead all morning," Pilot said, lowering his scarecrow frame into the chair opposite me. He pulled a pack of unfiltered cigarettes and matches from the inside pocket of his faded blue MurderLand blazer and lit up. "I saw you getting the crap beat out of you. You ought to let me look at those bruises of yours. I got some liniment in my locker."

"I'm fine," I insisted.

"I would have tried to stop them, but they'd only come back, and I didn't think you wanted me to call the cops."

"Everything's under control." I wondered how Pilot might have tried to stop them. I'd seen moderate winds almost knock him over on Victoria Avenue on his walk home.

"Frankie Argyll won't mess with you once your father's back on his feet."

My father had been semicomatose for six months since his stroke. The stroke had been triggered by someone ramming his car into the Niagara River. Pilot was the only person who believed Dad would come out of it. Not wanting to hear the miracles-can-happen shit, I changed the subject to more pressing problems.

"I need to raise some quick cash, Pilot."

"How much you talking about?"

"At least thirty-five grand. Forty or forty-five would be better."

He frowned. "You sell any more of the good stuff and you won't have enough to draw the crowds."

Crowds? What a joke. MurderLand hadn't drawn crowds in years.

"So what would you do?"

"Not for me to say. You're in charge until your old man gets back."

"All right, then what would my dad do?"

As far as I could tell, the attendance over the past few years hadn't been much different from my six months on the job. Yet, somehow, my father always made a pretty good living from the business—good enough to support four marriages, cover the costs of the museum, and live well.

Pilot just shrugged.

"So what does that mean? You don't know or you won't tell me?"

"How many times did your old man ask you to spend more time with him and learn the business instead of chasing nooky and get-rich-quick schemes in Toronto?"

How do you explain being young, full of testosterone, and wanting to do your own thing to a geezer like Pilot? How could someone as ancient as him understand that today is nothing like the past? You can't. Why bother? Instead I asked, "How many times did I hear Dad tell me he could never fire you because you knew too much? So, what exactly do you know, Pilot?"

"What I know is I didn't get no Christmas bonus like your old man used to give me, and I didn't get no raise."

"And I'm not drawing a salary."

He shrugged again like he could care less about my problems.

"Help me out here, Pilot. We're only having a temporary setback. To get back on our feet, we need to sell some of the old artifacts and create more contemporary exhibits." I was determined to revive MurderLand. It was in my blood. It had been in my father's and grandfather's blood. I felt a family obligation to keep the legacy alive. Besides, it was also the only thing I had going. If I could just get a little ahead, I could keep the doors open.

He took the cigarette from his mouth and spit a speck of tobacco into the wastepaper basket. "Ain't gonna be easy. All the good stuff in the display rooms has already been sold."

"There has to be more in the basement."

"You stay out of my goddamned basement. You've been messing things up down there since you came back. I can't find anything."

The basement had always been a mess, but Pilot had always considered it his mess. It was also the only place left where anything of value might turn up.

"If you don't want me down there, then bring me something I can use to raise money."

"Tyrant."

"Get Gina to help you. She can lock the front door. If any customers show up, I'll hear the buzzer and handle them."

"You tell her. That witch don't listen to me. This morning, I told her she should be studying the manual. She told me to go fuck myself. Ha. If I could fuck anything, I'd be happy."

The museum manual was an ancient employee guide that Pilot put together years before so the staff could answer visitors' questions about the displays. Pilot had been fighting with Gina for months, trying to get her to read it.

"When you see her, send her in. I'll have a word with her."

He stubbed out his cigarette in the overflowing ashtray and slowly stood.

"Fire the little minx. She's useless. You know what she told me the other day? She said, 'Hey, what's the big deal about this Kennedy guy anyway? So, someone shot him. Who cares?'"

Pilot went bug-eyed as he mimicked Gina's high, squeaky voice.

"Get me something good from the basement, and no one needs to be fired. And shut the door on the way out."

As soon as the door closed, I slid the nose off the old grizzly and retrieved the Soma I'd been saving for a special occasion. At the moment, nothing could be more special than easing my sore ribs.

I probably should have locked the door, but the thought of walking that far was too painful. So I just shook out enough Soma on top of the desk for a couple of lines and started chopping it up with the edge of one of my half dozen cancelled credit cards.

I was rolling a ten-dollar bill into a nose hose when Gina came through the door sooner than I expected and without knocking.

"The old fart said you wanted to see me," she snarled, then smiled as soon as she noticed what I was doing. She leaned over the desk, brushing her blond and pink dreadlocks over her shoulders. She eyed the Soma.

God, I thought, I love women, and everything about them—the way they look, the way they feel, their perfumes and aromas, all the different sizes and shapes, the way their minds work, and all the rest. Crazy Gina was no exception. Having a woman around the place seemed to brighten my spirits.

But womanhood wasn't the main reason I'd hired her. Gina was there to help me qualify for a special tax credit for the museum for hiring a student—Gina was studying at night to be a nail technician. She was also the only person I could find willing to work six days a week, five hours a day for minimum wage.

"You want to do a line?" I asked.

Hazel eyes sparkled. She held out her hand for the ten-dollar bill. We each did a line.

"That's it? That's what you wanted to see me about?" she asked, wiping the dust from her nose and licking her fingers with her plump, electric-pink lips.

"Sit down," I told her as I chopped up enough Soma for two more lines.

"Why? What're you gonna do? Quiz me? Like, what am I supposed to know about the Kennedy thing? It had something to do with the Nazis or something. Right?"

In a stretch, I thought, she was almost right. President Kennedy's father, Joseph P. Kennedy, had been a fan of Hitler. Old Joe had cozied up to Nazi sympathizers in England when he'd been US Ambassador to Great Britain before the US entered World War II.

"Something like that," I said, unable to suppress a smile.

"Then, I passed the test? What do I get?"

"I'd like you to help Pilot in the basement."

"It's not in my job description."

"You don't have a job description, Gina. You were hired as a general assistant. I want you to assist Pilot."

"I don't like him. He creeps me out. He keeps brushing up against me when he walks by. He pretends it's an accident. You should fire him."

"Nobody's getting fired."

She wanted to argue, but she couldn't keep her eyes off the drugs.

"Do me a favor. Be nice to Pilot and you can do another line."

"And I don't have to read the manual?"

"Read the manual when you're sitting at the ticket counter."

"I have to watch out for customers."

"There are no customers."

"Whatever." She stood, grabbed the bill from me, leaned over the desk, and snorkeled up the Soma.

As soon as she finished, she started to walk away with the ten-dollar bill still in her hand.

"The money," I said.

"Yeah, sure, whatever, and don't think I'm forgetting the raise that's supposed to be coming to me." She tossed me the bill and wiggled out the door, a Soma grin pasted on her lips.

A few seconds after I finished the last line of Soma, the phone rang.

What little euphoria I was feeling quickly evaporated when the caller ID flashed the name of my father's lawyer, Wally Lavaleer.

His secretary was on the line. "Mr. Lavaleer wants to remind you of your meeting in his office at two."

"Don't worry. I'll be there."

"I'll let him know." She hung up.

I felt a headache coming on just thinking about the meeting with Lavaleer and my stepmother. For months, the two of them had been cooking up schemes to wrestle the museum out of my hands. So far I'd been able to beat them back.

I had enough time before my meeting with Lavaleer to visit Dad at the nursing home. I grabbed a handful of painkillers, washed them down with a couple of swigs of scotch from my father's liquor cabinet, and headed out the door for my daily visit. On the drive over, I continued to rack my brain for a way to come up with Frankie's money before midnight.

CHAPTER 2

AS I HOBBLED INTO MY FATHER'S ROOM at the Graystone Nursing Home, Clive Elway looked up from his *manhua*, one of the Chinese comic books he read in his free time.

Clive Elway, a short, thin, twenty-something Jamaican-Canadian, had come to Niagara Falls a couple of years before to escape the gangs in Toronto. He wore a tan dread brim over his dark brown dreadlocks. As usual, his hat was pulled low in front over foxlike brown eyes.

Besides being the daytime orderly on my father's wing at the nursing home, Clive was teaching himself Chinese. He insisted the garish, 400-page comic books that focused on Kung Fu legends, were the best and quickest way to learn. He was convinced the Chinese intended to buy up the rest of Canada over the next decade.

I handed him one of the two veal cutlet sandwiches I'd picked up from Tony's Restaurant before coming to the nursing home.

Clive saw me wince as I lowered myself into the chair beside my father's bed.

"So why don't you ask me what happened, Clive?" Clive never missed a thing but was way too cool to ask.

"I already know," he said while unwrapping his sandwich. "A couple of thugs came by earlier looking for you. The big one said they were intending to rough you up. It appears they found you." In spite of the hip-hop look, he had ditched his Jamaican accent for a faux British one, though he could switch back and forth when it suited him.

"What's new with you?" I asked, nodding toward the empty bed beside my dad's.

"Mr. Peabody left us for another world this morning. I'm enjoying a bit of a rest until they bring me a new client." Clive called his patients *clients*. One of his many dreams was to work his way into business somehow. When he wasn't busy with one of his Chinese comic books, he was reading *The Economist*, a magazine I had recommended when I found out he was interested in finance and world affairs. For a kid who hated school and had dropped out at sixteen, he was nevertheless determined to better himself.

"How's my dad doing?" I asked as I unwrapped the second sandwich and left it on the bedside table as close to Dad as possible.

"You father's condition remains the same," Clive said as he munched on his sandwich.

It was almost incomprehensible for me to see my dad at death's door. My father, the athletic, always healthy-looking guy with the quiet voice and a smile for everyone, now looked like a waxy, gray corpse.

The car accident had put his right arm and both legs in casts. His bones had healed, but he hadn't recovered from his stroke. He had been lying in a semicomatose state for six months, asleep more than he was awake. Even with his eyes open, he didn't appear to recognize anyone or anything.

I reached out and held his hand, a hand that once could have crushed anyone's in a handshake if he'd been that type of guy. Of late, it had the feel of the cold, dead gerbil I'd accidentally stepped on when I was eight. My father had given me the gerbil—the only pet I ever had—out of guilt after my mother dropped her radio into her bathtub and electrocuted herself when I was seven.

"Hey, Dad, it's me, Harry." I bent close to my father's ear. "How are you doing?"

Out of the corner of my eye I could see Clive shaking his head as he continued to work his way through his sandwich.

I ignored him and leaned closer, listening to Dad. Sometimes, I thought I could hear him speaking. The gerontologist said it was just his irregular breathing, but I was sure it was more than that.

I listened hard.

What he usually seemed to be saying was, "Okay, Jenny. Not in the face"—whatever the hell that could mean. I wanted to believe the sounds were words and not just gurgling.

"Look, Dad, I brought your favorite sandwich." I held his sandwich closer, almost touching his nose.

If anything would shake Ralph Holiday out of his coma, it would be a whiff of a veal cutlet and spicy tomato sauce sandwich from Tony's. For nearly six months, since my father had been moved from the hospital to the chronic care facility, I'd brought him his favorite sandwich, the same sandwich he had eaten for lunch for as long as I could remember.

Even if it didn't shake him out of his coma, I hoped the smell would stir some pleasant memories for him.

I had my own memories of eating at Tony's with my father when I was a kid. Dad took me there for lunch whenever he brought me to work on Saturdays. I was intrigued because Tony, the owner, never let my father pay. I always thought it was because my father left such large tips for the waitresses. I only learned recently from the owner's son, Tony Junior, who had since taken over the business, that Tony Senior's wife had amyotrophic lateral sclerosis (ALS), a progressive neurological disease that disables and kills its victims. My father arranged to have Pilot fly Tony Senior and his wife to the Mayo Clinic in Minnesota in Dad's plane on a number of occasions and refused to take any money for it. I found out that Ralph Holiday had done scores of good deeds like this for friends over the years. There wasn't a charity in town that he hadn't contributed to.

I looked up just as Clive finished his sandwich and dusted his hands off.

"You want the other sandwich?" I asked.

Clive usually ended up eating the second sandwich as well.

"Later, Harry. I have work to do." He got to his feet. "If you really want to bond with your father, may I suggest you help me change his diaper?"

I suddenly remembered my appointment with Wally Lavaleer and my stepmother. I hightailed it out of there in a hurry.

CHAPTER 3

WALLY LAVALEER'S LAW OFFICE WAS LOCATED on Queen Street in a two-story brick building in the old downtown. Like many small-town main streets, Niagara's once-bustling town center had taken a hit from which it had never recovered. The newer malls and shopping centers built in the suburbs had gutted the business district. The lawyers only remained downtown because the police, courthouse, and city hall were still there.

My stepmother, Carlene Holiday, my father's fourth wife, was already in Lavaleer's office when I arrived. She was a head-turner in her late thirties with flawless ivory skin and wavy, shoulder-length, platinum blond hair. Her face was heart-shaped with large brown eyes set over high cheek bones, an upturned nose, and a wide mouth with perfect teeth. A heavy gold and diamond necklace circled her long neck. She had a firm, healthy body, which she kept fine-tuned by obsessively patronizing half the yoga and fitness clubs in the region. She was dressed in a white blouse, navy blue sports coat, and gray skirt that showcased her long legs.

A former Miss Niagara Wine Region beauty contest winner and one-time day clerk at one of the local luxury hotels, she had snagged my father when he was taking his then-mistress to Carlene's hotel for lunchtime quickies while cheating on his third wife.

Carlene and I gave each other fake smiles.

"Let me guess, Harry," Carlene said, brushing a strand of hair away from her face as I limped to my seat, "your two friends, Joey and Pinkie, finally caught up with you."

"We did lunch." I said, reminding myself that adoring all women indiscriminately because they're women is just another form of sexism. It was a flaw I shared with my father. I was trying to overcome it, especially in light of my feelings toward Carlene.

The animosity was mutual.

Carlene and I had taken a dislike to each other from the moment she'd married my father and announced that she was moving into our house and redoing it. I was still living at home. I was about to enter a local university in the fall. I was expecting to commute, but she made short work of me. To keep the peace, my father sent me packing. I had to move out of the house and into one of the rundown dorms at the school. I was certain from the start that my old man, who was notorious for picking the wrong women, had married real trouble.

My feelings for Wally Lavaleer weren't much better.

"Always a pleasure," he said. Lavaleer was about six feet tall, fit, and broad shouldered with wavy brown hair combed straight back; thick eyebrows; heavy-lidded, condescending brown eyes; a Roman nose; a square jaw; and a rough, olive complexion. His gym-worked pecks pushed against the front of his white shirt and blue suit jacket as he stood to shake my hand. He gave me his best pretty-boy smile and squeezed my hand harder than necessary. Like my stepmother, he was in his late thirties and part of the circle of young movers and shakers around town.

"So, how are you two planning on screwing me today?" I asked.

"Oh, please, Harry. You're paranoid. No one's getting screwed." Carlene stared at me with disdain.

After the accident and after I returned home and began asking questions, I quickly found out that Carlene and Wally Lavaleer had been carrying on an affair for a year and a half before my father had ended up in his current state. Since the accident, Lavaleer and Carlene had dropped all pretenses and were using my father and stepmother's house for their late night hookups. When I had brought this up with the police, they shrugged it off and told me the case was closed.

The cops were convinced that no one, including Carlene, had made an attempt on my father's life. They thought my father had the stroke first and the accident second. The medical review was inconclusive. I, on the other hand, was certain the unidentified car, which had been seen racing away from the accident site, held the answer. I had convinced myself that my father's stroke was caused when his car had been run off the embankment and into the upper Niagara River. My instincts and Carlene's cavalier attitude toward my father made me certain my father's poor, grieving near-widow had her fingerprints all over the accident. Since returning home, one of my obsessions had been investigating the crash. I had hired a private detective, but he had been unable to find the other car or the woman who had anonymously called the police to report it speeding away. Despite the lack of hard evidence, I remained certain Carlene was involved.

"Let's get started," Lavaleer said, flashing beady shark eyes at me. "We have a lot to take care of. First and foremost we need to discuss new income generating prospects for the Clifton Hill property."

I jumped right in, lying through my teeth. "If you're worried about the rent, don't be. The museum's just experiencing the usual winter-spring slow season. Revenues should pick up nicely in the summer. I have a few new exhibits under consideration that should be real winners. I'm planning to add new artifacts and tableaus associated with a new roster of unusual celebrity deaths and recent terrorist attacks."

Carlene rolled her eyes. She had been whining for months about the shortfall in revenues from the museum. MurderLand, which was a separately incorporated business from the building itself, was supposed to pay rent and a percentage of its profits to the second corporation that owned the property. My old man had set up the two corporations and operated them through two separate trusts in order to protect his assets from his ex-wives.

"We'll talk about MurderLand in a moment," Lavaleer insisted. "Right now, I want to talk about the building. Carlene and I have discussed the property at great length and have come to the conclusion that we have better ways to maximize the return on those assets. To be specific, after months of careful planning and investigation, we've decided to turn over the assets to New Heights Hotels on a ninety-nine-year lease, terms to be renegotiated every twenty-five years at market rates. They already have plans underway to demolish the current structure and put up a twenty-story hotel. You will, of course, have to move the museum."

The proposal was new to me and outrageous. "You want me to move the museum while you rip down the building and put up a new one? What will that take—two or three years? You expect me to wait that long before

I move back?" My head reeled with the potential costs and disruption to MurderLand.

"Actually, we don't anticipate MurderLand returning to the new building."

My brain felt like it was exploding. "You're evicting me? You can't evict me."

"Your lease is up in three months," he insisted.

"But that's only a technicality between the two trusts. My father set it up so—"

"I know what your father did. My father was his lawyer and your grandfather's lawyer. The bottom line today is that the real estate trust is better off leasing the land to a major international hotel chain than a failing museum."

"I'll get the rent money."

"You should have thought of that before you started pocketing the receipts," Carlene piped in. "Though shall not steal."

Lavaleer gave her a sharp look.

Carlene ignored him and gave me her most righteous stare as if she wanted me to believe she had a direct line to God. The fundamentalist congregation she belonged to used scriptures to justify everything.

I kept calm. "Under the terms of my father's will—"

"Your father is still alive," Lavaleer cut me off.

"He's a vegetable."

"Exactly my point, Harry. In his diminished capacity, your stepmother and I have general power of attorney over his affairs. We can do anything with respect to your father's property that your father could do if he wasn't incapacitated."

Carlene nodded reverently.

"He wouldn't evict me."

"He wouldn't let you run the business into the ground and jeopardize my future," Carlene insisted.

"The bottom line is that we have no way of knowing what your father might do," Lavaleer said sweetly. "What we do know is that Carlene and I have been designated to oversee his affairs. We have a fiduciary responsibility to the trust."

The power of attorney part wasn't news to me. A few years before, when Carlene had been complaining about her future, my father, twenty-seven years her senior, had gone to Lavaleer to alter his will. I didn't care. I was living in Toronto promoting a couple of fly-by-night startups that were supposed to make me richer than Mark Zuckerberg. By then, I had already made, lost, and made again, several million. At the time, I had no interest in returning to Niagara or taking over MurderLand. To do what my father thought would be best for everyone, and on the advice of Lavaleer, Dad had made Carlene and Lavaleer co-executors of his will. He also assigned them co-powers of attorney over his property and health care. I was the alternate should either of them resign, become incapacitated, or die.

Killing both of them definitely crossed my mind at that moment.

"Of course, you'll be compensated," Lavaleer added.

I remained silent, not rising to the bait. Carlene glanced at Lavaleer. His eyes flickered in her direction for a second as if to tell her to keep her mouth shut.

"I would guesstimate that after the building is up, and after taxes, etcetera, you will be looking at two or three thousand a month as your end of the hotel deal," Lavaleer added.

So they were intending to hose me completely, I thought. "Two or three thousand a month sounds a little skinny to me for a twenty-story hotel on Clifton Hill a couple of blocks from the casino."

"The *old* casino, Harry. Who knows how long they'll even keep it open?"

The provincial government owned all the casinos in Ontario but ran them through private managers in privately leased buildings. The government had shelled out a billion dollars in taxpayers' money to erect the new hotel, a high-end indoor shopping galleria, and a Las Vegas-style casino and theater in the Fallsview district, a mile away from the old casino. Most of the newer high-end hotels were there.

"The action will come straight back to Clifton Hill if they turn the old casino into a convention center." The lack of a building large enough to hold massive, Vegas-sized conferences was one of the things keeping Niagara Falls from tapping into the international convention pie. Current rumors were floating around that if the government pulled the plug on the old casino, the owner of the property might convert the building into a conference center.

"The convention center's only a rumor. New Heights is already committed. They're ready to build regardless."

"That still doesn't explain why the payout to the trust is so small, especially since we're the only parcel of land on Clifton Hill not tied up with one of the big boys." The big boys were the four families that owned virtually all of the property around the two casinos.

"New Heights will have to invest a lot and defer its own profits for some time. They're planning to put up a very impressive building."

"Or—let me guess—the costs you talked about—the *etcetera* to be exact—also include fees for a separate management company to handle the transactions between the hotel and me." Management companies appeared to be one of the tricks my father used between his trusts and his actual business entities to siphon money into his own pocket.

Lavaleer cleared his throat. "As a matter of fact, we thought it best to operate a management company as an intermediary between the tenant and the trust."

"Let me guess. You and Carlene are the managers."

Lavaleer gave me the slightest smile as he handed me a document of a dozen pages. "This explains it all."

"You get to keep the museum," Carlene said sarcastically, "or what's left after you finish looting it."

"And you two think I'm going to agree to this?" I flipped through the pages. "I'll never sign this."

"I'm sorry, Harry. You misunderstand," Lavaleer said. "There's nothing to sign. What I gave you is simply a memorandum of what's happening. As your father's attorneys we're doing this in his best interests. Let me add, of course, that if he recovers and wishes to do something else, that's his prerogative."

"Fat chance," Carlene said, suddenly more interested in her lacquered green nails than me.

CHAPTER 4

GINA WAS SITTING at the ticket counter when I returned. She had only lasted five minutes in the basement before Pilot sent her upstairs again.

"He was annoyed because I couldn't answer any of his questions. He thinks I should know the difference between the First World War and the Second," she said. "Who gives a shit? They're both over, right?"

I had the feeling if I told her they weren't, she would believe me.

"Right," I said.

"Oh, and I got some money for you." She opened the cash register.

Sending Gina to the ticket counter had actually turned out to be the best thing that could have happened. Benny Cole, a local tour guide we had been paying under the table for years, had come through with a half full bus of German tourists. After Benny had skimmed off his take, we'd pulled in a couple of hundred bucks in cash, twenty of which I advanced to Gina on her salary so she could leave early for the veterinarian's to retrieve Cuddles, her pet boa constrictor.

After she left, I locked the front door and headed straight to my office to get a second opinion on Carlene and Wally's scheme.

The only lawyer in town I could trust not to go running back to Wally was Melanie Wickers. I dialed her number and got her voice mail. I left her a message to call me as soon as possible.

I might not like Carlene, I reminded myself, but I would be a fool to underestimate her.

My stepmother was shallow and vain but also determined and willing to do anything for power and money. Before she met my father, she tried to parlay her beauty contest win and her blind ambition into a career in politics. She became the youngest ever candidate for the America-Canada Unification Party, a fringe group that favored amalgamation of the US and Canada. Like the rest of her party that year, she came in last behind Canada's Rhinoceros Party.

My lawyer returned my call a couple of minutes later and said she was tied up in meetings until five o'clock, but she asked me to fax the document Lavaleer gave me. "I can meet you at my office after five," she said, "and bring some you-know-what."

I made a mental note to score some high-grade weed for her. In spite of the relaxed and changing reefer laws, Melanie didn't want any of her clients to see her coming or going from a cannabis outlet. She also didn't want her name on any lists associated with the government or its marijuana mail-order licensees.

My bruises were still bothering me, so I downed a couple of shots of whisky before I went hunting for Pilot.

I heard him banging around below as soon as I opened the door to the basement. I yelled down, "Pilot, I'm back. Come up here. Show me what you've found."

Five minutes later, he wandered into my office with a tattered, old shoebox under one arm and a couple of plastic shopping bags dangling from the opposite hand. He set the box on my desk. As he sank slowly into the chair opposite me, he asked, "You know how come there're so many theories about why President Kennedy was shot, don't you?"

"Of course. Because so many people wanted him dead."

Not only was the assassination of JFK a mainstay of the museum, but it was one of Pilot's favorite subjects. He had drilled the facts into me before I could read. At the time of President Kennedy's assassination, the people who were seriously angry at him included: Fidel Castro; most of the Cuban exile community in the US; about half of the CIA and the US military-industrial establishment; Chicago-based Sam Giancana, the mafia kingpin of the Midwest; Meyer Lansky, number two in the National Crime Syndicate; FBI Director J. Edgar Hoover; and Teamsters boss James R. Hoffa. Even onetime Kennedy pal, Frank Sinatra, was pissed to the gills at the president.

"Gina has no idea who Kennedy is," he said. "She thinks he was one of the Beatles. I'm losing faith in young people."

"Gina's not all young people," I said, trying to cheer him.

"I hope not. How's your old man?"

"About the same."

"Doctors say when he's coming back to work?"

"Soon," I lied, not wishing to try to explain to Pilot that the next stop for my dad was the funeral home. For a guy who was supposed to know too much, Pilot could be thicker than a brick at times. Maybe if Pilot visited my father once in a while, he'd see for himself.

As Pilot lit a cigarette, I pulled the box across the desk and lifted the lid. Inside, I found a half dozen chunks of bent metal and broken plastic, each about the size of my hand.

"What the hell is this supposed to be, Pilot?"

"David Burke. December 7, 1987. The schmuck had been fired from USAir for stealing. He booked himself on Pacific Southwest Airlines Flight 1771, the same flight as his boss. Burke shot his boss and several others with a .44 magnum while flying over San Luis Obispo County, California. The plane crashed into the Santa Lucia Mountains near Paso Robles and disintegrated. A total of forty-three dead. What you're looking at is debris from the crash site. I got a letter from the guy your old man bought it from." He handed me a handwritten letter.

"Sheesh, Pilot, this is no good. I need something with a little more pizzazz." I pushed the box aside. Even with the letter, I doubted I could get more than a few hundred bucks for the debris.

Pilot took a silvery charm bracelet out of a bag and handed it to me.

"What's this?" I asked, fingering the bracelet. The charms were a mix of large solitaire rhinestones in bezels and animal figures accented with smaller rhinestones and colored stones.

"Jean Harlow's platinum charm bracelet."

"Platinum?"

He nodded. "You know who Harlow was, right?"

"The original Hollywood blond bombshell." Jean Harlow was a socialite who liked to pose nude and never wore underwear. Years before, we had displayed a Harlow look-alike mannequin as part of a tableau on the ground floor. The exhibit was about mysterious Hollywood deaths and possible suspects. Paul Bern, Harlow's second husband, had died under mysterious circumstances two months after he had married the much younger twenty-one-year-old superstar in 1932. His death was ruled a suicide, but the rumors circulated for years that Harlow, her former lover, or some unknown person or persons had been involved in Bern's death.

"Do we have any paperwork on this?" I asked, realizing I should have known the bracelet was platinum because of its weight.

"Something just as good." He pulled a couple of large black-and-white photos from the bag.

Both were upper-body studio portraits of Harlow wearing the bracelet. Both photos were signed by famed Hollywood photographer Edwin Bower Hesser on the back. I studied the bracelet in the photos with a magnifying glass. All the charms were the same and in the exact same order.

"Her boyfriend, Abner 'Longy' Zwillman, gave the bracelet to Harlow when she was just beginning to take off in the movies," Pilot said. "She single-handedly revised the charm bracelet craze."

The second name was also familiar. "Longy Zwillman was one of the first crime syndicate bosses," I said, looking over the charms with new respect.

"Zwillman, Willie Moretti, Meyer Lansky, Lucky Luciano, Benny Siegel, Waxey Gordon, Joe Adonis, Frank Costello, and a half dozen others created the first crime cartel which divided New York, New Jersey, New England, and Pennsylvania into seven separate territories," Pilot said. There was little he didn't know about the early American gangster years, one of the mainstays of MurderLand. It didn't take much to get him to reel off facts, figures, and dates of just about any American crime of any significance in the twentieth century.

"You see that little pig charm?" he asked.

I nodded.

"Zwillman used to make fun of Harlow because she gained weight whenever she wasn't shooting a film," Pilot explained. "To keep her from getting too fat, he once delivered a half million in cash to Harry Cohn, the head of Columbia Pictures, to finance two Harlow movies. One of them was *Platinum Blonde*. Zwillman was the first of the mob to discover Hollywood, even before Bugsy Siegel or George Raft made the scene."

The connection between the bracelet and a notorious gangster explained what the bracelet was doing at MurderLand, but I still wanted to know, "How'd we get it?"

"It was lost around the time Harlow fell ill and died in '37. About twenty years later it showed up in a private sale. No one would say where it came from, but your father did some digging. He said it probably came from the daughter of a woman who worked in the wardrobe department of MGM on *Saratoga*. The woman either found it and never returned it, or stole it from Harlow."

"*Saratoga* was Harlow's last film, wasn't it?"

"Yeah. She died during the shooting from a kidney ailment, the result of childhood meningitis and scarlet fever. They filmed the rest of the movie with stand-ins. Clark Gable said it felt like his co-star was a ghost."

"The diamonds are real?" I asked, looking over the piece with increasing reverence.

"As real as your ass, and the best rocks money can buy. Colored stones on the animals are top quality rubies and sapphires as well. The rocks alone are worth maybe twenty to thirty grand retail. With the Harlow connection, the sky's the limit."

The piece had definite possibilities. I knew two collectors I could contact on short notice who were wild about gangster-related jewelry and another who liked anything to do with Hollywood. Maybe I could start a bidding war.

"What else?"

He reached into the second plastic bag and pulled out a large bell jar. Inside was a shrunken head.

"Now, what do we have here?" I asked. I held the jar, turning it so I could see the specimen from all sides. If I had learned anything over the years from Pilot, it was that only three kinds of shrunken heads existed in this world. The first were true *tsantsas*—from the Ecuadoran-Peruvian jungle, made by the Jivaro, a particularly fierce South American clan, which killed their enemies, cut off their heads, and shrunk them. Other tribes in Africa, Asia, and elsewhere practiced headhunting and taking enemy heads as trophies, but only the Jivaro had been headhunters *and* head shrinkers. The second type of shrunken head was mainly crafted in the late 1800s and early 1900s by medical personnel in Central and South America after tourist demands for real *tsantsas* had taken off. The makers used unclaimed corpses and methods learned from the Jivaro clan. The third were also fakes—often made from monkey or baboon heads, or stretched and shaped goatskin. The museum had displayed several real shrunken heads over the years. Other reputable museums around the world had done the same in their anthropology sections until laws and customs changed in the last few decades and made it illegal or politically incorrect to display Aboriginal body parts under most circumstances.

How many shrunken heads had been relegated to the basement of MurderLand was a mystery, but each time Pilot uncovered one, I felt like kissing him. A genuine Jivaro—of which this was definitely one—along with the Harlow bracelet, would pay off Frankie and help keep the lights on in the building for some time.

"Thank you, thank you, thank you," I said.

"Yeah, well, don't piss the money away. I'm too old to be looking for another job."

CHAPTER 5

AFTER PILOT WENT HOME, I got busy on the phone, trolling for prospective buyers for the two big-ticket items—the bracelet and the shrunken head. Since I needed cash immediately, eBay and other auction venues were out. It would take too long to run the auction and get my hands on the money. Besides, for tax purposes, not to mention my avaricious stepmother, I wanted as many sales as possible to fly completely under the radar with no paper trail.

I could only reach two people with serious money on hand for the shrunken head—a biker king in nearby St. Catharines, Ontario, who collected anything related to human heads, and a plastic surgeon in New York City, an eclectic connoisseur who collected shrunken heads and was also interested in the Harlow bracelet. The only other possible buyer for the bracelet was a Los Angeles-based rock musician with an enormous collection of Harlow material, but she was touring in Europe and unreachable.

For the shrunken head, I ran a mini-auction on the telephone until the biker stalled out at thirty thousand. "That's all I'm gonna do, dude," he insisted.

If I had time to put it in a well-advertised auction, which I didn't, I could get fifty or sixty grand even in a sluggish economy.

"You're passing up one of the finest Jivaro heads you'll ever see," I told him. "The only reason I'm not asking more is because I want to move this today. It's worth at least forty."

"Hey, dude, give me a break. For forty grand, I can get Hitler's skull with a light bulb in it."

After he hung up, I called the physician, who offered me thirty-five. I tried to squeeze a little extra out of him. "I got an offer for forty," I lied, "but I'd much rather see the *tsantsa* go to you. Give me forty-one and it's yours."

"I don't know, Harry. I got more *tsantsas* than I know what to do with. So, thirty-five is my absolute limit and that's only if I like it."

"I'll need fifty on the bracelet."

"I'm thinking more like twenty."

"That's way, way low, Doc. The stones alone are worth more than that."

"What can I say, Harry? Look, if I like the *tsantsa* and the bracelet, maybe I'll go a bit higher for the bracelet. But I have to see it first."

"Doc, you'll like it. You've purchased pieces from me before. You've never been disappointed, and as you know, the museum stands behind everything we sell."

"I know, and I'm looking at airline schedules on my screen as we speak. I can be in our usual place at seven o'clock tonight. Will that work for you?"

"Great. See you then."

I hung up and calculated what I'd make from the shrunken head and bracelet if I met him partway on the jewelry. It was enough to pay off Frankie and cover some overhead costs and debts for the museum. My future was looking brighter.

Before locking up, I made my own trip to the basement.

The two-story, hundred-and-thirty-year-old brick building that housed MurderLand had been built by a liquor manufacturer to make and store wine and other alcoholic beverages. My grandfather bought the building in the 1940s and converted it into a museum.

Over the years, the basement had been chopped into a warren of rooms and passageways crammed with old advertising material, exhibits that had fallen into disrepair, and artifacts that my father or grandfather had acquired but were no longer on display upstairs in the museum showrooms.

Utter chaos, I thought, spitting out cobwebs and dust. One nice feature of the basement was that it was remarkably dry, which meant that everything stored there remained in relatively good shape. Of course, finding anything was always a challenge. Any semblance of order had disappeared years before as new boxes were added and old ones were moved around.

As messy as the place was, I knew it well. I had worked at the museum after school, on weekends, and during summer vacations when I was young. I also had made plenty of recent forays when Pilot wasn't around.

I turned down one passageway and headed into the room where many of the old mannequins and their outfits were stored. As a kid, one of my old jobs had been in displays, which put me in the mannequin-and-costume storage room on a regular basis. So I was able to make relatively short work of my current expedition as I dug through boxes of costumes that had been designed to match clothes worn by killers and victims such as Blue Beard, Ivan the Terrible, Mary Queen of Scotts, Marie Antoinette, Rasputin, Pretty Boy Floyd, and a host of others—all currently passé and unknown to latest crop of kids.

It took me only fifteen minutes to find what I was looking for—the box of clothes containing the reproduction coronation outfit of Henry VIII's wife, Anne Boleyn, who had been beheaded when Henry decided to change wives.

I had no idea whether the rhinestone crown bore any resemblance to the real one she once wore. What mattered was that it was perfect for my purposes.

I was feeling pleased with myself and in a hurry. As a result, when I squeezed past a row of freestanding metal shelving units, my sleeve got caught on a bracket, tipping one of the units halfway over and showering me with mannequin parts. I took a couple of whacks on my head and body, but fortunately, Anne Boleyn's crown was untouched. Nevertheless I was blocked in. The only way to get out was to climb over a tangle of plaster and plastic arms, legs, torsos, and heads, or dig my way out.

Fearing a broken leg if I simply tried scaling the mess, I began to return the mannequin parts to their shelves. Several had broken in the fall. I was in too much of a hurry to think about that until I got halfway down the pile and found the plaster head and torso of the Babushka Lady. The top half of the mannequin had split into a dozen pieces, revealing a bunched-up old towel tied with packing tape that someone had stuffed inside it.

For me, one of the most endearing aspects of MurderLand was that everywhere I turned, it was a repository of not only history—which I loved—but personal memories as well. The Babushka Lady, dressed in her yellow coat and silk scarf, had been part of the President Kennedy assassination tableau on the second floor of the museum. The tableau had included mannequins of the Kennedys; a cutaway, fiberglass reproduction of the president's car; and some of the others around them and nearby. This allowed visitors to the museum to walk among the people in the crowd as if they were actually on the street on the day JFK was shot.

The Babushka Lady was the most enigmatic of the onlookers in Dealey Plaza on November 22, 1963. She was called the Babushka Lady because she wore her scarf in the style of a Russian peasant woman. The grainy photos of her from the cameras of other onlookers also showed her apparently holding a still or movie camera.

After a comprehensive investigation, the FBI said they were able to identify every person in Dealey Plaza that day with a camera—except for the Babushka Lady. As a result, the FBI was able to view every still and movie camera shot taken—except those from the Babushka Lady's film. Years afterward, a woman came forward, claiming to be the Babushka Lady, but her story didn't hold up. The real identity of the Babushka Lady and what may have turned up in her camera had remained a mystery ever since.

The reason the mannequin of the Babushka Lady was no longer on display upstairs was because a high school friend of mine and I were horsing around one day, and we plowed into the Babushka Lady and three or four other figures, destroying the Babushka Lady's legs.

Now, I've destroyed the rest of you, I noted.

Curious about the towel since it had some weight to it, I peeled off the tape.

Inside I found a gun and two boxes of shells. The gun was a ten-round High Standard .22 caliber pistol with a customized, shortened silencer. The same pistol with a longer silencer was used as an assassin's weapon by agents of the Office of Strategic Services (OSS), the precursor of the CIA, during World War II. Both of the boxes of shells had some age to them. The first was filled with hollow points. The second box had no shells at all but instead contained an old, hexagon ladies' watch and a note. The note in my father's handwriting said simply: "Return to Betsy."

It wasn't the first time I'd stumbled on notes my father had left with items in the basement. All of the notes appeared to be memory joggers, either shedding some light on the provenance of an item or a reminder to return a collectible to someone. I'd already returned a half dozen items once lent to the museum to their owners or heirs as a result of notes my father had left.

I had an easy time imagining how the second box with the watch and note had ended up with the gun. My father must have put the watch in the box along with the note, and then someone—probably Pilot—had stored everything together after assuming the box contained shells for the .22.

I took a closer look at the old timepiece. It was a Swiss-made Longines in 14-karat gold and about an inch and a half wide. A ring was attached on the bottom side of the watch under the six so the watch could be hung from a chain or pin upside down, allowing the wearer to glance down and see the right time without turning the watch.

I had no qualms about returning the watch to Betsy—if I could figure out who Betsy was and where she lived. The only Betsy I could even vaguely remember was a woman who had worked for the museum years before and might be dead for all I knew.

The .22 was, no doubt, a stray artifact, wrapped in the towel, and most likely hidden in the Babushka Lady's torso by Pilot in order to keep it away from me.

This was not the first time I had to deal with a rogue firearm. Not long after my father's accident, I sold the registered guns in his collection and in the museum's collection to bona fide dealers. After that, on several occasions I had stumbled on older unregistered firearms, sometimes with no serial numbers. Pilot seemed to know whenever this happened and chided me about selling the weapons under the table, especially to Americans, who were the most likely buyers of the oddball items lying around MurderLand. Bringing the guns into the US could earn me prison time, especially since sting operations had increased dramatically in recent years.

The .22 with the silencer would sell quickly, but it would only bring a few hundred dollars. The risk of selling it far outweighed the reward.

I'll deal with the gun later, I told myself. Pocketing the watch and the note, I wrote down the serial number of the gun, so I could check it against the master list of registered guns in my father's and the museum's collections. Before leaving the basement, I packed the gun and ammo into an old, unused ventilation duct where I hoped Pilot wouldn't find them.

Upstairs in the museum's defunct gift shop, I found a suitable box for the faux Anne Boleyn crown and put some packing peanuts around it to protect the rhinestones. I set the burglar alarm, went out the rear door, and drove to Lundy's Lane.

For all practical purposes, Lundy's Lane is the Canadian Gettysburg and Battle of Bunker Hill rolled into one. The Battle of Lundy's Lane was one of the bloodiest in the two-year War of 1812 and the deadliest ever fought on Canadian soil. The two sides sustained more than eight hundred casualties each, including eighty-four dead and 783 wounded, captured, or missing for the British, Canadian, and Canadian-aligned Indigenous forces, and 174 dead and 679 wounded, captured, or missing for the Americans. The six-hour battle on July 25, 1814 was a lethal draw, but it halted the advance of the Americans into Canada, so Canadians chalk it up as a victory.

Unlike Americans who celebrate such events with hallowed parks and inspiring statues, we Canadians had turned Lundy's Lane into a mishmash of factory outlets, fast food joints, cheap motels, nightclubs, and strip joints, which, when you think about it, is a celebration of life of sorts.

Sally Helman worked in the third-largest clothing store at the factory outlet mall. A part-time sales person, occasional theatrical wardrobe mistress, and five-foot-ten-inch transgender woman, Sally was the most reliable person I knew in the city when it came to scoring great pot at a discount. She was also the only person wacky enough to let me pay with something like a faux Anne Boleyn crown for a four-gram bag of the Niagara Peninsula's finest hydroponically grown bud.

"Oh, I like this," she said, adjusting the crown over her carefully coiffed, dark brown, Audrey Hepburn style, beehive wig and checking herself in the three-way mirror in the near-empty store.

"What do you think?" She cocked one hip and flipped her hair with her four-inch, purple nails.

"Like a real queen," I said. Like a cupcake from Mars, I thought.

She smiled, revealing a sizeable space between her two front teeth. "Oh, you." She fluffed my hair with her fingernails. "You know how to make a girl smile. Alice is such a lucky little devil. Now, if you'll excuse me, I'll go powder my nose."

The mention of Alice made me smile, too.

I watched Sally shimmy toward the employee change room.

Sally was still called Stephen when I first scored grass from her. I liked her entrepreneurial spirit and had no interest in switching to a corporate supplier. She was also my best source of information on Alice May.

Alice May was the latest object of my obsessive-compulsive affections. I was planning to stop by her place before I dropped off Melanie's drugs.

Sally returned a minute later and handed me a small baggy of weed. We air-kissed goodbye, and I was back in my Lincoln heading for Queenston and Alice May two minutes after that.

Alice was the current year's pretty young thing at the Shaw Festival, which was in early rehearsals for the grand opening in the spring. Posh Niagara-on-the-Lake, where the Shaw Festival was held each year, was a thirty-minute drive north from the earthier Niagara Falls. Alice had sixth-billing, playing Clara Eynsford Hill in *Pygmalion*.

Alice was renting a rundown, one-bedroom cottage in Queenston, a quaint village about two-thirds of the way from Niagara Falls to Niagara-on-the-Lake. Her house sat on a large lot that backed onto a patch of thick woods. Her place was dark when I arrived, but I suspected Alice was home. Her platinum-gray Jetta was parked in the driveway. I knew she was there for sure when I heard the familiar plink, plink, plink coming from the rear of the house.

"Don't shoot. It's only me," I said, turning into her backyard.

I could just see her upper body leaning out her bedroom window. As always, the sight of Alice fired me up. I was indiscriminately drawn to sexy women, but like my father, I always seemed to have one woman in my life who made me crazier than the rest. Alice was my crazy-time gal at that moment. I could barely think straight whenever I was in her presence.

She was plinking away with a semiautomatic CO_2 air pistol at three raccoons, which were ignoring her shots and methodically tearing away at the garbage strewn across her yard. The large, plastic, allegedly raccoon-proof garbage container lay open on its side nearby.

"Trying to rebalance nature?" I asked.

"Trying to teach these disease-infested shit-eaters a lesson. And what are you doing here? Stalking me?" The thing about intense infatuation is that it is not always mutual.

"I was in the neighborhood. I thought I'd drop by. How are rehearsals?"

"The director wants me to loosen up more."

"Pearls before swine."

She ignored me and fired off two more rounds. The raccoons were unfazed.

"You intending to invite me in?"

"You got any Soma?"

"A little."

"Then, I guess you can come in. Door's open."

I headed up the porch steps toward the back door. She fired the pellet gun a few more times, missing the raccoons, which continued to gnaw at the garbage.

As usual, Alice looked gorgeous even at her worst—long, silky blond hair, uncombed and slightly wispy; no makeup around her big, dazzling blue eyes; and perfect bone structure. An oversized men's work shirt and loose jeans tried their best to hide a wonderful, lithe, twenty-three-year-old body that was both feminine and well exercised.

As visually beautiful as she was, her house, as usual, looked like it had just been redecorated by a tornado. Dirty dishes lay all over the kitchen. Ditto empty wine bottles, cans of consommé soup, and takeout boxes from a variety of fast-food joints. She told me that one of the reasons she was so determined to get rid of the raccoons was because she feared the mess inside might attract them into her house. She was terrified she'd wake up one night with a furball on her chest, eating her face.

She cleaned off a corner of the kitchen table, took the Soma from me, and plucked a credit card and twenty-dollar bill from her purse. I sat down beside her, watching her cut up four lines and inhaling two of them without coming up for air.

"Hey, good stuff." She grinned. Her eyes sparkled with innocence and sex. "You want something to drink?"

"Sure."

"You have a choice. Prune juice in the fridge or tap water. Help yourself."

I was not especially interested in either. Besides, if I moved, Alice would snort the last two lines of Soma. I stayed put, leaned over, and used my own ten-dollar bill to siphon the dust up my nose.

"Got any more?"

"Not on me. Maybe later. You want to go out? Eat dinner somewhere?"

She looked at me with her head cocked a little to one side and the sexiest grin on her lips. I thought she might be considering it.

Then it got better.

She put her hands on my shoulders, and moved slowly toward me, straddling my legs and somehow avoiding the bruised parts of me.

Good, I thought. We're going to skip dinner and go right for dessert.

As she lowered her angelic face toward mine, I opened my mouth, expecting our tongues to finally meet.

But all she did was lick my nose.

"You had some Soma on your nostrils," she said, retreating to her own seat and firmly pushing my hands away.

"You don't know what you're missing," I said, hoping she'd reconsider.

Her mouth turned down at the corners. "Harry, you're really good looking, and I'm attracted to you, but don't fall in love with me. It isn't going to happen between us. You just can't give me what I want."

We had been over this before. She wanted a guy with lots of money.

"Money's no problem," I told her.

"Harry, you live at home. You're driving your dad's old car."

"A temporary setback," I said as I watched her ignore me to concentrate on reloading her pellet gun. I wanted to tell her how I'd once been an innocent history major at university. Halfway through my sophomore year, I'd headed to Toronto with two classmates who developed a software package that was a complete mystery to me. My claim to fame was figuring out how to sell it for three and a half million dollars to a big tech company, making all of us richer than we'd ever thought possible. I was a twenty-year-old millionaire. Within a few years, I helped create and sell three more companies for another few million. With all the loose money sloshing around, I believed I could sell anything; I could be anything; I could have anything. I was more popular with women than I had ever been. The drugs were plentiful. And I was sure the good times would last forever—until, of course, the recession hit when I was leveraged to the hilt. Overnight, I was broke again. I'd bounced back and crashed and burned two more times in as many years. Presently, I was banking on MurderLand for my salvation. I was determined to figure it out and make it hum again before I turned thirty, which, I reminded myself, was less than a year away.

If I thought explaining this to Alice would make a difference, I would have tried, but she was already too distracted by scratching sounds at the door.

"Those fucking raccoons. They won't leave me alone." She glanced at the door, then back at me. "Can you get me a real gun? The fuckers kept me up all night yesterday with their screaming and hissing."

A gun?

The Soma and my semi-woody were ready to overrule my better judgment. Maybe I could, I thought, reminding myself of the newly discovered pistol in the basement. "I might be able to do something. We could have dinner later, maybe talk it over?"

"Not tonight, Harry. I have to study my lines for tomorrow."

Of course, the more she refused me, the more I wanted her. It's no secret why guys chase women who don't want them. We're wired that way. It's Darwin's law of natural selection at its most primal best. The women who don't want us always appear to be the most desirable.

Darwin or not, I saw no advantage in pushing the point at that moment. Alice couldn't care less. She was already heading toward the door, pellet gun in hand, my presence forgotten.

CHAPTER 6

"OH-HARRY-OH-HARRY, KEEP GOING. Harder. Harder. That's it. That's it."

I was holding on for all I was worth, trying to stay focused as her hips pounded against mine. The headboard hammered the wall—thunk-thunk-thunk. The joints of the wooden bed groaned so loudly I was half expecting the frame to fly apart at any moment.

"I'm just about there. Don't stop, don't stop. Keep going."

I was on the bottom, barely moving, keeping my eyes shut and trying to pretend that I was screwing my brains out with Alice May instead of my lawyer, Melanie Wickers.

"I'm coming," I wheezed, not able to hang on any longer. As I started to feel my little swimmers getting ready to jump ship, she ground her hips even tighter and screamed, "Yes, yes, yes." Then all of a sudden, she started doing the one thing she promised not to do, which she always did when she came in that position. She started thumping her fists on my chest as her whole body convulsed with uncontrollable spasms, while she howled, "Oh, oh, oh."

I had no time to enjoy her pleasure or mine. I had to fight to keep from passing out from the pain as I wrestled her hands to a standstill, yelling, "Stop, stop, stop."

I was glad for the shots of Canadian Club, the Soma, and weed I'd had before sleeping with her, because they more or less eased the pain she inflicted on my already bruised chest.

Melanie was a large woman, a Rubenesque model, the Greek goddess Aphrodite, the blond in the clamshell in Sandro Bottocelli's painting, *The*

Birth of Venus. Melanie had always made it abundantly clear that I was nothing more to her than a love object. She and I hooked up often when she wasn't dating one of the men who were always screwing her around. She, like me, had a habit of picking the wrong ones.

Don't get me wrong. I loved making love to Melanie. I loved the give and take of great sex whenever we got together. But aside from an ancient obsessive infatuation that I once had for her, I wasn't *in love* with Melanie. And I certainly wasn't obsessed with her at the moment like I was with Alice.

"You're...really...fucked," she finally said as her breathing gradually returned to normal.

"Yeah, you, too," I said, thankful for the dim light so I could still pretend she was Alice.

"No," she said. "I mean...Lavaleer...Carlene...MurderLand."

We had yet to discuss the main reason why I was there. I hadn't quite forgotten about the fact that my stepmother and my father's lawyer were about to steal my inheritance. I had just been avoiding the subject, hoping it might disappear if I didn't think about it.

"I went over the papers you sent me, and I made some calls around town." Melanie propped an extra pillow against the headboard and rested against it. "By the way, do you know who the largest investor in the New Heights Hotel chain happens to be?"

"Who?"

"A pension fund related to one of the American transportation unions and a Buffalo investor with alleged ties to the mob."

"That's just fucking great."

"The agreement with Wally and the hotel appears to be a done deal. It looks like your stepmother, Lavaleer, and the hotel people have been working on this for nearly six months behind closed doors. Even the building preservationists have given their blessings to the new project. You're screwed unless a miracle happens or your dad gets better and says no to the deal."

She knew as well as I did that my father wasn't getting better. Melanie had already shed a few tears over him. Her late parents were close friends with my father, and Melanie had idolized him. She had also been my babysitter when I was a preteen. Later, when I was in high school, she had been my first sexual experience.

"What if my father dies?" I asked. "The estate gets split fifty-fifty, right?"

"Yes, but if any disagreement occurs between the heirs, the executors are empowered to settle the agreement—meaning Wally and Carlene."

"I could sue."

"You could, but you'd have no guarantee of winning. I doubt it would slow down their project. A lawsuit would take years to work through the courts and cost you a fortune. You'd likely lose everything."

"What about the planning committees? The twenty-story hotel complex they're proposing is taller than any other building in the Clifton Hill district."

"Don't even go there, Harry. Wally has all the right people in his pocket. The various government agencies want this to go through. The city has fast-tracked it. About the only way you could stop them is if Carlene dropped dead. Then, as the alternate executor *and* heir, you'd have control over everything."

I'm in a fucking war, I thought. I'm fighting for my life. I tried to make fun of my anger. "What if I could knock them both off?"

"You'd be in the pink." Melanie nuzzled her face against my neck and slipped her arms around me, trying to get me to cuddle.

I gently extracted myself from her. I wanted to sulk by myself. "I gotta go, Melanie. Sorry. I have a meeting on the other side of the river in a half hour. I can't be late."

"You could come back later. I could make you dinner. You could sleep over. I could look after those bruises of yours." This wasn't so much a sexual invitation as a motherly one. Melanie had never quite stopped thinking of me as a kid, especially since I had grown up without a mother.

"I'll take a rain check."

"If you change your mind, just come by." She reached for the half-smoked joint in the ashtray on her bedside table, lit it, inhaled, and handed it to me.

I took one last toke and flew out the door, fantasizing about ways my stepmother might drop dead.

I drove down the hill from Melanie's place to the Whirlpool Rapids Bridge. The bridge had the advantage of being open to NEXUS traffic only. NEXUS is a joint US-Canadian program for low-risk, prescreened, and approved travelers to cross the border. Drivers use a special identity card and dedicated NEXUS lanes that usually allow them entry to the bridge on one side and exit on the other without being questioned by US or Canadian customs and immigration authorities.

NEXUS wasn't a complete get-out-of-jail-free card. The authorities on either side could still stop and question you at any time, but since the Whirlpool Rapids Bridge was used by locals, the chances were pretty good that I wouldn't be stopped, which was important since I didn't want to try explaining the shrunken head or the charm bracelet to US customs when I drove into the States.

On the other side, I wound my way through Niagara Falls, New York, the shabby sister of Niagara Falls, Ontario.

Dr. David Danielson and I met in our usual spot, a near-empty parking lot behind an Italian restaurant a few blocks from the bridge.

I had done business with Dr. Danielson before. Most recently, he'd bought a houndstooth check sports jacket that belonged to murdered crime boss, Benjamin "Bugsy" Siegel, the Brooklyn wise guy who had brought the mob to Las Vegas. Siegel had been murdered in the living room of Virginia Hill, his mistress, after he was caught stealing from his fellow gangsters.

Danielson was a slight man in his late fifties with narrow eyes, a diamond stud in his left ear, and pale, spotty skin that looked like the head of a much-beaten snare drum. We sat in the backseat of his airport rental car while he examined the items.

He had brought along his own Harlow photos, which he placed beside the Hesser photos. He studiously examined the bracelet against each photo while I filled him in on the bracelet's history.

When I finished my little talk on its provenance, he asked, "Did you know that Zwillman never got over Harlow?"

"Yeah," I said, reaching into my memory bank for one of the many stories that Pilot had drilled into my head. "When they found him hanging in the basement of his West Orange, New Jersey mansion, he still had a photo of Harlow in his pocket."

The official version of Zwillman's death was that it was a suicide. The government had been cracking down on his finances. They had him on tax evasion and more. He'd been leading a respectable life in 1959 and didn't want to end up in jail for tax fraud like Al Capone or Waxey Gordon. So he killed himself. Unofficially, it had been rumored for years that the national crime bosses were afraid he would try to make a deal with the feds. His old buddy Meyer Lansky allegedly ordered the hit.

The doctor placed the bracelet and photos on the seat between us. "Way I heard it, Zwillman got the bracelet back after Harlow died and carried it in his pocket like a talisman."

And maybe the hit man who killed him stole the bracelet and gave it to my old man, I thought wearily. *Stories.* Everybody had one.

"Anything's possible," I told him. "What I told you is what I've been told. The bottom line is that this bracelet is a perfect match for the one in the photos."

He nodded thoughtfully. Without replying, he pulled on rubber gloves, took the shrunken head out of the bell jar, and began examining it with a small, handheld microscope. He held the *tsantsa* to his nose and sniffed. The real ones had a distinct, funky odor. When he was done, he returned it to the jar, screwed on the cap, and handed it to me.

"It's genuine. Don't worry," I told him.

"It probably is." He removed his gloves. "Do you have any paperwork on it?"

"No."

"Too bad." He picked up the bracelet and the photos. "I'll take the bracelet and the Hesser photos, but I'm going to pass on the *tsantsa*. I have too many already, Harry. Besides, I'm trying to narrow my collection to Hollywood-related memorabilia."

I was disappointed but played it cool. I held the jar to the car's inside light and pretended to admire the shriveled specimen. "It's one of the finest genuine Jivaro heads you'll ever see."

"I understand. I just don't need it. I'm going to say *no*."

The *tsantsa* was off the table, but I sensed he had his heart set on the bracelet.

"If you're not taking both items, I'm afraid I can't be very flexible on the bracelet," I said.

"I can understand that." He spoke like he didn't really care, but his eyes kept dropping toward the bracelet. "What are you thinking?"

He wasn't much of a poker player. On the other hand, I had no idea at what price he'd fold and just walk away. I needed as much money as possible to settle with Frankie and have enough left over to pay some bills.

"Forty-five grand is the best I can do," I said.

"That's steep, Harry." He rocked his head from side to side. "How about thirty?" he asked halfheartedly.

"Forty. That's the lowest I can go. I'm giving it away at that price. It's a piece of Hollywood history."

He hesitated, but I sensed I had him. All I needed to do was reel him in. "If you don't want it that's okay." I reached to pick it up, but he beat me to it.

"No, I want it." He put it into his lap and held it there while he counted out the forty thousand dollars in bank-wrapped bundles of US hundreds.

I recounted the money and stuffed the wads into the deep pockets of my overcoat. I shook hands with the good doctor and returned to my car as he drove off.

Five minutes later, I headed across the Whirlpool Rapids Bridge with the shrunken head in my trunk and my pockets stuffed with greenbacks. I was happy. I could pay Frankie and have a little left over to celebrate. And I still had the shrunken head.

Just when I was sure my troubles were over, the unthinkable happened. Customs forced me to stop.

CHAPTER 7

ACTUALLY, IT WAS NESSA WILEY who flagged me over.

"Well, well, well. Look who we have here. I saw you drive past earlier. I was hoping you'd come back my way." Her grin was just wide enough for me to see her slightly crooked front teeth. Her dark, narrow eyes felt like they were drilling holes through me.

She had been a regular sex monkey in high school. Later, after dropping out of university and trying and failing to reinvent herself as a fitness instructor in Toronto, she joined the border guards. A few years back when I was visiting my father, I'd seen her photo in the local newspaper announcing an award she had won for border guard of the year or something like that. I had to admit, Nessa was looking pretty sweet as she hovered beside my car.

"Hey, Nessa. Nice to see you. Thought you'd transferred to Windsor-Detroit."

"I did, and then I transferred back. I've been working the Peace Bridge for the last two months. This is my first night working the Whirlpool Rapids Bridge. I got married." She wiggled her left hand at me, showing off a modest gold wedding band.

As a teen, Nessa was a scrawny hippie girl with skin problems who excelled at the harp, consumed excessive amounts of alcohol and weed, and had screwed me with great enthusiasm throughout my junior and senior years whenever we'd both run out of other options.

"Congratulations."

"Yeah, and you know what would be a nice wedding present? You could pay me what you owe me."

I was afraid of that. Not all of my business dealings in the heyday of my stock hustling career were related to computers and telecoms. One was a biotech outfit promoting elastic panty hose with a special chemical coating that was supposed to eliminate cellulite without exercise or dieting. I'd charmed her into investing twenty-five grand when I'd run into her in Toronto.

"It was an investment, Nessa. I lost a heck of a lot more than you did." Rumors had it her money came from a porn film she'd been in or a mobster boyfriend who'd died or been killed.

"You said the product had been properly tested and was market ready."

"That's what I'd been told." The magic fat remover not only didn't work but left a yellow-green tint on your skin that glowed in the dark. Nessa and her two sisters ended up with yellow-green bums. The dye took about six months to wear off.

"I asked you to put the money in something safe. You said you personally guaranteed it."

"A figure of speech. We've been through this before. I can't change history. I thought we agreed on that." I was itching to get going so I could pay Frankie.

She eyed me coldly. "I never agreed to anything. I could use that money right now."

"Business is bad, Nessa. I'm a little short of cash these days. Why don't we talk about this on your next day off?"

I saw a hardening in her jaw that I hadn't seen before. I wondered if her marriage had changed her.

She leaned closer and said in a low voice. "What's it worth to you right now to not have your car searched?"

"You're kidding, right?" I started to sweat.

"What would I find if I searched your pockets?"

Not good, I thought. Nessa knew me well enough to know that I was probably carrying something illegal. I knew her well enough to know that she wasn't just fucking with me. She could definitely do some damage since I had the shrunken head in the trunk. Technically, I was simply taking it back where it came from, but I had no documents to prove that. So

I could be smuggling ancient body parts, which could be iffy at the best of times at an international border without proper papers. If she searched me she'd also find the wads of hundreds.

I decided to try to finesse my way out.

"Nessa, I have enough cash on me to pay you off, but I'm not sure we should do it under the watchful eyes of the cameras. We could meet later, and I could give you the money." I took a packet of hundreds out of my pocket and held it below the steering wheel where she could see it but the security cameras couldn't.

"I have a better idea. I'll call my significant other. We'll arrange a pick up. That way, I'll have my money by the time I get off work."

"Sounds like a plan," I said, playing for time. Anything that would get me away from the border checkpoint was worth a shot.

She made a call on her phone and spoke in a low voice. I could only hear her end. "Val? You still in the area?" She paused and then spoke again. "Yeah, that little business I told you about earlier just came together." She described my car, listened for a few more seconds, and then added, "Good. I'll tell him."

"You had this all figured out, didn't you?" I said as she hung up.

She pointed toward the exit. "Drive up Bridge Street. Val will meet you."

"How will I know—"

"Get going." She waved me through as she stepped away from the car.

No sense arguing, I thought as I drove off.

Once clear of the border, I drove straight west and up the hill on Bridge Street, weighing the consequences of making a run for it, not paying Nessa, and taking care of my obligations with Frankie first. Nessa could wait. She had invested of her own free will, and I lost plenty of my own money. On the other hand, I didn't want to piss her off. If she red flagged my name at customs, the long-term, negative ramifications could hurt my cross-border business. Then, again, I didn't want to piss off Frankie either.

Before I could make up my mind, a patrol car with lights flashing pulled behind me and tapped its siren.

This is all I need, I thought as I pulled to the curb. A tall, broad-shouldered cop stepped from the squad car and came toward me as I lowered my window.

"What's the problem, officer?" As I spoke, I realized that the cop was a female officer with short blond hair and large blue eyes set over high cheekbones. Sort of reminded me of the handsome Swedish Viking woman out of an Ingmar Bergman movie.

"You Harry Holiday?"

"Yes."

"I'm Constable Valerie Runge. You have something for Nessa?"

I nodded, noticing she wore a gold wedding band that matched Nessa's.

So, Nessa's switched sides. Interesting, I thought, unable to keep myself from checking out the Nordic goddess. I wondered what it would be like to have a threesome. I liked women so much I sometimes imagined I had been a lesbian in a former lifetime.

I halfheartedly tried to strike up a conversation as I counted out the money, making adjustments for the difference in the exchange rate. Val was all business. She said nothing but a polite thank you when I handed over the cash.

No fun here, I concluded as I took off again.

I pushed the thoughts of sex from my mind and returned to my real problem. It was getting late, and I was short ten grand Canadian for Frankie.

I still had a few hours before meeting my bookie at Pole Catz, a gentleman's club and strip joint on Lundy's Lane in which Frankie had an interest.

I headed to the museum to drop off the shrunken head and try to find something else to sell.

I returned to the old mannequin storage area and began to dig through the junk. After shaking old mannequins in the basement for a half hour, I found another gun inside the head of a mannequin of Jack Ruby, the nightclub owner who had gunned down JFK's assassin, Lee Harvey Oswald, in the Dallas police headquarters two days after the president's assassination. The killing of Oswald had been shown live on television while it was happening. The face of the Ruby mannequin was missing its nose. The second gun was wrapped in a tea towel inside a wad of yellowed newspaper. It was a five-shot .38 Smith and Wesson Terrier with a two-inch barrel, a gun favored by plain-clothes detectives in the 1930s and later. Along with it was a full box of cartridges. Definitely not the gun that killed Oswald since I knew that one was in another collection.

The .38 was worth at best a few hundred dollars, and definitely not worth the bother of trying to sell it. I jotted down the serial number and put the .38 with the .22, reminding myself to check both serial numbers against the master list later. Returning to my office, I continued to rummage through the dark recesses of my mind, trying to think of someone to call to scare up more cash.

The only possible person who might help keep me from getting beaten to a pulp was Melanie. But I probably owed her ten or fifteen grand already. I'd lost track.

Still, any port in a storm. She was unlikely to have that much cash on hand, but maybe I could talk her into writing a check and hope that Frankie was in the mood to accept it.

I was just about to reach for the receiver when the phone rang.

The caller ID said it was a private number, but as soon as I heard the voice on the other end of the line, I knew my luck had suddenly changed.

It was Big Mo, the St. Catharines biker king.

"I been trying to get you on your cell phone all evening. I left a dozen messages."

"Cell's broken. What can I do for you, Big Mo?"

"You still got the shrunken head?"

"It's still in my possession, but it's spoken for," I lied.

"I need it."

I pretended to be doing my own contemplating.

"Hey, you still there, Holiday?"

"You should have taken it when I offered it." I feigned exasperation. "I have an offer pending for fifty-two thousand and that's cheap."

"I have forty grand in cash on me that says it's mine but only if you bring it by right now."

"Forty-eight," I countered.

"Forty-four. Canadian."

"You're killing me."

"That's it. Take it or leave it. I'm having a party. Be here before nine. It's my old lady's birthday. I want a present that's gonna make a statement. You're bringing it."

"I'll be there." This is my night, I thought. I was already starting to plan big. Head buzzing with excitement, I began thinking beyond paying off Frankie. I was suddenly in the mood to take a little detour and visit Alice May again after I dropped off the shrunken head. I thought about bringing a little something along to sweeten the surprise. I checked out the serial numbers of both guns. They weren't on the master list of guns for my father's or the museum's collections. Both handguns were probably acquired before they needed to be registered. It gave me a sliver of comfort to know that if my little gift ended up in the hands of the police for some reason, it couldn't be traced officially back to the museum, my father, or me. I returned to the basement, picked up the .38, and filled the cylinder with bullets. It was just what Alice May had asked for.

What a surprise the weapon was going to make, I thought gleefully, imagining the grin on her face as I headed north to St. Catharines on the Queen Elizabeth Way (QEW) to close the deal with Big Mo.

It took me twenty minutes to reach his large, two-story, brand new, Georgian-style mansion. It sat behind a wrought iron gate on five acres of manicured grounds. I stated my business over the intercom before being buzzed in.

The circular driveway in front was busier than I had seen it on past visits. I counted two dozen motorcycles and as many Mercedes, Beemers, and luxury SUVs.

A couple of thugs draped in leather and steel studs patted me down at the entrance. No problem. I'd left the .38 in the trunk of my car.

The party was raging in the living room and out onto the back deck in spite of the chilly air. A live rock band that sounded a little like Barenaked Ladies wailed away in the living room while a half dozen scantily clad babes, who looked like they were auditioning for Hooters, milled about with trays of beer, food, and drugs.

One of the doormen led me up a side stairway, and delivered me to a room at the end of the hall on the second floor.

Big Mo was there with his chief enforcer, Goose, a thin, ghoulish guy with a Fu Manchu moustache and a black patch over his left eye. They were watching near-naked, female pro wrestlers tossing each other around on a TV screen the size of a billboard.

Big Mo lowered the sound with the remote and stood as I entered the room.

"How's my man doing?" He held out a hand the size of a catcher's mitt. Big Mo was all muscle and tattoos except for the huge paunch that hung over his belt. He wore his trademark wraparound sunglasses and leather Confederate kepi over his long, stringy, gray hair.

Goose looked at me with his one good eye but made no gesture of greeting. He had been on trial three times for murdering rival gang members, but the trials had been cancelled when the witnesses had recanted or disappeared.

The walls of the room were covered with Nazi and biker paraphernalia, including an impressive collection of Nazi helmets, uniforms, and photos of Hitler and his pals. I recognized an armchair in the corner that had once belonged to Heinrich Himmler. I had been forced to sell it to Big Mo during a previous financial crisis at MurderLand.

Big Mo took a long time to study the shrunken head through the jar before taking it out and looking at it even closer under one of the table lamps.

Finally, he held it to his nose, closed his eyes, and took a deep whiff.

"Ah, the smell of death. My old lady's gonna love this." He opened his eyes and flashed small yellow teeth at his pal. "This is going to make Candy horny as hell, don't you think, Goose?"

Thinking didn't appear to be part of Goose's job description. He nodded without taking his eyes off the big screen.

Big Mo and I took care of the money. Then in a separate transaction, I bought an ounce of Soma to take with me to Alice May's.

I stayed for the singing of "Happy Birthday," the cutting of the cake, and Big Mo's presentation of his gift to Mrs. Big Mo, a large brunette with no waist and swastikas tattooed on each of her knuckles. Mrs. Big Mo went apeshit over the skull, jumping up on Big Mo with her thighs around his waist and screaming at the top of her lungs. She even gave me a hug that damned near broke my already sore ribs.

Big Mo pulled me aside. "She's been bitching at me about not including her in my skull collecting activities. This should get her wet."

Not sure about wet, but she insisted on doing a couple of lines of Soma with me off the glass mantle of the fireplace.

I left immediately afterward, smoking a joint that I had filched from one of the candy trays in the living room.

I was happy. I had more than enough money to pay Frankie and enough left over to keep my head above water for a few of weeks.

But the real thing that was cranking me up was the thought of the look on Alice May's face when I arrived at her place with drugs, a .38-caliber raccoon killer, and enough money to take her to the craps tables. The one thing that made Alice May horny was gambling with other people's money.

With the Soma, gun, and cash, I would be irresistible.

I was happy as a cockroach at a salad bar until I neared her place and spied the magma red Mercedes SL500 parked in her driveway behind her Jetta.

As I cruised slowly by I read the vanity license plate on the rear of the car—RCHLWYR. Wally Lavaleer.

CHAPTER 8

I PARKED MY CAR down the road and walked back. I tried to keep my anger in check by telling myself that Wally Lavaleer was there to give Alice May legal advice.

The lights were out at the front of the house.

I went around back. I saw light peeking around the edges of the drawn curtains. I could hear voices coming from inside. A raccoon was sitting a few feet away from the porch, snacking on a pile of garbage. We ignored each other. I walked up the steps to the porch as quietly as possible.

I grew increasingly pissed as I heard Wally and Alice laughing.

Looking through the crack between the curtains and the window frame, two things instantly struck me. First, with the exception of a bottle of wine and two nearly empty glasses on the kitchen table, the kitchen was spotless. Second, Wally Lavaleer was sitting where I had hours before. His shirt was half unbuttoned, and he was smoking a cigar while Alice May straddled his lap exactly as she had straddled mine earlier in the evening. She was also nibbling on Wally's ear. The hand of Wally's that wasn't holding the cigar was halfway down the rear of Alice's jeans. Though I couldn't be a hundred percent sure, one of her hands appeared to be sticking down the front of his pants.

The thought that Wally Lavaleer, the guy who was trying to screw me out of my inheritance, as well as screwing my father's wife, was also playing kissy face with my girl, set my brain on fire. Never mind that Alice May wasn't my girl. Obsession is not a rational condition.

Who knows? If I hadn't left the .38 in the trunk, I might have been tempted to shoot both of them. Instead I must have shifted my weight on the rickety porch in a way that made Alice stop and turn toward the window.

Thankfully, I was able to get off the porch, and in spite of my injuries from my beating earlier, I managed to run like hell, suddenly feeling like the dumb shit that I was. I succeeded in reaching the shadows at the rear of her lawn moments before the back door opened and Alice began blasting the backyard with pellets from her semiautomatic.

A couple of the slugs zinged close to me. For a moment, I wondered if she had me in her sights. I was damned glad I hadn't driven by earlier and lent her the .38.

Any thoughts that she might have spotted me vanished when Lavaleer joined her at the door and asked, "What are you doing?"

"Damned raccoons are driving me nuts."

He laughed. "Come inside." He pulled her away from the door and covered her mouth with his. The kitchen light went out.

On the way back to town, my head reeled.

Fuck Wally. Fuck Carlene.

I didn't have any trouble imaging what life would be like if Wally and my stepmother were pushed into the Niagara River like my father had been.

My feelings for Alice were more ambivalent. I hated her, and at the same time, I wanted her even more.

I felt a sudden need to get high. Correction. Higher. I was already pretty wasted.

Anyone who has ever wanted sex, or money, or another person, or anything else that they were obsessing over probably already knows everything they need to know about drugs, including alcohol. It's no secret why drugs are attractive. They make you feel better. The bad thing about them is that they don't make you feel better long enough. So you take more, and more, and pretty soon you turn into an idiot.

That's exactly where I was heading that night. I was rapidly losing IQ points by the minute.

I drove straight to Pole Catz and went inside, determined to have a good time until the witching hour.

The doorman told me Frankie was upstairs in the VIP lounge.

I stayed downstairs, went to the bar in back, and started drinking and watching beautiful young women strip bare-assed for the half dozen guys scattered around the room who had nowhere better to be at eleven thirty on a Monday night.

At twenty to midnight, Joey Angelo, the onetime boxer, came downstairs and told me, "Frankie knows you're here. He sent me down to tell you to go upstairs and tell him what your problem is. If you don't want to go see him, I'm supposed to take you out back and give you a repeat of this afternoon."

"Tell Frankie I got until midnight," I said, running a hand over my rubbery, drunken lips.

Joey shook his head wearily. It wasn't the answer he wanted to hear. "Look, Harry. I'm gonna give you a break. I'm gonna go upstairs and tell Frankie you went to the can to bleed your lizard and you'll be up in a few minutes. If you don't show, and he sends me looking for you, I'm bringing Pinkie with me, and you know Pinkie don't like you."

"Pinkie can go fuck himself. And you, too. And Frankie, too. I got 'til midnight," I said, trying not to slur my words.

Joey was shaking his head as he climbed the stairs.

I finished my drink while a top-heavy blond named Bonnie with a tattoo of a rose at the base of her spine made love to the pole in the middle of the stage.

At three minutes to midnight I headed up the rear stairs. Joey and Pinkie were just coming down to get me. They met me halfway and glued themselves to my sides like maggots on a corpse.

"I'm gonna enjoy this," Pinkie said as he and Joey accompanied me the rest of the way.

Frankie was nursing a drink at his usual table in the VIP lounge on the opposite side of the room from the bar. A lanky, nude blond was sitting on a towel beside him, trying to keep her behind from collecting bacteria. A skinny redhead wearing a black G-string and tank top, lounged in the corner on the other side of Frankie, playing with a swizzle stick in a tall glass filled with a blue-tinted drink that reminded me of toilet bowl cleaner.

In his early sixties, Frankie Argyll looked more like someone's schoolteacher uncle who had wandered into Pole Catz by accident, than someone who could send guys like Joey and Pinkie around town collecting bad debts the easy way or the hard way. Frankie was five nine or five ten, medium build. His egg-shaped head was bald on top with close-cropped gray hair around the sides. His face was clean shaven with a long, straight nose and fleshy lips. He was dressed in a tweed jacket with a blue dress shirt, open at the neck, and dark slacks.

He had once run most of the illegal gambling operations in town, including off-track and sports betting and floating card games, which my father was fond of. Some people said his gambling business was way down since the casinos had opened. If it was, he wasn't letting anyone know it. He'd recently moved into a new McMansion on the north side of town.

Frankie told the two girls to get lost, dismissed Joey and Pinkie, and told me to sit down beside him.

"Harry, I'm letting you come here to talk to me for your father's sake. I hate seeing you like this. So if you got something to say, say it." Up close, his large, brown, hangdog eyes were as dead as an undertaker's.

When he finished his little sermon, I began pulling packets of hundred-dollar bills out of my various pockets until I reached thirty-five thousand. He thumbed through a few of the wads.

"It's all there," I said.

"I'm sure it is. I'd offer you a drink, but you've already had enough."

I smiled and counted out another twenty grand, telling him, "Put half on the Bulls over the Wizards, half on the Nets over the Blazers."

I started to get up, but he stopped me.

"Hold it a second, Harry. I want to talk to you." He rested a hand on my shoulder.

"About what?"

"You. You're out of control."

"For gambling on basketball? I'm keeping you in business."

"You're in here too much. You're gambling too much. You insult me. I try to help you. I tell you to stay away from the bets for a while, and you tell me, 'Frankie, if you don't take my bets, I'll go somewhere else.' So then you run three weeks late on your payment. I give you an extension, and you miss that. If I don't try to collect, you make me look bad to my other customers. Then, when you finally come to pay me, you hold out until the last minute. What? So you can show me how tough you are? I'm trying to help you here, Harry."

"Frankie, if you want to help, tell me what happened to my old man."

"I already told you. Check yourself into Carlene's Place, and when you straighten yourself out, then, start looking around."

Carlene's Place was a local, tough-love drop-in center for addicts that my stepmother had helped found through her congregation.

"Don't worry about me, Frankie. I know I'm out of control, but right now, I need to be."

If I ever needed help sobering up, Carlene's Place was the last place I would go. Frankie had to know that. "Tell me something else. Tell me something about Carlene."

When I first returned to the Falls, Frankie told me he heard that Carlene was involved in my father's accident. He said he wouldn't ever tell me more, and if I went to the police, he'd deny it.

"I told you, I don't have anything else to say about your father's accident, but I will tell you a story about your grandfather. When I was young and was just starting out, I went to him for business advice. I thought he could tell me what I needed to know about buying a bar. I knew he once owned a bar in New York. He told me, 'Everything's like pool. Check all the angles before you take your shot.'"

I couldn't help wondering if Frankie was going a little soft in the head. "That's the exact same story you told me last time."

"The next time you ask, I'll tell you the same thing. Your grandfather also told me. 'Some lessons are best learned on your own.'"

Enough of the fortune cookie shit, I thought. "Okay, if you won't help me with Carlene, tell me what you know about my father's business."

"Your father and I are friends. I placed his bets. We never talked business."

"Do you know if he knew anyone named Jenny?"

He thought for a moment and then said, "Doesn't ring any bells."

"Or Betsy?" For all I knew, the watch in my pocket belonged to one of Dad's old lovers. He had no shortage of those in the Niagara region. Maybe one of them could shed some light on Dad's financial affairs.

But Frankie shook his head. "I don't recall anyone named Betsy either."

"Think on it. If anything comes to mind, let me know."

"Sure thing, Harry. And you think about being nicer to your friends and staying out of trouble. Your old man would want that for you."

It was good advice, but I wasn't looking for advice. I was still dealing with the impact of finding Alice May and Wally Lavaleer together.

I went downstairs, drank shots of tequila, and watched beautiful women dancing naked while I stewed. In between, I slipped off to the restroom to share a couple of lines of Soma with one of the girls.

I was still feeling cocky by the time I left. After selling the Harlow bracelet, settling with Nessa, selling the shrunken head to Big Mo, buying the Soma, paying off Frankie, placing my latest bets, paying my bar bill, and tipping everyone in sight, I still had more than twelve grand left thanks to the exchange rates. I drove to the Fallsview Casino with the remaining money burning a hole in my pocket. I was up ten grand at one of the craps tables in the first twenty minutes. I should have quit while I was ahead, but I was way too loaded. I dropped the ten I'd just made and another eleven in under an hour. Easy come, easy go, I told myself. I still had more than a grand in my pocket and twenty grand on the two basketball games for Tuesday night.

With the good times still eluding me, I drove to Queenston to Alice May's place again.

Both cars were gone. The house was dark.

I had a pretty good idea where they were not—at Wally's place—because his wife wouldn't exactly like it. Nor were they likely at my father's place, since my stepmother would hardly welcome the duo. That left maybe sixty or seventy hotels and motels in the area.

I decided to give up before I even started.

On the return trip to Niagara Falls, I got a craving for a cigarette, a habit I'd kicked months before.

I pulled into a gas station, but the attendant, a young kid with a pierced eyebrow, had already closed out the cash for the night and was just setting the alarms on the front door.

"The convenience store on Victoria should be open," he said.

It was a good suggestion except for the fact that Victoria Avenue was a mess. Half the street was torn up for sewer repairs. I had to park a block away and walk back.

Just as I approached the front of the convenience store, I heard a muffled POP.

Even half crocked, it sounded to me like a gunshot. I ducked behind a backhoe, just in case. I was still pretty high, not to mention jumpy and paranoid. I wanted to get the lay of the land without exposing myself. If someone had tried to knock off my father, I reasoned, they could just as easily be after me.

I looked around but couldn't see anyone on the street. The only lights along the block were from the convenience store and the street lamps.

I had a good view of the front window of the convenience store. Unfortunately, the shopkeeper had jammed the window with merchandise and advertising posters, so I couldn't see in. I sat tight and waited.

I was just getting ready to continue toward the store when the front door swung open, and a big guy in a dark leather bomber jacket stuck his head out and peered up and down the street.

The light from the street lamp over the store gave me a perfect view as he stepped outside. He tucked what looked like a handgun into his pocket and walked down the street in the opposite direction from me.

Interesting, I thought, especially since I recognized the guy.

CHAPTER 9

DUANE MORTHWELL, ANOTHER LOCAL I had gone to elementary and high school with, was dressed in a shabby, black leather bomber jacket, jeans, and weathered cowboy hat.

Like Joey Angelo and Pinkie, Duane Morthwell had dropped out of high school before graduating. Last I'd heard, he'd been caught with a hundred pounds of weed and had done some time at the Maplehurst Correctional Complex in Milton.

I watched him cross the street. He pulled the brim of his cowboy hat lower over his eyes. He got into a dark, ancient, rusting Camaro and drove north.

Much soberer than I had been a few moments before, I decided to see what had taken place inside.

Once through the door, it took me only seconds to take it all in. The night clerk was lying in a pool of blood with the top of his head blown off. His right index finger was stuck through the trigger guard of a pistol.

I had seen dead people before—my grandfather, my mother, deceased friends of my father, and a high school pal who'd died of leukemia, but they had all been laid out, coiffed, and sanitized. Even the dead at the museum had been mummified, shrunken, stuffed, or in some way abstracted. This was the real deal. The smell of human waste permeated the air.

I glanced quickly at the blood and gore on the walls behind the dead man, then away.

I kept expecting to hear sirens, but the only noises were the buzz from overhead florescent lights and the whir of the refrigeration equipment at the rear of the store.

The normal thing to do would have been to call the police or leave, but I wasn't feeling very normal.

For better or worse, I had already made the leap into a different world. How can I explain it?

Maybe it was the idea of killing Carlene and Wally, which had been rattling around in my brain for some time. Maybe it was just something inside me that was misfiring.

One of my university professors had once asked our class: "What would you do if someone offered you a billion dollars, and all you had to do was push a button and a stranger on the other side of the world would die? The only cost to you would be a guilty conscience—if you had a conscience. Would you do it?"

We all said *no*, but I remembered wondering if any of my fellow students were secretly thinking, like me, about whether they could do it under the right circumstances.

I was suddenly in the midst of the right circumstances. I was facing someone who was ruining my life, might want to kill me, and for all practical purposes, had ended my father's life. And all I had to do was manipulate the circumstances a little and my problem would go away.

Could I do it?

I had so many mood-altering substances and so much adrenaline pumping through me I felt invincible.

I forced myself to look at the murder victim again. The gun in the night clerk's hand drew my attention. I squatted down to take a closer look, careful not to step in the bloody footprints surrounding the body. Duane Morthwell's prints no doubt.

With a population of about 85,000, Niagara Falls is small and relatively peaceful. Armed robberies and armed night clerks in convenience stores weren't unheard of, but they were rare in a small town like the Falls. Getting a license to pack a pistol in public isn't very Canadian.

The gun was no toy. It was a .44 Magnum Colt Anaconda. My father had had one of the big-bore shooters in his collection. This was a serious killing machine.

I wanted to know more.

I slowly glanced around at the shelves above me.

It took me a few moments to spot what I was looking for.

The surveillance camera was well hidden and mounted on the underside of a shelf in the far corner beside a stack of canned goods.

I hunted around for the control box for the system. I finally found it in a cabinet behind a carton of candy bars.

Whoever installed the system had done a reasonably good job. I wasn't an expert, but I knew a thing or two about surveillance systems from the museum.

The convenience store system consisted of an entry-level camera and single channel digital video recorder similar to the ancient system at MurderLand.

Since the video was stored on the hard drive, my only option was to detach the cables and plugs, and pull the machine out of its hiding place. Even with my gloves on to prevent me from leaving fingerprints, it took me less than five minutes to detach everything and walk out of there with the recorder cradled under one arm.

The night air outside was clean and fresh compared to the stench of death in the store. As I hurried toward my car, I felt a renewed sense of purpose.

Only afterward on the drive home did I remember that I'd forgotten to get cigarettes.

CHAPTER 10

I TOOK THE RECORDER TO MY OFFICE, plugged it into my computer, and with a few quick adjustments to accommodate the difference between the store's recorder and the ones at the museum, I honed in on the last part of the video beginning with Duane Morthwell entering the convenience store.

I immediately ran into a few disappointments. The audio had been turned off to increase the number of hours that could be stored on the hard drive. All I had was a silent video. To save more storage, the camera had been recording at a frame rate of one a second compared to the thirty frames a second needed for real-time imaging. As a result, the video was a jumpy sequence of shots that had more in common with an old-time slide show than a movie.

The one thing that really mattered—the image quality—had been set to high, which made the individual pictures crisp and detailed.

As I watched, I got my first big surprise when Duane came through the front door of the store.

I assumed the incident was a robbery gone wrong. The video suggested something else.

Duane Morthwell stepped to the counter and nodded at the middle-aged night clerk, a stocky man with short, black hair, coarse features, and a narrow, black moustache. A silver cross dangled from the ear visible to the camera.

For nearly a minute, it seemed that Morthwell and the clerk carried on a civil conversation, but then it appeared to grow heated, and the clerk pointed a finger at Morthwell like he was accusing him of something or telling him to fuck off.

Morthwell pointed back and looked like he was shouting.

That's when the clerk pulled the .44 from under the counter.

Was it his gun? Was it the store owner's?

Morthwell immediately raised his hands in submission and started walking backward toward the door. The clerk said something more. Morthwell responded, and then waved a hand in disgust and appeared to be heading out.

The clerk seemed content and lowered the gun to his side. He was smiling broadly enough so that I could see he was missing a couple of teeth on one side.

Morthwell didn't open the door. Instead, he turned around. His face was contorted with rage. In the next couple of frames, he pulled from his jacket pocket a handgun, pointed it at the clerk, and appeared to be yelling at him. Maybe he was telling the clerk to drop his gun. Even in frames spaced one second apart, it looked as if Morthwell didn't fire until the clerk tried to raise the Colt .44 again.

Morthwell shot the clerk in the face. The back of the clerk's head exploded as he flew backward to the floor. I couldn't be sure, but it appeared that the gun Duane used was a revolver, not much different than the .38 I'd found in the basement.

Morthwell stood over the victim for a few seconds, switched the gun to his opposite hand, and then did something completely unexpected. Instead of going for the cash register, he began rifling through the clerk's pockets, all the time glancing over his shoulder at the front door. Finally, he found the guy's wallet, searched it, and stuck it back in the clerk's back pocket without apparently taking a dime.

Morthwell then stood and glanced around the store like he was thinking about searching somewhere else. He took one last, long look at the dead man, shook his head in apparent frustration, and headed out the door.

As I reran the video a second and third time, I kept wondering, what was Morthwell looking for in the clerk's pockets? Why didn't he touch the cash register?

I did a quick search to see if I could find anything on Morthwell online, which might give me a clue, but all I turned up was an address and phone number for him on a couple of different sites that listed landlines and addresses.

I extracted the part of the video I was interested in and stored copies of it on two different memory sticks. I also made some individual prints of the frames showing Morthwell shooting the clerk. Last, I erased the hard drive on the recorder and removed it from its housing. I smashed the hard drive flat with a sledgehammer in the workshop in the basement.

When I was done, I labeled three bubble envelopes one, two, and three.

Into the first and second ones, I put a memory stick and copies of the stills.

Into the third one, I put the remainder of the drugs I had bought from Big Mo. I needed a clear head, but I wasn't about to throw a thousand bucks worth of Soma down the drain.

When I had all three envelopes sealed, I wrote a note to Melanie, instructing her to put them in a safe place and only open them if something happened to me. The memory sticks and photos would be self-explanatory. She'd know what to do with the drugs.

When that was done, I drove to Melanie's place and dropped the note and the envelopes through the mail slot of her law office on the ground floor of her house.

After that, I drove south along the Niagara River through the village of Chippawa and past the Chippawa Battlefield—another bloody encounter in the War of 1812. The battle on July 5, 1814 produced 415 dead, wounded, and missing for the British, Canadians, and Canadian-allied Indigenous forces, and 328 for the Americans.

Reports of seeing ghosts of dead soldiers on foggy nights by motorists driving along River Road were commonplace.

I continued past my father's house to a turnoff a few miles south, near where my father had been run into the river. I parked and chucked the battered hard drive and recorder into the swift moving waters.

When that was done, I drove home.

I felt bone-tired but content. Even the sight of Wally Lavaleer's Mercedes parked next to my stepmother's Lexus in the driveway of my father's house couldn't bring me down. After all, if Wally was inside having sex with my stepmother, then he wasn't with Alice May.

My living arrangements at that moment left a lot to be desired. My father had purchased a large, modern, two-story home on a couple of acres along the Niagara Parkway before marrying Carlene. The Niagara Parkway, also called the River Road, ran for thirty-five miles along the Canadian side of the Niagara River between Lake Erie and Lake Ontario. British Prime Minister Winston Churchill once called it the prettiest Sunday drive in the world. My father's house not only had a spectacular view of the river but a separate two-bedroom guesthouse on the side and to the rear of the main house under a large horse chestnut tree. I had taken up residence there when I'd returned from Toronto. My return to the family compound had made Carlene furious. She had tried and failed to get me evicted.

The property was worth a cool two and a quarter million. The trouble was that my father had always used his houses like chess pieces in his financial games. At the time of his accident, the property was carrying a first, second, and third mortgage. Had he not been turned into a vegetable, he would, no doubt, have cleaned up his debts like he had done on so many other occasions.

For the moment, the mortgage payments, taxes, and house expenses were being covered by my father's disability policy, but that money would dry up once he died, which, as much as I didn't want to think about it, was likely to occur sooner rather than later. Unless I figured out how to make MurderLand pay, I could well end up homeless.

Unless, of course, something really bad happened to Carlene.

Given all that had happened, not to mention the alcoholic and pharmaceutical additives I'd put into my system that day, it didn't surprise me that my head was still spinning when I crawled under the covers.

Before falling asleep, I made a mental note to buy a new smart phone.

TUESDAY

When I awoke the next morning, I was so hungover I thought I had dreamt my whole life.

My eyes were stuck shut. My mouth and the front of my face felt numb.

When I finally got my eyes open, I saw Carlene and panicked. She was rooting through my pants. I knew exactly what she was looking for—money.

By the time I reached her, she had a wad of bills in her hand.

"That's mine. Give it to me," I yelled, grabbing for the money.

I was quick, but in my battered state she was quicker. She shot a knee into my groin while I was physically ripping the bills out of her fist.

I went down, but I wouldn't let go. She dropped on me, knees first. The onetime Miss Niagara Wine Region and consummate workout queen pushed an elbow into my already black-and-blue ribs.

I let out a yelp, then another as she yanked my hair.

What could I do? I had to fight back. With my free hand, I shoved her hard, knocking her on her butt, producing a loud yelp of pain. More importantly, she let go of the money.

"You fucking bastard," she hissed, fighting back tears as she rubbed her rear.

"There, there, Carlene. You know how the Lord feels about profanity."

Her glare was pure fire and brimstone. "God is always with me. He knows what I'm doing. If I'm doing it, it's with his approval."

"God must be rolling over in her grave every time you open your mouth."

"Blasphemer. God has a special place in hell for sinners like you."

My father used to say the one thing consistent about Carlene was her religious conviction. After she married my father, she used his money and her newfound status as Ralph Holiday's trophy wife to become a board member of her congregation and help found Carlene's Place. I had never had the pleasure of meeting her God, but I doubted her good deeds cancelled out attempted murder.

"What place in hell does your Almighty reserve for a wife who put her husband into a fatal coma?"

"You are so ignorant." She stood, still massaging her behind.

In all the time I'd been accusing her of trying to kill my father she'd never really denied it.

"And don't forget about your latest attempt to rip off my inheritance. Thou art stealing."

"Fuck you. Your father married me on false pretenses. I could have done much better than marrying him."

I knew the story by heart. When her political ambitions fell apart, she entered the junior management program at the luxury hotel where she was clerking when she met my father. At the time, she was also being hotly pursued by the son of the owner of a fledging winery. My guess was she chose my father over someone her own age for two reasons—because she thought my father and MurderLand were worth far more than the winery at the time, and because she thought my father would die sooner than the younger guy, meaning she'd get her hands on Dad's money faster. She never failed to remind my father that the son of the winery owner had taken over the winery a couple of years later and turned it into one of the most profitable businesses in the region.

"Your father said if I married him, I'd never have to worry about money again. If I had to count on him now, I'd be worried sick. I wasn't born like you with someone paying my way. I have to look out for myself, and I intend to do just that." She headed toward the door, and then stopped and shot me the meanest, nastiest, little smile. "Just so you know, Harry. The hotel deal was my idea, not Wally's. Nothing would make me happier than to see you out on the street and homeless."

"The game ain't over until Elvis leaves the building."

"You're not Elvis, and it's over, believe me, it's over." She curled her lips, displaying teeth that had charmed my father out of his wits. Her smile made me think of a rabid coyote.

I locked my door after she left and made a mental note to remind myself to lock it in the future. Then, I headed into the bathroom and took a long, hot shower, hoping that Carlene wouldn't set fire to the place while I was soaking.

Later, while getting ready for work, I listened to the radio accounts of the convenience store killing.

The first accounts were sketchy.

The night clerk at the Happy Convenience Store on Victoria Avenue in Niagara Falls has been shot and killed according to police reports. The homicide was discovered at seven this morning by the store owner, Kim Lee, when he arrived at work to relieve the night clerk. The name of the victim is being withheld until notification of next of kin. The police are asking anyone with information about the shooting to contact them.

Hmmm, I thought, that would be me.

CHAPTER 11

PILOT HAD ALREADY OPENED THE MUSEUM by the time I arrived. He was sitting at the ticket counter. He'd switched the museum sound system over to the local jazz station. Bessie Smith was singing a sultry "Need a Little Sugar in My Bowl" while he studied his racing form. As usual, he was underlining statistics and jotting down numbers in the columns with a pencil.

"You look like shit, sonny boy," he told me when I stopped at the ticket counter.

"Out late." I stifled a yawn with my fist.

"You hear about the shooting on Victoria Avenue?"

"On the radio. Probably some crackhead."

He raised his chin and looked at me with eyes slightly narrowed. "You didn't have anything to do with it, did you?"

It struck me at that moment that Pilot lived only a block away from the convenience store.

I looked right back at him. "Me? What the heck would that have to do with me?"

"It's not the kind of thing you should be messing with," he said in a warning tone.

"I couldn't agree more." Could he have been out for a walk at three in the morning?

Nah, I told myself. Stop being paranoid. I glanced over his shoulder at his racing form. "See anything interesting?"

"Maybe a nag in the third race at Santa Anita on Thursday. I'm still thinking about it."

"Let me know. Maybe I'll throw in a few bucks." Pilot was one of the best handicappers I'd ever met. The problem was that he rarely found a horse that he liked, and when he did, the odds were so low that it was difficult to make much of a return.

"You should be saving money to keep this place going, not pissing it away on the ponies."

"Not to worry, Pilot. Gina late again?" She was supposed to be manning the ticket counter.

"She's been in the can all morning. Your old man would never put up with a lazy chippy like her. I tried to explain to her the connection between Kennedy, Sinatra, and the Chicago mob, but she didn't even know who Sinatra was. What's wrong with her?"

I ignored the complaint. "Any customers?"

"*Nada.*"

"When Gina comes back, come see me in my office."

"Oh, boy," he said sarcastically. "I'm gonna get my Christmas bonus. Finally."

I went to my office and retrieved my one message. It was from my lawyer Melanie. She wanted me to call her right away.

"I'm a little curious about the packages you left here." She sounded downright worried. "Are you in trouble, Harry?"

"None whatsoever, sweetheart. It's just a little business situation that might come up between the tax department and me. I thought it would be better if I left some of the documents in your care. Don't worry. It's nothing. Really."

"Okay. And if you're not doing anything tonight, we could get together."

"I'll see. I have a pretty busy day. I'll try calling you later."

"Sure. Whatever." She tried to sound casual, but I could hear the disappointment in her voice.

"I'll try to call," I repeated, just to make her feel better.

After I hung up, I thought about the guns and pendant watch I found with the note to return it to Betsy. I was fairly certain that Pilot originally had hidden the guns in the two mannequins after I'd begun scrounging in the basement for items to sell over the past six months. Not wanting to

get into an argument with him over unregistered firearms, I wasn't about
to ask him who Betsy was. Instead, I hunted through my father's old telephone book. I found an entry for a Betsy Stein. I was fairly sure it was the
same Betsy who worked at MurderLand when I was a kid. All I could remember about her was that she smelled like soap and had arms that jig-
gled when she laughed. Under her name was an address in Virgil, a village
a short drive away. The phone number was crossed out. I tried finding a
number for her online but came up empty. My guess was that my dad or
someone had found the old watch, recognized it as one that Betsy had
lost, and Dad intended to return it. Maybe he had tried to return it already
and the old lady was dead.

Writing the address down on a slip of paper and sticking it in my wallet, I told myself the next time I was near Virgil and had some time to kill,
I'd drive by her house and see what I could find. In the meantime, I began
filling out some new government forms. They were supposed to help
small businesses like mine but were simply a way to waste my time and
keep more bureaucrats working in Queen's Park, our provincial parlia-
ment in Toronto. As I worked, I switched on the television with the remote.

The local news was broadcasting new details of the murder story on
Victoria Avenue. The name of the night clerk had just been released—
John "Johnny" Johnson, 49, of Niagara Falls—and surprise, surprise, he
had a police record for burglary, fraud, and receiving stolen goods.

Time of death was set between two thirty and four in the morning.

The police downplayed Johnson's criminal record and stressed that
they were working on several leads. They were also hoping someone
might have seen something and would come forward.

They mentioned that one resident of the area had reported hearing
automobiles starting up on Victoria Avenue around the time of the shooting.

One curious note made me smile. The shopkeeper, Kim Lee, made it
sound like Genghis Khan and his Mongolian hordes had marched
through his shop. He claimed that all the money in the cash register had
been taken as well as several cases of cigarettes and his surveillance recorder. He estimated the loss at eight thousand dollars.

Of course, I had taken the recorder, but I had seen no signs of any
money disappearing from the cash or cases of cigarettes walking out the

door. On the other hand, maybe the guy was telling the truth, and somehow Johnson and Morthwell were working a scam that hadn't appeared on the recorder.

Heck, maybe the shopkeeper was involved in whatever had gone down.

Let the police sort it out, I told myself. If Johnson and Duane Morthwell were known associates, it wouldn't be long before Morthwell was picked up and nailed for the crime.

I flicked off the TV and returned to my paperwork. A few minutes later, Pilot appeared, puffing on a cigarette. As he sat down, I pulled out the remaining money from my pocket and counted out five hundred dollars.

I shoved the money across the desk and told him, "Merry Christmas. This is an advance on the money I owe you."

His pale, bony hands recounted the money before tucking it into the inside pocket of his frayed blazer.

"Things are going to be different from now on," I said brightly.

"Is that the drugs talking?"

I ignored the crack. "I'm thinking about ways to boost sales for the summer. One good summer, and we're back on our feet. But I'll need your help. I need cash. Lots of cash. Cash to keep things going. Cash to buy new artifacts and build new exhibits."

He raised an eyebrow. "You already blew through the stuff I gave you last night?"

I ignored his question. "We need to get the younger generation talking about us. I'm thinking we need objects and displays relating to more recent murders and mysterious deaths, especially ones featured in movies, TV, the media, or on the net. We have to modernize, innovate. Make ourselves more relevant."

"How do you figure on doing that?"

"We find some way to bring back the teenagers. We lure in the ones full of angst or madly in love and want someone to cling to in the middle of something scary. We want a place little kids can see frightening things at a time in their young lives when they're learning to fight against their fears. We want a place where parents and grandparents want to take their children and grandchildren because the kids want to go there."

He took the cigarette out of his mouth and lit another from the butt. "Fucking waste of time. You're talking about a roller coaster for the whole family, but at least you're showing some balls."

"I need your support. I want you in the basement full-time looking for stuff we can sell."

He took a long drag on his cigarette and spoke without taking it out of his mouth. "I hate to rain on your parade, but there ain't much left down there worth selling."

"Whatever you can find, let's put it to work," I said. "What do we have to lose?"

"The whole goddamned history of this place," he said. "You still remember what happened between Sinatra and Kennedy, right?"

It was all there in Pilot's manual. Of course, I remembered. If I felt like showing off, I could have spit out the whole enchilada. JFK's father, ex-Nazi-loving US Ambassador and millionaire, Joseph P. Kennedy, got his old pal from his bootlegging days, Chicago crime boss Sam "Momo" Giancana, the most powerful mobster in the Midwest, to get his good buddy Frank Sinatra to support JFK during the 1960 presidential race between Kennedy and Richard Nixon. Sinatra, arguably the most influential force in Hollywood at the time, went all out, raising over a million dollars for JFK and hooking him up with Marilyn Monroe and Judith Campbell Exner, who also happened to be sleeping with Giancana. The loose screw in the motor was FBI Director J. Edgar Hoover. The president and his younger brother, Attorney General Robert Kennedy, wanted to fire him. Hoover began blackmailing the president about his connections to Giancana. The only thing JFK could do to protect himself was cut his ties with Giancana and Sinatra. The break with Sinatra came at a very bad time for the singer. President Kennedy was planning a trip to Palm Springs, California in 1962 and had promised to stay with Sinatra. Sinatra made massive renovations to his Palm Springs home in preparation of the trip, even referring to it as the new Western White House. JFK went to Palm Springs but snubbed Sinatra and stayed at the home of rival crooner, Bing Crosby, a Republican, who hadn't even supported Kennedy during the election. Frank was mortified in front of all Hollywood and the world.

"I remember, Pilot. But fewer and fewer young people care."

"We can teach them."

"They want to be entertained, not educated."

"Yeah, whatever. You're the boss."

He took a long time to get up and a longer time to reach the door. There, he stopped and looked at me with a tiny smile on his face. "Just don't ever forget who you are. You're Ralph Holiday's son, and Julian Holiday's grandson, sonny boy."

"I won't," I said. I was determined to forge ahead and keep Murder-Land going no matter what.

Even when Gina asked to leave a half hour later, I remained unflappable.

"You just came on duty, Gina, and I need Pilot in the basement."

"Yeah, well, the place is dead anyway. No one's going to miss me. I'll be back after lunch."

"What's the rush?"

"I got something stuck up my vagina last night. I gotta go see my doctor. You want me to show you?"

"I believe you." I said quick enough to keep her from pulling her skirt up any farther. I already knew way more than I needed to know. "Tell you what, Gina. Read a couple of pages from the manual and you can go."

"I can't remember where I put it."

I plucked a copy from the stack of MurderLand manuals on the credenza behind me and handed it to her.

"Here. Read this section about Frank Sinatra and Kennedy. Make peace with Pilot."

She rolled her eyes but marched out of my office carrying the manual.

The ticket counter was vacant when I passed by a half hour later. The manual was on the floor under her chair. I locked up and went outside. On my way to pick up sandwiches for my father and Clive, I wondered if the police had picked up Duane Morthwell yet.

CHAPTER 12

"OKAY, JENNY. Not in the face," Dad seemed to gurgle when I told him that I had plans for boosting attendance at the museum.

Clive Elway shook his head as he munched on his sandwich.

"Go on, Clive. Say it. You know you're dying to say it."

"I hold my views in reserve. Like the three monkeys. Hear no evil, see no evil, speak no evil."

"That doesn't stop you from thinking. Spit it out."

He smiled. "All right. Nothing personal, but I think you're a damned fool. Not that I'm blaming you, but your father doesn't know what you're telling him, and he doesn't care. All he cares about is whether he's fed and his diapers are changed."

"I think he understands," I said.

"Believe what you want. It's a free country."

"The doctors gave him a month to live when they sent him here. That was five months ago. Maybe the doctors are wrong about him coming out of his semicomatose state."

"Your father's a strong one. I'll give him that." He nodded toward the other bed, which had been filled overnight with a frail, bony man. "My new client? He'll be cashing in his portfolio in less than a week."

"What's he in for?"

"What's he in for?" Clive chuckled softly. "What's he in for? *Dying*, brother. That's what he's in for. What else do you think is happening here? Resurrection?"

Death. The great equalizer. The final cut.

"There has to be more," I insisted.

"Why? Just because you want it, doesn't make it so. Just because society wants it, doesn't make it so. Let me ask you something, brother. If your father knew he would end up like this until his death and he could tell you his thoughts right now, do you think he'd tell you to leave him like he is or put a pillow over his face and put him out of his misery?"

I didn't answer. I couldn't answer. I didn't know.

I doubted very much I could end my dad's life, even if he asked me to. Carlene? Now, she was another story. The idea that I might have found a way of getting rid of her kept me in a buoyant and somewhat reckless state of mind.

On the return drive to the museum, I went along Victoria Avenue. The roadwork was in full swing. I was forced to drive slowly, giving me plenty of time to check out the front of the Happy Convenience Store. Yellow police tape was strung across the front door.

A police car was parked at the next light. A policewoman was standing in the road, routing traffic around the construction mess.

As I got closer, I realized the traffic cop was Constable Valerie Runge, Nessa's partner, the person who had collected the money for Nessa the previous night.

I flipped down the sun visor as I went by hoping to shield my face. She was busy with a string of cars coming the other way. I didn't think she saw me.

That was stupid, I thought as I returned to the museum. Stay away from the convenience store.

Gina had returned from her doctor's appointment and was looking through the manual. "If I read this, will I get a raise?"

"We'll talk about it," I said, not sure Gina could read. "Any customers?"

"No customers, but a couple of cops are waiting for you in your office. They showed up about five minutes ago."

"You let them in?"

She shrugged, and then brightened, "Maybe it has something to do with the convenience store killing. My mom was once married to some guy named Johnson. Wouldn't it be weird if I was related?"

Weird wouldn't begin to explain you, I wanted to tell her.

"You want to hear what my doctor said?" Gina called after me as I headed down the hall to my office.

I didn't bother to answer.

I was expecting the police. So I wasn't completely unprepared.

As soon as I entered my office, I recognized Detective Sills, the larger of the two plainclothes officers. I hadn't seen the other officer before. They were standing in front of the credenza, looking at a row of celebrity photos.

Sills was about six feet two or three and weighed a couple of hundred pounds. I guessed he was in his mid-forties. A bulbous drinker's nose over a sloppy brown moustache and heavy-lidded, dark, puffy eyes gave him a permanently sour appearance. What was left of his receding hair was dyed a shade of reddish-brown that only looked good on shoes.

The other detective, who I estimated to be in his late thirties, was perhaps an inch shorter and twenty pounds lighter with a neck that was as wide as his jug-eared, shaved head. His eyes were a pale blue, set over a long, pointed nose and thin lips. A light red, circular scar on his cheek looked like someone had once taken a bite out of it. He was dressed in an expensive, black leather coat and gray slacks.

"Well, if it isn't Harry Holiday," Sills said. "This is my partner, Detective Mallard. I was just telling him what a popular guy your old man was. Too bad he can't protect you any longer."

My father had many friends in high places. He'd made sure that none of the charges against me for pranks in my teen years ever stuck.

"What can I do for you, officers?"

"Start by telling us where you were last night between midnight and four in the morning?"

I had a pretty good idea who had connected me to the convenience store murder, but I wasn't a hundred percent positive. So I decided to say as little as possible until I'd figured out where they were coming from.

"I was at Pole Catz having a few drinks and then at the casino losing money at the craps tables. Afterward, I drove around for a while and went home to sleep."

"The attendant at the gas bar off the QEW says you were at his place between two fifteen and two thirty."

I rubbed my hand over my chin. "Come to think of it, I might have gone over there, but he was closing up."

"He called our hotline. He said you were looking to buy some cigarettes. He sent you to the convenience store on Victoria Avenue."

"He must be mistaken. I stopped for gas. I quit smoking months ago."

Sills and his partner both glanced at the overflowing ashtray on my desk.

"Then, you're a lousy housekeeper."

"They're my butts," Pilot said from the doorway, a lit cigarette dangling from his lips.

He entered the room.

"You got nothing better to do than pick on the kid?" Pilot asked as he emptied the ashtray into the wastepaper basket beside the desk. "You should be ashamed of yourselves. Go on, get out of here."

Sills looked like he might just go. Mallard stepped up to Pilot. "Who are you, old man?"

"The guy who kidnapped Jimmy Hoffa. What's it to you?" Pilot puffed out his sunken chest.

Mallard was about to say something, but Sills stopped him. "Forget it, Mallard. It's just old man Pringle. We hated him as kids. Geezer was always coming up behind you in the museum and trying to scare the shit out of you." Sills turned to Pilot and asked, "You still telling the kids about how you whacked Albert Anastasia?"

"I said I saw him whacked. Kids now-a-days don't even know who he is," Pilot grumbled.

I knew who Anastasia was. The highlight of the Anastasia exhibit was the original barber chair with a mannequin of Anastasia sitting in it and two mannequins, representing his shooters, pumping him full of bullets. Pilot loved scaring the ten-year-olds who got out of line by telling them he'd whacked this guy or that.

"Go take care of your own business, Pops, before you have a heart attack," Sills told him.

Pilot gave Sills and Mallard one last dirty look and walked out with the wastepaper basket under his arm.

Sills turned to me. "So, tell me again, Holiday, after you were at the gas station, where did you go for cigarettes?"

"I told you, I didn't go for cigarettes. The gas jockey's mixing me up with someone else."

"So you went where?"

"Home."

"So you went home. About what time was that?"

I shrugged.

"But you went straight home."

"I drove along the river to the place where my father's car was run off the road. I parked there for a few minutes, thinking about how you guys never found the car that ran him into the river."

Sills ignored my jab. "What time was that?"

"I don't remember exactly."

"Your stepmother says she heard you pull in around three thirty."

Again, I gave them a shrug. "I didn't look at my watch. All I was interested in was crawling into bed. I had way too much to drink."

Sills scowled, maybe remembering one of his own drinking binges. "You mind if we test you for GSR?"

Gunshot residue, I thought. So they definitely had me pegged for the shooter, but they didn't quite have enough to haul me in.

"No problem," I said, surprising both of them. I was sure they were hoping to use my refusal as another piece of circumstantial evidence to talk some judge into issuing a full-blown order to search me and everything connected to me.

While Mallard went to get his briefcase from his car with his testing equipment, Sills kept up a pretense of interrogation by halfheartedly telling me, "Don't think we don't know about you borrowing money from Frankie Argyll."

"So?"

"And you want to tell me about the little trip you made over the border last night?"

They must have checked the NEXUS logs. I doubted whether Nessa or her partner, Valerie, would have said anything about our little transaction. So I felt no qualms about lying.

"I went to look at buildings in Niagara Falls, New York. I'm thinking about branching out or relocating."

"And the name of your real estate broker is?"

"I don't have a New York broker. I'm just looking at potential locations. I drove around."

Mallard returned just then with his field kit and gave my hands the once over. When I asked him about the kit, he explained it was a new kind that used a fiberglass swab and a special liquid that could show the results instantly.

Even I could see from the look on Mallard's face that I tested negative. Mallard also took a set of my fingerprints. I wasn't worried. I'd had my gloves on the whole time at the convenience store.

"You're not home free, Holiday," Sills insisted as Mallard packed up his equipment. "We're keeping an eye on you. You're still a person of interest. So don't be taking any long trips out of town."

"Be sure to let me know how I can help," I said, walking them to the front door and seeing them out.

Gina stopped me as I passed the ticket counter on my way to my office. "I gotta leave early this afternoon. I gotta give Cuddles his pills."

"How early?" I asked, not knowing why I should even care about her or her pet snake.

"I'm thinking like now."

"It's two thirty. We don't close until five."

"It's only this once. You want him to die?"

Actually I didn't give a shit if he died or lived, but I was in a better-than-average mood. "Yeah. Go ahead. Leave. But just this once."

"Oh, thank you, thank you. I'll never forget." She pressed her hands together like she was praying. She was way too excited to be going home to dump pills down her boa's throat.

"You can come in on Sunday if you really want to pay me back," I called after her.

She flipped me the bird before disappearing into the employee change room.

CHAPTER 13

AN HOUR LATER, REGGIE BAKER WAS IN MY OFFICE sitting in the chair opposite me scratching his armpit through his sweater while his digital recorder sat idle on my desk.

Reggie Baker was the crime beat reporter for a new daily newspaper called *The Falls*. It had been started by a couple of right-wing businessmen who'd been frozen out of the local radio and TV market and had enough money to fight a media war with *The Review*, the other daily local. Reggie had once been a top crime reporter in New York City but had been implicated in a police cover-up scheme. He had been fired and had his Green Card revoked. He had been bouncing around the local newspaper circuit on the Canadian side of the border ever since.

"Don't blame me, Harry. I have to check you out. I heard you were involved in the Victoria Avenue shooting."

"How'd you hear that?"

"I got a tip."

"From who? Sills, Mallard, my stepmother?"

"From whom, Harry, from whom? And you know I'm not going to reveal my sources."

He picked up the glass with two inches of my father's best thirty-year-old Glenlivet in it and drank an inch more. That made four inches already in not many more minutes. Neither of us was kidding ourselves. He was there as much for the free booze as he was for the story. I was happy to feed him booze in return for information.

"So what exactly are they saying about me?"

"That's it, Harry. That's why I thought I'd come over and check it out. Everyone's blowing smoke, but no one's got anything on you." He turned on his recorder. "Were you ever in that convenience store?"

"No. Never."

"Did you ever have anything to do with Johnny Johnson?"

"Never heard of the guy."

"So, it's just a coincidence that you asked the gas station attendant where to find cigarettes right around the time of the killing?"

"I don't smoke. The attendant's mixing me up with someone else."

"That's what I had to check out." He clicked off the recorder and peered at me through thick, lightly tinted glasses. He finished the last inch of his scotch and reached for the bottle, but I grabbed it first.

He had a day's growth of beard on his face. His hands were trembling.

To think, he and my dad used to go hunting together.

"What else are you hearing?"

"About you?"

I nodded. He eyed the bottle.

"I'm hearing that Wally Lavaleer and your stepmom have a hotel chain interested in your property."

"You heard they're trying to screw me?"

"I heard her main interest is herself."

"What else?"

"Joey Angelo and Pinkie beat the crap out of you yesterday. And from somewhere you got the money to pay Frankie, and that was before Johnson got killed at the convenience store."

It didn't surprise me how much Baker knew. He was a drunk, but he was also one hell of a reporter.

The one thing he hadn't been able to find out was who ran my old man off the road.

"What else?"

"Nothing about you."

"What about the convenience store shooting?" I waved the neck of the bottle above his glass. Baker knew that hell was likely to freeze over before he got another crack at free liquor that good.

"Preliminary ballistics report indicates the murder weapon's a Colt Detective Special .38 revolver."

He hesitated like he was done.

His tidbit of information dovetailed with the images of Morthwell's gun in the surveillance video, but the news didn't give me anything useful. I held onto the bottle. "Come on, Reggie. You can do better than that. I'm not going to scoop you."

"Police are checking out something else. Some neighbors of Johnson said he seemed to have more than a casual interest in preteen boys."

"A regular Michael Jackson. Police have anything definite?" I poured another couple of inches into his glass.

"Just people saying they had their suspicions. Who knows? Maybe the father of some kid he diddled decided to work it out himself."

"What do you think?"

"I try not to think. I just report what I hear." He drained his glass and set it down a few inches closer to me.

"The next time you're talking to your friends in the police department, maybe you should ask them about progress on the investigation into the murder attempt on my father," I suggested.

"You know I tried to help you out on that one."

"Yeah, but maybe you should tell them they should be looking at who's benefiting most."

"Can't hurt to ask. Can I quote you?"

"I don't see why not."

"You mind repeating it?" he asked as he turned on the recorder again.

I repeated what I'd said. Then, to show my gratitude that someone—anyone—was listening to me about my father's accident, I poured the rest of the bottle into his glass.

After he'd emptied it, he pocketed his recorder, pulled on his overcoat, and left.

Right after Reggie Baker exited, Pilot appeared carrying a couple of plastic bags. He sat opposite me.

"You have more stuff?" I asked.

"Yeah, I have more, but I want to tell you something first. Stay the hell out of the basement. That's my bailiwick. Understand? Every time you go down there, you mix everything up. You're driving me nuts."

"Sorry."

"You better be." He eyed me suspiciously before reaching into the bags, pulling out new items, and giving me a little spiel on each one.

Inside a clear plastic sleeve was a lock of hair that had been allegedly dug up at the site of one of the victims of serial killer Ted Bundy.

Pilot identified a thin green, hardcover book on birds as belonging to Robert Stroud, the Bird Man of Alcatraz. Pilot pointed out pencil notes in the margins by the self-taught scientist and two-time killer.

The next item, a ten-dollar gold certificate, had been part of the ransom for the baby of the famed aviator, Charles Lindbergh. The baby eventually turned up dead. The recovered ransom money was used as evidence to send Bruno Richard Hauptmann to the electric chair.

The pair of sunglasses belonged to Reverend Jim Jones of Jonestown, Guyana. After his disciples killed a US Congressman and several others, Jones flipped out and incited the mass suicide-murder of some 900 of his followers by encouraging or forcing them to drink poison-laced Flavor-aid.

A camel-colored, felt Dobbs fedora with the initials "OM" on the sweatband had belonged to New York gangster, Owney "The Killer" Madden.

For me, Madden had always been one of the most intriguing gangsters of Prohibition Era America. He was a British-born gangster of Irish parents. He got his start in crime as an immigrant kid in the Irish gangs of New York's infamous Hell's Kitchen. He was called "The Killer" because he'd murdered two people before he was out of his teens. Later, he spent eight years in prison for one of about a half dozen known murders he committed. He then went into the liquor business, making beer and operating bars throughout Hell's Kitchen and elsewhere in New York. He was the owner of the Cotton Club, and a boyfriend of Mae West. He bankrolled her first Broadway play and was an investor in her first movie. He represented the Irish gangs for the newly emerging national crime syndicate until 1935 when he retired and moved to Arkansas.

"Didn't Grandpa Julian buy one of Madden's bars after Madden retired?" I asked Pilot, recalling the family connection.

"Good for you, Harry. That's right. Your grandfather managed a bar for Madden on Eighth Avenue and then bought it when Madden went to Arkansas. He sold it when he came up here to open MurderLand."

That's why my grandfather happened to have a signed photo of Mae West, I recalled. Still, while the Madden fedora was a sentimental favorite, it wouldn't bring much.

"That it?" I asked, surveying everything Pilot had found. He was right. We were getting down to the dregs.

"Don't look so glum," he said, digging into the last bag and pulling out a blood stained undershirt and pair of boxer underpants. Both were yellow with age. The shirt had holes in the front and back.

"What's this?" I asked.

"The pièce de résistance. They belonged to Alberta Anastasia. He was wearing them the day he got shot at the Park Sheraton in New York. Your grandfather bought them off one of the morgue attendants." Talking to Detective Sills about Anastasia must have jogged Pilot's memory.

"You have any documentation on these?" I asked, seeing dollar signs before my eyes.

"Nothing in writing, but you can take them to the bank. I was there when your gramps bought them."

It wasn't the best of situations, but I could always write up a certificate of authenticity on museum letterhead. That usually was enough for most collectors.

The rest of the items had pretty good documentation. The letter authenticating the Bundy victim's lock of hair came from one of the volunteers who helped the police comb the Washington State mountainside looking for the remains of women Bundy had killed. The note was exceptionally lurid, describing how Bundy had dumped the bodies of various victims, then returned periodically to masturbate on the corpses. I knew of one collector who was a huge Bundy aficionado. He would definitely want the lock of hair.

"You did great, Pilot," I said, rummaging through my brain for the appropriate collectors who'd pay top dollar for the rest. I had a feeling that the bloody Albert Anastasia clothing could turn into a nice little bidding war between one freak who collected memorabilia related to Murder, Inc. and another who specialized in clothing of victims and killers, especially if soiled.

"We're getting to the bottom of the barrel."

"Keep looking."

Pilot fingered the Owney Madden hat. "It's a shame you gotta let stuff like this go."

"We'll get newer, better stuff. Don't worry."

After Pilot left the office, I began phoning collectors for the unsold items he had pulled from the basement over the last two days. I soon had payments by cash and money orders on the way for the Jim Jones sunglasses, the Birdman book, and the Lindbergh ransom money. The same collector, who purchased the lock of hair from Ted Bundy's victim, also bought the Paso Robles plane crash debris. The doctor in New York, who'd bought the Jean Harlow charm bracelet, scooped up the Owney Madden hat sight unseen because of Madden's connection to Mae West, the Cotton Club, and Madden's onetime bouncer, George Raft, who went on to Hollywood fame. The bidding war for the bloody Anastasia items was going to take longer to conclude because one of the collectors wanted to fly in to see the items but couldn't make it for a few days. That was okay with me as the items I'd already sold were more than enough to cover overhead for the next few weeks.

I was on a natural high. Everything was working out perfectly. I was feeling omnipotent.

Pilot and I locked up early. I got in my car and drove toward Niagara-on-the-Lake, listening to the radio. The convenience store killing had already slipped to the third story behind another suicide bombing in the Middle East and new allegations of kickbacks to a Canadian politician from a defense contractor.

I drove to the Festival Theatre on Picton Street, the biggest of the three Shaw Festival theaters. I snuck in a side door that was always unlocked during rehearsals for cast and crew members who needed to get out of the smoke-free building to feed their nicotine habits.

Once inside, I slipped up to the balcony to watch the closed-set rehearsal, and more specifically, to see Alice May.

I was in luck. They were rehearsing *Pygmalion*, Act I.

Alice (playing Clara), her stage Brother (playing Freddy), and stage Mother (playing Mrs. Eynsford-Hill) had just come from Covent Garden and were ducking the rain under the portico of St. Paul's Church.

I watched Clara's brother, Freddy, run to get a cab and collide with the young flower girl, Eliza Doolittle, whose flowers were ruined in the crash.

The snobbish, social-climbing Clara was appalled when the flower girl tried to hit up their mother for money to pay for the ruined flowers. Professor Higgins (played by the crusty old Sir Gallagher Duckworth) hovered in the background, taking notes, studying the language of the interchanges between Mother, Daughter, and the Flower Girl.

You had to give Alice credit. In a few short years, she had pulled herself out of a world of foster homes, and into a credible acting career where she had already won a coveted spot at the world-renowned Shaw Festival. To my eyes, Alice's performance seemed flawless. Her voice was like silk. I wanted to applaud.

Apparently, Derek Sotherland, the director, a tall, skinny, forty-something guy with a Hitler moustache and a shrill voice, couldn't agree less.

He jumped up from his orchestra seat halfway through Alice's big part and yelled, "STOP, STOP, STOP. Alice, you have it all wrong. This isn't one of your beverage commercials." Alice had made a big name for herself as the party girl in a recent blitz of beer ads. "You're Clara. Wealthy. Sophisticated. Upper class. And a snob. You despise Eliza. She's vermin to you."

"But her brother just knocked down the poor flower girl and wiped out her business," Alice protested.

"Eliza ran into *him*, stupid."

Even from the balcony, I could see Alice's eyes smoldering.

Tell him to shove it, I wanted to yell.

"You're a bitch, Alice. Be a bitch. You know how to do it," he said, and then to everyone, "All right, let's try again."

The director sat down, and the cast returned to their positions and started over.

From the way the director shook his head each time Alice spoke, I knew we were in for another outburst.

"Stop," he shouted again. "Alice, you're destroying the play for all of us."

"Fire the dumb bitch," Sir Duckworth called out in disgust.

Alice gave the grumpy, old actor a fuck-you look that made him bare his teeth.

"Calm down, calm down, everyone," the director shouted, clapping his hands. "Alice, you can do this. I know you can, sweetie. Try to focus."

Sally Helman, my pot dealer, told me that Alice had gotten the job in part because her agent was the director's boy toy.

"Okay, everybody, begin, and Alice, show me your inner bitch," Sotherland demanded.

Apparently, Alice and the rest of the cast did it better on the next go-around, though I couldn't tell the difference. They were a little more than halfway through Act I when I felt a tap on my shoulder. I turned and was surprised to find Wally Lavaleer standing over me, grinning.

"Hey, hotshot, what are you doing here?" he whispered. "Don't you know this is a closed rehearsal?"

"You're not supposed to be here either," I whispered back, my blood already boiling.

I figured he'd sit down quietly and leave me alone. Instead, he leaned over the balcony railing and yelled, "Hey, Derek, did you know that you have a trespasser in the balcony?"

Everyone on stage stopped in their tracks.

I had a sudden urge to throw Lavaleer over the rail.

"Who is that?" the director yelled, peering at the balcony.

Lavaleer didn't respond.

Derek called over his shoulder to some unseen crew member. "Get me a goddamned spotlight up there."

I was pissed. "He'll throw us both out now, asshole."

Lavaleer stood tall, a shit-eating grin on his face.

As the spotlight found both of us, Lavaleer spoke to me out of the side of his mouth. "The only one who's going to get bounced is you, sweet pea. Derek thinks I'm financing his next play."

He laughed as he lifted a hand and waved at the director. "Hi, Derek. It's me, Wally Lavaleer. I just found Harry Holiday up here. Didn't you say you'd barred him from rehearsals?"

The only thing worse than hearing my name echoing through the huge theater was seeing the look of chagrin on Alice's face as she marched offstage.

"Thank you, Wally. I appreciate it," Derek shouted. To other forces hidden from sight, he called, "Get someone up there and have Holiday thrown off the premises. This time for good."

Not knowing the size of the posse coming to get me, I headed for the nearest exit, while Wally yelled after me, "By the way, you were parked in a handicapped spot. I had the police tow your car."

Shit, I thought as I ran down the stairs and crashed through the door to the parking lot.

My car was indeed gone.

That was only part of my problem. I was halfway to the street when two oversized stagehands came running after me.

I was still sore from the beating I'd taken from Joey, so I wasn't about to try to outrun them.

I stopped and decided to make a stand with my back against the trunk of an old tree.

The fact that I was no longer running made the two thugs more cautious.

They slowed to a walk as they continued to approach me. The bad news was that one of them had a nail gun in his hand. The good news was that they stopped a few yards from me. Even from that distance I could see their pupils were completely dilated. Both were stoned out of their gourds.

"Hey, dudes, you really want to do this?" I asked, holding up the peace sign. "Derek's a shit. He isn't worth it."

"But you keep coming back, man," the guy with the nail gun said, still trying to catch his breath.

"You're getting us in trouble. Derek's gonna make our lives miserable if we don't kick your butt," the other one added, contorting himself into a half-assed kung fu stance. He kept readjusting his legs to avoid tipping over.

These guys were serious potheads, not bouncers. "Just tell Derek you beat the crap out of me. Who's to know, dudes?"

They stared back. Then, almost like lights going on in all four of their eyes, their eyebrows went up. They turned and glanced at each other, then back at me.

"So, we tell him we kicked the shit out of you?" the guy with the nail gun asked, lowering his weapon.

"Right."

"And you don't say anything?" the guy without the nail gun asked, rubbing his arms. Both were wearing only T-shirts. Their teeth were starting to chatter.

"I know how to keep my mouth shut."

They looked at each other again and nodded, and then the guy with the nail gun said, "Just don't come back. Okay?"

"Okay."

I wasn't planning on coming back. But the incident did give me one more reason to think about getting rid of Wally and Carlene.

Retrieving my car only added to my reasons. It cost me two hundred bucks and the rest of the afternoon to get it out of the police pound.

Enough is enough, I told myself as I drove away from the pound and headed toward the most recent address I'd been able to find for the one person who might just be able to completely turn my world around.

CHAPTER 14

DUANE MORTHWELL, THE CONVENIENCE STORE KILLER, was going to be my fixer. So far, it looked like the police hadn't nailed him.

I would have been smarter to wait a few days to see what the police did before checking out Morthwell, but I was growing increasingly impatient. Who knew? Maybe the fact that I hadn't had any drugs all day was making me jittery.

It was nearly dark by the time I reached Duane Morthwell's place in Silvertown, a Niagara Falls neighborhood of rundown houses, light industrial warehouses, and manufacturing plants. His small bungalow was a couple of houses away from a quiet intersection with four-way stop signs controlling traffic in all directions.

Duane appeared to be home. His Camaro was parked in the driveway. Unfortunately, the shades on the house were drawn so I couldn't see in.

I drove around the block and past Duane's place a second time. The house on one side of Duane's had its doors and windows boarded up and a for sale sign on the front lawn. On the other side of his place was a house with a chain-link fence around it and a couple of Dobermans behind the fence. They barked at my car as I went by.

I drove around the block again and parked just before the intersection where I could watch Morthwell's place without being conspicuous.

I got lucky. I hadn't been sitting there more than twenty minutes when Duane came outside and got in his car.

I followed him across town to a cheapo parking lot six blocks from the Fallsview Casino and Resort complex.

I drove to a nearby lot, parked, and watched Duane walk up the hill toward Fallsview Avenue. Over the last dozen years, the billion-dollar Fallsview Casino Resort—with its Vegas-style casino, hotel, theater, and luxury shops and restaurants—had turned the Fallsview district into Niagara's newest center of gravity. Surrounded by a dozen high-rise hotels, the hill gave its hotel and restaurant guests one of the most spectacular views of the Horseshoe Falls. The buildings also had an unexpected impact on the environment. By altering the wind patterns, the new structures appeared to have caused an increase in the amount of mist that hovered over the falls. The new buildings had also turned the hill into a series of mini-wind canyons, which funneled the air into ice-cold jets that made my face ache.

Hunched over, I kept my distance, walking a couple of hundred feet behind Duane. He was busy holding his hand on top of his cowboy hat to keep it from flying off in the fierce wind.

At Fallsview Avenue, he turned in the opposite direction from the casino and headed toward the row of hotels to the south.

He continued past the first hotel, then across the front driveway of the second one, stopping in front of the side door where the shuttle busses picked up and dropped off passengers. He lit a cigarette and hunched in the doorway.

When the next shuttle bus pulled to the curb a few minutes later, he waited for a couple of elderly ladies to get off. Then, he approached the open door of the bus and talked to the driver while he continued to smoke. Less than a minute later, the driver got out. Duane ground out his cigarette on the sidewalk, climbed into the bus, and sat in the driver's seat.

He's on the night shift for one of the shuttle busses, I told myself. Very interesting. He could have been coming from work between two thirty and three in the morning when he shot Johnny Johnson.

I ducked into the recess of the hotel's main entrance fifty feet from the shuttle bus. I could see him, but he wouldn't likely see me since he was concentrating on the side door of the hotel where the shuttle passengers departed and returned.

He sat in the driver's seat for another couple of minutes. Finally, he checked his watch and headed out on his route with an empty bus.

The round trip from the new hotels to the Clifton Hills hotels and back with a half dozen stops in between, would take him thirty minutes. He would do the run a dozen times by two thirty when the shuttles dropped off their last passengers for the night.

He would definitely be tied up long enough for what I had planned.

I drove back to Duane's house, feeling high on adrenaline. I parked on the next street. Before I got out, I took a handful of tools and a flashlight from my glove compartment.

I went down the driveway of the boarded-up house, crossed the side lawn to Duane's side door, and knocked on it just as a precaution.

When no one answered, I tried the door. It was locked, but the lock was so loose, I had it open in a matter of seconds with nothing more than a little pressure from the screwdriver between the door and the frame. The side door opened into a tiny kitchen.

Once inside, I used the flashlight to give myself a tour, careful not to shine the light on the curtains.

Duane wasn't much of a housekeeper. The sink was filled with a mismatched collection of dirty dishes and glasses. The frying pan on the stove had a thick layer of grease in the bottom.

The kitchen table was stacked high with opened and unopened mail. I leafed through the opened mail with my gloved fingers.

According to his latest bank statement, he had a hundred and sixty dollars in his checking account and four hundred and seventy-eight dollars and change in a savings account. Duane was living from paycheck to paycheck, if you could call it living.

From evidence in the refrigerator and garbage can, he had been subsisting on no-name-brand macaroni and cheese, bacon, beer, and cigarettes.

The living room had the funky smell of a cheap, furnished rental. The ancient couch was covered with a blanket. An old analog tuner and tape deck sat on a board held up by a couple of cinderblocks. A large collection of old rock 'n' roll and country and western tapes sat beside them, half of them by Elvis, Roy Orbison, or Patsy Cline.

The only surprise was the pet gold fish in a small bowl sitting on a side table next to a can of fish food and an old photo of an elderly woman who looked to me like the grandmother who'd raised him when we'd been in school together.

The bathroom smelled of mold. It contained what I expected—soap, shampoo, shaving gear, toothbrush, paste, a comb, and a couple of filthy old towels. I took off the top of the tank behind the toilet bowl, wondering what might be stashed there.

Nothing.

The bedroom was furnished with a bed, an old painted dresser, a nightstand, and lamp. The bed was unmade. An ancient, cheapo, combination tape cassette player and TV and a stack of porn videos sat on the dresser.

I looked through the closet and the drawers of the dresser.

Nothing but clothes.

An answering machine that must have been twenty years old sat on the nightstand next to a cheap telephone. The guy was in a serious need of a techno makeover.

Inside the nightstand drawer were a couple of packages of rolling papers and a roach clip but no drugs.

It didn't look like he had much of a sex life either. A box of unopened condoms sat in the back of the drawer. I wondered if he knew they'd expired two years before.

The ringing phone made me jump.

The ancient answering machine picked up on the third ring. The outgoing message was in Duane's voice, plain, and to the point, "Hey, this is Duane. What can I do you for?"

The caller was a telemarketer selling carpet cleaning services. He didn't appear to realize he was talking to a machine until halfway into his spiel when the machine beeped.

After the telemarketer hung up, the machine reset itself. I noticed that the tape was half full. I pushed the button to replay the messages from the beginning.

They were all from telemarketers. There must have been twenty of them.

Sheesh, I thought as I reset the tape. What a life? Not much mystery here.

And yet as I locked up and headed to my car, I couldn't help wondering—what had last night been all about? I found no gun, no hoard of cigarettes, no other contraband. Of course, he or his confederates could have the booty stashed somewhere else.

But why had Duane Morthwell shot Johnny Johnson?

Maybe I didn't need to know. It wouldn't matter one way or another to my own plans.

CHAPTER 15

IT WAS STILL EARLY. But I had finished everything I dared do that night concerning Morthwell.

What I had undertaken left me pumped. I turned on the radio, found a channel in Buffalo playing old rock 'n' roll, and sang my lungs out to the Rolling Stone's "Sympathy for the Devil."

I drove with the car windows down and the cold air numbing my face, but it didn't cool me off.

The sensible thing would have been to go home and call it a day, but I was way too out of control for that. I wanted to get high and get laid.

I drove to Queenston and cruised by Alice's house. Her car was gone. The lights were out.

From there, I skipped over to Niagara-on-the-Lake and cruised along Picton Street to Queen Street with detours up and down several side streets. I drove past all the elegant Victorian buildings, which had been turned into upscale hotels, bed and breakfasts, gift shops, restaurants, and bars.

I stopped in a few of the bars that were struggling through the lean winter months. The only patrons were locals and a handful of actors and crew who had already arrived in town for rehearsals for the upcoming season.

Alice was not among them. No one I asked knew where she might be.

On the return trip to the Falls, I remembered that I'd promised to call Melanie and hadn't. Well, I still didn't. I went to Pole Catz first and got loaded to the gills doing vodka shots with an older Romanian stripper who'd managed to slip into the country before the ban on foreign peelers went into effect. In years past, Canadian owners of exotic dance clubs had been so desperate for talent they began hiring girls from all over the world. At one time, the number of non-strippers trying to use this route to gain entry into Canada was so large that immigration officials required the applicants to submit fully nude performance photos of themselves to be considered for a work permit. The practice of granting temporary work permits to strippers ground to a halt when a federal cabinet minister got caught fast-tracking a residency application for a dancer who helped in her election campaign.

What a country, I thought as I headed over to Melanie's.

As usual, Melanie was glad to see me. I reassured her that the three envelopes I'd dropped off that morning were nothing to worry about. We smoked a joint and went to bed.

What can I say? With my eyes closed, Melanie made a good substitute for Alice May.

"I just love making love to you," Melanie said afterward, still nuzzled against me on the damp sheets.

"You're the greatest," I said, "but I should be going."

"Actually, I think your little fellow would like to stay." She gripped me tighter.

I was getting hard again in spite of plans to leave. "I have to get up early and work. So do you."

"All I have is a ten o'clock with a couple of gay clients." She shifted her position so she could face me and tease me at the same time. "I love gay marriages. They get hitched, and then they have to come in and get their wills redone. I get an extra week at La Costa."

Melanie's greatest pleasure, besides screwing and smoking grass, was going to the most expensive spas in the world. La Costa in southern California was her newest favorite.

"Stop thinking so much and just do it to me," she said, rolling on her back and yanking me on top.

The second time lasted longer than the first. I was so exhausted afterward that I must have passed out. I only woke up when she began to wiggle out from under me.

"Don't go," she insisted as I started to sit up. She stuck her hands in my crotch and tried to resurrect me a third time. I was at risk of turning into her bitch.

"I have to go."

She leaned over and kissed me. "You're a beautiful lover."

"You, too," I said, and meant it, but I still couldn't help silently asking, why can't you be Alice May?

I got dressed. I kissed Melanie good night and promised to call.

I checked the car radio for the basketball scores and got some bad news. Both of my picks, the Bulls and the Nets, had gone down in flames in their respective games. I should have been a little pissed but even dropping twenty grand wasn't going to bring me down.

I was still in a good mood when I pulled the Lincoln into my driveway. I didn't give Wally Lavaleer's Mercedes a second thought.

At least I know where he isn't, I told myself as I entered my place and went to bed.

I read a couple of chapters of Machiavelli's *The Prince*, which I had picked up from my father's collection, hoping it might give me some insight into how he ran his business.

If I dreamed, I don't remember.

WEDNESDAY

I woke to the sound of the telephone ringing. It reminded me I still hadn't gotten a new cell phone.

I picked up the receiver and heard Melanie on the other end.

"I thought you said there was nothing to worry about." She sounded grumpy.

"What's the problem?" I took the portable phone into the bathroom so I could relieve myself while I talked. In the mirror, I noted my bruises had turned a psychedelic purple-yellow.

"*The Falls* has an article about the convenience store murder. It says you were questioned by police."

"A lot of people were questioned, Melanie. Stop worrying." I tried to aim my stream at the side of the bowl so she wouldn't hear me.

"Are you peeing while I'm talking to you?"

"I didn't think you'd mind."

"This is serious, Harry. We have to talk. You could come here right away, or I could cancel my ten o'clock, and you could meet me."

"Melanie, trust me. There's nothing to worry about. I was out late."

"Doing what?" She sounded scary, like a wife.

"On the night of the convenience store murder, I was at the casino, then, home in bed."

"An unidentified police source says you stopped in a gas station for cigarettes and the attendant sent you to the convenience store."

"I stopped for gas. I haven't smoked in months."

"What about the envelopes?"

"An entirely different matter. Stop fretting. This will all blow over as soon as they catch the killer. I guarantee you, it won't be me."

"Promise me you'll call me before you do anything crazy."

"Crazy, how? Like last night? Was that crazy enough for you?"

She giggled. "I wish you were here. I could cancel my appointment."

"I have to work. You have to work. You don't want to miss your next spa vacation."

"You're right. Speak to you later."

I hung up. I crossed the living room and opened the front door. My free copy of *The Falls* was on the porch. Every house along the parkway had been getting a free subscription as a promotional effort to boost circulation. I turned to the front page and began reading about the murder while I made some instant coffee.

Reggie Baker had opened the article by quoting an anonymous police source saying that Harry Holiday, president of the Niagara Falls' landmark museum, MurderLand, had been questioned extensively by police about the convenience store killing after a gas station attendant had reported sending him there for cigarettes around the time of the murder. Good old Reggie.

What really pleased me most was the last paragraph.

Holiday is the son of Ralph Holiday, former president of MurderLand and a prominent local businessman, who has been in a coma following an accident from unknown causes six months ago on the Niagara Parkway. The younger Holiday continues to insist that the police have been derelict in their duties by not pursuing the investigation. In other interviews, Holiday has claimed that,

"All the police have to do to find out who ran my father's car off the road is to look at who benefits from his death."

I was just finishing my coffee when the door flew open, reminding me once again that I had to remember to lock it.

"You bastard. I'll sue you," my stepmother screamed as she charged into my place wearing her mink coat over her workout clothes. She tried to swat me with her copy of *The Falls*. I had trouble keeping the table between us.

"Fucking rotten creep," she wailed. "Who the hell do you think you are?"

"Definitely not the person who ran my father's car off the road."

She shoved the table at me, hitting my thighs, but not hard enough to do any serious damage. "You think it's easy being your father's wife?"

"You could have divorced him. Or died, like my mother."

"I worked hard for what I'm going to get."

"So my father was a job to you?"

"You don't know much about your old man, do you? What if I told you your father was thinking about getting rid of me?"

"How? Like having you killed?" I joked.

"You don't believe he could do something like that, do you, you simpleton?"

I wished he could, I thought.

"He didn't deserve what you did," I told her.

"Anything I get I deserve." Her voice was like ice.

"They should bring back hanging just for you."

"Fuck you." She turned to go, then stopped and faced me again. "Think about this, you little dope fiend. If I could do what you say I did to your father, then I could do it to you, too. Couldn't I?"

Her eyes were beyond angry. They had reached the dead zone. I felt the chill all the way down my back. Carlene was capable of murder. For my father's sake, I wished I could capture that look and take it to the police.

"Are you threatening me?" I asked.

"What do you think? Try me again and find out." She held my gaze for several seconds, making sure that I would never forget that look. She was threatening me.

I probably should have been scared, but I wasn't. I couldn't be. I was already steeling myself to kill her. It felt good in a weird sort of way to know she was responsible for my father's accident. I had no doubt she was coming for me if I got in her way.

I intended to get in her way.

Any doubts I may have had about Duane Morthwell and my plans for Carlene were gone.

We are at war. It won't end until one of us is dead, I told myself.

CHAPTER 16

As I expected, by the time I arrived for work at eleven, the museum was enjoying an increase in attendance. *The Falls* was distributed free to the hotels and motels in the area. The publicity from the article on the convenience store killing had produced a slow but steady stream of tourists visiting the museum.

Gina told me she'd sold eighteen tickets that morning, all of them senior discounts, almost all in cash. She also said Pilot was pissed that I hadn't shown up at opening time.

"Glad you could make it," Pilot said sourly as soon as I found him. "We've been swamped."

"I wouldn't call eighteen customers a tidal wave, Pilot."

"They came to see the convenience store killer, sonny boy. You ought to stay in the lobby and talk to people. Good word of mouth. We could print fliers. Maybe Gina could pass them out on Clifton Hill."

"You're kidding, right?"

He sucked in his lips until they nearly vanished.

"You and Gina take care of the customers," I said. "I have things to look after."

"What things?"

"I thought you were the guy who knew too much?"

"Up yours. I'm on a cigarette break." He shuffled off toward the employee lounge while I headed to my office.

My morning turned out to be busier than I expected.

FedEx delivered checks and cash for the remains of the Paso Robles plane crash, the Jim Jones sunglasses, the lock of hair from one of Ted Bundy's victims, Owney Madden's fedora, the Birdman book, and the Lindbergh ransom money. I started packaging and labeling the goods.

Since all the buyers were in the US, I was planning to take the parcels over the border myself and send them from the other side through the US Postal Service to avoid customs.

I was hurrying to finish the packaging to try to beat the midday rush at the post office, but before I could finish, my two new admirers, Detectives Sills and Mallard, showed up. Gina brought them to the office and seemed eager to stay until I sent her back to her station.

Sills explained, "We have a witness who says they saw a car down the street from the convenience store around the time Johnson got shot. They say the car was a light colored Lincoln, an older model."

I said nothing. I waited.

Sills was watching me watch him. I looked away to check on Mallard.

The bags under his eyes suggested he hadn't slept much since the last time we'd talked.

Sills leaned over the desk. "Come on, Holiday, talk to me. You know I'm okay. I was a friend of your father's. Tell us about the car."

My instincts told me they were just fishing. "I already told you. I wasn't there."

"Maybe you forgot?" Sills coached me with his head slightly tilted as if he was being sympathetic.

"I wasn't there," I repeated respectfully. "I'm sorry. I can't help you."

"But you were driving around in a light blue Lincoln around the time we're talking about."

"Detectives, I have a lot of work to do. I'd like to help you, but I can't. I don't know anything. If you want to pursue this, I would be happy to call my lawyer.

"You could talk to us now without a lawyer."

"Right now, I have to get back to work."

I walked them out and returned to sealing my packages, convinced the cops were kicking tires.

I drove over the Whirlpool Rapids Bridge with no delays and got my packages off in the mail—no insurance—just like the diamond and jewelry people do. Insurance is red meat to the thieves inside the post office.

Happily, I breezed over the bridge back to Canada with no problems and no sign of Nessa Wiley.

I picked up two sandwiches at Tony's and headed to the nursing home.

I sat in the room beside my father, listening to him mumble what I still was willing to swear sounded like, "Okay, Jenny. Not in the face."

Was Jenny possibly a wild distortion of Deirdre, the name of my mother? Was it the name of one of my father's countless other babes? I had ruled out Helen and Marla, the names of the two wives he had married and divorced between my mother and Carlene. Neither of those names sounded anything like Jenny.

I thought about Betsy Stein, who may or may not have been the woman to whom I was supposed to return the pendant watch. Maybe she could help. Somebody had to know who Jenny was. Why not an ex-employee?

While I was making a mental note to remind myself to try to find Betsy Stein, Dad's roommate was blowing the loudest, smelliest farts that I'd ever encountered. Even after I opened the window, I could still barely breathe.

Clive showed up twenty minutes after I arrived. He was carrying a copy of *The Economist* under his arm and a scowl on his face. "Please don't open the window without permission," Clive scolded me. "You risk freezing my clients to death."

He closed the window before sitting down. Once seated in the chair on the other side of the new guy, Clive removed the wrapping from his sandwich, took a bite, and began leafing through his magazine without speaking. Something was bugging him.

"Sorry about the window."

He looked up. "If you are in the mood to ask for forgiveness, then you could apologize for not telling me you are moving your father to another facility. Were you planning to simply vanish and not say goodbye?"

"What are you talking about?"

"As if you don't know."

"Know what?"

"Your stepmother and Dr. Patek were here this morning talking about transportation for your father to Maple Creek."

My brain switched to high alert. Patek was the head of the Graystone Nursing Home.

"Tell me you're kidding."

"I wouldn't joke about that. Go ask Dr. Patek or your stepmother. She said she wanted your father out of here by the end of the week."

The end of the week? That miserable....

The Maple Creek Chronic Care Rest Home was one step up from a morgue. They had been closed down so many times for vermin, patient abuse, and fraud that I was surprised to hear that they were still in business. After deducting the part of the expenses the government picked up, Maple Creek was also about half the price of Dad's present accommodations. Carlene was no doubt working some new scam to skim off part of the money from his insurance and personal funds. Or she was just getting ready to finish him off.

"I have to do something about this," I said.

"That is your business," Clive said. He was licking his fingers when he suddenly let out a little, "Uh-oh" jumped to his feet, and bent over my dad's roommate. The old guy was staring at the ceiling with his mouth and eyes open. Clive felt the man's neck for a pulse.

"Stone cold dead. I have to get back to work," Clive sighed. "I thought he'd been too quiet these last few minutes. Hope the cold air didn't kill him."

I left while Clive called the nurses' station.

CHAPTER 17

DOWNSTAIRS IN THE ADMINISTRATION WING, I managed to squeeze in a few minutes with Graystone's CEO, Dr. Patek, a short, round, well-dressed man in his fifties.

At first, Patek didn't sound very encouraging. The arrangements to move my father had already been made, and another patient on the facility's waiting list was already scheduled to arrive on Friday. When I told Patek my father's roommate had just died, he brightened. "I'm sorry to hear that, but I think this may be a blessing in disguise for you. Give me a moment." He turned away from me and tapped on his keyboard for a couple of minutes before looking up again with a toothy smile. "I have good news. We will be able to keep your father here and in the same room. We will move him, of course, to the bed closer to the window."

"Why can't he stay in his own bed?"

"Because that bed has been reassigned. Corporate policy."

Ridiculous, I thought but I decided to let it go. The only thing I really cared about was keeping my father at Graystone. I suspected my father wouldn't know the difference. "Mail the paperwork to me. I'll make sure that any costs not picked up by the government are paid by me personally."

I'll find the money, I told myself as I drove to the museum. I couldn't let Dad go to Maple Creek.

Gina and Pilot were both wiped out from the afternoon rush of another two dozen people. My employees were both grumpy because I'd left them on their own.

"We should hire more people," Pilot insisted, sitting in my office. "You can't run this place with a skeleton crew."

"We should have a union, ask for more pay, and get rid of these smelly uniforms," Gina added, hovering over Pilot's shoulder.

"Here." I divided the day's receipts between the two of them. "Enjoy it while it lasts. By tomorrow, the convenience store murder and its connection to the museum and me will be old news, and we'll be begging for customers."

"Suits me." Gina counted her money and stuffed it in her blazer pocket. "You think I can go home now?"

"Yeah, both of you can go home. You did a great job. I'll see you tomorrow."

As soon as they left, I sat back and tried to think. Would I really be able to keep the museum afloat? Would my plan for Carlene and Wally really work? Or would I be better off letting everything fall apart, let my father go to the glue factory, and forget about Carlene? If, as I believed in the deepest recesses of my heart, Carlene had been responsible for my father's current condition, could I forgive and forget?

Don't quit, I chided myself. Show some guts. I'm Ralph Holiday's son and Julian Holiday's grandson.

I had no drugs on hand to give me a lift. So, I settled for a couple of shots of scotch from my dad's liquor cabinet.

Feeling refreshed, and ready to put the next part of my plan into action, I locked the front door and turned on the alarm. Just before heading out the back way, I glanced out the rear window and noticed two hulks huddling in a dark corner of the parking lot.

I couldn't make out their faces, but I could see they were facing the rear door like they were waiting for me to come out.

I was pretty certain they weren't cops. If I was under surveillance, the cops would be sitting in a nice warm car instead of freezing their asses off standing in the parking lot.

I'd paid Frankie what I owed him. So they were unlikely to be his people. I could think of a few other people around town I owed money to, but none were the type to send muscle to collect.

Carlene was another possibility. Maybe she was planning to take me out sooner than I imagined.

Calling the police was not an option.

I decided to handle the situation on my own.

I went to the basement to the old ventilation duct where I had stored the two guns.

I was pleased to see that Pilot hadn't found them. The first one I took out seemed about as good as any. It was the five-shot snub nose .38 Smith and Wesson Terrier. I stuck it into my coat pocket and returned upstairs.

By the time I looked outside again, whoever had been there was gone. Even so, I kept the gun in my hand inside my pocket as I went through the door. It made me feel more at ease. For all I knew, the hulks were still waiting to get me.

I drove to Melanie's, keeping an eye out for the hulks and anyone else who might be tailing me.

Melanie buzzed me in. I found her upstairs in her bathroom with the door open. She was dressed only in her bra and pantyhose. She flashed me a quick smile as she continued to fuss with her hair and makeup.

"Hot date?"

"I have to meet a client for a drink."

I sat down on her bed next to a pretty silver-blue evening gown and began rolling myself a joint from her diminishing stash. "Got time for a quickie?"

"Not now, sweetie. I'm already behind schedule. And if you want to smoke, please take it into the living room. I don't want my clothes to smell."

I moved to the living room, sat on her couch, and lit the joint.

She entered the living room a few minutes later wearing the silver-blue evening gown. The cloth looked almost wet clinging to her skin. Her lips were blood red and moist.

"You can stay if you want, but I have to leave," she said, pulling at the bottom of her bra through her dress.

"I have to go, too, but I need to pick up two of my envelopes first."

"Can it wait until tomorrow? I really must get going."

"I need them tonight."

"All right. We'll get them on the way out." She checked herself in the mirror on the wall over the sofa and frowned slightly.

"You look fabulous," I said, meaning it and also feeling a twinge of jealousy. She never dressed like that for me.

"Thanks." She smiled.

"Must be an important client."

"We'll see."

"You want some?" I held up the joint.

"No." She waved the smoke away.

Grabbing her fur coat off the railing, she started down the inside staircase that connected her living quarters to her office. The strong scent of her musk was making me horny.

"You sure you don't have time for a quickie? You'd be more relaxed for your meeting."

"Fuck off, Harry." She laughed, but I could hear the edge in her voice.

I watched her cross the room to a wall of filing cabinets on the other side of her desk. She took a key from her purse and opened a drawer.

"Just envelopes two and three," I said as she flipped through the folders.

She removed the two envelopes and relocked the cabinet.

"Sorry, hon, but I really do have to fly. Wish me luck." She buttoned her coat, air-kissed me, and led me outside.

"Break a leg," I told her as she hopped into her SUV.

As I watched her drive away, I almost felt like following her, just to see what the big meeting was all about. Instead, I sat in my car, finished the joint, and pocketed the Soma from envelope number three.

I drove to Pole Catz and killed some time drinking scotch and buying lap dances from a stripper named Bambi from Moose Jaw with big hair and crooked teeth. By the time I headed to the Fallsview district on the hill I was ready for anything.

I pulled into the same parking lot I'd used the night before when I'd followed Duane Morthwell. While I was waiting for him to show up for work, I went through envelope two, sorting through the photos of him at the convenience store. I picked one of the tamer ones showing him entering the store before he blew Johnny Johnson away. I folded the photo in half.

I wanted to whet his appetite but not scare him off with the more gruesome shots.

At a quarter to seven, his rusty Camaro pulled into the parking lot beside mine just as I expected. He was an unrepentant creature of habit.

I hung back as I followed him on foot to the shuttle stop in front of the side door of the hotel. I watched him smoke a cigarette.

I was in luck. No one else was waiting for the shuttle.

When it arrived, it dropped off an old man and two old women. After the riders departed, the other driver exited and shot the shit with Morthwell for a couple of minutes before leaving Morthwell and heading in the direction of the parking lots.

Morthwell continued to smoke for another minute until he finally ground out his cigarette and hopped on the bus.

I checked one last time to make sure no one was hurrying down the side corridor to try to catch the shuttle. When I was sure I was the only passenger, I stepped quickly into the bus.

Up close, Morthwell looked ten years older than he did in the surveillance camera photos. His skin was lined, pale, and pimply.

"Can I see your pass, please?" he asked politely looking up only partway.

"Sorry. I don't have one, but this should do." I fished a twenty out of my pocket and dropped it into his tip bucket.

He glanced into the bucket and then raised his head a few more inches, studying my face. His hair could use a good washing.

"Remember me?" I asked.

"Yeah. Harry Holiday. From high school. Your father owns Murder-Land. I used to beat you up and steal your lunch money in elementary school."

"Good memory."

"What do you want?"

"A ride."

I sat down in the seat on the other side of the aisle kitty-corner to the driver's seat.

A man of few words, he simply shrugged and drove the short block to his next stop.

Again, I was in luck.

No one got on. A minute later, we were on the road, heading toward the Fallsview Casino two blocks away.

Halfway there I got up and stood beside him.

"You're supposed to stay behind the white line until the bus stops," he said. He pointed to the sign overhead.

"I want to talk to you."

"I can't talk. I'm on duty. Some other time."

"You see my name in the papers this morning?"

"Why would I see your name in the papers?"

I was sure he'd been following to the news, waiting for the ax to fall ever since he'd shot Johnson.

"The police have been questioning me about the convenience store killing."

He remained silent as he pulled into the passenger loading area at the rear of the Fallsview Casino complex.

When no one got on, I took the folded photo out of my pocket and handed it to him. "Here. Open this when you're by yourself. If you want to find out more, then be at Brock's Monument at Queenston Heights tomorrow at four. I'll meet you by the tower."

"What is this? Some kind of joke?"

"No joke. We'll talk tomorrow."

I stepped into the stairwell and walked down a step. He pulled the lever. The door swung open. Before getting out, I reached over and plucked the twenty-dollar bill out of the tip bucket.

His mouth fell open, but he didn't say anything.

"For the lunch money you stole. Now, we're even." I was hoping it would show him he wasn't dealing with some kid he used to bully.

CHAPTER 18

THE ENTIRE INTERACTION WITH DUANE MORTHWELL took no more than ten minutes.

I surprised myself by how calm, cool, and collected I'd been.

I was on a roll. I fingered the gun in my pocket as I walked along the near-deserted streets to the parking lot. No one was going to get in my way.

I drove to Queenston, hoping to catch Alice at home, but she was out. I cruised through Niagara-on-the-Lake. She wasn't there.

I drove to Melanie's, but she hadn't returned from her meeting. Just for the fun of it, I hit a few of the other strip joints around town, looking for the elusive good time. I ended up at strip club at the edge of town buying shooters for a dancer from the Maritimes. She was having a miserable time because her boyfriend had dumped her and run off with another woman, and her brother had just been diagnosed with cancer and had three months to live. I felt lucky because I could fix most of my problems.

I drove to Queenston again, but Alice was still out, and I was too beat to wait around hoping she'd return.

I finally arrived home around two in the morning. The one bit of good news was that Wally Lavaleer's Mercedes was parked in the driveway, meaning he wasn't with Alice.

Eat or be eaten, I told myself as I slipped off to sleep. Darwin was right. The urge to kill or cower is innate in each of us.

THURSDAY

I woke up at three forty-five when Wally peeled out of the driveway.

Prick, I thought, turning over and letting out a little yelp when I hit one of my bruises the wrong way.

I tried to get back to sleep, but I was too wired.

I remained in bed and read until seven, got up, showered, dressed, and headed to the main house to steal Carlene's newspaper. In addition to *The Falls*, she also got *The Review*.

My timing couldn't have been worse. Carlene opened the door just as I got there. She was in her bathrobe, holding the hem closed with one hand as she reached for her papers.

Had I been just a little quicker, I might have arrived in time to step on her fingers. Instead she snatched both papers from the stoop. She would have slammed the door in my face if I hadn't grabbed it.

She stared at me like she was thinking about whether or not to take a swing.

I struggled to keep my voice under control. "Moving my dad to Maple Creek is really sick. The worst part is that you're doing it so you can get more of his money."

She glared at me. "Get real. He's old. He's in a coma. The secret of happiness is money, Harry. Your father can't give it to me anymore. I'm taking what I need."

"He wouldn't be where he is if you hadn't put him there."

"Run this by me again, Harry. Am I supposed to be quaking in my boots because of what you think?"

"That's up to you."

"Yeah, well, your days are numbered. Enjoy them."

I started to walk away, wondering if she might be referring to the two hulks from the night before.

"I can't wait until your father's dead," she screamed at me.

I kept going, afraid if I turned around I might pull the gun out of my coat pocket and blow her away. I couldn't imagine enjoying anything more than watching the expression on her face.

No, I reminded myself. I could imagine something sweeter—to see her and Wally Lavaleer out of my hair forever. That was worth waiting for.

I read my copy of *The Falls* while sipping a cup of instant coffee. When I finished, I turned on the radio and the television.

If the convenience store killing was still lingering in the media, it was doing a pretty good job of hiding from me. I suspected the story was gone for good unless the police caught someone. My plan called for making sure that never happened.

After breakfast, I headed to work. The increased attendance the day before was a blip. Gina was changing her tongue stud at the reception desk.

"That is truly disgusting," I said. "Why don't you go to the ladies' room to finish off?"

"Disgusting? Pilot just showed me a Jap ear from World War II. It looked like a potato chip. Gross." She made a gagging sound.

"Where is Pilot?"

"Who knows? Probably in the change room playing with himself. Oh, before you leave, which of these do you think looks best?" She pointed to the three tongue studs laid out on the tissue on the desk. The first was a large steel stud; the second, a ruby; the third, a diamond.

"I just can't decide. You choose." I felt queasy as I walked away.

"You're no fun," she called after me, giggling.

Pilot was in my office on his hands and knees, digging through the lower half of the liquor cabinet.

"What're you doing?" I tried to see over his shoulder into the cabinet.

He pulled his head out. A cigarette was dangling from his lips. He glared at me with watery eyes. "I see you broke the Babushka Lady."

"She was already broken. Besides, it was an accident."

"What'd you do with the guns?"

"Guns?"

"Don't be cute. The .22 High Standard and the .38 you found in Jack Ruby's head."

"Don't worry about the guns, Pilot. I took care of them."

"You didn't sell them, did you?"

"No. I hid them."

"Where?"

"They're safe. Here, let me give you a hand up."

"I don't need your damned help," he spat. "Do I look helpless to you?"

"Suit yourself." I headed for my chair, patting Old Smokey on the head as I went by.

Pilot was huffing and puffing by the time he pulled himself to his feet and sat down opposite me.

"You didn't sell the guns, did you?" he asked again as soon as he caught his breath.

"Pilot, I told you. I moved them to a safe place. If you can't find them, it's a pretty good hiding place, right?" I couldn't help wondering what he would do if he realized the .38 was in my coat.

"I just hope you're not stupid enough to sell them."

I think he was most pissed because he couldn't find them. I couldn't help pulling his leg.

"What's the big deal, Pilot? What are they? The guns that rubbed out Albert Anastasia and were never found?"

"You don't remember anything, do you?"

I had him going. "Refresh my memory."

"Albert Anastasia. October 25, 1957. The Park Sheraton Hotel. One gunman with a .32 Smith and Wesson. The other with a .38 Colt revolver. Both guns *were* found two blocks away. Killers were never identified."

Pilot was like the elevator music of homicide—a litany of facts that he used to reel off when he led the tours.

"So, maybe it's the gun that killed Arnold Rothstein." Arnold "The Brain" Rothstein was the gambler best remembered for allegedly fixing the World Series in 1919. He was shot in 1928 in the Park Sheraton Hotel and died a few days later, twenty-nine years before Anastasia was shot in the same hotel. Both murders were unsolved.

"The gun that killed Rothstein was found a block away in the subway with five unfired bullets in it. It was a .38 Colt Detective Special. The Smith and Wesson Terrier, the one you stole from the basement, wasn't introduced until 1936. How can you forget that?"

"Call me stupid. What about Sam Giancana? They never found his killers."

"June 19th, 1975. In the kitchen of his basement, in his home in Oak Park, Illinois outside Chicago. Shot dead with a .22 while cooking pasta. A week later, the murder weapon was found in Florida, you dumb kid. You're supposed to know all that."

A flicker of anger lit his face. For a moment, he looked ten, maybe twenty years younger. I felt like God awakening the dead.

"So why are these guns important?"

"Because they'll get you in trouble. Just don't go selling or using them for any of your shit. You hear me?"

"You have to learn to trust me, Pilot. The proof is in the pudding."

"Stupid boy. That's what you are. The proof ain't in the pudding, you dimwit. If I was your old man, I'd give you a smack on the side of the head to wake you up."

"Find me stuff I can sell, and I won't have to sell the guns."

"I'll see what I can do. Just promise me you won't sell them."

I nodded. I had no intention of selling the pistols, but now that he knew I had them, I could ask him another question that had been rattling around in my head. I took the watch and the note to Betsy out of my pocket and asked him what he knew.

He studied the note and the watch and shook his head. "I don't recognize the watch, and I don't have any idea who Betsy is. My advice? Sell the watch, and don't say nothing to nobody."

"Wasn't there a Betsy Stein, an old woman who worked here years ago when I was maybe ten or twelve?"

"Forget it, kid. She's probably dead." He handed the watch and note back to me. "Just do what I say. Don't sell the guns."

"Okay, but only if you give me something I can sell."

"You're the boss." He reached in his side pocket and pulled out what looked like the dried ear he had shown Gina. It had a yellowed label attached to it by a string.

Before I could read the label, Pilot pulled a round, silver-colored medallion and chain from another pocket and held it in front of me. The medallion was about the size of a silver dollar.

"Do you know what this is?"

"I do." I smiled, recalling the little talk Pilot made me memorize when I'd worked under his tutelage as a teen tour guide at MurderLand.

The medallion had a four-leaf clover etched deeply into it. In the center of each leaf was an evil eye. The talisman was supposed to repel danger. The amulet and chain had been part of our exhibit on the life and death of Bessie Starkman, one of the most powerful crime bosses in North America during the Roaring Twenties. Along with her husband,

Rocco Perri, the Al Capone of Canada, who provided the muscle, Bessie operated as the CEO, business manager, and unrefuted brains behind a major Canadian crime syndicate that supplied booze to Americans during Prohibition. Bessie was the only female and one of only a few Canadian crime bosses of either sex to rise to the heights of a mafia chief or syndicate boss in North America. The exhibit was one of MurderLand's only Canadian displays, which made it a sentimental favorite of mine. The exhibit had also included a flapper dress made of 14-karat gold beads and pearls worn by Starkman at the height of her power in the 1920s. The favorite parts of the exhibit for the kids, who once flocked to the museum, were the bloody handbag she was carrying when she was killed and the crime scene photos of Starkman's Hamilton, Ontario garage where she was gunned down by persons unknown in 1930.

"You remember what you were supposed to tell the boys when you showed them the display?" Pilot asked me.

"I'd point out the lucky charm and the murder scene photos and say, 'You can wear all the magic medallions you want, but they won't stop a speeding bullet.'"

"And what did you tell the girls?"

"Bessie proved women could do anything a man could do—even bad things."

Pilot beamed. "You speak the words just like I wrote them, sonny boy. Music to my ears."

The amulet couldn't be found when I sold off the dress, handbag, and photos a month after I took over the museum. Seeing the talisman in Pilot's hands made me hope for a small miracle.

"Platinum?" I asked hopefully.

"You tell me." He handed me the amulet and chain.

It felt too light for platinum. "Silver?"

He nodded. "You're learning. Now, I gotta get back to work." He stood and headed toward the door.

Too bad about the Starkman piece, I told myself. The silver amulet and chain wouldn't bring very much even with Starkman's name attached to it. The market for artifacts related to Canadian gangsters was tiny compared to their American counterparts.

I picked up the severed ear and read the label:

Taken off a dead Jap, Battle of Tenaru, Guadalcanal, August 21, 1942.

Pilot was gone by the time I looked up.

He was right. We were running out of good stuff to sell. I returned the watch and note to my pocket. I was still hoping to find out who the watch belonged to. It had also become a talisman of sorts for me. I'd found it right around the time my current scheme had begun to take shape.

I paid a few more bills, visited my father in the nursing home, and went over some more paperwork with Dr. Patek. Returning to Murder-Land, I let Gina go early to see a guy about cut-rate live mice for her snake.

I called Melanie to ask how her evening had gone.

"It was all right," she said offhandedly.

"What? Like you got laid?" I was glad for her.

"It was a business meeting." Her voice was cool, distant. "Listen, I have a ton of catching up to do. I have to go."

"Maybe I'll stop by later."

"Uh-huh." She wasn't really listening to me. I could hear her clacking away on her keyboard.

I hung up.

Pilot showed up and asked me about the guns again. I told him not to worry and asked him once more if he knew who Jenny was or what my father could mean by "Okay, Jenny, not in the face." As he had over the past several months when I had asked him the same questions, he dismissed them with a wave of his hand. "Stop wasting my time and yours on nonsense."

He was right. I had more important things to think about. I sent him home early and got down to the real business of the day. I went over and over in my mind what I was going to say at my meeting with my new buddy, Duane Morthwell. During the peak of my stock market wheeling and dealing when stupid money was chasing deals, the trick was to sketch out the entire model for the business you were trying to sell to investors on one page. The reason was simple. You wanted to get their money before they asked too many questions. Murder, I figured, was just like that. Keep it simple.

I locked the front door, set the alarm, and headed out the back way.

My mind was pounding away with details and possible contingencies that could derail everything.

Just as I closed the outside door behind me and slipped the keys in my pocket, the two hulks appeared.

I mentally switched gears and watched them emerge from the driveway.

The bigger of the two was over six feet tall and must have weighed two hundred and fifty pounds. The other one was only slightly smaller. Both were wearing long leather coats and black hats with wide brims pulled over their eyes—like thugs from a bad Bogart movie.

Fuck you, assholes, I thought, jamming my hand around the .38 in my coat pocket. I was in no mood to be messed with.

"What the fuck do you want?" I snapped, deciding in that instant I was going to take out the bigger of the two with a shot in the face at the first sign of trouble.

My finger tightened on the trigger as the bigger of the two came toward me.

CHAPTER 19

"Harry, it's me, Tommy Mancuso."

He stopped in front of me with his hand extended.

Under the mounds of flesh and multiple chins, I made out the outline of Tommy Mancuso's face, right down to the five o'clock shadow that he'd sported as a twelve-year-old. Tommy was shaving when the rest of us were still counting our pubic hairs on one hand.

"Tommy Mancuso." He repeated it like he was talking to an idiot. "We used to live across the street from you when we were kids. This is my little brother, Vinnie. You remember Vinnie? Pumpkin Head?" He nodded toward the other hulk beside him. Pumpkin Head grinned at me with the unmistakable round head and pumpkin teeth that we used to make fun of.

Tommy was still holding his hand out to me. The only reason I hesitated was because my fingers were cramped around the .38. I was having trouble letting go.

Finally, I retrieved my hand from my pocket and shook his. "Tommy, I'm sorry. I didn't recognize you. You gained a few pounds." The last time I saw Tommy he weighed a hundred pounds less.

"I got married. To Dolores Fuccio. She's the best cook." He patted his belly.

"I remember her. Bobby Fuccio's sister."

"Yeah, and remember the time you, me, and Bobby broke those mannequins?" Tommy asked.

Bobby was the guy I'd been horsing around with when we broke the Babushka Lady. I didn't remember Tommy being there.

"You were there?"

"Yeah. Don't you remember?" He sounded hurt.

"Sure." Not really sure.

"Bobby's teaching computer sciences at Waterloo," Tommy went on, "and Vinnie married Dolores's little sister, Mia."

She must be a hell of a cook, too, I thought. Last time I'd seen Pumpkin Head he was a skinny little kid.

"Congratulations. So what brings you to my parking lot?"

"Mancuso Demolition. Our dad's company. Me and Vinnie, we're partners now with Dad. We're looking over your building. Getting ready to put in our bid to tear it down. Bidding closes at the end of next week."

"I think you heard wrong, Tommy. No one's going to tear down this building."

"With all due respect, Harry, I heard about the problems with your father's business, your stepmother, and Wally Lavaleer. Believe me, I sympathize, but I'll tell you something between you and me. The deal's done. Everyone at city hall and the planning board who's supposed to be paid off has gotten what they wanted. Am I right, Vinnie?"

Vinnie nodded with his eyes half closed. "They wanna start demolition as soon as possible after Canada Day. Six months from now, this is gonna be a hole in the ground."

Tommy added, "Harry, if you could put in a good word with Lavaleer, there could be something in it for you. Think about it, okay?"

I was shocked. Carlene and Lavaleer were moving even faster than I thought.

"I'll do what I can to help both of you, but right now I have a lot on my mind. I have to go. It was nice seeing you guys," I shook hands with both of them.

"Don't forget what I said. Put in a good word. We'll make it worth your while."

I smiled. I was afraid if I said more I'd start screaming at them to get the fuck off my land.

Instead, I got in the Lincoln and drove off, leaving them in the alley, checking out ways to rip down the building at the lowest possible price.

My brain was having a meltdown.

A hole in the ground in six months?

Yeah, right. Over my cold, freaking, dead body. Pushing the button on Carlene was no longer an option. It was a necessity. I had to do it.

I drove to the Queenston Heights Park, another one of those little reminders that Canada and the US weren't always such good buddies.

The Battle of Queenston Heights is Canada's story of David versus Goliath. It was similar to how I was feeling. I was the little guy, striking back against all the big guys.

During the War of 1812, the Americans decided to cross the Niagara River at Lewiston, New York, downriver from Niagara Falls. Their plan was to take the Canadian headquarters at Fort George outside Niagara-on-the-Lake. Queenston, on the Canadian side, was considered impregnable. So the Americans decided to try to cross the river farther south of Queenston and scale the 350-foot cliffs of Queenston Heights to launch their attack on what was then called Upper Canada, later, Ontario. The Americans had 6,000 soldiers. The Canadians had 1,000 soldiers, including British regulars, battle-hardened Indigenous warriors, and local farm boys and townies formed into local militias. At the end of the battle on October 13, 1812, the Americans had lost 500 killed or wounded and 1,000 captured including a brigadier-general, a colonel, four lieutenant colonels, and hundreds of frightened American militiamen, who had been hiding in the bush waiting for the battle to be over. The British, local Canadian militias, and Canadian-aligned Indigenous warriors, mainly Mohawks, lost a total of fourteen killed and seventy-seven wounded. The biggest loss for the Canadians was the death of one of their boldest and brightest leaders, Major-General Sir Isaac Brock, the top ranking British officer in Upper Canada.

The battlefield park was at the top of the cliffs overlooking Queenston. It had a giant tower in the center of the park commemorating Brock's death. Brock and one of his aides-de-camp, Lieutenant-Colonel John Macdonell, who was also killed in the same battle, were buried at the base of the monument.

I spotted Duane Morthwell's Camaro in the parking lot. In the summer, the park would be packed. That afternoon, fewer than a dozen cars were there. As I headed toward the tower, I could see small groups of tourists in twos and threes scattered around the park reading the plaques that commemorated the battle.

No one paid attention to me. I was pretty sure Morthwell wouldn't try anything stupid with potential witnesses milling around. Just in case, I kept one hand in my pocket firmly gripping the .38. The other was carrying the envelope with the extra set of the convenience store photos and a memory stick with the duplicate copy of the relevant parts of the surveillance video.

I walked along the escarpment with its breathtaking views. I could see across Lake Ontario all the way to Toronto thirty miles away. By land Toronto was nearly eighty miles away. Looking down at the foot of the cliffs, I could see Queenston. If I had the time, I could have picked out Alice's house. Instead, I kept going toward the monument.

The giant monument in the middle of the park was the second of two towers built on the heights to honor General Brock. The first, a 135-foot-tall column, had been blown up by Canadian terrorists in 1840 in support of the Mackenzie Rebellion. The new granite one with the huge bronze statue of Brock at the top was completed in 1856 and stands 185 feet tall to the plume on Brock's hat. During the summer, when the tower is open, you can walk to the observation deck inside the stone column on a dizzying, circular, stone staircase. In winter, the monument was closed off with industrial fencing.

Duane Morthwell was standing beside the fence, eyes riveted on me as I approached. His hands were stuck deep in the pockets of his bomber jacket. His coarse, grim features and his cowboy hat gave him the appearance of a scruffy bad guy in a spaghetti western.

He was nearly a head taller than me and forty pounds heavier. Not someone I'd choose to tangle with in a fistfight.

His eyes were narrow and angry.

"I'm glad you decided to come." I offered a pleasant smile, trying to put him at ease.

"What's this about?"

"I think you know." I held out the envelope.

He just stared at it.

"Go on. These are yours," I said. "I have copies."

He finally produced his hands from his jacket pockets and took the envelope. He held it in front of him without opening it.

"Copies of what?"

"Open it."

He pulled open the flap and glanced inside.

I watched as he extracted the photos and began fingering through them, stopping every so often to spend time on a particular shot before continuing.

"Where'd you get these?"

"From the surveillance camera at the convenience store. There's a complete copy on the memory stick in the envelope. Just so you know, I have copies of the photos and video in a safe place. Anything happens to me, and they'll be sent straight to Niagara's finest."

"How'd you get them?"

"I was in front of the store when you shot Johnny Johnson. I went in right after you left and found the surveillance system. I guess you missed seeing the camera on the back wall."

"I guess. What do you want?"

"I'm thinking that maybe you and I can help each other. I can keep the video out of the hands of the police. All you have to do is a small favor for me."

He scowled. "Like what?"

"First, let me tell you the problem."

I gave him a brief rundown of my troubles with Carlene and Wally Lavaleer.

When I finished, he said, "You should kill the bitch and the lawyer. Fucking animals." He took a pack of cigarettes out of his pocket and lit one.

"I'd like to, Duane, but you see, I'm the first person the cops will suspect."

"That's a real shame."

"It's not quite as bad as all that, because they don't know about you."

"Me? What's that supposed to mean?"

"Think about it, Duane. If you kill Carlene and Wally for me, no one would ever suspect you. I'm home free. I'll forget what I saw at the convenience store, and you're home free, too."

"You're fucking crazy. I'm no killer."

"Two words, Duane. *Johnny Johnson*. He's dead. You killed him. I'm not asking you to do anything you haven't done already."

"Fuck Johnny Johnson. He fucking deserved what he got. And fuck you, too. I ain't no murderer."

He took a deep drag on his cigarette, eyeing me defiantly.

Progress was slow but moving in the right direction. Believe me, if I had a choice, I wouldn't have picked a moron like Duane to work with, but I had to work with what I had.

"I'm curious, Duane. What were you and Johnson arguing about?"

"Who said we were arguing?"

"It's right there on the video. Only the video didn't have any sound. But you two were arguing about something."

"You really want to know?"

"I do."

"The fucker was trying to cheat me. Big time."

"How?"

"You wouldn't believe it if I told you."

"Try me."

"All right. Johnson sold me some speed a couple a months ago. I use it to stay awake when I drive at night. Only it turned out it wasn't speed but some shit that made me puke my guts out. I lost three days of work."

"So you whacked him for that?"

"I should have, but I didn't. I'm not that desperate. We're talking a couple of hundred bucks worth of shit. I told him I'd bust his head if he didn't give me my money back. He said he didn't have it, but he'd make me a deal. He'd pay me half and work off the rest. He knew I bought lottery tickets. So he said he'd buy me a 649 with an Encore twice a week until he'd paid me off."

"So, he didn't buy the tickets?"

"He bought the tickets all right. He used my numbers." He spat out the six numbers. "Four, five, and thirteen for my initials. D-E-M for Duane Edward Morthwell. And nine, eight, thirty-two, for Patsy Cline's birthday, September 8, 1932. Johnny showed me the tickets after each draw. We used to run into each other around town once in a while. I never went to the store. He didn't want anyone going there to buy drugs. Then, my numbers came up. Me and four other people had the same numbers. I was supposed to split eight million bucks with the other winners. A five-way split. That's fucking one point six million apiece, tax free."

"Whew." Unlike American lotteries where there's always some bullshit catch, Canadian lotteries were all cash, no taxes. The winners receive the whole enchilada right in their hands.

"Yeah, fuck, *whew*. That fucker Johnson pretended like he hadn't played the numbers this time. Told me he forgot."

"Maybe he did."

"You on his side now?"

"I'm just saying, if he did win and he was ripping you off, why go to work? Why not just go to the lottery office, pick up the money, and split. Seems to me a guy like Johnson didn't have that much to hold him here."

"He thought he could scare me off before he collected. Then, he wouldn't have to go anywhere. You saw the video. You know what he did when I went to see him. He pulled a fucking gun. Know what he told me?"

"What?"

"'Get the fuck out, motherfucker. Leave me alone. If you come in here again, I'll shoot you and tell the police you were trying to rob me. If I see you following me on the street, I'll shoot you and say you were trying to mug me. Who's going to care?' And that's when I knew he had the ticket. He'd have no reason to be afraid of me if he wasn't planning on collecting my winnings. He was laughing at me. He thought he was hot shit. I got ripped off good by the motherfucker. Fucking animal deserved to die."

"You searched him, but you didn't find the lottery ticket."

"That's right. I should have stayed and looked harder. I know it was there somewhere." His eyes glistened with rage. "I can't fucking believe it. One point six million, and now it's gone."

He pulled a dirty handkerchief from his jacket pocket and blew his nose. "On top of that, I'm coming down with a fucking cold, and my asshole boss wants to cut my hours. That means I'll be working only part-time until Easter. I can't fucking live on nothing, can I?"

"Hey, I know about money problems, friend. If you help me, I can help you."

"I ain't killing no more fucking people. I can tell you that right now."

"Duane, Duane, Duane. Don't ever say never. Besides, you said so yourself. These aren't people. These are animals. You'd be doing the world a service. You'd be doing me a favor. You do this for me, and you'd get the other copy of the video—"

"You threatening me?"

I held up a hand. "Duane, just a second. Let me finish. I'm a business-man. I'm making a win-win deal for both of us. You take care of my little problem, and you win, too."

He stared at me for a few moments, and then asked, "How much?"

"You get the videos—"

"I said *how much*? I got to make something from this if I'm even going to consider it, don't you think?"

Progress, I thought. "You have a number in mind?"

"Yeah. How about one point six million fucking dollars?"

I laughed. "You have a good sense of humor, Duane."

"Yeah, well, fuck my sense of humor. How much you thinking?"

"I'm thinking like ten thousand dollars, and don't forget the video. That's worth something."

"Ten thousand for each of the ones you want killed?"

"We could talk about that if you're really interested."

"How much up front?"

"I already explained my situation. Until I get Carlene and Lavaleer off my back, and get the business on its feet again, I have a little cash-flow problem. Besides," I pointed to the envelope in his hands, "getting this monkey off your back should be a big reward by itself."

"This is crazy, man. I can't do it."

"Yes, you can."

He took a drag off the remains of his cigarette and blew a long jet of smoke out of the side of his mouth. "I gotta think about it, man. I need some time."

"I understand." We started to walk toward the parking lot. "Think about it. But I don't have much time. If you think about it too long, the museum's going to be a hole in the ground, and Carlene's going to move my dad to Maple Creek, and that'll kill him."

"I gotta think," he repeated.

"I need an answer by tomorrow night. We'll meet at the Drummond Hill Cemetery. Go to Laura Secord's grave and wait for me. Let's make it six."

"If I'm not there?"

"You do what you have to do, and I'll do what I have to do." I broke away from him and headed to my car without looking back.

CHAPTER 20

As soon as I left Duane Morthwell, I drove to St. David's to the nearest convenience store I could think of. There I checked the lottery numbers for the 649. Morthwell's numbers had come up on the day he claimed they had.

Poor fucker, I thought.

I left the store and drove to Alice May's. I found her car in the drive-way. Thankfully, Wally Lavaleer's Mercedes wasn't there.

Things are returning to normal, I mused as I headed around back and found Alice leaning out her bedroom window with her pellet gun, firing at the raccoons in her backyard. She was wearing a heavy wool turtleneck and a black baseball cap pulled tightly over her hair. She had both hands on the gun as she trained her sights on the furballs.

I spotted five raccoons in all, four adults and a half-pint. If the adults were suitcases, they would have been too big to qualify for carry-on luggage at the airport. They ignored the shots that splattered around them as they waddled through the garbage-strewn yard.

"Maybe you should try some traps," I suggested.

"Maybe I will." She swung around and fired a shot that winged so close to my ear it sounded like a bee.

"Hey, what the hell was that for? You could have taken out my eye." I touched my hand to my face. The only reason I wasn't running for cover was because she'd lowered the gun and folded her arms on the window ledge.

"I'm really, really pissed at you," she said. "Derek told me if you show up at the theater again, he's going to fire me. You're going to ruin my career. Then, I will kill you."

"Derek's not going to fire you. He's screwing your agent."

"They had a spat. Tyler left in a huff and went back to Toronto."

"They'll kiss and make up."

"I hope so. Derek's in a much better mood when he's getting laid regularly. They were talking about getting married."

"Are you going to ask me in?"

"You have the gun you promised me?"

"Not yet." I'd already decided that handing a loaded gun to Alice was a terrible idea. I'd parked the .38 in the trunk of the car before driving over. Gunshots in a quiet little village like Queenston would likely bring the cops to her door in a hurry. She would crack under interrogation and finger me, and the last thing I wanted was to talk to the cops about guns when I was getting ready to have my stepmother and her lawyer bumped off.

"Do you have any Soma?" she asked.

"I might."

"Then, I might ask you in." She flashed her electric smile. "Door's open. See you in the kitchen."

I went inside.

"Where's the Soma?" she asked before I had my coat off.

"I'm a little pissed at you, too," I said, ignoring her question as I sat down at the dining table, which, as usual, was covered with dirty dishes.

"Why are you pissed?" She straddled my thighs and dug into my pockets trying to locate the drugs. The friction of her crotch against mine was turning me on.

"I came by a couple of times in the last few days. You weren't here."

"I was at rehearsals."

"At two in the morning?"

"I stayed over at my girlfriend Loretta's place. We were helping each other practice our parts. She has a small part in the Ibsen play at the Court House Theater. She also has a fabulous place with a view of the lake. Better than this dump. Her husband owns a diamond mine in Nunavut. They're loaded."

I took her hand out of my pocket and puckered my lips, hoping for a kiss. She hit me in the chest, not nearly as hard as Joey, but it still made me wince.

"Stop that, Harry. That's not the kind of relationship we have."

Since she stayed put on my lap, I held her wrists so she couldn't hit me again.

"What about Wally? I drove by two nights ago and saw his car parked out front. Exactly what were you rehearsing with him?"

"Wally's fun. And he's loaded."

"He's married."

"Of course, stupid. All the good ones are married."

"I'm not."

"Exactly my point. Wally took me to the casino. He's going to finance a movie with some Hollywood big-shot friend of his when the season here is over. He's putting me in it. When the movie's done shooting, he's taking me to Bali. I've never been to Bali."

"You slept with him because he lied to you?"

"I didn't sleep with him. I gave him a hand job. I'm saving my virginity for Mr. Right. I've told you that a million times already." She sounded annoyed as she got off my lap and sat in the other chair.

"Wally's sleeping with my stepmother in addition to his wife. Did you know that?"

"That should bother me because...?"

"You, me, Wally, my stepmother—it's like something out of a redneck soap opera."

She lifted her baseball cap and ran her fingers through her long, shiny locks. "There is no *you and me*, Harry. So stop worrying about it. Now, do you have any good stuff or not?"

Sucker that I am, I sighed and dug in my pocket for the Soma, knowing full well that was all she really wanted.

When we'd finished off what I had on me, she told me she had to leave to rehearse with Loretta.

I left, but I didn't go far. I parked down the road, waited until she drove away, and then followed her. She parked in the driveway of a big house on Front Street in Niagara-on-the Lake behind a silver Porsche Targa with vanity plates that said, "SPOYLT." I waited a respectable five minutes before approaching the house. Through the living room window,

I could see Alice and a busty, dark-haired woman—Loretta, I had to assume—pacing back and forth on the hardwood floors, throwing lines at each other.

They were busy. I needed something to do. It was still early. I thought of the pendant watch in my pocket. I was barely three miles from Virgil. I wondered if a visit to the last-known address of a dead woman might tell me something. I definitely had some time on my hands.

I pulled the last-known address of Betsy Stein out of my wallet and drove to Virgil, a tiny crossroads village three miles west of Niagara-on-the-Lake. The house was on a narrow country road in the middle of nowhere. The gravel laneway to the house was unmarked and easily missed.

A hundred feet up a small hill, I came to a white, Cape Cod-style cottage in what appeared in the moonlight to be a small orchard of cherry trees. The Niagara Peninsula had once been famous for all kinds of fruits and vegetables, but a lot of the fruit trees had been cut down in recent years in favor of more lucrative vineyards that had sprung up everywhere.

A dark Chrysler sedan was parked in the carport. The porch light and a light in one of the front rooms of the house were on.

I rang the bell.

Moments later, the door opened and a stocky, elderly woman with short, blue-white hair and chubby cheeks stood in the doorway. Sparkling blue eyes gave me the once-over through gold wire rim glasses.

"Whatever you're selling, I don't want any," she said in a pleasant but firm voice.

I smiled. I recognized her in an instant even though I hadn't seen her in nearly twenty years. Betsy Stein was definitely not dead.

"Betsy. It's me, Harry Holiday. Ralph Holiday's son. You used to work for my father at MurderLand."

My words took a second to register. She opened the door wider and looked me over from head to toe.

"Harry? Harry Holiday? My goodness. The last time I saw you, you were just a child. What are you doing here? Come in, come in."

She held the door open. I stepped into the house.

"I'm sorry I wasn't able to call first, but your number's unlisted," I explained.

"Actually, I don't have a phone, Harry."

I didn't say anything, wondering if she had fallen on hard times and had to give it up.

She picked up on my concern and smiled as she led me into the living room. "I can afford a phone, Harry. Don't look so worried. I gave it up years ago so no one would bother me. I swore off newspapers, television, and radio as well. I prefer my solitude, photography, and my books."

She certainly had enough books. Two of the walls of the living room held floor-to-ceiling bookshelves crammed full of paperbacks and hard covers. On the other walls were four large, framed and matted colored photos of a single cherry tree on a hillside taken during each of the four seasons.

"Are these yours?" I asked, studying the photos.

"Yes. My little hobby." She smiled. "Please sit down, Harry. Make yourself at home. Would you like something to drink? Coffee or tea?"

"No thank you. I'm fine." I sat on the couch. Despite the clutter, the house had a warm, clean smell like someone had just taken a bubble bath.

She removed a book from the stuffed wing chair and sat across the coffee table from me.

"You're lucky, Harry," she said, "You ended up with the best features of both your parents. They were such a handsome couple."

"Thank you."

"So, what brings you to my neck of the woods, and how is your father?"

"I'm afraid he's not very well." I explained what had happened to him and his ordeal over the past six months.

She was genuinely moved. She pulled a tissue out of the box on the side table and dabbed at her eyes. "I'm glad you stopped by, or I never would have known." While she wrote down the name of the nursing home, I took the watch out of my pocket.

"The main reason I wanted to see you was that I was hoping you could tell me something about this." I held the watch out to her. "I found it the other day with the note from my father that said, 'Return to Betsy.' You were the only Betsy I could think of."

She took the watch in her hands like she was holding a bird's egg and examined it for several seconds. "Yes, I know exactly what it is. It belonged to your mother. I gave it to her for her thirtieth birthday. Your father threw a big party for her. She adored these older style watches. She used to wear it from a little gold pin. A couple of years later, she was wearing it while visiting the museum, and it must have come undone and slipped off somewhere. We looked all over but never found it. I suppose after I retired, your father must have found it, and thought it should go back to me. My guess is that he never got around to delivering it."

"That would be like him," I said. "Well, at least the mystery is solved."

She held the watch out to me.

"It's yours," I said. "My father wanted you to have it."

"That's sweet of you, Harry, but I'm an old lady. I have no heirs, and my quartz watch never needs winding." She held up her wrist to show me the watch she was wearing. "I'd like you to have your mother's watch as a keepsake."

I hesitated.

"Please?"

Except for some old photos, the truth was that everything else connected to my mom had disappeared over the years as my father kept getting remarried.

I reached out and took the watch.

"That's really nice of you. Thanks. I'll treasure it." I tucked the watch into my pocket. "If I'm not keeping you, I have a few other questions."

"Not at all. Ask away."

"Do you know if my father had any other business interests besides MurderLand?"

"What do you mean?"

"I'm not sure." I explained about the attendance and the cash flow. "I'm wondering if he might have been a silent partner in other businesses or properties around town."

"I'm afraid I can't be much help, Harry. I was never involved in the money side of the business, just in exhibits."

"What about anyone named Jenny? After his stroke, he seems to be repeating the same thing over and over again. *Okay, Jenny, not in the face.*"

She shook her head. "I'm sorry, Harry. No one named Jenny comes to mind. Anything else?"

"One last question." I'd saved the strangest for last. "When I found the watch, it was wrapped in a towel in an ammunition box along with another box of ammunition and a .22 High Standard pistol with a silencer. Do you happen to know anything about the gun?"

She laughed. "Me? Oh lord, no. MurderLand was always full of guns, but I'm afraid I don't know anything about them. The guns were all handled by Pilot, your father, or grandfather. I was just told where they went. Too bad Pilot isn't around or he would likely know."

"Oh, he's still around. He comes to work every day."

"You're kidding me. He must be in his nineties. I can't believe it. How is he?"

"Not as spry as he once was but just as grumpy."

"I'm glad to hear that. I should drop by the museum and see him one of these days. You've brought back a flood of memories, Harry. Thank you."

"Thank you," I said, getting to my feet. "You've been really kind."

"My pleasure." She walked me to the door. "I am so sorry about your father. Please give Pilot my best."

I returned to my car, drove to Loretta's place, and found Loretta and Alice still pacing the floor.

My best bet to get any action was Melanie.

I returned to the Falls.

Melanie was still out. I thought about sneaking into her place, hopping into her bed, and surprising her when she came home. In the end, it sounded like too much work. I headed to Pole Catz. Before heading home, I sprung for hamburgers, fries, and beer for a couple of dancers just finishing their shift.

Back at my place, I watched the end of a basketball game on cable, and then, tumbled into bed. I read several more chapters of *The Prince* before finally falling asleep around midnight.

I only woke up twice, once around two thirty when Wally arrived in our driveway tooting his horn and once an hour later when he peeled rubber on his way out.

FRIDAY

When I finally woke up for good, it was seven o'clock. I checked for news about the convenience store killing in *The Falls*, and then stole *The Review* from Carlene's front steps before she got up. Not a word in either paper about the murder. It was as if it never happened.

The temperature had dropped below freezing again, but the sun was out, sparkling off the crumbling ice in the Niagara River, making it look like the world's largest collection of precious jewels.

As soon as I got to work, I told Pilot about finding Betsy and discovering the watch that belonged to my mother.

"Stop wasting your time," he grumbled. "Get me the guns. I'll dispose of them, and you can concentrate on putting the museum back on its feet."

Pilot showed no interest in visiting Betsy, even when I offered to drive him there. "She ain't going to tell me a damned thing I don't already know, and she ain't going to tell you anything you need to know."

After Pilot left the office, I did paperwork until just before noon when Tommy and Vinnie Mancuso showed up with a brown paper bag.

"When I told Dolores I ran into you yesterday," Tommy said, "she insisted on making you her favorite dessert."

He took a large plastic container out of the bag and opened it on the desk. Inside were a dozen cannolis.

He sat on the chair opposite me. Vinnie sat on the couch.

"Harry, the contract for tearing down this place would put a real feather in our caps with our old man. Anything you want, you just name it." He gave me a half wink.

I glanced at Vinnie. He gave me the same half wink.

"Tommy, I'll see what I can do," I said, hedging my bets. Maybe a kickback on the demolition contract would look good if everything else fell apart.

"You won't regret it." He helped himself to a pastry. Vinnie took two.

"Regret what?" Pilot asked, coming through the door with a scowl on his face.

Before I could answer, Tommy got up and began shaking Pilot's hand.

"Pilot, it's me, Tommy Mancuso. I used to come here with Harry when we were kids. Vinnie, this is the guy I keep telling you about. The guy who said he was on the grassy knoll when President Kennedy got shot."

Pilot gave him a sour look. Tommy led Pilot to the chair he'd just vacated. Once Pilot was seated, Tommy held the container of cannolis under his nose.

"Take one. They'll grow hair on your chest. They're cannolis. Like Italian cream puffs."

"I know what they are, you meatball. I'm on a diet." He shrank from the container and Tommy.

Tommy just grinned. "See, Vinnie? He remembers me."

Pilot frowned. "How could I forget you? You broke the Babushka Lady."

Tommy smiled, apparently validated by the recognition. He turned to Vinnie. "Pilot used to tell us he was one of the guys who whacked Bugsy Siegel. Remember I told you that when we saw the movie *Bugsy* with Warren Beatty?"

Pumpkin Head nodded.

"Who else did you whack, Pilot?" Tommy asked.

"I don't remember."

I did. Pilot loved taking credit for half the unsolved murders in America. At one time or another, I'd heard him say he'd been there when Anastasia got it in New York and Giancana got it in Oak Park. If he thought anyone would believe him, Pilot would have probably taken credit for shooting Abraham Lincoln.

"Harry, what was the guy's name who flew out the window on Coney Island?" Tommy asked. "You used to have photos of him upstairs. It had something to do with a canary."

"Abe 'Kid Twist' Reles. The first field commander of Murder Incorporated," I said. We had photos upstairs of his death as part of the Sing Sing electric chair exhibit. Reles's testimony had sent Louis "Lepke" Buchalter and six others to the electric chair. Peter Falk played Reles in the 1960s movie *Murder, Inc.*

"You killed him, right?" Tommy said to Pilot. "You shoved an ice pick in his ear."

"He fell out a window. He died of internal injuries, you dumb shit," Pilot muttered as he pulled himself to his feet. "I'm out of here."

"It's good to see you, Pilot," Tommy said.

"Don't trust these palookas, Harry. They don't have your best interests at heart," Pilot called over his shoulder as he went through the door.

Tommy acted like he hadn't heard the last remark. "So we got a deal, Harry?" He leaned over the desk and grabbed another pastry. Vinnie took two more.

"I'll see what I can do."

After they left, I took the remaining cannolis out front and asked Gina if she'd like some.

"I can't. My tongue is infected." She stuck her stud-less tongue out. The end looked like a large, rotten strawberry. "I have to leave early to see the doctor."

"I need you here until three. Can you hold out until then?"

"Three?" she whined. "And do what?"

"Read the goddamned manual."

"In case of what? In case we get a customer?"

I ignored her, knowing that no matter what I said, she'd leave when she felt like it.

No sense docking her pay since that would cut off the credits I was getting from the government to cover most of her salary.

When I arrived at the nursing home after picking up sandwiches for my father and Clive, I found Clive asleep in my father's old bed with a Chinese comic book draped over his face. My father had been moved to the bed that had been occupied by the old guy who kicked the bucket on Wednesday.

Clive woke while I was unwrapping the sandwiches.

"I thought you were getting a new guy in this morning?"

"We almost did. He died on the way over."

"Tough break."

He sat up, yawned, and stretched. "Not all bad. I got to catch up on my sleep."

"Partying again all night?"

He ignored me as he walked to the nightstand where I'd placed the container of pastries.

"Ah, cannolis."

"Yeah. They're homemade. Help yourself."

He took one and sat down on the chair beside my father's new bed, finished off the first one, and began working his way through the second one.

When he was one bite from the end, he looked up and said, "Ginnie."

"Ginnie?"

"Yes, Ginnie. Short for Virginia." He finished the last bite and licked his fingers.

"Who's Ginnie?"

"How should I know? I'm just telling you, it's *Ginnie*, not *Jenny*, that's all. Like 'Okay, Ginnie. Not in the face.'"

I was all ears. "So you heard it?"

"I don't know what I heard, but whatever it is, it sounds like, 'Okay, Ginnie, not in the face.' That's all I know."

"When did you hear it?"

"Yesterday, when we was moving your father to his new bed."

"You heard him speak?"

"I heard something."

"Okay, Ginnie, not in the face," I said. "What the hell could it mean?"

"Maybe it doesn't mean anything."

I took Dad's hand and listened closely to the sounds coming out of his mouth. If I blocked out the noise from the highway and the heating system, I could just make out my father saying, "Okay, Ginnie, not in the face."

"Who's Ginnie?" I asked my father. He showed no sign of hearing or understanding me, but something was rattling around in the back of my mind that sounded familiar.

CHAPTER 21

"I DON'T GIVE A FLYING RAT'S ASS who Ginnie is," Pilot told me when I arrived back at three. "You got four toilets in the ladies' room overflowing and shit all over the floor, and I ain't cleaning it up,"

Gina had already left for the day, and six plumbers had already refused to come by until their old invoices were paid in full. "You have to see this to believe it."

"I don't need to see it." I pulled out the last of my cash and handed it to him. "Find someone to fix it."

He began counting the money as I headed toward the office. "I'm gonna hire someone to come in and mop up as well," he called after me.

"Whatever. And if you think of who Ginnie might be, let me know."

"It ain't nobody. Forget it."

I went into my office and closed the door.

Sheesh. Maybe I was making a mistake. Maybe I should get out of the business and let Carlene and Wally screw me. I was worried that Duane Morthwell wouldn't show at the appointed spot or he'd try to kill me.

Everything will be all right, I told myself. Think positive thoughts.

My three thirty appointment showed up on time. Roger Mosswood was a heavyset florist from Omaha, Nebraska with warm, brown, puppy dog eyes and an Abe Lincoln beard. He had a wallet full of cash, which he was quick to flash at me as soon as he finished fondling and sniffing the bloody undergarments of the murdered gangster, Albert Anastasia. He'd flown into Buffalo and driven across the river to view the gangster relics.

"I can smell shit *and* blood," he said, holding the underpants toward me. "Here, smell."

"I already smelled them," I said, thinking he was most likely smelling the shit backed up in our ladies' room.

"I have ten thousand in cash."

Money in the hand sounded good, especially since I was on the ropes again, but I wavered. My other bidder was unreachable for at least a few more days. Who knew how high the bidding might go if the other guy was as eager as this one?

"I'll have to make a phone call or two. I have offers for eleven-fifty already."

"I'll go to twelve thousand. I'll write you a check for the extra two. Look, I already have Sharon Tate's bloody slipper, a bra that belonged to Ethel Rosenberg before she was electrocuted in Sing Sing, and the underwear Ma Barker was wearing when she was gunned down in Florida in '35. These would be a great addition to my collection." He caressed the cloth with his fingers, looking over every inch of the garments with greedy eyes.

For guys like Mosswood, the secret of happiness was a satisfied fetish.

I was just about to go for it, but when I looked up, Pilot was standing in the doorway. I thought he was going to interrupt and tell me something about the toilets, but instead, he drew a finger across his neck, which I took to mean *don't do it*. Then, he put his finger to his lips indicating that I shouldn't mention that he had been standing there. Finally, he mouthed, "I'll be right back," before disappearing.

"I should make those calls."

"I can't go any higher than twelve," Mosswood said.

I didn't want to close the deal until Pilot returned. I killed a couple of minutes pretending to look up numbers of other bidders. Then, I dialed my bank, certain my call would be picked up by their automated system.

Once the automated receptionist began her spiel, I had a long conversation with "Mr. J," the made-up name I'd given the other bidder, so Mosswood wouldn't be able to figure out I was faking the call.

As soon as I hung up, Mosswood tried guessing who Mr. J was.

"Is it Jamieson, the plumbing supply wholesaler from St. Louis?"

"No."

"Jack Jeller from Dallas?"

"No." The circle that Mosswood traveled in—high-end collectors of famous soiled undergarments—wasn't very big. I was glad when Pilot returned, so I could quit lying.

Pilot shuffled in with a couple of plastic bags in his hand, looking a little gray and sweaty, most likely from an unusually fast trip to the basement and back.

"Mr. Mosswood, this is Felix Pringle, our resident expert." Mosswood offered his fleshy, liver-spotted hand to Pilot without getting up.

"Nice to meet you," Mosswood said sourly, waving the smoke from Pilot's cigarette away from the Anastasia garments.

"Charmed," said Pilot.

"I thought this place was nonsmoking," Mosswood said to me.

Pilot took the hint and sat down on the couch away from Mosswood. Once settled in his seat, Pilot butted out his cigarette and then removed a lemon yellow, one-piece bathing suit from one of the bags and held it up.

"When Mr. Holiday told me that such a distinguished connoisseur of historic garments was coming to visit," Pilot said, "I went through the inventory to see what else you might be interested in. This is a Marilyn Monroe bathing suit. Summer of 1952. She wore it when she was here filming *Niagara*. It's unwashed."

He handed it to Mosswood who began to look it over inch by inch, pausing periodically to sniff various parts. Something must have stimulated his olfactory senses. Mosswood's eyebrows kept arching up like goosed caterpillars.

"Did she wear it in the movie?"

"Not in the movie. When she was relaxing after work."

"You guarantee it?" He looked from Pilot to me. I was sure he was already hooked.

"The museum stands behind everything we sell," I said.

"You could probably get DNA off the pubic hairs in the crotch," Pilot added.

Mosswood tightened his grip on the garment. No doubt he had already seen the hairs but hadn't wanted to let on, fearing I would jack up the price.

"It's interesting, but I don't really need it." He tried to appear uninterested. He placed it on the desk beside the Anastasia garments. "But out of curiosity, what would you want for it?"

Behind his back, Pilot held up ten fingers, then two fingers.

I thought he was way too high, but I decided to go with it.

"The swimsuit would cost you twelve grand."

"The same as the Anastasia clothes?" His high voice suddenly rose higher with indignation.

"Mr. Mosswood, the final bids aren't in on the Anastasia items. Your twelve thousand might only be the floor, not the final selling price. The Marilyn suit is only twelve."

His Adam's apple bobbed up and down. "What's the best you can do?"

Pilot held his thumb and forefinger about an inch apart to signal me not to go down too much.

"Eleven-fifty and no tax."

"Canadian," he insisted.

"Let's make it ten US. That's the best I can do, Mr. Mosswood."

"I'll take it," he said.

Ten minutes later, Mosswood was on his way to the Buffalo airport with Marilyn's swimsuit, and I had ten grand US in cash, the equivalent that day of twelve thousand five hundred Canadian, and no paper trail.

"Good work," I told Pilot after I'd seen Mosswood off and returned to the office.

"Give me three grand." Pilot held out his hand.

"What for?"

"Plumber's got three men on the job. It's gonna cost more than I thought. Just hand it over."

I could hear the plumbers pounding away in the ladies' room down the hallway. But I wasn't completely taken in. I'd seen that sly look on Pilot's face before. It wasn't all going to the plumbers. Still, I forked over twenty-four hundred US. Pilot had saved the day. I was feeling generous.

"Where'd you find the swimsuit?" I asked. Even though Marilyn Monroe's death was shrouded in mystery, to my knowledge we'd never displayed anything of hers except for the autographed photo on the office wall.

"Marilyn and Joe DiMaggio came by your grandfather's house a couple of times for a swim when she was filming. Your grandfather still had the big place down the road from where your father is now. It had a big pool in back. Remember?"

"That's where my father taught me how to swim. Marilyn Monroe and Joe DiMaggio were there?"

Pilot nodded. "The last time Joe and Marilyn stopped by Marilyn spent the afternoon lounging by the pool. Joe and Marilyn left the next day, and a few days later your granddad found the suit in the cabana. He called Joe and asked him where to send it, and Joe told him to keep it. He thought it looked too skimpy on her anyway."

"No shit. So Granddad kept it?"

"You know how he could never throw anything away."

I nodded. My grandfather and father had both been pack rats.

Pilot reached into another bag and took out a small, clear plastic display box with a signed baseball inside. "Here's something else you might like." He held the case out to me. "My advice? Don't sell it. You could build quite a display around it."

I looked at the signatures. On one side, inscribed in DiMaggio's hand were the words, "To Julian Holiday, One hell of a guy," and signed, "Your pals, Joe DiMaggio and Marilyn Monroe." Joe and Marilyn had signed separately. On the other side, it said in Marilyn's handwriting, "Thanks for the memories. The most fun I had all summer, Love, Marilyn Monroe. 1952."

Each signature alone would be worth maybe three to five thousand. Together, they were incredibly rare. The ball might be worth between fifteen and twenty-five thousand. Maybe more, if the right buyers could be found and pitted against each other.

"I think I'll hang onto this." I put the case on the credenza beside my desk.

"Maybe there's hope for you yet," Pilot said before walking out the door with a rare smile on his face.

Right after he left, Melanie called and asked me, "Can you get me some more you-know-what?"

"So quickly?"

"Hey, I have a lot on my plate. What can I tell you?"

"Sounds like more than something on your plate. I swung by last night. You weren't around. I'm beginning to think you're being unfaithful."

She laughed. "Listen, my little lothario, can you do me the favor or not?"

"Of course. I'll swing by around eight."

"No can do. Sooner would be better."

"You sly thing. You really are stepping out on me."

"It's business, Harry. Stuff it. Yes or no?" She sounded huffy.

She'd done a lot for me. The last thing I wanted to do was rain on her parade. Everyone deserves a little happiness. "I have to meet someone at six. Not sure how long that will take."

"Can you make it before your meeting? Please?"

"I could be there in a half hour."

"Thank you, sweetie. I won't forget you."

Pilot was still looking after the plumbers. He said he'd lock up, which was a good thing because I was starting to run late.

I had no time to go hunting in the basement for something pretty for Sally Helman. I'd pay cash instead. I jumped in the Lincoln and drove to Sally's store. I had to cool my heels for ten minutes while she cashed out a customer.

"By the way," Sally told me after we'd completed our transaction, "in case you're interested, your little girlfriend, Alice, is cheating on you with Wally Lavaleer. She told a girlfriend of mine that she really likes you but she doesn't think you're decisive enough."

"I'm decisive."

"Be more decisive," she said, poking me in the ribs. "Now, get out of here before I get a crush on you myself."

I reached Melanie's place by a quarter after five. She was still in her office. I rolled a couple of joints and asked her if she wanted to toke up.

"I have work to finish."

I didn't. I smoked half of a joint, and headed outside. I was getting in the Lincoln when I noticed a dark, midsized car parked up the street with someone in the driver's seat. I couldn't see who it was.

My pleasant high turned instantly into a paranoid buzz. Were they watching me or just sitting there?

I started the Lincoln, but instead of heading in the direction I had been pointed in, I did a K-turn, intending to drive by the midsized car and driver and check them out.

While I was turning, the other car drove to the intersection and turned. By the time I reached the intersection, the other car had vanished.

I'm just jumpy, I told myself. Stay focused.

I patted the revolver in my pocket and felt better as I headed for the Drummond Hill Cemetery.

CHAPTER 22

CANADA'S PAUL REVERE WAS A WOMAN NAMED LAURA SECORD who lived in Queenston during the War of 1812. A candy company adopted her name nearly a hundred years later in the early 1900s. Most Canadians think of miniature chocolates when they hear her name. In fact, her fame has nothing to do with candy. On the evening of June 21, 1813, thirty-seven-year-old Laura Secord overheard a conversation among the American soldiers who had taken over her house in Queenston. They were talking about an attack on the Canadian forces, which had been harassing them throughout the Niagara Peninsula. Laura snuck out of her house and walked twenty miles through enemy lines and treacherous terrain to reach the Canadian headquarters in Thorold. Forewarned by Laura, two-hundred-and-fifty Canadian-allied Indigenous warriors, mostly Mohawks from the Kahnawake Reserve near Montreal, with support from eighty British regulars, ambushed an American force twice as large, killing eighty and capturing the rest to win the Battle of Beaver Dams on June 24. Laura Secord died fifty-five years later, the year after Canada became a country. She was buried in the Drummond Hill Cemetery.

Also buried there was Karel Soucek, who, in 1984, became the first Canadian to go over the falls in a barrel. He died in a freak stunt in the Houston Astrodome a few years later.

The cemetery, which bordered on Lundy's Lane, was the resting place for many of the soldiers slaughtered in the Battle of Lundy's Lane. It was also one of the most haunted cemeteries in North America. The ghosts of dead soldiers were reported there so often that the graveyard was the featured stop on many haunted tours of Niagara Falls in the summer.

Duane Morthwell was already there when I arrived. He stood between the church and Laura Secord's grave, smoking a cigarette.

We nodded at each other but didn't shake hands. Up close, his face was even more broken out than the day before. If this kept up, he'd be one giant zit in a few days.

"I take it you're happy with our arrangement," I said.

"Happy? I'm thinking maybe there's another way."

"You have another idea?"

"I was hoping you might."

"If I had another idea, would I need you?"

"No."

"Duane, I am trying to help you."

"Yeah. Right." He flicked his still-lit cigarette at a nearby tombstone. It hit with a small shower of sparks. "So how do you want this done? You got a plan, or are you expecting me to wing it?"

"We'll work it out together. The last thing I want is for you to get caught."

"So what are you thinking? I hit this Marlene and what's-his-name separately or together."

"It's Carlene. Carlene Holiday and Wally Lavaleer, and the best thing to do would be to get them together. The most likely place would be at my father's house most nights between two thirty and four thirty in the morning, give or take a half hour. That should be good for you since that's right at the end of your shift."

"So what does that mean *most nights*? Like I gotta make an appointment? And what about you? Maybe you can call me when they're there."

"No. I have to be out of there for the night."

"Call me when they get there. Then split."

"No. First, no phone calls. We don't want any calls between us. They're too easily traced. Second, I have to be gone the entire night. I need an airtight alibi."

"So, give me a call when you have this all worked out." He started to walk away.

"Wait."

He stopped.

"I have it worked out."

"Okay, hotshot. Tell me. How do I kill what's-her-name and what's-his-name?"

"Carlene. Carlene Holiday and Wally. Wally Lavaleer."

"Hey, fuck you. Don't get mad at me. Why do I need to know their names? All I need to know is when to hit them and how. Right?"

"Right."

"Okay, so tell me what you got worked out."

I thought quickly. I could drag it out, but the longer I dragged it out, more things might go wrong.

"I think I can get something lined up tomorrow night."

"Tomorrow night's too soon. I need a gun. And I need five hundred dollars to get one that's reliable and untraceable."

"What happened to the one you used on Johnson?"

"Never mind. All you need to know is it's gone."

"I can get you a gun."

"What kind of gun?"

"A handgun," I said, fingering the .38 in my pocket but not sure yet which gun I wanted to give him.

"It's gotta be unregistered."

"It'll be unregistered. We'll meet at the same time tomorrow. I'll give you the gun and tell you whether or not I'll be at the house." I gave him the address. "Once I'm sure everything's set, I'll give you the green light. Then, you'll swing by the house after you finish work, make sure they're both there, and do your thing."

"Give me the number of the house again." He pulled a ballpoint pen out of his pocket and a scrap of paper from his wallet.

I gave him the address. He wrote slowly and made me repeat it two times before returning the paper to his wallet.

"Okay. Let's say they're at the house," he continued. "What next?"

"Don't park in the driveway. Use the driveway one house to the south. No one's there during the winter. Walk through the hedge on the side of the house and go to the back of Carlene's. She keeps a key under the flowerpot beside the door because she's always losing hers. Go in the back way using the key so you won't make any noise. As soon as you get inside, you'll see a staircase to your left. Go up the stairs and down the hall to the end. They'll be in the bedroom. Go in and do your thing. Carlene has plenty of jewelry lying around. She'll likely have some cash in her purse. Take it all. Make it look like a robbery. Dump the jewelry in the river."

"Why would I do that?"

"It's too easy to trace. Keep the cash. That's your bonus."

"All right."

"And now, this is important. Remember what I'm going to tell you. Before you leave, open the front door and leave it partly open like you went out that way in a hurry. When you leave, use the back door but leave it unlocked. Return the key to where you found it. Then, break the window on the door from the outside. That way the police will think that's how the intruder got in. Leaving the front door open will give me an excuse to go inside in the morning and discover the bodies."

He was shaking his head by the time I was done.

"What's the matter? You have a better idea?"

"Yeah. You do it. This is stupid."

"Duane, do you want to go to prison again?"

"No."

"Then, stop complaining."

"How do I know you'll keep your word?"

"Think about it, Duane. If I turn you in, you'll rat me out. What am I going to gain? You have the most to gain. Or, of course, you could turn yourself in. Tell the cops what you did. Make a deal with them. You'll probably be out in what, ten, twelve years? And you never have to see me again. Or you can do me a favor and walk away from the Johnson problem with the photos, memory stick, the cash you find at Carlene's, and ten thousand dollars."

"Twenty, I'm going to need twenty. Ten for the bitch. Ten for the shyster. After this is over, I'm gonna split and start over. And I don't want to ever hear from you again."

"All right, twenty." No sense arguing. It was a win-win for both of us. He was not only willing but eager to leave town once the job was done. I stuck out my hand. We shook on it. "We'll meet tomorrow. Same time."

"Fine with me, but we need to pick another place. This one's creeping me out. Too many ghosts."

CHAPTER 23

I LOCATED ALICE at her friend's house in Niagara-on-the-Lake. Alice's car was parked in the driveway. I could see her and her friend rehearsing inside. I was thinking about crashing the party and offering to take them both to dinner, but my plan collapsed when a chicken delivery wagon arrived.

I split and returned to the Falls. I dropped by Pole Catz and bought a half dozen lap dances from a Miss Nude Northern Europe named Ursula, who had one side of her face tattooed like a Viking warrior.

I switched to a beautiful, young woman who called herself Delicious and actually danced like someone who had been professionally trained. She had long, straight, raven-colored hair that hung halfway down her back, skin like milk, narrow blue eyes, big pouty lips, and a tattoo of a butterfly over her right breast. She was just a little too serious looking to pull in the big money. She had the look that said she was grinding her pelvis for tips until Les Ballets Jazz de Montréal or the National Ballet called. Fortunately, she was still fresh enough in a sultry sort of way to do all right, though I imagined that most of her tips came from the rescuers—guys who imagined they could find true love in a peeler pub by rescuing one of the lost souls. Me, I was there for a good time and to spend money on the working girls.

I drank heavily but stayed surprisingly sober as I contemplated my new career as a double murderer.

I felt unusually calm about the idea of killing Carlene and Wally. My problem was Duane Morthwell. I tried to think of a way to cut him out and take care of Carlene and Wally myself. The trick was not getting caught. No matter how I looked at the possibilities, nothing better came to mind.

"I like your butterfly. It matches your eyes," I told Delicious. I'm not sure whether the large tip or the compliment was most responsible for putting a big smile on her face. I was glad to help out whenever I could.

Before I left, I discovered I still had time to place five thousand with Frankie on the Vancouver Canucks to beat the Calgary Flames that night on the West Coast.

I spent the rest of the evening being a model citizen. I drove to a restaurant on the hill and had some ribs and a beer. Afterward, I drove home and tried to decide whether to continue reading *The Prince* or tackle another book I had recently uncovered in the basement of MurderLand— *The Outsider*. The small paperback was a rare but more accurate translation of the Albert Camus novel best known as *The Stranger* in the English-speaking world. I ended up reading Camus until one in the morning when I must have dozed off.

As usual Wally arrived around two thirty and left at four, waking me both times.

SATURDAY

I got up at eight and checked the hockey scores. My Canucks had won. I'd doubled my money. I got dressed for work. I was just putting on my overcoat to go out the door when I heard a dull thud out front. I dashed out in time to see Carlene speeding away. She made the turn onto the parkway without even slowing down.

I looked at the side of my Lincoln and noticed that the rear door on the driver's side had a large, new dent.

On an ordinary day, I might have hopped in the Lincoln, given chase, and rammed the shit out of her car.

This is no ordinary day, I told myself.

I was feeling mellow. I was certain nothing could touch me. If karma existed, then the relevant elements had lined up just right.

All the hocus pocus about good and evil is horseshit, I thought as I drove to the office feeling good about everything.

When Gina said she needed a dollar an hour raise, I gave it to her. I think she was miffed that she hadn't asked for more, but when I told her to take the afternoon off, she perked up.

Pilot showed up with two old, eight-by-ten, black-and-white photos of a big bell jar with what looked like a foot-long, white worm floating in it.

"I'll trade you," he said laying the photos on the desk in front of me. "This for the guns."

I picked up the photos. On closer inspection, I could see that the worm was almost certainly a penis.

"Holy shit. This isn't what I think it is?"

"It's exactly what you think it is. John Dillinger's cock in formaldehyde."

The Dillinger dong was one of the holy grails of gangland collectibles. We once had a tableau on the ground floor showing Dillinger being gunned down by FBI agents.

John Dillinger was Public Enemy Number One. He was killed on July 22, 1934 outside Chicago's Biograph Theater after the FBI had been tipped off by one of his girlfriends, the legendary Romanian madam, Anna Sage, known as the Woman in Red. For years, rumors had circulated that Dillinger's penis had been removed while his body was in the morgue and taken to the Smithsonian Institute in Washington, DC where it was stored. Pilot once told me it was a lie; it was stored in our basement. I thought he said it to scare me. My father said it was true, but I thought he was just playing along with Pilot.

"Your grandpa got this off a relative of the morgue employee who stole it," he said, pushing a yellowing sheet of paper at me. It was the letter from the employee. "Your grandpa bought it in the late 1940s. Everything checks out. You give me the guns. I turn Dillinger over to you."

"I have to see the specimen first," I insisted.

"When you give me the guns." He held out his bony, nicotine-stained hand like he expected me to pull the guns out of my pocket and hand them to him.

"What's with the guns anyway?"

"I'm just trying to keep you out of trouble."

"You have to trust me."

He remained stony faced.

"Look, Pilot. The guns are in a safe place. Let's just leave them there. Now, why don't you go get the jar?"

"No guns, no deal."

"Hey, I thought I was the boss around here."

"Fire me." He crossed his arms and glared at me. "If you think you'll find the jar, forget it."

"We'll talk later," I said.

"Stupid fuck. There's no hope for you." He wandered off.

I wasn't worried. Either he'd come around or I'd eventually find the jar in the basement. I could only imagine what something like that would be worth to the right collector.

Who knows? I thought. Maybe the Smithsonian would want it.

I was definitely on a roll. The next thing I needed to do was set up my airtight alibi.

I telephoned Melanie and asked her to spend the night with me.

"I'm sorry, Harry. I can't. I'm tied up."

"Melanie, it's important. Drop everything. I'll take you to the best restaurant in town. We'll go to the casino and rent a suite. We can fuck and gamble without losing any time in-between. It'll be total debauchery. Just what you like."

"It sounds like fun, but I'm busy."

"The new lover?"

She didn't respond.

"Come on, Melanie. Be smart. You're acting like a lovesick teenager. You know what's going to happen? What always happens when you give too much? The next thing you know your lover will be taking you for granted. Then, he'll dump you. If you're really in love, then you have to show him who's in charge. Stand him up."

"Harry, do me a favor. Mind your own business."

"Melanie, I'm telling you—"

"Fuck off, Harry. I'm not available tonight. That's it. Sorry, sweetie. Do you need anything else?"

"No. I'm fine. Thanks."

I was fine. After paying the plumbers, laying my bet with Frankie, paying my bar bill, and tipping several strippers the previous night, I had almost four grand left from selling the Marilyn Monroe swimsuit. In the worst case scenario, I could simply go play craps at the casino all night and let the surveillance cameras be my alibi.

I called Tommy Mancuso and told him I'd decided to support his bid to demolish the museum.

"I won't forget you, Harry. This means a lot to me," he said.

"We'll talk about how you can remember me when you land the contract."

"Sure, sure, Harry. Anything you want. We'll talk."

One more piece to my cover story is in place, I thought as I hung up.

My confidence was still on the rise when Nessa Wiley showed up.

As she entered the office, she looked around like she was taking inventory. I had to admit she was looking even better in the light of day in her red leather jacket and short skirt than she had in her border guard uniform under the harsh lights of the bridge. In spite of my instant arousal, I had to remind myself that she had just beaten me out of a substantial amount of cash.

"So how's the customs and immigration business?" I asked. "Isn't this a little off your beat?"

"I'm not on the job now. I was in the neighborhood. I thought I'd drop by." She patted Old Smokey's head. "I've been thinking a lot about you." The sexiness in her voice chipped away at my guard.

Stay focused, I told myself. "You got your money back, didn't you?"

"Yeah. We're cool, Harry. On that account. Val and I were in a bidding war on a house, but even with the extra twenty-five grand we came up fifty thousand short."

"Better luck next time."

"We decided to go a little slower. Think things through. Not get in debt over our heads."

"I could put the money to work for you," I said, thinking about what it would be like to have sex with her again.

"I'm not here for investment advice, Harry. I'm thinking about something else."

She flashed her bedroom eyes at me like she was thinking the same thing as me, and then she did something that made the hair on the back of my neck stand up. She pulled Old Smokey's nose off, revealing the cavity where I normally stored my drugs.

Her smile turned into a grin. "I pulled apart a stuffed grizzly just like this in Windsor last year and found ten grand in heroin inside the head."

"Would that be Canadian or US dollars?" I asked. Thankfully, I still had the rest of the Soma I'd scored from Big Mo in my coat.

"Hey, lighten up, Harry. This is a friendly visit." She replaced Smokey's nose and sat down on the chair opposite me.

"Friendly? How so, Nessa?" I was still telling myself to be cautious, but I was also growing hornier. I had to admit, she had always turned me on for some crazy reason. The marriage thing made her less available but more desirable.

"Friendly-friendly, Harry." She put her elbows on the desk, rested her chin on one hand, and gave me the same pout that matched Marilyn Monroe's in the signed photo on the office wall. In high school when she gave me that smile, it was meant as a joke. This time I found it surprisingly carnal.

"Seeing you the other night made me remember the old days. You ever think about the good times we used to have together?" she asked.

"Sometimes. But you're recently married."

"Sometimes I like a little variety. What about you?"

"Sometimes. You thinking a threesome?"

"Just you and me. Val's busy. The rest of my day and night are free."

"Trouble in lesboland?"

"Variety, Harry. I want to fuck you. I don't want to marry you."

I hesitated. I'd committed adultery before but never with half of a lesbian couple.

"It's just a fun night. A onetime thing. You always liked fucking me. Admit it. You have the start of a woody right now under your desk just thinking about it."

She was right. I could use a good lay and a good alibi. She would be perfect for both. I decided to go for it.

"I'm busy until this evening. Then we could party all night."

"Sounds like a plan, Harry. I've already booked us into a penthouse suite with a Jacuzzi and fireplace at The Cliffs on the hill overlooking the falls under a fake name." She handed me a card from Niagara Falls' newest luxury spa and hotel with her fake name written on the back. "What time do you want to meet me?"

"You little minx. You knew I'd say *yes*."

She smiled.

"Can I call you?" I wanted to wait until after my meeting with Duane Morthwell to set a time.

"Yeah. Call my cell." She gave me the number.

"I'll see you then." We shook hands. Strangely, a kiss seemed out of context.

"Oh, by the way," she said, pausing at the door, "that thing about finding the heroin in the nose of the bear in Windsor? I made it up. You showed me that trick when we were in high school. We came here, drank ourselves silly, and fucked our brains out on that couch." She glanced at the office couch with a crooked smile. "I had such bad couch burns on my bum I couldn't sit for a week."

I had vague memories of a number of drunken sex nights with Nessa in the office.

"I always had a good time with you, Harry. See you later."

"Before you go, could I ask you something?"

"Sure."

"Where'd you get the money you originally invested with me?"

"Why do you want to know?"

"Just curious."

She smiled. "Let me guess. You heard the rumors that I made an adult film or that I was a gangster's mistress?"

Before I could answer, she said, "Maybe I'll tell you one day. Maybe tonight." She winked, and then, she was gone.

Maybe the secret of happiness is to just go with the flow, I thought.

Everything works out when it's supposed to, my father used to say. I thought he was full of crap, but I was starting to become a believer.

CHAPTER 24

RIGHT AFTER NESSA LEFT, I phoned a real estate broker I knew and spent a half hour talking to him about renting a new place to house MurderLand.

Two of the places he suggested sounded interesting. I made an appointment to see them right after I visited my father. The real estate search was to be another part of my alibi. I would be able to say with a straight face that I had accepted Wally and Carlene's proposal and was making plans to move the museum. To add further credibility, I made a call to my bank manager and told him I wanted to come in the following week to talk about a bridge loan to accommodate the move.

After that, I picked up sandwiches for my dad and Clive and drove to the nursing home.

The empty bed beside Dad was filled with a stocky, old, bald guy with a face the color of oatmeal. He looked at me with big doe eyes. When I said hello, his only response was to begin to cry softly.

Clive came in a few minutes after I arrived. He was limping.

"What happened to you?"

"Went dancing."

"Strain a muscle?"

"Met a woman. I think I'm in love."

"Lucky you. How's my dad been?"

"The same. Ginnie this, Ginnie that. He doesn't make any sense to me." He rubbed his crotch. "By the way, an old lady named Betsy visited your father around ten."

I was delighted Betsy had visited Dad. While Betsy didn't know who Jenny was, she might know who Ginnie was. I made a mental note to stop by Virgil the next time I was in the neighborhood, thank her for visiting my dad, and ask her if she knew anyone named Ginnie.

"Who's the new guy?" I asked. His crying had grown louder after Clive arrived.

"A gentleman with Alzheimer's. He's petrified of people of color."

To demonstrate, Clive walked slowly toward the guy. The closer he got, the louder the guy whimpered and the harder he pulled at his covers, trying to cover his head. The way the sheets had been tucked in, they only came to his chin.

"This fellow has Ku Klux Klan written all over him," Clive said, backing away. The whimpering grew softer as Clive retreated.

Clive returned to his chair near the door and sat down slowly, pulling at his crotch. "Tongue studs. Oh, man." He laughed a big, hearty laugh.

After the nursing home, I met with the real estate agent. The first building he showed me was modern and had a good layout but was way too expensive and too far from Clifton Hill.

The second one was about half the size of MurderLand but was just close enough to Clifton Hill to pick up the foot traffic. It was also rundown and needed a lot of work. I gave the agent a lowball offer and demanded extravagant improvements before I leased it.

"The owner will never accept that, Harry."

"Let him make a counteroffer." All I needed to make my story solid was an indication that I had accepted Carlene's and Wally's demands and was serious about moving.

I headed to the museum with another piece of my plan in place.

Gina had already left.

I called Frankie and told him to take the winnings from the previous night, double them, and put it all on the Raptors' home game.

I felt like the Teflon man. I wasn't bothered in the least when Pilot emerged from the basement as grumpy as ever.

"Where'd you put those damned guns?" he asked as soon as he saw me.

"Why are they so important?"

"They're not registered. You'll end up with your ass in a sling if you sell them."

"Forget about the guns. I won't sell them. I want to talk to you about something else. I've decided it's going to take too much energy to fight Carlene and Wally. I'm going to move the museum to another location."

"You're so full of shit."

"I'm serious. I put in an offer this afternoon to rent a place a few blocks from here on Ferry Street."

He knew I was lying. He took his cigarette all the way out of his mouth, lowered his eye brows, and glared at me without saying a word.

I didn't care. I wanted him to be able to tell the police with a straight face that I'd informed him we were moving.

"It's a good move for us. We'll have less space to manage. It's all on one floor so you won't have to go up and down stairs."

"Stairs don't bother me. I like stairs. Stairs keep me young."

"Maybe we can put in a small exercise room for employees."

He stuck the stub of his cigarette between his lips, leaned forward over the desk, and said in a low voice, "When you're ready to tell me what you're really up to, then I'm all ears. Until then, stop wasting my time with bullshit."

"I'm not bullshitting you."

He pulled himself up to his full height. "Just be careful, sonny boy. You're not half as smart as you think you are."

As he headed toward the door I remembered something from the day before.

"Virginia Hill," I said.

He stopped. "What's that supposed to mean?"

"Virginia Hill. *Ginnie*. The name my father keeps repeating." One of the museum's most gruesome tableaus was a recreation of Virginia Hill's Beverly Hills living room, where her lover, Bugsy Siegel, had been shot several times with a high-powered rifle by a hit man hiding in the bushes outside on the evening of June 20, 1947. Bugsy had stolen money from the casino he had built and was operating for the mob. Meyer Lansky, his old partner and boyhood friend, had sanctioned the hit. Pilot had recreated the bloody scene from police photos right down to using a glass eye to represent the one that had been blown out of Bugsy's head and sent flying a dozen feet across the room. The one thing that wasn't accurate was the mannequin of Virginia Hill standing beside the body with her hands in the air, mouth open as if screaming her head off. She hadn't even been home at the time, but Pilot thought it added to the effect.

"Stop with the guesses. You're not even close," he said, with a wave of his hand as he headed out the door.

"Wait. Then, who is Ginnie?"

"I'm going home," he yelled from the hallway. "You lock up. I'm outta here."

He knows, I thought.

The phone rang.

CHAPTER 25

"HEY, HARRY, IT'S MELANIE. How's it going?"

"Great. What's up?"

"I was just calling to see if you found a date for tonight, because if you haven't, I might be able to help you out." She sounded as bubbly as day-old ginger ale.

"Got dumped?"

"Let's not talk about it, okay?"

"Melanie, I'm sorry, but I made other plans."

"You could always break them."

"Gee, I'd like to. Really I would, but I can't. Maybe another time."

"Yeah, sure. Another time."

"And Melanie, next time, pay attention when I tell you how to treat men. Listen to me. I always have your best interests at heart."

"Thanks for rubbing it in. Have a good time. If you change your mind, you know where to find me."

We blew each other kisses over the phone.

When it rains, it pours, I thought.

I locked the front door and returned to the office. While I waited for the clock to run down for my meeting with Duane Morthwell, I went over and over everything that was supposed to happen during the next twelve hours.

I kept returning to the same question. Should I give Duane the .38 or the High Standard .22 with the silencer? The .22 would be the quietest, but it was unlikely anyone would hear Duane fire a .38 inside my father's house. Even if the sound penetrated the walls, the neighbor to the south was away and the one on the north was an old woman who was deaf even with her hearing aids turned up full blast.

The .38 was more deadly and a better weapon for an amateur. On the other hand, the .22 might make it look more like a mob hit.

I couldn't decide.

I went to my hiding place in the basement and took out the High Standard .22 and loaded it with .22 hollow points, which rip apart on impact. The ripping made them good for head shots because the pieces tumble around inside the brain and scramble it.

I decided to take both guns along and make up my mind on the way.

This is it, I thought as I locked up and headed to my car.

As the car warmed up, I felt surprisingly calm, knowing that once Wally and Carlene were out of the way, I had a shot at saving the family business.

Once on the road, I had the feeling that a dark, midsized car might be tailing me. During a few moments of paranoia, I even wondered if it might be the same midsized car I'd seen in front of Melanie's the day before. It was always just too far away for me to identify the make or the driver.

Does Morthwell have an unknown friend who might be tailing me?

Nah. It's nothing but frayed nerves, I reassured myself. Nevertheless to be on the safe side, I took Dorchester Road instead of the QEW so I could have a clearer view of who was behind me. By the time I'd zigzagged the last couple of miles to Firemen's Park, I was sure I wasn't being followed.

The wooded park on the Bruce Trail sat on a hundred and thirty-five acres at the north end of town. It was mainly used by locals and usually deserted late in the afternoon in winter. As expected, Duane's car was the only one in the parking lot.

I made a last-minute decision just before getting out of the car to give Morthwell the .38 and keep the .22 for myself. The .22 would eject its cartridges at the scene. I didn't want Morthwell worrying about collecting them after the shootings.

Morthwell was waiting for me at one of the picnic tables a short walk from the parking lot. His hands were wrapped around a takeout coffee cup on the table in front of him.

He nodded at me but didn't say anything.

"Been here long?" I stopped on the other side of the table.

"Long enough. You gonna sit down?" He looked cold, miserable, angry, and impatient.

I sat opposite him.

He took a sip of his coffee. "You're a crazy motherfucker, you know that?"

"Not crazy. Determined."

"You got the gun?"

"Yeah."

"Give it here." He held out his hand.

I handed him the .38.

He began to check it out carefully.

"Looks okay," he said, sticking the pistol in his jacket pocket and replacing his hands around his coffee cup.

"You know what to do?"

"Why don't you go over it one last time?"

"All right. You drive to my stepmother's place on the parkway." I gave him the address again. "You park in the driveway of the house to the south."

"You're sure the neighbors are away?"

"Positive. No one can see you there from the road or from my stepmother's house. You cross over to her house through the hedge. You look for Lavaleer's car, which is a brand new, bright red Mercedes SL500. License plate is R-C-H-L-W-Y-R. Rich lawyer. Get it?"

"Yeah. Ha. Ha. Maybe I should steal the car after I finish." He grinned, revealing small uneven teeth in need of some serious dental care.

"Not a good idea. The car would be way too hot."

"And if there's no car in the driveway?"

"Carlene's car will be there. A silver Lexus. So there will be at least one car. But if Wally's car isn't there, then abort, and we'll try again another night. We want to take them out together."

"What's the chance he won't be there?"

"Maybe one in ten. The odds are way better than winning the lottery a second time."

He cracked a smile. "Yeah. Okay, so the Mercedes is there. So, then I go around back and look for the key what's-her-name left outside."

"Carlene. The key will be under the flowerpot beside the door."

"Okay, give me a visual picture of what it's like inside or I'm gonna be stumbling all over the place."

"You won't have to worry. Carlene keeps a night-light on in the kitchen, which is where you'll enter the house. There's a back staircase between the kitchen and dining room to the bedrooms on the second floor. Carlene and Wally like to fuck with the lights on and the door open to the bedroom. You should have plenty of light to get up the stairs. Oh, and they like to crank up the music. Hip-hop or jazz, depending on the mood. So they won't hear you until you want them to. And don't be surprised if one or the other of them is handcuffed to the bedposts."

"Kinky."

"Yeah, among other things."

"How do you know all this?"

"Just do your job. Wear gloves. When you're done, do what you can to make it look like a robbery. Leave the front door open slightly like you went out that way in a hurry. Go out through the back door, and replace the key under the flowerpot. Break the window in the back door from the outside, so it looks like that's how you got in. Wipe the gun clean and throw it in the river. Throw the jewelry in, too. Go home, wash up, wash your clothes to get rid of any gunshot residue, and do what you normally do. I'll be in touch in a few weeks."

"Don't worry about me. You just remember our deal. I want my money, the photos, and any copies of the video. Don't try to screw with me."

"I won't. Just stay cool afterward. The police will suspect me right off the top. They'll rake me over the coals. But the case will go cold quickly. Once things settle down, I'll contact you. And no phone calls in the meantime. They're too easily traced. Understand?"

"All right. But don't cross me."

"I won't." I got up. He stayed seated. "You coming, Duane?"

"In a bit. Gonna finish my coffee." He raised the cup to his lips.

I returned to my car and just sat there for a minute, breathing slowly in and out.

It's done, I thought, staring at the orange slice of moon hovering overhead in the sky. I'd pushed the button. Now, all I had to worry about was whether or not Wally and Carlene would get together in the next twelve hours.

Everything will work out, I reassured myself.

CHAPTER 26

I SHOULD HAVE KEPT MY PROMISE to call Nessa right then, but instead, I decided to drive to Alice May's place in Queenston. I was already halfway there and feeling omnipotent.

Alice's Jetta was parked in the driveway. She was leaning out of her bedroom window in back shooting and ranting at her raccoons.

The varmint population had increased to six with the addition of one more adult.

"Any luck?" I asked, watching her in profile as she sighted down the barrel and fired off pellet after pellet.

"One of them ripped the screen off my window last night."

"You're not going to do much damage to them with a pellet gun."

"Did you bring the gun you promised me?"

"Maybe."

She held out her hand. I just grinned at her. Her eyes were too crazy for me to trust her with a gun.

She frowned. "Stop making promises you can't keep. If you're not going to help, go home, Harry. Get lost."

She was bumming me out. I was feeling decisive.

This is my night, I reminded myself. Either I'm going to be lucky or not.

I was in the twilight zone.

"I'm going to take care of your problem," I said, deciding to show her how decisive I could be.

I pulled the pistol out of my pocket and fired off six shots before she or the raccoons realized what was happening.

Without the silencer, the .22 long rifle hollow point bullets would have made a small racket. With it, the only noise was a hissing sound that was quieter than opening a can of warm soda. Her pellet gun was louder.

I'm what is called a natural shooter—someone who can just aim and hit the mark without much effort or any glimmer of buck fever. It's something I, no doubt, inherited from my father and grandfather. Both were equally endowed. I had never had an aversion to killing things. What had kept me from being a willing participant on their hunting forays had been a pathological aversion to black flies, mosquitoes, and being wet and cold all the time.

"Cat got your tongue?" I asked, retrieving the spent cartridges. I glanced at Alice, who was staring at me with her mouth open.

Before she could reply, I walked toward the raccoons to examine the carnage.

Five of the six were stone cold dead with holes in their heads. One had been shot through the side, because it had turned in a way that hid its head. It appeared to still be moving. I gave it a *coup de grâce* through the ear and retrieved the cartridge.

Alice joined me as I returned the gun to my pocket. She put her arm through mine and used the toe of her boot to nudge the raccoon corpse closest to her.

"I'm kind of hungry," I said. "Let's get something to eat."

"Whatever you'd like." Her voice was thick and husky.

"Let's get your coat. We're going out on the town."

The last thing she'd ever call me again was indecisive, I mused as we headed into the house.

She threw her arms around me as we went through the door. Standing in her kitchen, we made out for the first time.

I could have tossed her over my shoulder, caveman style, carried her into the bedroom, and screwed her brains out. Instead, I played it cool.

"Come on," I said, breaking away from her. "Let's go."

I led; she followed. It's no secret why. Some women crave powerful men the way some men crave sex.

I wanted to laugh. It was all so simple.

CHAPTER 27

Did I remember my date with Nessa?

Yes, for one fleeting moment, but I wasn't about to waste time calling her and breaking the spell between Alice and me.

I stopped at the museum and left Alice in the office while I went downstairs to hide the .22 in the air duct.

When I returned to the office, she was gone. I located her on the second floor, standing where the Babushka Lady used to be, staring at the Kennedy tableau.

"God, this is so real," she said.

"You know what it is?"

"Of course, I do, Harry. I'm not stupid. My grandmother talked about it sometimes. Kennedy's assassination changed everything."

"Did you know that Richard Nixon, the guy who lost to Kennedy and later became president, was in Dallas the morning of Kennedy's assassination?"

This largely unknown detail was one of Pilot's favorite ways to get a rise out of visitors.

"No, really? Did he witness the assassination?"

I was pleased that she seemed to know who Nixon was. She was getting better and better all the time. "No. He had been there at a board meeting. He was in private law practice at the time. He flew out earlier in the morning."

"You think he was involved?" She pressed herself close to me.

Ask Pilot and he'd reel off dozens of people who were involved in the Kennedy assassination and why. Castro wanted JFK dead because the CIA, via the mafia, had tried to assassinate him and because Kennedy had allowed the Bay of Pigs invasion of Cuba to take place. The Cuban exile community in America wanted Kennedy dead because he hadn't provided the promised air cover for the Bay of Pigs invasion and most of the invaders were killed or captured. Ditto certain factions of the CIA, which had participated in the Bay of Pigs and thought Kennedy was soft on Communism. The US military-industrial complex—the same guys Eisenhower warned the nation of in his farewell address at the end of his presidency—wanted Kennedy dead because he refused to commit combat troops to Vietnam. Chicago mafia boss Sam Giancana wanted him dead because Giancana had helped elect JFK and was under attack by the president's brother, Attorney General Bobby Kennedy. Ditto Teamsters boss, Jimmy Hoffa, a Republican who had supported Kennedy on behalf of Giancana and was also under attack for criminal activities by the attorney general. Ditto Meyer Lansky, second in command of the National Crime Syndicate, who was pissed because Kennedy had failed to kill Castro and restore the mob's Cuban casinos. FBI Director J. Edgar Hoover wanted JFK dead because the Kennedy brothers wanted to fire him. Nixon wanted him dead because Kennedy had used mafia money and influence to win votes. Even Sinatra was pissed enough to want him dead, because Kennedy had publicly humiliated him. These weren't just figments of Pilot's fertile imagination. Many of the names of Kennedy's enemies and their motives leading up to the president's assassination appeared in Senator Church's Committee Reports, the report of the House Select Committee on Assassinations, FBI wiretaps and memos, and CIA documentation.

"I don't know who was involved," I told her truthfully.

"Let's get out of here," she said. She hugged me tighter. "I'm getting creeped out."

I took Alice to one of the best restaurants on the cliff overlooking the falls.

"It's like flying over the falls in an airplane," Alice said, staring down at the brim of the falls from our window seats.

I explained to her that Niagara Falls is really three falls: the American Falls and the small Bridal Veil Falls on the New York side, and the U-shaped Horseshoe Falls on the Canadian side. At night, the falls are lit by twenty-one xenon white and colored lights, each producing a brilliance of 250 million-candlepower. They illuminate the cascades of water pouring over the 1,000-foot brink of the American Falls and the 2,600-foot brink of the Horseshoe Falls.

"The drop from the brink of the falls to the boulders at the bottom of the gorge is about two hundred feet, about the height of a twenty-story building," I explained.

We watched the spectacle as we pigged out on lobster and steak. Despite all the kitsch surrounding them, the falls remain one of the world's most awesome natural wonders.

"I wonder how much water goes over the falls?" she asked between bites of her food, mesmerized by the sight.

"On average about 750,000 gallons a second. Another 750,000 gallons a second are streamed off through underground tunnels under Niagara Falls, Ontario and Niagara Falls, New York to power plants downstream on both sides. This isn't just a natural wonder, Alice. It's a strategic resource."

"A potential terrorist target?"

"Definitely. The hydro plants on the two sides of the river are producing enough electricity to light nearly four million homes."

"Scary. I should have known you'd know so much about the falls." Her eyes sparkled with awe and excitement. "It must have been fun growing up here with your father owning MurderLand."

"It was, but I never really appreciated it as much as I do now."

"Do you mind if I ask you a personal question?"

"No, not at all."

"What I don't understand is how you're going to resurrect MurderLand," she said. "I checked it out when you first started hitting on me and I still thought you might be loaded. The museum was once very famous. Now, it's on its last legs. The only customers I saw there were old people."

"It's struggling," I admitted, "but I keep telling myself, there's a business hiding in there somewhere. I just need to figure it out. What about you? What are your future plans?"

"TV commercials pay the bills. I also like live theater. It's a great way to learn my craft, but it doesn't pay much. I'd like to do more theater, but I'd also like to do a TV series and break into feature films."

Then, she asked me a question about the museum that surprised me, not because she asked it, but because most people assumed they knew the answer.

"Do you ever find yourself questioning what you do for a living?"

"Do I feel guilty about making money by exploiting other people's prurient interests in misery and gratuitous violence?"

"I'm sorry. I didn't mean it like that." Then, she corrected herself. "No, I'm *not* sorry. That's exactly what I meant."

"You think MurderLand is creepy?"

"Strange."

"Is it really so different than reading a crime novel or watching a movie like *JFK* or *Bugsy?*"

"Are you calling what you do art?"

"Art, archeology, theater, history. What's different from what we do than what, say, the Dada artist Marcel Duchamp did in 1917? He turned the art world on its head by exhibiting a urinal as art. Art is about the sensation. It's the sensations that keep us feeling alive—the craving to witness and attach ourselves emotionally to earth-shattering events— whether the events are good or bad."

"What about redemption? Isn't the difference between art and pornography the redemption we experience from art?"

"The redemption's there to make us feel less guilty about craving sensation. Redemption's the hypocritical part of art, the excuse, the cover-up. MurderLand is the urinal. We don't try to fake it. We don't try to cover it up. We're sex, not love. We know why you're paying your money to see what we have. We leave it to you to discover your own higher order. All business, including the art business, trades on human misery, desire, or need in some way. In our business, we just don't have Academy Awards or froufrou literary awards to sanitize what we do. We're right there at the edge of death, demonstrating, like the urinal, the dirty part of life, the part that feeds into your vital organs. Like sex, like car racing, like roller coasters."

"Like a traffic accident on the highway."

"Exactly," I said, pleased she got it. "We're helping you relive and recapture the most famous traffic accidents on the human highway. We attract and repulse—we make you feel alive, but most of all we make you *feel* and that validates you."

"You're scary. I like that." She squeezed my knee under the table. "But what about beauty? Love?"

"The sugarcoating of reality. It's the pause between all the rest. In the end, it's just another sensation—not much different than wallowing in the frightening, or the horrible, or the tragic, or finding relief because something bad or ugly isn't happening to you. It's good because it makes you feel something." I drank some wine and savored the smile on her face. "What about you? Does acting make you happy?"

"You mean pretending to be someone else, so I don't have to worry about who I really am?"

"I didn't mean it like that."

"Yes, you did." Her smile broadened. "Harry, what makes me happy is being twenty-three years old and attractive to the people I want to attract. What could possibly be better? Right now, all I want to do is experience it all."

"All?"

Alice slipped off her shoe and stuck her toes in my crotch. When I reciprocated, she started to moan loud enough for the maître d' to give us a dirty look.

This has to be happiness, I thought.

After dessert and coffee, when we were alone in the elevator on the way downstairs, I asked her if she preferred that we rent a room or go to the casino.

"What do you think?" she asked with her hand on my crotch. "You choose."

"The casino." When her mouth turned into a pout, I added, "We'll save the best for last." I gave her a peck on the cheek, and then whispered in her ear, "I want it all, Alice."

What I really wanted was to be seen out and about for a good portion of the night. The casino, with its eyes in the sky, would provide me with a foolproof alibi.

I had taken Alice to the casino a couple of times before when she still thought I had money and I thought she would sleep with me. I knew she liked the craps tables as much as me.

Like all the games in the casino, the odds in craps are in favor of the house. But every once in a while the stars align and a player can win big in spite of all mathematical logic.

That's what happened to us. The dice turned hot whether we were shooters or betting from the sidelines. By midnight I had turned the thirty-five hundred I had left after dinner into sixteen grand. Alice kept asking whether or not we should quit and rent a room. I said *no*. I wanted to keep going. By one o'clock, we had made the round trip up to twenty-two thousand and back down to fourteen grand. At one thirty, we had twenty-three grand in chips in front of us. I cashed in enough to pay five hundred for a luxury suite so we could disappear upstairs to do a few lines of Soma. We were back at the tables fifteen minutes later.

In addition to the surveillance cameras, the casino was filled with box men, dealers, stickmen, and floor men who would remember us. Alice, with her drop-dead good looks and our winning streak, had also attracted quite an audience of onlookers and gamblers who followed our every wager as we moved from table to table. We spread our action among the tables on the main floor as well as the more upscale Salon Privé where the minimum and maximum bets were the highest.

The critical hour was two thirty to three thirty, when Morthwell got off work. That's when Wally would arrive at my stepmother's place and Morthwell would do his thing.

The craps tables provided an excellent distraction. We were down to twenty grand by three o'clock. I wanted to keep going, but I was starting to fade. Not wanting to be out of sight of the cameras, I dragged Alice to a roulette table where we could sit and place bets without much thinking.

By four, we were sitting on twenty-seven thousand, making everything from outside bets on black and red and odd and even, to straight-up bets on favorite numbers that would have turned our pockets inside out on a normal night.

This was no normal night.

By six, we called it quits. I tipped lavishly so everyone would remember me, and cashed out with thirty-one thousand dollars. Alice and I were both bushed but still running on adrenaline highs as we headed to our suite.

We finished the Soma, and finally, finally got naked and hurled ourselves into bed.

In the nude, she was even more beautiful than I had imagined. A pure goddess with flawless skin and a perfect body.

Alice made me lie on my back and slowly nibbled her way down my torso to my groin. I felt my mercury rising and gently pushed her head away. She covered my mouth with hers. I moved down her body and focused on her breasts and her pussy. She was as wet as I was hard.

When I tried to go down on her, she lifted her head and said, "No. I want you inside me now. I want to give you the prize."

"I want the prize," I said, taking her into my arms as she lay back on the bed with her knees up and her legs spread wide.

"Be gentle," she whispered in my ear as I positioned myself over her. She squeezed my butt cheeks in her hands and pulled me to her.

She claimed to be a virgin, so I was expecting a barrier that would bend my dick in half. But it was nothing like that. The entrance was more like slipping through warm butter.

"Yes," she said with more of a sigh than a yelp of pain.

Maybe she'd lost her hymen horseback riding, I thought as I began to move back and forth.

As I moved my hips against hers, she seemed to be mildly enjoying herself as she continued to grip my butt with both hands.

"Does it hurt?" I whispered.

"No, no," she whispered back. "It's wonderful. Don't stop."

I kept going, speeding up, slowing down, moving from side to side, moving in circles, doing the twist—it all seemed the same to her. She just lay there, breathing heavily, with her eyes shut tight, not moving a muscle.

Finally, it hit me. She's using me like a giant dildo.

To paraphrase Lenny Bruce, guys will fuck mud if they're horny enough. This was like fucking mud.

When she came, she produced the most annoying, little chirping sounds. It made me think of a baby sparrow that had fallen out of its nest.

The chirping was so irritating I was surprised I was even able to come. When I finally did and rolled off her, she threw her arms around my neck, and said, "Wasn't that wonderful?"

"Yeah. Wonderful." I tried not to sound ungrateful. This is what she'd been saving? This is her idea of ecstasy?

"I knew if I waited I'd find someone who really and truly appreciates me." She wrapped her arms and legs around me. "Was it really good for you?"

Didn't she know? Did I really have to lie?

"Wow," I managed to say.

"Can I tell you a secret?"

I didn't have to answer. I knew she would tell me anyway.

"I'm not really a virgin. I slept with my drama teacher when I was in high school. We did it about a dozen times. Then, he dumped me for someone younger. The other girl told me he thought I was a terrible lay. Of course, she just said that to hurt my feelings. But I couldn't help it. I took it to heart. I just never wanted to have that happen to me again. I never told anyone until now. I feel like I can tell you anything. I feel so close to you."

"That's a pretty sad story." I tried to not sound too disinterested. Sheesh, I thought, what have I gotten myself into.

"We should go to sleep now and then get up and do it again. We have the room until eleven o'clock, and Sunday rehearsal doesn't start until noon," she said in a lazy voice.

"Maybe we should get up and have breakfast." It was nearly seven o'clock.

"Go to sleep," she whispered in my ear.

Before I could say more, she was snoring in the same annoying, chirpy way that she emitted during her orgasm.

CHAPTER 28

SUNDAY

THE STORY OF SISYPHUS should be tattooed to the inside of every man's eyelids. The trouble with being on top of the mountain is that it is inevitably transitory. I should have realized right then that I was already on the way down. But I was still basking in the rays of naïve optimism.

Even finding out that Alice was awful in bed hadn't dampened my spirits. In the scheme of things, if Duane Morthwell hadn't screwed up, my stepmother and Wally Lavaleer were both dead.

What I needed to do was get my dick to leave my brain alone long enough to think.

I needed to focus on the upcoming murder investigation.

For that, sleep wasn't such a bad idea. I managed to get in a couple of hours and then got up and had a long, hot shower.

At ten, I called the museum and told Pilot I was running late and wouldn't be in for a few hours. It was Gina's day off. He was holding down the fort by himself, which always made him grumpier than normal.

"Hang in there, Pilot. I'll be in as soon as possible," I assured him.

The hotel maids were hovering in the hallway like buzzards ready to pick apart the room by the time I got Alice up and out the door. "I could say I'm sick and skip rehearsal," Alice suggested. "We could keep the room for the rest of the day and screw ourselves silly."

"You need to go to your rehearsal. I have business to take care of," I said, sounding more decisive now that I didn't give a shit whether she liked me or not.

I drove her to Queenston and took the time to throw the carcasses of the raccoons into garbage bags along with the other garbage in her backyard.

"Best you don't talk about what happened to the raccoons, Alice. The animal rights people might end up boycotting your play."

"Good thinking. You're right. I'll see you when I finish rehearsing. Okay?"

"Call me. We'll figure something out." I played along, wanting to keep her on my good side. I expected all hell to break loose once I went home and discovered the bodies of Carlene and Wally. The last thing I wanted was to have Alice as an enemy. She was a necessary part of my alibi.

If I was to be suspect number one, I also needed to be prepared to take whatever the cops threw at me. Before leaving Alice's, I went to the trunk of my car, retrieved a different set of clothes, and went back inside and changed into them. I was sure that the shower at the hotel had washed off any remaining gunshot residue on my face and hands from the .22, but just to be on the safe side, I dropped my old clothes off at an old clothes collection bin on the way home.

That should have been the biggest of my worries.

When I pulled into the driveway, I was surprised to see Carlene's Lexus parked out front but no sign of Wally's Mercedes.

Duane must have aborted the plan, I told myself. Fuck.

I approached the main house, feeling a deep sense of disappointment. Then I saw that the front door was partially open, raising my spirits.

As soon as I stepped inside, I was hit with the same foul, human waste odor floating in the air that I'd smelled at the convenience store after Johnny Johnson had been shot.

Then I saw a naked leg on the floor through the arch between the living room and the dining room.

I crossed the living room and peered into the dining room.

Carlene was lying on the hardwood floor with arms and legs splayed like a bent swastika. She was wearing a white, blood-soaked bathrobe. It was open, revealing her nude body. It appeared she had been shot at least a couple of times in her chest.

I had no doubt she was dead. Her eyes were open, staring at the ceiling. Her skin was white and waxy. I avoided the large pool of blood as I approached her and felt the carotid artery in her neck. She had no pulse. Her skin was ice cold.

Feeling a little dizzy as I stood up, I wondered what the hell Carlene was doing downstairs, and where the hell was Wally?

My greatest fear was that Duane had driven off in Wally's Mercedes—a car that would be so easy to spot he'd likely be arrested before sundown.

I took a quick tour of the house. Carlene's best jewelry was gone from the dresser.

Good, I told myself. But I still saw no sign of Wally.

I cruised through the entire house. Still no Wally.

Shocked and shaken, I did what I could to keep the plan moving in its original direction. Hoping for the best, I picked up the portable phone in the living room, dialed 9-1-1, and told the dispatcher that I had a suspicious death to report and needed immediate assistance.

The dispatcher told me to wait outside.

I stayed on the portable phone with the dispatcher fielding questions until the first two patrol cars arrived with two cops in each one.

The driver of the second patrol car was Constable Valerie Runge, looking even grimmer than when she had pulled me over to collect the money for Nessa. She had to recognize me, I thought, but she avoided eye contact and let the other constables do all the talking.

After I'd briefed them, the driver of the first car told me to stay outside while he and his partner headed around the side of the house. Constable Runge and her partner went inside to see if the killer or killers might still be hanging around.

As more police cars and medical personnel arrived, I used the portable phone to call Melanie. I got her voice mail and explained what I had found. I told her the police were already on the scene. I left it to her imagination to figure out what she'd need to do.

I also called Pilot. When I told him what had happened, all he said was, "Don't say nothing over the phone," and hung up. Somehow, it felt comforting to know that someone was more paranoid than me.

The person I didn't dare call was Duane Morthwell. I was dying to know why he had changed our plan, but any contact with him was out of the question.

The last person I called was Alice. I left a message on her voice mail, telling her briefly what had happened and promising to try to call her later.

Just as I hung up the phone, Detectives Sills and Mallard arrived. After they interviewed me on the front steps, they accompanied me into the house to see if I could identify anything that might be missing. I mentioned to them that my father had given Carlene a lot of jewelry. I gave them descriptions of some of Carlene's better pieces. They had me go upstairs with them and wait while they looked in the dresser where I said I thought she kept her jewelry. I acted surprised that all her good jewelry was missing.

I accompanied them outside, and Mallard did an on-the-spot gunshot residue test on me, again, which, of course, I passed.

Neither Sills nor Mallard was satisfied. They asked me to go with them to the station. I went without a fuss, but I also told them, "I've read enough mysteries and seen enough cop shows to know that the first 48-to-72 hours after a crime are crucial. If you guys spend all your time with me, then you'll never catch who really did this."

"You and your stepmother were at war with each other," Sills said. "You think we wouldn't find that out? We found out plenty about you when we checked you out for the Johnson murder, remember?"

"And by now, you know I had nothing to do with the convenience store killing."

They both fell silent until they had me in the windowless interrogation room sitting on an uncomfortable metal chair, staring at them across a scarred wooden table.

"What we don't know is how you, Johnny Johnson, and your step mother all fit together," Sills said.

"If you do find out, let me know."

"What we do know is that you had a motive to kill your stepmother. She was about to bleed your inheritance, demolish the museum, and put you out on the street."

"No disrespect meant, but you guys have been public servants too long. You don't understand business. Whatever she was planning wasn't the end of the world. I still would have had a piece of the hotel lease, and I was free to move the museum to a new location. I own the MurderLand brand. Only yesterday, I was out looking at buildings to lease. I put in an offer on a new location. You can call my broker if you want." I gave them his card.

Sills and Mallard exchanged glances.

"That's real convenient," Mallard said, "looking at real estate the day before your stepmother gets killed."

"I was looking in New York State a week ago. Remember?" Again *the look* passed between them.

"Your stepmother was planning to move your father to another facility. We understand you went against her wishes and arranged to have him stay at Graystone, even though you didn't have the authority."

Damn, I thought. They had been looking into my affairs even more closely than I thought. Maybe someone had been following me. I had to be careful and not say anything that would box me in later. "My stepmother and I spoke about it. I convinced her to hold off on any decision for a few weeks. She said she would think it over. She was still thinking it over as far as I know." I decided to get creative. "Look, detectives, I know you want to solve this, but maybe you are looking at this all wrong. Maybe I'm not the only one with a motive. First of all, Carlene's good jewelry is gone. Maybe it was a burglary gone wrong. Second, the last time I spoke with Carlene, which was yesterday, she told me she was getting a funny feeling about Wally Lavaleer. She said she wasn't sure she could trust him."

"They were screwing each other," Mallard said matter-of-factly.

"Yeah, but maybe he was screwing her financially more than she wanted. She said she thought the people he was dealing with might be connected to Buffalo mobsters. If I were you two, I'd be checking out Lavaleer. Carlene and I weren't best friends, but nobody deserves what happened to her."

Neither officer looked particularly sympathetic.

"Just so you know. We still have you as a person of interest for Johnson," Sills said. "So don't go too far."

"I have no intention of going anywhere. I want to see the killer or killers caught as much as you," I lied.

CHAPTER 29

AFTER THE POLICE INTERROGATION, I visited my father. I forgot it was Clive's day off. His replacement popped his head into the room for a couple of seconds and then vanished. Dad's roommate was asleep in the next bed and snoring softly. I ate one of the sandwiches and threw the other one out. I thought about telling my father what happened to Carlene, but since she rarely visited, I figured he wouldn't miss her.

The front door of MurderLand was locked, but I knew Pilot was still there because the lights were on. Once inside, I yelled down the basement stairs to him.

"Be there in a minute. Hold your horses," he yelled back.

I went to my office. While waiting, I checked my computer for the score for the game I'd bet on the night before. The Raptors had lost. I owed Frankie Argyll ten thousand, but I could easily cover it from the money I'd won at the casino. Besides, I reminded myself, I was still on a roll. I called Frankie and told him to put two thousand on the underdog Colorado Avalanche over the Minnesota Wild.

Pilot showed up a few minutes later. He was carrying a small paper bag.

"What's in the bag?" I asked.

"It can wait. Tell me about Carlene."

I filled him in on my day. His only change in expression was when he opened his mouth to stick another cigarette in it.

"What's in the bag?" I asked again, having no more to add on Carlene's demise.

He pulled out an old ice pick and handed it to me.

"You remember this?"

It brought back a slice of an old memory—one that I hadn't thought of in years.

"It looks like the old ice pick that sat on Grandpa's desk." I could see where my grandfather had carved his initials into the pick's wooden handle.

"It's the same one," he said. "You remember what you did with it?"

It was right after the funeral for my mother. I was visiting my grandfather at the museum. He was retired but still had his own office down the hall from my father's office. My grandfather had left me alone for a few minutes, and I had found the ice pick on his desk. I was still mad that my mother wasn't ever coming back. I had gone around the office stabbing everything in sight, including the leather couch, which I really liked stabbing because the hide made a little popping sound, almost like a cap gun, each time the blade penetrated it.

"I remember."

"You remember what happened when your father caught you?"

I nodded. My father came into the office before my grandfather returned. He was pissed, and it appeared he was going to tan my behind, but just then Pilot and my grandfather showed up. They all had a little powwow, and the next thing I knew, my grandfather was squatting down at eye level with me, explaining to me how I could hurt myself with the pick.

"What did your grandfather tell you?"

"That I could poke my eye out."

"What else?"

I pointed to my ear. "He said if I poked it in my ear, it could go in my brain and turn it into scrambled eggs and kill me."

"What did I tell you when you were eleven or twelve about ice picks? Who used them?"

"Hey, Pilot, where exactly is this going? I was out all last night. My stepmother was just murdered, and I spent half of today being interrogated by the police."

"Yeah, and you seem really broken up. Just answer the question."

I could see the stubborn look in his eyes. It was easier to go along than argue.

"Murder Incorporated. Abe 'Kid Twist' Reles was their first field commander—one of the most vicious killers who ever lived. Everyone was afraid of him. The ice pick was his favorite weapon. He was so good at sticking the pick through a guy's eardrum and twisting it, that a lot of his murders went undetected because they appeared to be strokes."

"What happened?"

"Reles was hanging tough on a murder rap when an underling ratted him out. He tried to save himself from the electric chair by making a deal with Thomas E. Dewey, New York's special prosecutor. Reles turned state's evidence and testified against not only some of his old childhood friends, but his boss. In the end, his testimony sent seven men to the Sing Sing electric chair, including Louis 'Lepke' Buchalter, the only organized crime executive to die in the hot seat."

"What else?"

I reached deep into my memory bank, recalling the stories Pilot had drilled into my head over the years. "Reles was the guy who coined the terms 'hit' and 'contract.'"

"How did he die?"

"He was being held in protective custody at the Half Moon Hotel in Coney Island, guarded by more than twenty cops manning round-the-clock shifts. He fell, jumped, or was thrown out the window and died on the roof below. The mob called him the canary who could sing but couldn't fly."

"Was it a mob hit?"

"Nobody knows. They found some sheets tied together and strung out the window, and also some broken wire beside him. Maybe he tried to climb out. Maybe he committed suicide. Maybe the cops turned their backs long enough for mobsters to go in and throw him out the window and position the sheets and wire to make it look like a suicide. Or maybe some bought-off cops threw him out."

"What's the lesson?"

He had never asked me this part before. "Don't rat out the mob," I answered.

"No. Try again."

The phone rang. Melanie's name popped up on the call display. "Excuse me, Pilot, I have to answer this."

He scrunched up his face, clearly annoyed. "I forgot to tell you. Your lawyer called earlier." I gave him a sharp look as I answered the phone.

"Harry, it's Melanie. I'm so sorry. Terrible news about Carlene."

"I'm just going to have to live with it." I tried not to sound too glib.

"I called earlier. Did you get my message?"

"I just got it."

"I understand the police may have found the murder weapon."

"Oh?" That was news to me. Scary news, since Duane was supposed to throw it in the river. "Where'd you hear that?"

"I made some calls. A friend of mine in the prosecutor's office told me on the QT. They received an anonymous phone call. Someone said they saw a man in a Mercedes drive through the laneway a block from Wally Lavaleer's office and throw something into a dumpster that looked like a gun. The weapon's been shipped to the forensics center in Toronto. The police took Wally in for questioning about an hour ago. He's still there."

Yes, I thought, yes, yes. There is a God.

"Wow, that's heavy, Melanie. I don't know what to say."

"I know. It's just awful. If you feel like company, stop by later."

"Still having trouble with the new lover?"

"Let's not talk about that. If you want, I'm here."

"Thanks, Melanie. It's been a pretty hectic day."

Good old Duane Morthwell, I mused. Somewhere in that thick skull of his lay a functioning brain. He may not have killed Wally, but he had done the next best thing—he'd thrown the suspicion on him by dumping the gun close to his office, then telling the police he'd seen someone in a car like Wally's dump it there. I strongly suspected Morthwell of being the person who had made the anonymous telephone call to the police.

I told Pilot what Melanie had said, and then asked, "So, what's the answer, Pilot? If it isn't 'don't rat out the mob,' what is it?"

"The answer is: Nothing's ever what it appears to be."

"What's that supposed to mean?" I asked, genuinely puzzled.

"You need to learn a lot. Think about what I told you." He pulled himself to his feet.

"Okay."

It made no sense to me, but I didn't have the heart to tell him.

CHAPTER 30

"Chirp, chirp, chirp."

The little noises that Alice made when she came grew more annoying the more I heard them.

"Oh, darling, wasn't that wonderful?" she asked, slipping out from under me, then noticing that I was still hard. "Uh-oh. Didn't you come? Wasn't it good for you?"

"It was wonderful," I told her. How do you tell a woman the truth about something like that?

"But you didn't come," she said.

"I came a little bit," I lied. "Maybe oral sex would do the trick."

She started to cry. "You're just like my drama teacher. You think I'm terrible in bed."

"No, no, no." I can't stand it when women cry. Hers was more like a little mew-mew of a shivering kitten—even more grating than her chirping. "It's not your fault. I have a condition. I can't come all the time. I was afraid to tell you."

She brightened. "Oh, Harry, you can tell me anything."

She held my penis in her hand and scrutinized it. "That's terrible. Is it hereditary? Will it affect our children?"

Children? I wanted to scream. And run.

I would have bolted, but she decided to go down on me. Except for the same little chirping noises she made while blowing me, she gave passable head. The strangest part for me was that while I watched the most beautiful face in the world nibbling on me, I had to pretend it was Melanie or I probably would have gone soft.

"There, that's better now." She patted my penis afterward.

I wanted to get up. She wanted to cuddle. "After all you've gone through today, you should try to get a good night's sleep," she whispered.

"I can't sleep."

"I'm sorry I'm not enough for you." She started to whimper again.

"Please don't cry."

"Okay. Just don't be mean or I'll tell the police what I really think."

The quick change of attitude got my attention.

"What do you really think?" I asked cautiously, wondering just how stupid it was of me to forget that she was a professional actor.

She put her finger to my lips to shush me, and then put her arms around me and pulled me to her. "Let's just cuddle."

We cuddled.

She fell asleep. My arm under her fell asleep. I didn't. I lay there staring at the ceiling wondering what had I gotten myself into, and more to the point, what did she think she knew?

A little after one o'clock in the morning, I managed to extract my arm without waking her. I got out of bed and went to the living room at the front of her house.

Peeking through the curtains, I could see a dark-colored car with one or possibly two shadowy occupants sitting a half of a block away. I was almost certain it was the police. I wondered if they wanted me to see them or if they were so stupid that they thought I might not. I wandered into the kitchen and opened a bottle of red wine. The empty boxes of Chinese takeout, which Alice had ordered and I'd picked up on the way over, were still on the kitchen table along with our dirty dishes and glasses.

Failing to find a clean glass, I drank the wine straight from the bottle as I returned to the living room. I searched around for a book to read, but the only reading materials Alice seemed to have were glamour magazines. I settled for the TV. I turned it extra low so I wouldn't wake her and have to go back and cuddle. I watched *The Shape of Things to Come*—not the 1930s sci-fi classic, but the 1979 remake with Jack Palance, Carol Lynley, and Barry Morse. The film was so bad that it had become a cult classic as one of the ten worst movies of all time. It was the third time I'd seen it. Canadian stations loved playing it late at night as filler because it had been shot in Canada and helped Canadian TV stations meet their annual quota for Canadian content.

I finished the wine and dozed off on the couch.

MONDAY

When I woke again, I guessed that it was around eight by the light peeking around the edges of the curtains. I had a blanket over me and a hangover. The television had been turned off, and a note lay on the coffee table under the empty wine bottle.

Hi, Sweetie.

You looked so peaceful I didn't want to wake you. I'm off to an early rehearsal. Last night was delicious. See you later.

Love, Alice.

P.S. I took some money from your pocket. I'll get something nice to wear for your stepmother's funeral.

I'm not sure what bothered me more—the fact that she dotted the "i" in Alice with a happy face or that she was already acting like a wife. She'd taken fifteen hundred from my stash for her little shopping spree.

I looked out the front window. It was pouring rain and sleet. The trees were covered with a thick bark of ice. I also noticed that whoever had been out there in the parked car was gone. If I was still being watched, the cops were using a smarter surveillance team.

The bathroom was a pigsty. The last thing I wanted to do was clean up in Alice's mess.

I drove home to my own pigsty through the sleet, ice, and rain—the weather couldn't seem to make up its mind. I took a shower at my place.

The top story on TV and in *The Falls* and *The Review* was Carlene's murder. Theories abounded. Even my suggestion that the Buffalo mob might be involved had made it into the news. It looked like everyone was floundering to come up with a motive.

Good, I thought. The more muddied the waters, the less chance of the police finding Duane or me.

The hockey score from the previous evening wasn't so good. Colorado lost by a goal.

I was flying through money like a man on fire.

I can handle it, I told myself. Just keep the forward momentum going. Damn the setbacks.

I picked up the phone, called the police station, and asked to speak to Detective Sills or Mallard.

I needed to keep up the impression that I was concerned about Carlene's death.

When Sills answered, I asked, "Have you located the killers yet?"

"We're making progress. We'll let you know when we have something definite. If you hear anything, make sure you let us know. Even the smallest thing."

The good cop.

"Of course I will," I assured him. "I also wanted to let you know that you still have the crime scene tape on my stepmother's house. When can I go in? I'd like to look for her will and her address book. She has a cousin in California. I'd like to contact him."

"You can go in whenever you like. The forensic team's done. They must have forgotten to take the tape down. As for the will, Wally Lavaleer told me he has a copy of it."

"Thanks."

"When you get the phone number for this cousin, give it to me. I'd like to speak with him and see what kind of light he might shed on things."

"I'll give you the number as soon as I find it."

"Oh, and one last thing, we talked to your girlfriend."

It didn't surprise me. Alice was part of my alibi. She was in all the hotel and casino surveillance videos.

"I hope she was helpful," I said.

"She was."

I said goodbye and hung up. I was pretty sure if Alice had incriminated me in some way, the police would have delivered their news in person.

The cousin was not likely to have much to say either. He was a forty-year-old geek. Carlene couldn't stand him. A couple of years before, when the geek and his wife called to say they were planning to visit Niagara Falls, my father took the phone call and invited them to stay at the house for a few days. Carlene was livid and faked a migraine the whole time so she wouldn't have to deal with them.

I was just about to call Wally Lavaleer when I heard a car drive up.

I peered out in time to see someone in a raincoat and porkpie hat getting out of a brown Toyota Corolla. One headlight appeared to be held in place with duct tape.

I threw on a raincoat, grabbed an umbrella, and went outside.

Nearing the front door of my father's house, I caught the profile of Reggie Baker, my favorite reporter. He was fiddling with the front door handle as if hoping it might pop open.

"Hey, Reggie, what's up?"

He backed away from the door, sticking his hands in the pockets of his wet trench coat. He looked up at the house, more like a prospective house buyer than a break-and-enter man.

"Hey, Harry. Didn't know you were here. Where's your car?"

"On the other side of the guesthouse. What're you looking for?"

He shrugged. "I don't know. Just thought I'd come by and pick up some atmosphere."

"Hoping to keep the story alive for a while?"

"It should be good for a few days. I hear you found her when you came home."

"What else did you hear?"

He gave me the old silent smile.

"Reggie, I'll make you a deal. You tell me something I haven't read in the papers or something I don't know, and I'll let you look inside."

"And take some photos?" He pulled his smart phone from his coat pocket.

"If you tell me something worthwhile."

"Okay. How about this? Sills has a hard-on for you for the convenience store job. He's sure you're the missing link between Johnny Johnson and your stepmother."

"I already know that. I also know I'm innocent. Give me something new."

"I'm hearing the convenience store killing might be about money, a lot of money, and something about a winning lottery ticket."

Duane Morthwell's story. I pretended I was hearing this for the first time. "Sounds interesting. I'd like to win the lottery. What are they saying?"

"That's all I got so far about that. Sills isn't saying much. I'm getting it in roundabout ways."

"What else?"

"Sills likes you for your stepmother and Johnson, but Mallard is leaning toward Wally Lavaleer. Seems Mallard is interested in the backers of the hotel chain and their links to organized crime. Of course, Wally's denying he's connected to organized crime or the murder of your stepmother."

I forced myself not to smile. "What do you think, Reggie? Is it possible that Carlene wanted to back out of the deal, and Wally was in too far?"

"I'm looking into it. You have enough to let me in the house?"

"Sure." I tore down the tape and opened the front door with my key. The foul smell had lessened but was still present.

I gave Reggie a quick tour, showing him where I found Carlene. The blood was still there. He took a few photos. I showed him the bedroom and the bed. He was particularly interested in the nightstand drawer. The investigators had left it half open. Inside were two pairs of handcuffs, a two-headed dildo, and a tube of lubricant. I told Reggie I didn't know anything about them, but I let him take all the photos he wanted.

While Reggie was wandering around, I located Carlene's address book and copied the number of her cousin on a slip of paper and pocketed it.

Not surprisingly, Reggie ended up in the living room in front of the liquor cabinet. "How about a drink? Then, we can and talk, like gentlemen, and I'll tell you something else that I really shouldn't tell you."

He didn't seem at all bothered by the smell or the close proximity to the crime scene in the next room. He had his eyes riveted on a thirty-year-old silver presentation bottle of Glenfiddich that belonged to my father. Carlene had never touched it. She only drank white wine.

"You want to give me a hint?"

"You want to give me a drink?"

"Let's go to my place where it doesn't smell," I said, grabbing the bottle and heading out. He followed, carrying a couple of clean glasses.

At my place, I poured the amber liquid into his glass nearly to the top and poured myself a finger full. We clinked glasses. He chugged his drink down in two quick gulps without taking the glass away from his lips.

"Breakfast of champions."

He started to reach for the bottle, but I clapped my hand around it. "You were going to tell me a story."

"Sure. The big news is that the coroner dug two different kinds of slugs out of your stepmother. The fatal shot apparently came from one gun. The second shot was from another gun entirely."

"Two different guns?" I asked, trying to comprehend what that could possibly mean.

"Two different guns, and probably two different shooters unless the shooter was the two-gun type." He raised his eyebrows to show me that he was skeptical about that possibility.

"What kind of guns?" I wondered what kind of stunt Morthwell had pulled.

"Don't know right now. That's all the details I have, but by the time forensics is done, they'll likely know the makes of the guns. The damned shame of it is that I can't write it up or the cops will know exactly who gave me the information, and my contact will get fired."

"Too bad." I poured him another inch of scotch, wondering if it was possible that Morthwell had used the gun from the convenience store shooting as well. Or equally as bad, had he brought someone else into the equation?

Or had someone else shot Carlene?

Baker finished his drink and started to reach for the bottle again. I pulled it away.

"I got something else," he said, eyeing the liquor.

"It better be good."

"Oh, it's good. Show me good faith, Harry." He pointed to his glass. I poured him another shot. He downed it.

"Now that Carlene's dead, people are starting to talk. They're saying that little drop-in center she set up, Carlene's Place, was a front to confiscate opioids from vulnerable seniors. She made her walking-around money selling the pills to people at the half dozen fitness places she belonged to."

"Who told you?"

"Police sources. I can't tell you. But I can tell you I also talked to a few of the elders in her congregation. They all said the same thing. Carlene was an outsider at the church. She didn't have a religious bone in her body. They knew she was just trying to buy respectability through her membership in their community. Their creed says they have no right to judge her. They went out of their way to accept her, because they were hoping she would eventually find her spirituality, or some crap like that. The way I figure it, nobody wanted to rock the boat on the congregation's biggest donor."

I topped up my own drink and then pushed the rest of the bottle toward Reggie.

I downed the liquor in my glass, hoping it would sober me.

I was still reeling from the information after Reggie Baker left.

I was stunned by how much I didn't known about Carlene, and even more stunned by my ignorance about her murder. I also couldn't help wondering what Frankie Argyll knew. I told myself to ask him the next time I saw him.

The good news was that according to Baker, the police were looking at Wally Lavaleer as much as they were looking at me.

I called Pilot and discovered that Wally's secretary had just phoned the museum. "She told me to tell you she wants to set up a meeting with Lavaleer within the next few hours. She said it was urgent."

"I'll go see Wally right now unless you need me there,"

"Gina didn't show, but the place is dead. Weather's the shits. You go ahead. Do what you have to."

"Did Gina call in sick?"

"Not a peep out of her. I told you, get rid of her."

"Don't worry. We have a lot of changes to make once the estate is settled."

"You hear me worrying?"

I hung up, content to know that the place was secure in his grumpy old hands. I was equally delighted at the prospect that I might actually be able to fire Gina one day soon because I would no longer need her as a tax dodge.

CHAPTER 31

LAVALEER STOOD TO GREET ME. "Harry, Harry, Harry. What a terrible trag-
edy, eh?" He extended his hand. I ignored it.

"How can I help you?"

"Have a seat."

I sat down. He looked dutifully sad with just a hint of a friendly smile.
"Harry, I understand the police are hassling you. If you run into any trouble, I'm here."

"That's interesting. I heard the police are hassling you."

"Just a little misunderstanding. Nothing I can't handle. What we need
to talk about now is how you're doing and what your plans are."

"Gee, Wally, frankly, I was expecting you to be a little more broken up
about Carlene. Don't you even miss her a little?"

I could see a little spark of anger in his eyes, but to his credit, he managed to keep it under control.

"Harry, I know how you felt about Carlene. I'm sorry about what happened. But no one can do anything for her now."

"I don't know. I'm thinking maybe someone should collect her remains and bury her."

He raised a hand, palm up. "It's all under control. I drafted a new will
for Carlene after your father fell ill. I'm the executor of her estate."

I wanted to scream: Fell ill? My father didn't fall ill, you moron. Someone tried to murder him.

I held my temper.

"Oh, good. I presume that means you get to look after the funeral and call the cousin in California. Be a pal and call the police, too. Give them the cousin's name, if you don't mind." I handed him the slip of paper with the cousin's telephone number on it.

"Your stepmother wanted to be cremated." He spoke solemnly, glancing at the slip of paper before placing it on his desk. "She made no stipulation about a ceremony, but I'm sure she'd want a memorial service of some kind. Maybe in a couple of weeks. I'll set something up with her congregation." He clearly seemed uncomfortable with his role.

I wasn't about to offer any help. "Good. Let me know what you're planning so I can get my suit cleaned."

"Harry, I didn't call you here to fight. We need to talk about you."

"Wally, a week ago, you and my stepmother were not only screwing each other but screwing me, too. Now you want to kiss and make up?"

"The relationship between Carlene and me was business. What we did after hours was an arrangement between two consenting adults and no one else's concern."

"Tell me, Wally, what does Mrs. Lavaleer think about all this? I'm curious."

The fact that he hadn't thrown me out or even lost his temper suggested he needed me badly. But for what?

"For starters, it's none of your business, but since you ask, I'll tell you. My wife knew about Carlene. She approved of it. My wife spends half the winter in Palm Beach. She understands that I have to work hard to support our lifestyle. As far as she's concerned, I'm entitled to a little recreation."

"Okay, but tell me one thing. Who used the handcuffs on whom?"

He sat back and folded his hands on his stomach. "The trouble with you, Harry, is you don't know the difference between being smart and being a smart ass. I'm trying to help you."

"I didn't know I needed your help. The way I understand it, my father arranged his trusts with multiple options in case of my death or Carlene's. With Carlene predeceasing my father, her share of my father's assets should just about equal the clothes in her closet, any jewelry that wasn't stolen, and any bank accounts in her name."

"That's right."

"And control of the trusts now goes to me."

"They're still the property of your father, but you have co-power of attorney as the alternate now that Carlene is deceased. You also share the power with me."

"Yes, but my understanding is that as an executor and sole heir, I have the power to encroach—to basically do what I want with the money. All I have to do is inform my co-executor—you—in writing."

"Why wouldn't you want my advice?"

"Maybe because I don't trust you?"

"Harry, regardless of how you feel about me, what I set up for your father's property is best for everyone. With Carlene no longer in the picture, you step right into her place. Everything she was to get, you get."

"And everything you were to get, you still get."

"I'm going to make you rich enough so you won't have to worry about money again for the rest of your life."

"Maybe I'm rich enough the way I am."

"And what? You're going to keep running the museum? Be angry at me all you want, but don't be a fool. As a business, MurderLand is finished. The mom-and-pop exhibits are history. The chain operators are eating you alive. Redevelop the Clifton Hill property. Close MurderLand. Become a landlord. That's your ticket to true happiness."

"What happens to you if I back out? And whose happiness are we really talking about here, Wally? I'm hearing that this deal has to go through or you're in trouble with the mob."

"I don't know where that horseshit is coming from. First of all, we're dealing with a reputable hotel chain. Second, if this deal goes south, I'll lose some time. But I don't have any capital invested."

"What about your reputation?"

"There's always another deal, Harry. I know your business inside and out. My father was your grandfather's and your father's attorney. I've done the numbers. MurderLand is through."

"My father was making a good living from it."

"Your father had his fingers in a lot of pies."

"Such as?"

"I don't know. I never knew. All I know is MurderLand is dead. It's hemorrhaging cash. When your dad got sick, Carlene tried to talk to you about it, but you kept insisting she tried to kill him."

"My father didn't get sick. Carlene tried to murder him."

"Who knows? Maybe she did. The point is that if your father hadn't ended up in the nursing home, I'd be having the same conversation with him."

"He'd never sell out."

"Believe what you want. What's important is that you do the right thing or you'll end up with nothing. I'm willing to let you take your anger out on me up to a point, but at some time, you're going to have to shit or get off the pot."

I had no intention of selling out, but I had no reason to show my cards to Wally. I would enjoy letting him squirm. I told him, "I'll need some time to think about it."

"You do that, Harry. Take all the time you want. But you need to know that we have papers to sign in three days. You miss the deadline and the whole deal collapses."

I wondered what that would mean for him. If Reggie Baker's information was correct, first prize for Wally might mean a trip to the bottom of Lake Erie in cement galoshes. I could only hope.

We both stood. Neither of us offered to shake hands. "Don't worry about me, Harry. I can look after myself. You think about what kind of future you want for you. I can help you."

"I'm sure you have nothing but my best interests at heart. Oh, and by the way, if you're thinking about making a play for Alice May, be my guest."

He laughed. "What are you, nuts? She has to be the worst sex I've ever had. Knock yourself out, pal. She's all yours."

CHAPTER 32

THE WEATHER WAS HAVING A DIFFICULT TIME deciding what to do. It had already dumped an inch of rain on the town, then three inches of snow, and then enough rain to turn the snow into slush. Then, the temperature dropped ten degrees, turning everything to ice again. I nearly broke a leg slipping on a patch of black ice in the nursing home parking lot.

Clive was there, and the first thing he said was, "I am truly sorry for your loss, Harry. I read in the papers about your stepmother's demise."

"Thanks, Clive." I handed him his sandwich and unwrapped the other one for my dad. Dad's roommate was whimpering softly in the next bed with his back to us.

"You will be happy to know that I told the police you and your stepmother had a perfectly civil relationship. I had nothing else to tell them. They questioned me for twenty minutes. First thing this morning. They talked to Dr. Patek, too. And some of the nurses." He took two business cards out of his pocket. "Detectives Sills and Mallard. They asked me if you did a lot of drugs."

"What did you say?"

"I told them I knew nothing about drugs or you. We only know each other from the nursing home. The only thing we ever discussed was the welfare of your father. I said I have learned to tune out everything that's said around me. Otherwise, I would go insane."

He smiled when he got done reciting what he had told the police.

"Clive, you're a good man. Thanks."

"The way you look after your father is touching."

"You mind if I ask you a question?"

"I'm at your service."

"What do you think the secret of happiness is?"

He thought for a moment before answering.

"Look after your physical and mental health, be in love if you can, keep learning, and keep chasing a good dream."

"What's your biggest dream now."

"Everything, man. I want to experience it all."

When we shook hands at the end of my visit, he showed me an elaborate handshake that ended with a big hug. He also gave me a joint to smoke in the car on the way to the museum. Clive told me months before that he smoked weed when he was on duty because it put him on the same wavelength as his clients.

The temperature was a couple of degrees below freezing when I left the nursing home. The road was like a skating rink.

Despite the nice buzz I had off the joint, I got a very bad feeling when I approached the MurderLand and saw two fire trucks pulling away.

In the lobby, I spotted a guy in a green jumpsuit working on the control panel for the electrical circuits. Pilot was talking to two other stocky guys wearing trapper hats and down coats with yellow stitching on the back that said, "Ray's Roofing."

"What's up, Pilot? What's with the fire engines?"

"We got a leak on the roof. It ran down the insides of two walls, shorted out the smoke detectors, and set off the alarms. Electrician just got the lights back on."

"So everything's back to normal?"

"Not quite. These guys are from the roofing company. I'll let them tell you the bad news."

The older of the two roofing guys began explaining. Water had been leaking through the roof in several places. It had been seeping between the outside stone walls and the inner plaster walls on the front and the south side of the building for months, maybe years. Until that morning, the water had been able to find a way outside. The freezing, thawing, and freezing of the past day had upset the balance. The water had backed up all the way to the roof. Part of the roof and ceiling beneath it had caved in. We needed a new roof immediately and some work on two of the walls.

"Bottom line?" I asked.

"About a hundred grand."

I felt nauseous. The roofing contractor wanted fifteen grand to start the job.

The only two pieces of good news were that the water had exited the building before entering the basement and the roofers could begin work the next day.

"Go ahead. Do what you have to." I forked over the money.

"We'll be back tomorrow. First thing," the boss of the roofing company assured me before leaving.

Pilot stayed in the hallway to supervise the guy working on the electrical panel while I went to the second floor to take a look at the ceiling. Even from inside the building, it was easy to see how bad things were. Chunks of plaster the size of small cars had fallen from the ceiling. One large chunk had landed on the Kennedy tableau, smack on the back of Jackie in her pink suit as she crawled over the trunk of the fiberglass reproduction of the president's car. The falling plaster had squashed her flat.

For a moment, I thought about Lavaleer's offer but only for a moment. The thought of doing business with him made my flesh crawl.

I'll get through this. Somehow.

Pilot hit me for another three hundred to pay the electrician.

I called my bank manager.

He informed me he was not lending any more money to MurderLand, and our line of credit was under review. He said he could almost guarantee that the bank would be severely cutting back on its commitments.

"Thanks," and fuck you, I wanted to add, but there was no point.

Nor was there much point in seeing any of the other legitimate financial institutions around town. I really had nothing to secure the loan against unless I was willing to sell the property for redevelopment.

I still wasn't ready to capitulate.

By the time I got off the phone, Pilot was getting ready to leave.

"What did the bank tell you?" he asked.

"They're going to think about it," I lied.

"You'll need a backup plan. In the meantime, you ought to call Gina. Tell her not to bother coming in tomorrow. No sense throwing away money if we're closed."

"Let her come in. She can help you in the basement. We'll have to sell more things."

"I told you there ain't much left. The easy money's gone."

"What about the Dillinger penis?"

"What about it?"

It dawned on me that Pilot had been bluffing. "All you have are the photos. You don't really have Dillinger's cock, do you?"

"It's somewhere." He waved his hand in the air, avoiding eye contact.

"If you find it, let me know."

"You want me to go look now?"

"No. Go home. I'll lock up."

After he left, I finally got around to checking my voice mail from that morning. There were six calls. Five were from Alice, telling me she loved me, that she couldn't wait to see me, and that I should call her as soon as I got in. I definitely was in no mood to call her.

The sixth call gave me a nice lift. It was from Harvey Glendon, the other collector who was interested in Albert Anastasia's bloody underwear. I returned his call, and we agreed to meet on the US side of the border the next day.

I also called Roger Mosswood, the Nebraska florist. "It's Harry Holiday. How are you?"

"I've had a bit of stomach flu for the past few days. Other than that, I'm fine. What's up?"

He knows what's up, I thought. He's playing cool. "I'm meeting with the other buyer tomorrow for the Anastasia clothes. I thought I'd give you a call and make sure you're around so you get a chance to top any price he might offer."

"Harry, I've been thinking about that. The Marilyn swimsuit ate up my spring budget."

"You're not unhappy with the purchase, are you?"

"No, no. Nothing like that. I'm delighted. I'm just a little stretched right now. We had an ice storm two nights ago, and you'll never guess. I have to put a new roof on the store. If it isn't one thing, it's another."

"Tell me about it." I tried not to sound too desperate. "I understand, Mr. Mosswood, but artifacts like the Anastasia clothes don't come along every day."

"Granted, but I can't afford to get into a bidding war."

"Just give me a number, Mr. Mosswood. You offered me twelve when you were here. Why don't we call it fourteen? I'd like to see it go to your collection."

"That's way out of my range, Harry?"

"What are you thinking?"

"I could give you a bid, but I don't want to insult you."

"Mr. Mosswood, tell me what you can pay. If it doesn't add up, I won't sell it."

"I could go to seven."

"Seven? You know they're worth more than that."

"I'm sorry, Harry. That's the best I can do, and even that's a stretch. You want to call me in six months from now, maybe I could do better."

"Let me think about it."

"By the way, I figured out who the other buyer has to be. Harvey Glendon from Cleveland. Am I right?"

"Sorry, Mr. Mosswood. I treat all bidding and sales confidentially. I'll get back to you."

"Looking forward to hearing from you, Harry."

Glendon will bid way over that, I assured myself.

Realistically, even if he went to fifteen or sixteen thousand, it wouldn't make a very big dent in the cost of a new roof.

I glanced around the office. I still had the baseball with Marilyn and Joe DiMaggio's signatures, the MurderLand posters on the office walls, the signed photos of the celebrities, the hunting trophies, the Japanese soldier's ear from Guadalcanal, the Starkman amulet, and even Old Smokey.

I felt depressed. Was I really sinking this low? Getting rid of Carlene was supposed to be the end of my troubles, but I wasn't much farther ahead.

Deep down I continued to feel I still had no real idea how to draw the kids and teens back to MurderLand. I needed new ideas. I needed money.

I went to the basement and began hunting through boxes. In a half hour, all I managed to do was accumulate an inch of dust up my nose. Coughing and sneezing, I came upstairs and checked my messages one last time. I had two more from Alice. The first was the same—sweetie-I-miss-you crap. The second seemed to be a little more ominous and curt—"Harry, I hope you're not trying to ignore me. Please call. We have to talk."

I was definitely in no mood to talk. I locked up and headed outside. More bad news was waiting.

CHAPTER 33

FRANKIE'S TWO THUGS, Joey Angelo and Pinkie the Lizard, were sitting in Joey's Buick beside my Lincoln.

"Frankie sent us over to collect the money you owe him," Joey said, stepping from the driver's side.

"I was just going to see Frankie."

"You don't need to see him. You need to give us the money." Pinkie hovered over me, breathing garlic fumes in my face.

"He said if you didn't have the money we was to bring you to him," Joey added.

"Fine. I'll follow you over."

"We'll take you."

"I'd rather drive myself."

"You want to do this the hard way?" Pinkie gripped my upper arm and squeezed, cutting into the muscles and nerves. He shoved me in the backseat and piled in beside me.

We rode in silence to Manny's, a small Italian restaurant on Stanley Avenue near the casino. The parking lot was nearly empty, making it easy to spot Frankie's dark gray Cadillac.

Frankie and Bambi, the stripper with the big hair and crooked teeth from Pole Catz, were sitting in a semicircular booth in the far corner of the back room eating dinner. They were the only patrons in the room. Word on the street was that Frankie owned a piece of Manny's.

Bambi had had her hair cut into a cute pageboy, taking five years off her looks. If she recognized me, she showed no sign of it. Instead, she returned to her plate, sawed off another hunk of what looked like veal marsala, and chewed disinterestedly with her mouth slightly open.

Frankie looked genuinely sad.

"Harry, Harry, Harry, what am I gonna do with you, eh?"

"For starters, Frankie, you can count your money." I pulled out a roll of bills and counted through the money I still had from my casino winnings. By the time I finished, I was down to my last two thousand dollars.

He looked at the money, then at his two hoods, and said to me, "I told them to bring you here if you didn't have the money."

"Boss, we told him that," Joey said.

"It's true, boss," Pinkie added.

"If you had the money, Harry, why didn't you say something?" He tucked the money away without counting it. "What's with the fuckin' drama all the time?"

"They didn't ask nicely, Frankie. You should teach them better manners."

Frankie flashed them a dirty look. Pinkie and Joey lowered their heads.

"Besides, I needed to see you," I said.

"All right. Sit down."

"Alone." I remained standing.

He turned to Pinkie and Joey. "You two make yourselves scarce."

"And don't go too far," I told them. "I'll need a ride when I'm done."

"Wait in the bar, and take her with you," Frankie said. "Up, sweetheart. Make room for Harry."

Bambi looked very unhappy, but she did as she was told, taking her plate and silverware with her.

"I like your new hairdo. It suits you," I told her as she went by. She gave me a small smile and a wink.

The waiter stuck his head into the room as I slipped into the booth beside Frankie.

"You want something to eat?" Frankie asked me.

"Nothing."

"A glass of wine? An espresso? They make a good espresso here."

"I'm fine. Thanks."

Frankie dismissed the waiter with a wave of his hand.

"So, what do you want to talk about?"

"First of all, Frankie, explain to me why you sent your goons to find me. You could have picked up the phone."

"To tell you the truth, Harry, I didn't think you had the money."

"And my credit's no good?"

"Nothing personal. It's business. The cops still like you for the murder of your stepmother. If they charge you, I don't want to be standing behind your lawyers and the rest of your creditors trying to collect."

"You think I did it?"

"Doesn't matter what I think."

"I'm hearing that the police are looking into Wally Lavaleer and his investors. Maybe Carlene was getting cold feet about the deal. You hear anything about that?"

"Situation like this, you hear all kinds of things. Me? If I was in your shoes, I'd be inclined to go along with Wally Lavaleer's offer or I'd watch my back."

"Is that you talking or your friends from Buffalo? Or do you know something about Wally Lavaleer that I don't know?"

"Harry, never mind what I know. It's you who has to think smart. I just heard you need a new roof. Now, where are you gonna get the money to fix that?"

Niagara Falls is a small town. I wasn't surprised that he would hear about my roof. I was just surprised he heard so quickly.

"That's what I want to talk to you about. I'm hoping you'll provide me with a short-term loan."

"No can do, Harry. Like I said, if anything happens to you, by the time your other creditors are paid off, I'd be out of luck."

"First of all, nothing's going to happen to me. Second—"

"Harry, Harry. Let's not argue. You want to place a small bet with me, I'll give you a float. But that's it."

"How much of a float?"

"One, maybe two grand. If you lose, just be sure you pay up. I don't want to send my boys looking for you. That's the best I can do."

"After all these years, this is what it's come to?"

"Like I said, Harry, it's business. Nothing personal. I don't want to see you hurt, but I don't want to see *me* hurt even more. Now, you do what you have to do."

I took him up on his offer and bet two grand on Arizona over Anaheim. It was a long, long shot, but if I won, I'd turn the two grand into eight.

Before I left, I tried to ask him about Carlene.

"You knew about Carlene's drug business, didn't you? You wanted me to go Carlene's Place and do exactly what you told me to do. Sober up and look around. You knew I'd figure it out. You—"

He held up his hand to stop me.

"Harry, all you need to know is that I don't like to get involved in other people's business. Now, get out of here. Get back to your life. Good luck with your bets."

CHAPTER 34

PINKIE AND JOEY DROPPED ME OFF AT THE MUSEUM.

Feeling restless, I hopped in the Lincoln, drove over to Pole Catz, and had a couple of drinks. Zena, a brunette from Calgary, shared a joint with me in the ladies' room. Afterward, when I went upstairs, Danny, the VIP-room bouncer, pulled me aside and said, "It ain't any of my business, but a couple of guys were in here earlier asking if anyone knew where to find you."

"What did they look like?" I asked.

"White males. Six two or three. One guy was heavy. One guy medium build. Both were wearing leather coats and sunglasses."

"Americans?"

"Hard to say."

"You tell them where they could find me?"

He smiled. "I told them I didn't know you."

"Good man." I slipped him a fifty. "If they come back, do me a favor. See if you can get their names."

"Will do."

I ordered a drink, but I didn't finish it. The idea that a couple of goons, most likely from Buffalo, were looking for me made me jittery.

What I needed was a little protection. I got in my car and headed toward the museum to retrieve the High Standard .22 I'd stashed in the basement on Saturday night.

On the way over, I thought I saw someone following me. To be on the safe side, I hopped on the QEW, took the exit for Niagara-on-the-Lake, and zigzagged east to the Niagara Parkway.

During the summer tourist season, the two-lane road along the river gorge was usually filled with cars. In February, I had the road to myself. If someone had been following me, I'd lost them.

Or so I thought.

Suddenly, from out of nowhere, I saw lights barreling toward me from behind. It was a no passing zone, but I figured the fool would pass anyway. So, I slowed down.

The next thing I knew, a van hit me from behind and seemed to be trying to push me across the road toward the unguarded edge of the gorge.

I'm a goner, I thought as I skidded toward the edge. The drop to the bottom was more than a hundred feet.

I don't quite know how I kept from going over the cliff. Somehow, I managed to spin my car around as I pulled hard on the wheel. The van sideswiped the driver's side of the Lincoln as it went by.

I saw clearly into the van for the few seconds while I was careening out of control. Only one person was inside—the driver. I had never seen him before, but I was sure I'd never forget him. He had a long, thin, clean-shaven skeleton-like face framed with dark, scraggily, shoulder-length hair. He was grinning at me as he went by.

As soon as I came to a stop, I glanced over my shoulder and realized the van had halted a couple of hundred feet away. It was a dark-colored Ford. I saw the parking lights go on, but before he had backed up more than a few yards, another car came around the bend. The van sped away.

The other car stopped opposite me. A white-haired woman wearing a heavy down coat got out and approached me.

My car was still running.

"You okay?" the woman asked.

I didn't have to roll down the window, because the van had taken it out. "Yeah, thanks."

"You want me to call the police?" She took her phone from her coat pocket.

"Let me see if I can still drive the car." With the no-fault provincial insurance system, the police don't show up unless someone is injured or the car can't be moved.

I did a U-turn and pointed the car in the direction I had been going. The woman insisted on following me to the museum in her car. I was happy to have the company. With a witness trailing behind, I suspected the skeleton-faced prick in the van would have second thoughts about taking another shot at me.

The cold air blew in through the open window, turning my face to ice by the time I reached the museum. I parked in front and discovered the driver's door wouldn't open. I exited on the passenger side, and waved to the Good Samaritan as she drove away.

Once inside, I locked the front door and went straight to the basement. I retrieved the .22 with the silencer and the box of hollow point shells.

I reloaded the gun, locked up, and returned to my car. I took a few moments to walk around it to see just what damage the van had done.

The driver's side door and the rear door on the driver's side needed replacing. The rear bumper and trunk lid would need work. The rear door window on the driver's side remained intact, but I couldn't lower it. I was looking at probably ten grand worth of repairs for a car that would probably *Bluebook* at not much more than that. No sense calling the insurance company. They'd either cancel my insurance or jack up my premiums.

Whoever you are, thanks a lot, I thought as I climbed in through the passenger side, started the Lincoln, and headed home.

I was half frozen by the time I reached my place.

I parked between the guesthouse and my father's house. I got out gripping the gun as I glanced around the yard.

Once safe in the guesthouse, I read a few more chapters of Machiavelli's *The Prince*, and then switched to an old translation of *The Count of Monte Cristo* by Alexandre Dumas, another book I'd uncovered in a box in the basement of MurderLand. I was reading a chapter at a time to make it last as long as possible. Like my copy of *The Outsider* by Camus, this copy of *The Count of Monte Cristo* was a rare and unabridged English translation, not the one usually read in North America. In my copy, the Count spends part of his time on his secret island in the Mediterranean smoking hashish to help him formulate his plans for revenge against the people who had him thrown in prison for life on fake charges.

I was asleep with the lights out when I heard a car in the driveway.

It was two in the morning. I got up and peered through a crack in the curtains. It was Alice's Jetta.

I continued to watch from behind the curtains as she stepped from her car and headed toward the front of my father's house. She must have thought I lived there.

When she got no answer at the front door, she began tossing pebbles at the upper windows, yelling, "Harry, Harry, if you're in there, let me in. We need to talk."

I didn't want to talk. I remained hidden.

After tossing a dozen stones, she returned to her car and sat there with the motor running for a half hour before driving off.

I returned to bed and lay awake for another couple of hours, listening for more cars until I finally fell asleep.

CHAPTER 35

TUESDAY

I WOKE AT NINE. The newspaper told me I had something to be happy about. Arizona had trounced Anaheim. Hooray for hockey. I was in the black again.

I called Frankie, woke the sonovabitch, and told him to put everything on another long shot for that night—the Dallas Stars over the Chicago Blackhawks.

After I finished my coffee, showered, and dressed, it occurred to me that I didn't have to freeze my ass off driving around in the Lincoln. Instead, I took Carlene's Lexus to work.

Pilot had opened MurderLand. The roofing guys were already at work.

Gina wasn't there. Maybe she saw the mess and went home. The sign on the front door said we were closed for repairs

I went to the office and called the phone number she had written on her application. The line was disconnected. There was no referral number.

Six new calls had accumulated on my voice mail from Alice. I ignored them. I had other things to think about. Top on my list was my meeting with Harvey Glendon at eleven. I checked his flight from Cleveland to Buffalo. It was on schedule.

Before I left, I wrote a letter to Lavaleer terminating all agreements with him and his firm. Whatever I ended up doing, I wanted him out of the picture.

I gathered the Anastasia underwear. The big question was what to do with my gun. I was a little nervous about traveling around without it, especially in light of the night before. On the other hand, I was driving the Lexus, which I figured might buy me a few days of anonymity. I was also traveling to the US, so I stashed the gun in its hiding place downstairs along with the extra shells.

Before heading to the US, I stopped at a postal substation and sent the termination letter to Lavaleer by registered mail.

I sailed over the Whirlpool Rapids Bridge and found Harvey Glendon already waiting for me in his room at his hotel on the New York side. He was a stocky man in his fifties, with a low brow; thick, curly, brown hair; and chunky facial features. He owned a chain of grocery stores in Ohio and Indiana. I'd done business with him before. We didn't waste a lot of time with preliminaries.

He took the garments to the desk beside the window and studied them under a magnifying glass.

I sat on the couch, reading the room-service menu, watching the small smile on his face, and trying to figure where I should start the price.

The thing about selling something where all the value is in the story—whether it's a stock or a collectible—is to be able to price it just right. Too high and the client might walk. Too low and you rob yourself. You may also create a suspicion that you're desperate, and either the client will try to wheedle you down even more or walk away, thinking the item might not be what you say it is.

Harvey finished his examination with a little sigh, which I couldn't quite read.

"So, what do you think?" I was contemplating asking fifteen thousand, which was just a little above the number that Roger Mosswood almost went for before I sold him the Marilyn swimsuit.

Harvey turned to me and said, "Sorry, Harry, but I'm not interested."

"What? Why not?"

"The provenance. It just isn't enough," he said, placing the certificate of authenticity I'd printed up on top of the clothes. "If you had some other paperwork, maybe."

"You know that I guarantee everything a hundred percent or your money back."

"I know. I didn't fly here from Cleveland because I didn't want the garments, but word is out that you may be going out of business. Then your certificate is just a piece of paper."

"MurderLand will be around for a long, long time, Harvey. Any rumors you may have heard to the contrary are lies." I tried to sound like I was laughing it off.

I could feel him seeing right through me.

"I'm sorry, Harry. I'm going to pass."

"No problem." I tried to remain upbeat. "Thanks for taking a look." There was always the possibility of another sale to him another time. I wasn't about to burn any bridges. Besides, I still had Roger Mosswood.

As I headed over the bridge toward Canada, thinking about how much I could squeeze out of Mosswood, Nessa appeared and pulled me over.

"Hey, Harry, how's it going?" She looked inside the Lexus as she leaned in the window. She had dark circles under her eyes and a painful looking pimple on her nose.

"About the other night—"

"You stood me up."

"I got hung up. I'm really sorry."

"Let me guess. You never heard of a phone?"

"I misplaced your number."

"That was...let me see...how many days ago?"

"Three. I apologize. I don't know if you heard, but my stepmother was murdered that night. I've been kind of busy."

"I heard. Now, would you mind opening your trunk?"

"Why are you pissed off? I thought our date was just supposed to be fun?"

My questions were greeted with an icy stare.

Women, I thought as I popped the latch on the trunk. Don't argue with her.

I tried not to think about what she might find in the trunk. Carlene was always zipping over to Buffalo to shop and smuggle clothes into Canada without paying taxes. My worst fear, of course, was that she might have stashed her drugs in the trunk.

Stay calm, I told myself as Nessa opened the trunk and rummaged around inside.

Moments later, she returned to my window, carrying an orange thong and a Louis Vuitton handbag, both with their price tags still attached.

"These were purchased in Buffalo," she said. "Were you planning to declare them?"

"They belong to Carlene, my late stepmother. This is her car. I'm borrowing it," I said, thankful Nessa hadn't found any dope.

Nessa didn't say anything but simply walked to the trunk, replaced the purse and thong, and closed the lid.

I could see by the swagger in her walk that she wasn't done yet. She walked to the passenger side, opened the door, and picked up the bag with Anastasia's bloody shirt and underpants.

"Now, what do we have here?" She took the clothes out of the bag.

"Laundry."

"Really? I'm thinking these are new purchases for your museum, and they're worth a small fortune."

"They're just old clothes."

"I could take them home and wash them for you. I have a really good way of getting out stains."

"I'd rather do them myself."

"A domestic side to our Harry Holiday. You're full of surprises, aren't you?"

She stuffed the clothes into the plastic bag and dropped it on the floor. "I'm still pissed at you, Harry. Don't forget it. I'd bust you, but I'm too lazy to do the paperwork. So, fuck off, and don't mess with your friends, okay?"

"Lesson learned, Nessa. I'm sorry. I owe you."

"Yes, you do. Now, get out of here." She closed the door.

Sheesh, I thought, what a strange woman. I had no idea whether she was serious or not, but oddly, she'd given me half of a hard-on. Sex and danger had always been aphrodisiacs for me.

As soon as I returned to the museum, I looked up her address and was going to send flowers, but then I remembered Constable Valerie Runge, her significant other. The last thing Nessa would want to do was to try explaining flowers to her spouse.

After that, I tried to reach Roger Mosswood, but all I got was his voice mail. I left a message that I'd call back. I retrieved my gun and the ammunition before picking up a couple of sandwiches for my father. I certainly wasn't forgetting about the van that nearly bumped me off the road or the two hoods who had been looking for me at the strip joint.

Clive wasn't around when I arrived at the nursing home. Dad's room-mate was curled up on his bed with the blanket over his head, moaning softly. My father seemed unaffected. When I put my ear close to his mouth, I could hear him repeating the same sentence over and over, "Okay, Ginnie. Not in the face."

I told my dad that the museum was doing just fine and that Pilot and I couldn't wait for him to come back. I made up stories about how we'd been put on a preferred list of tour bus operators and had increased at-tendance over the past six months.

I was rattling away like this when Dr. Patek poked his head into the room and said, "Ah, Mr. Holiday. The receptionist told me you were here. I'm sorry about your stepmother. My deepest condolences."

"Thank you. She'll be deeply missed."

"Yes, and I understand you've had to close the museum."

"Just temporarily. We're working on the roof."

"Yes, of course." He fluttered his long eyelashes at me. "And I have al-ready changed the records to show that we will be dealing directly with you on all matters concerning your father from now on."

"That's right."

"And so I want to remind you about the payment that's due next week. When your stepmother decided to switch your father to the other home, she cancelled the direct deposit payments."

"Send me the bill."

He pulled a legal-sized envelope from his inside jacket pocket and handed it to me. "If you prefer, you can pay by check or credit card before you leave."

Or what, I felt like asking. You'll wheel my father outside and leave him there?

"I'll look after it." I pocketed the envelope.

"Thank you. I appreciate it."

Another chunk of change gone from my ever-dwindling funds.

Clive arrived a few minutes later and went right for the extra sand-wich. "Dr. Patek is looking for you," he informed me after he'd taken his first bite. "You can slip out through the service entrance. I can show you the way."

"He already saw me."

"Money troubles?"

"Nothing I can't handle." I smiled bravely.

"I am in contact with someone who has come into a large sum of money and is looking for a way to invest part of it. I could set up a meeting."

"Thanks, Clive, but I need a lot of money right now."

"My contact would like to put at least a hundred thousand to work, maybe more."

Drug money, I suspected. Then, again, I wasn't in any position to be a snob. "Sorry, Clive. You're right. I could be interested."

"If I set you up, I get a finder's fee."

"Of course. If it works out."

"Thank you." He wrote an address down on a slip of paper and handed it to me. "There's a party tomorrow. I'll introduce you to the investor."

I tucked the address in my pocket and finished my visit with my dad. I told myself that drug money or whatever kind of money Clive's friends had to invest couldn't be any worse than borrowing from Frankie. It couldn't hurt to check it out.

When I returned to the museum, I tried to reach Roger Mosswood again but got his sister instead.

"I'm sorry, Mr. Holiday," she told me in a soft, shaky voice, "but my brother went to the hospital last night with acute appendicitis. He passed away this morning just after nine o'clock."

"I'm sorry." My mind was already spinning. Mosswood was one of the all-time great collectors of homicide-related garments. No doubt he had some gems in his collection. If I could scoop up his collection for a song and flip it, I could make a bundle. "I'm the president of MurderLand, the world's largest museum of objects connected to famous gangsters and murders," I explained. "Your brother's collection of homicide-related artifacts is world class. If I can be of any help to the estate in evaluating or disposing of any items, please let me know."

"That's rude and disgusting," she said. "My brother would never have anything to do with something like that."

She slammed the receiver down before I could give her my phone number. I wondered what would go through her mind when she discovered Roger's stash.

I didn't have long to think about it. The front door buzzer sounded enough times to let me know that Pilot was too busy elsewhere to answer it. I went to the front and peered through a side window to make sure it wasn't Alice, or the two guys in the sunglasses, or the guy who had tried to run me into the gorge, or anyone else I didn't want to see.

Reggie Baker was pacing back and forth on the front steps.

I let him in since the alternative seemed to be to disconnect the buzzer.

"What's up, Reggie?"

"Got a drink for a tired old man?"

"Only if you have something good to tell me. I'm kind of busy."

"Guaranteed good."

I led him into the office, opened a new bottle of Johnny Walker Black Label, and filled a highball glass. He drank it like he was guzzling a can of soda.

"You ever hear of Billy McCasters or Mark Patterson?"

"No. Why?"

"Then I got a story for you." Grinning, he reached across the desk, grabbed the bottle, and refilled his glass. "It's the damnedest thing, Harry. Billy "Mick" McCasters was a Teamsters enforcer and small-time hood from Buffalo. Back in '69, I was a cub reporter working in Buffalo. McCasters got arrested for killing another small-time hood. While Mick was in the lockup, he was trying to work out a deal on the murder charge. He claimed to have information on President Kennedy's assassination. Someone from the DA's office apparently leaked the story of the deal he was trying to make, and the next thing you knew, the Kennedy connection was headlines all over the place. Then, the murder case against him fell apart. Something about one witness recanting and another disappearing. A few days later, Mick was back on the street. A week later he got whacked. Supposedly in retaliation for the small-time hood he killed. The police never found his killer."

"And Mick never revealed what he knew about President Kennedy's assassination," I offered.

"Exactly."

"Why should I be interested?"

"Mark Patterson."

I shook my head. "Never heard of him."

"Patterson's a retired forensic investigator. He's also one of the world's leading experts on ballistics analysis. His records of solved and unsolved murders go back decades. The forensic labs use him and his databank to check on guns used in crimes to see if they match any old crimes. He happened to get ahold of the ballistics information they got off the two bullets they recovered from your stepmother. Guess what? The gun they found in the dumpster was the same gun that killed McCasters in 1969. A .38 Smith and Wesson Terrier."

Uh-oh. It was also quite probably the gun I had found hidden in the basement and given to Duane Morthwell.

"What about the other gun?" I asked.

"That one hasn't turned up, but they can tell from the slug it's a Chinese knockoff of the Soviet T33 Tokarev 9 millimeter."

The gun that had killed Johnny Johnson had been a Colt .38. So it wasn't that one. Did Morthwell have a collection of guns? I hadn't seen any guns at his place. Did he have help? Reggie Baker was the last person I wanted to confide in. I let him finish his drink and showed him out.

Pilot showed up after Baker left.

"What did the reporter want besides your old man's best scotch?"

"Baker? Nothing really. He wanted to know if I'd heard anything new from the detectives." I wanted to ask Pilot about the .38 that the police found. I wanted to ask if he had ever heard of Billy McCasters, but Pilot knew I had the .38 in my hands. I didn't want him connecting the dots between me and Carlene's death.

"I hope you kept your mouth shut. First rule when the police are hanging around is never, ever talk to the press."

"Reggie's all right."

"Reggie's not all right. He's a drunk and a liar, and he'd sell his mother down the river for a story or a drink. He's nobody's friend." Pilot glared at me with narrowed eyes.

"All right."

"I ain't going to be around forever, Harry. It's time you learn what you need to know. So don't ever forget what I'm telling you. Don't trust anyone."

The tone in his voice was different than his usual grumpy old self.

"Pilot, are you all right?"

"I'm fine." He shook a finger at me. "You just remember what I'm telling you."

His words were still resonating in my brain fifteen minutes later when the phone rang. I picked up the phone without thinking and said, "Hello. MurderLand. How can I help you?"

The last person in the world I wanted to hear from was on the other end of the line.

CHAPTER 36

I RECOGNIZED THE VOICE AS SOON AS I HEARD IT.

"Hey, man, you know who this is, so don't hang up."

It was Duane Morthwell.

I needed to get him off the line and fast.

"I'm busy. Maybe we can talk another time."

"We need to settle our accounts." His voice grew more forceful as if he wanted me to know he was ready to boil over.

"You'll just have to be patient. I'll be in touch. Don't call back."

I hung up.

I checked the caller ID. The name and number were blocked.

Asshole, I thought.

When the phone rang again, I let it ring.

What the hell is he thinking, I wondered. My stepmother had been dead only a couple of days. For all I knew, the cops had a tap on my line or his.

Like everyone else, he'll have to stand in line for his money, I told myself. If he had a brain in his head, he'd realize that he'd be the last person I'd want to stiff. I had to look after Duane so neither of us ended up in prison.

Alice called a couple of times, but she stopped leaving messages.

I spent the rest of the afternoon calling buyers across the continent who might be interested in the Anastasia clothes. I had no luck. By five, the roofers were gone.

Pilot was still in the basement. I told him to go home. He said he was still looking for the guns. I didn't have the heart to tell him they weren't there. Besides, maybe he'd uncover something else of value.

I put in another half hour making phone calls, but I had hit a black hole. I couldn't give the Anastasia undergarments away.

By five thirty, I was finished.

I called Melanie to see if she was up for a date. All I got was her voice mail.

I checked on Pilot one last time. "If you're ready to go, I'll give you a ride home."

"I don't need a ride, and I'll leave when I'm ready. You go ahead. I'll set the alarms."

I checked the lock on the front door and then checked outside in the parking lot through the rear window. The lot was empty except for my car.

Besides, I had the .22 for protection.

I stepped outside and locked the back door. I was halfway across the parking lot before I sensed something behind me. Before I could turn, I took a punch to my back that felt like a shotgun blast. I fell to the ground. The ache was so great it disoriented me. I struggled to clear my head.

Glancing up, I knew I was going to be hit again at the very least when I saw the two hulks in sunglasses with the leather coats, jeans, and leather boots hovering over me.

It took me a second to recognize them behind the smoky, wraparound glasses—the biker king, Big Mo, and his chief enforcer, Goose.

"Hey, what the hell are you doing?" I tried to get to my feet.

Big Mo kicked me in the chest, sending me sprawling backwards. I curled up in a ball while Big Mo and Goose each kicked me a couple of times.

"Hey, stop. What's this all about? Whatever it is can be fixed," I shouted at the two bikers.

Big Mo and Goose leaned over me. I could see the outline of Goose's eyepatch behind his shades.

Big Mo took my jaw in one of his enormous hands and squeezed, making my mouth ache. "That shrunken head you sold me? It's a fake, asshole. You think I wouldn't find out?"

"That's impossible," I protested.

"Impossible?" he spat. "You tell that to my old lady. The same old lady I gave it to for a birthday present. She took it to two of the top experts in the field in Toronto. They ran lab tests. And guess what, shithead? The thread used to sew the lips, eyes, and back of the neck is nylon. Now, you tell me how someone in the middle of the jungle in South America got their hands on nylon in the nineteenth century?"

"I don't understand." I was genuinely surprised. "If there's a problem, I'll give you your money back. I'm sorry."

"You can't fix my problem with money, *hombre*. You embarrassed the shit out of me with my old lady. You embarrassed my old lady. You're a dead man, motherfucker. But first we have plans to see how much we can hurt you before you die."

He kicked me again, and then turned to Goose, "Watch him while I go get the rope."

The negotiations were over. I wasn't going to talk my way out of this one. They were going to kill me. As Big Mo walked away and Goose bent over to pull me to my feet, I did the only thing I could think of. I pulled the .22 out of my pocket and shot Goose once in the chest and once in the face.

He took a step backward but didn't go down. I started to wonder whether or not I'd done any damage. Then, he keeled over to one side, hitting the driveway with a thunk. Out of the corner of my eye, I saw Big Mo turn around.

"Fuckhead," he shouted, drawing a gun from his belt.

I shot twice, once at his chest and once at his head before he could get off a round. He spun to one side, caught himself and raised the gun toward me. I shot him dead center between his eyes. He went down instantly falling backward with his hands thrown out to his sides.

To be sure, I put another bullet into each of them.

Take that, I thought, feeling a strange mix of anger, relief, and power.

As I retrieved the casings and reloaded the .22, I was surprisingly calm for someone who had just shot his first two humans. I circled around the bodies, barely breathing, realizing how different it felt from seeing Carlene's body on the dining room floor or Johnson's body at the convenience store. This was my work. Adrenaline made me feel like I was on speed.

I glanced down the driveway and saw that they'd backed their SUV halfway in, presumably to make it easier to throw me in the back.

My best bet was hoisting them into their SUV, driving their bodies somewhere where I could get clear access to deep water, and sinking them and their vehicle. I knew a pretty good spot on Lake Erie. It would take me two hours to drive there. It was the only place I could think of where I could run the car off the road and land it in deep enough water to sink it. I had no idea how I'd get back.

I'll think of something, I told myself as I lifted Big Mo under the arms and started to drag his body toward the SUV.

Halfway there the rear door to the museum swung open.

Pilot stood in the doorway. I followed his gaze as he took in the carnage.

"Well, now you've gone and done it," he said, taking his cigarette out of his mouth. "Just like your father."

CHAPTER 37

"What do you mean 'just like your father'?" I asked.

"Never mind. What do you want me to do?"

"Go home, Pilot. This doesn't concern you. I don't want you involved."

"Stupid kid. I ain't going nowhere. You need me."

"I don't need you. Go home."

"Tell me what happened."

I was wasting time arguing with him. I continued dragging Big Mo to the rear of the SUV, giving Pilot a brief rundown as I went. He listened quietly, attaching himself to me like a puppy.

I was grateful for the adrenaline. It was masking the pain from my latest beating. Without it, I probably couldn't have lifted a finger, much less a couple of hundred pounds of dead weight.

As I got Big Mo to the rear of the SUV and began to maneuver him inside, Pilot went to the front of the vehicle and pulled a plastic bag from the floor. Inside the bag was the bell jar containing the shrunken head I'd sold to Big Mo. "They were probably going to shove this up your ass before they killed you," Pilot informed me.

"I wish I had known it wasn't a genuine Jivaro head," I said.

"You blaming me?" he asked, following me as I went to get Goose.

"I'm not blaming anyone. You said it was the real deal. You made a mistake."

"Harry, I never said it was genuine. You never asked. You just assumed it was. I know what it is because it's one of mine."

"One of yours?" I grunted as I pushed Goose part way into the SUV. "What's that supposed to mean?"

"At one time I had an arrangement with a guy who was running the mortuary at a medical school. He was getting more bodies donated than he could use. He sold off spare parts."

"Great. So you bought a head and shrunk it?" I gave Goose one last push to get him all the way into the rear of the vehicle.

Pilot watched in silence.

"Big Mo was right about the thread. It's nylon."

"It's easier to work with."

I stuck Big Mo's gun in his pocket and covered both bodies with a tarp that had been in the rear of the vehicle, probably to be used to wrap my body before dumping it somewhere.

"Next time tell me." I slammed the rear door shut.

"Next time ask. If not me, then ask someone smarter than you. You gotta get used to not thinking you know everything. Now, what are you planning to do with the two stiffs?"

"Don't worry. Go home."

"I'm not leaving you. I'm supposed to be looking after you."

"You're not coming with me," I said, heading for the driver's door.

Pilot tried to block my way. "Harry, listen to me for once in your life. What are you planning?"

I told him.

"You ever sunk a car before?"

"No. Have you?"

He ignored my question. "And then what? You're going to walk back seventy miles, or maybe you're going to call a cab? And then in the summer some weekend scuba diver's going to find the SUV, and the cops are going to check the cab companies and find you?"

"You've been watching too many police procedurals. Besides, do you have a better idea?"

"I know a spot where no divers are ever going to find them, and it's a lot closer than seventy miles from here. I'll take you there. Then bring you back. No one will ever know."

"I don't want you involved."

"I'm already involved. I'm a material witness. You have to trust me, Harry. Your father and your grandfather trusted me to watch their backs. I never failed them."

"What do you mean *watch their backs?*" I asked.

He pressed his lips together like he had already said too much.

What am I missing, I wondered. My mind was still spinning.

"If I let you—"

"Just give me the goddamn keys to the Lexus," he said, holding out his hand. "And follow me."

"All right. But if I get stopped by the police, you keep going."

"Don't worry about me." He said, grabbing the keys and heading toward my late stepmother's car. I got in the driver's side of the SUV.

I followed him along surface streets through town and then into the countryside along local roads that wound through farmland and bush.

Strange night, I kept thinking as I drove along, trying to ignore the smell of the two dead guys in back. But it wasn't just the bodies of Big Mo and Goose that had my attention. Pilot showed less reaction to the dead guys than he had to the overflowing toilets and the leaking roof. And what did he mean "just like your father" and "covering your father's and grandfather's backs"? Why did they need covering?

Somewhere near one of the local First Nations' reserves, he turned onto a gravel road and drove through thick woods. He finally stopped along a nondescript stretch of road in the middle of nowhere.

I parked behind him. He got out and climbed into the passenger side of the SUV.

"We'll leave the Lexus here. No sense making more tracks than we have to. Now, drive up ahead slowly, and I'll tell you when to turn."

I drove another hundred yards and turned where he said, onto a dirt road that went up the side of a steep hill and wound through more woods for a couple of hundred feet to a turnaround at the edge of a precipice.

"Park here," he said. As soon as I stopped, he got out. I followed him to the edge of the cliff. I could see a small lake twenty feet below us. The cold breeze coming toward us across the water had a strange, unpleasant, acidic smell.

"What is this place?"

"It's an old quarry. Been flooded for years. Goes down a couple of hundred feet."

"What's the smell?"

"Factories in St. Catharines and Hamilton used to come up here and dump their toxic waste. Your friends will probably dissolve long before they're ever discovered."

We'd both been wearing gloves the whole time, but we wiped down the SUV anyway just as a precaution. As much as I hated to do it, at Pilot's insistence, we left the fake Jivaro head in the SUV.

"I'm opening the windows and vents enough," Pilot explained like he was teaching me to tie my shoes, "to make it easier for the SUV to sink but not enough for the bodies to float out."

When he finished, we pushed the vehicle over the edge.

It hit with a tremendous splash and settled halfway down in the water.

At first, I was afraid that it might not sink, but the weight of the engine took the nose under first, and then slowly, the vehicle went deeper and deeper until it finally disappeared.

When the bubbles stopped, we walked down the dirt road to the Lexus. The ground was frozen enough so that we wouldn't leave footprints.

"I'd like to go see your father now if you don't mind," Pilot said when we finally reached the Lexus.

CHAPTER 38

PILOT SHOWED ME AN EASIER ROUTE BACK, and we were soon on the QEW, heading toward Niagara Falls.

"What did you mean when you said, 'Just like your father'?" I asked.

"Nothing."

"You meant something, Pilot. And how did you 'cover' my father's and grandfather's backs? You didn't even blink when you saw the two dead guys in the parking lot. What are you not telling me?"

"Let me ask you something, sonny boy. When you shot the two mooks, what did you feel?"

"What do you mean?"

"Inside your guts. What did you feel?"

"I don't see what—"

"Just answer the question."

I thought for a moment. "I don't know. I guess I felt anger. Relief."

"But no regrets. No remorse."

"No."

"That's what I thought."

"What do you mean, 'That's what I thought'? Thought about *what*?"

"Figure it out, Harry."

"Figure what out?"

He fell silent, again. In the dim light from the dashboard and the highway, his profile was like a weathered wood carving with deep, craggy cuts. The cigarette smoke coming out of his nose and mouth was the only indication he was alive.

The clown, I thought. Always the clown. How many times had I laughed at him when he'd scared one of my friends by telling them he'd been there when Bugsy Siegel or Alberta Anastasia had been whacked? Was it even remotely possible that Pilot had been on the grassy knoll the day Kennedy was shot? Was it possible he had had something to do with the mysterious disappearance of Teamsters power broker James R. Hoffa? What about my father and grandfather? Were they connected to these unsolved crimes? Could the answers have been hiding in plain sight all these years?

And what about me? Why didn't I feel anything? I had just shot two people in cold blood. Granted, they were about to kill me. But I felt no remorse, no guilt. All I wanted to do was get away with it.

Was I inherently evil?

And what did Pilot mean when he said, "Just like your father"? From some deep, dark spot inside me, I knew his words were not to be taken lightly.

How was I like my father? What was I supposed to figure out?

"Pilot, when you said the other day, 'Nothing is ever what it appears to be,' what did you mean?"

"Not now, sonny boy," he said. "We're almost there. I gotta get ready."

He turned the rearview mirror so he could view himself. He slipped a comb out of his pocket and carefully began combing his wisps of white hair as I slowed for the upcoming exit for Graystone.

CHAPTER 39

Visiting hours were almost over. I went into my father's room with Pilot, but we were only there a minute or two when Pilot asked if he could be alone with my dad. I went to the cafeteria, grabbed a coffee, and returned to the car. Pilot returned after twenty minutes looking like he'd aged ten years.

I watched him out of the corner of my eye as I started the engine. I wasn't sure if his eyes were just a little more watery than usual or whether he was crying until I saw a single tear roll down his cheek. He didn't bother to wipe it away but let it fall to his coat.

As we drove toward downtown, I asked, "Pilot, would you like to have dinner? I'd really like it if you would." I'd eaten with him and my father on countless occasions in the past when I was a kid, but it never occurred to me to even offer to go out with him on my own.

"I could use some grub."

"Just name your favorite restaurant. My treat."

"Doug's."

Doug's was a 24-hour greasy spoon that had been old and greasy when I was a kid.

"Come on, Pilot. We can do better than that." I rattled off several fine restaurants around town.

"Doug's."

Ten minutes later, we were tucked in the rear of the near empty restaurant with soup, sandwiches, and mugs full of coffee.

"I just couldn't bring myself to see your father like that," he said after taking a small bite of his roast beef sandwich. "All these months, I just couldn't go visit him. I feel like shit."

"You can come with me anytime," I said, trying to make him feel better.

"Maybe I will." That seemed to perk him up. He smiled between bites. "You're not half bad, Harry. Not half bad."

"Thanks, Pilot." I was a little surprised to feel my face flush.

"Listen, you mind if we blow this joint? I'm having a nicotine fit."

"Are you sure you don't want to finish your food?" He'd only eaten a few spoons of soup and not even half of his sandwich.

"It's way too much. Sitting and eating like this makes my legs cramp up."

"Maybe you should see a doctor."

"Doctors. What the hell do they know?"

I paid the bill and followed him out.

He stopped just outside the door. I thought he was stopping to catch his breath, but he pulled out his cigarettes and lit up. Instead of returning to the car, we walked along the empty sidewalk while he smoked.

"Pilot, Reggie Baker told me something today that I need to check out with you. He heard from the police that one of the guns that shot Carlene was used years ago to kill someone named Billy 'Mick' McCasters, a small-time hood in Buffalo who said he had information about President Kennedy's assassination."

He stopped, took the cigarette out of his mouth, and shook his head. "Damn. I knew this was going to happen. I told you not to sell that gun."

"Knew what, Pilot? How did the gun get to MurderLand?"

"How did it get out? You tell me that." He glared at me for a second, then stuck the cigarette back in his mouth. "Figure it out. You're the smart guy."

"Figure what out? Did my father know the guy who shot McCasters?"

"Jesus, Harry. It wasn't supposed to happen this way. I wasn't supposed to be the one to tell you any of this."

"Tell me what?"

He didn't answer.

"If you weren't supposed to tell me, who was?"

He remained silent.

"Was it my father?"

More silence but I could see the *yes* in his eyes.

"What was he supposed to tell me?"

"Not tonight, Harry. Not tonight." He took one last, long drag off the remains of his cigarette before flicking the butt into the street. "Take me home. I'm starting to get cold and cranky. We've both had enough excitement for one day."

What could I do? His eyes were already half shut. He looked like he was going to fall asleep on his feet. Once I got him into the car, he started to doze. His chin dropped to his chest.

I parked in front of his low-rise apartment building and helped him out of the car, but when I tried to walk him inside, he stopped me. "I'm fine, Harry. I don't need your help, just a good night's sleep."

"Sleep in, Pilot. You never take time off. I'll open up tomorrow. You don't have to worry about anything. And Pilot, thanks for all your help this evening."

"Get lost, Harry. Go home. I'll see you in the morning."

"You sure you don't want me to walk you upstairs?"

"Go home. See you tomorrow." He waved one last time without turning around as he entered the building.

CHAPTER 40

ON THE DRIVE HOME, I couldn't stop racking my brain, trying to figure out what Pilot kept telling me to figure out. How was I just like my father? How and why did Pilot have to cover the backs of my father and grandfather? And why hadn't I felt any guilt over the deaths of Carlene, Big Mo, and Goose? And what about the .38 that had been used to kill McCasters? The possible answers sent shivers down my spine.

Or was Pilot just toying with me?

Pilot used to babysit me after my mother died when my father was busy with one of his lady friends. I hadn't been in Pilot's apartment since I was nine or ten years old, but I could still recall all the animal trophies with their innocent looking glass eyes. He used to tell me ghost stories, tales of animal attacks on humans, and stories about serial killers until I was scared out of my mind, but I never let him know it. After a while, I started to think that all he was doing was making up stories to see me react. Once I figured that out, I no longer needed to be afraid.

I was thinking about this as I drove into my driveway and noticed a light peaking around the edges of the curtains in my place. As I got out of the Lexus, I reached into my pocket for the .22, thinking about Duane and the guy who nearly ran me off the road.

I was still trying to decide whether to investigate or get in the Lexus and drive off, when the front door swung open.

My finger tightened around the trigger.

I can't really say what kept me from firing off a round into the person framed in the doorway. It would have been the normal thing to do after the course of events that evening.

For whatever reason, I held back. A second later, the porch light came on illuminating Alice. She was standing in the doorway in my bathrobe. A strange odor drifted toward me as I approached the front door. It smelled like burnt food.

"What are you doing here?" I asked.

"Some greeting. I was waiting for you. I must have fallen asleep."

"How'd you get here? Where's your car?"

"I parked in back. What happened to the Lincoln?"

"Careless driver." I held up my gun. "I could have shot you. You should have told me you were coming,"

"I tried, but you wouldn't return my calls. The old woman next door was outside looking for her cat. She told me you lived in the guesthouse, not the main house."

I walked past Alice into the living room.

"How'd you get in?"

"I just pushed hard. It's not much of a lock."

"What smells?"

"Dinner. I wanted to surprise you. I burned everything and had to throw it in the garbage. I guess it's too late to order a pizza?"

It was past eleven. Except for the casinos, a few coffee shops, bars, and convenience stores, Niagara Falls was closed for the night.

By the time I'd finished hanging my coat in the closet, Alice had turned off the lights, lit several candles, and sat down at one end of the couch as if expecting me to join her. On the coffee table was a plate with cheddar cheese cubes, an open bottle of red wine, and two glasses; one was half full, the other empty. Just what you might expect from a twenty-three-year-old trying to play house.

"You tidied the place," I said, noticing she had cleared away my old dishes.

"I was bored. I had nothing better to do."

I was afraid to thank her. It seemed like too great a commitment. Her attempt at domesticity scared me. I sat opposite her in one of the stuffed chairs and grabbed a cheese cube and popped it into my mouth.

"You want some wine?" she asked.

I nodded.

"How was your day?" She topped up both glasses.

"The usual. What about yours?"

"Derek was in one of his moods. He called me a dumb shit. The good news is my agent called. He said that he might have a cable series for me—a cop show for the mystery channel. I have to audition in Toronto. The series is being shot in Vancouver. If I get it, I can quit the festival and move there. They start shooting in less than a month."

"I hope you get it." I took a sip of wine.

"You didn't even ask me if I wanted the part."

"Do you want it?"

"I don't know. I told him I'd think about it. Do you want me to take it?"

"I want you to do what makes you happy."

"Are you breaking up with me?"

"I didn't say that."

"If I took the job, would you come with me?"

"I have a business to run."

"If I stayed here what would happen to us?"

"I don't know. I understand the police interviewed you."

"Yes. Twice. Once on Sunday late in the afternoon, and then again on Monday. They came to the theater both times. I tried calling you, but you were too busy to answer your phone or call back."

"I saw you on Sunday night. You should have told me."

"I started to, but you were grumpy. I didn't want to make it worse."

She had mentioned the police. I did have a lot on my mind.

"What did they ask you?"

"All kinds of things to try to get me to say that I thought you might have killed your stepmother or you were somehow involved. Don't worry. I've had experience with these things. My mother stabbed one of her boyfriends to death when I was ten. The police tried to make me say it was my mother's fault. I kept my mouth shut. My mother went to prison anyway, and I went to a foster home, then to my grandmother's."

She took a sip of wine and nibbled on a cheese cube. "You have any drugs?" she asked.

"No."

She smiled and produced a joint from her purse.

"I got this from one of the stagehands. Why don't we go to the bedroom," she suggested after lighting up, taking a hit, and handing it to me. "I put on clean sheets."

"All right. But can I ask you something first?"

She nodded.

"Can you try not to make those little chirping sounds?"

She giggled. "Sure. I thought they were a turn-on. I'm an actor. I can do anything you want, be anyone you want me to be."

For the moment, all I really wanted was to get laid and feel something to reaffirm my own life after the day I'd just had. I put my arm around Alice on the way to the bedroom and hugged her to me. She felt warm and good. Her lips tasted sweet from the wine.

WEDNESDAY

I woke up early. Alice was already gone. I found her note on the kitchen table beside her cell phone.

Darling,

Last night was the best ever. So sorry. I have to run. Busy day. The dress I bought for your stepmother's funeral is hanging in the closet. I was going to model it for you last night, but I didn't want to spoil the mood. I'm leaving my cell phone with you so I can reach you later wherever you are.

XXOO
A.

PS I forgot to tell you, the raccoons are back. I borrowed your gun. I'll take care of them and return it later.

Shit. Double shit.

I double-checked my coat pockets in the closet and found the ammunition, but the gun was gone.

The only thing of Alice's in the closet was her dress, a skimpy black thing with the price tag still on it. It always amazed me how much women paid for clothes.

I had her phone. So I couldn't call her. It was too early to call the theater.

I found a roach in the ashtray, lit it, took a hit, and smoked the rest of it as I drove to Alice's. I was hoping to retrieve the gun before she did any serious damage.

The car radio gave me some good news. The Dallas Stars won a squeaker against the Chicago Blackhawks in overtime. I was up over sixteen grand. A few more good picks and I'd have the money to pay for the roof.

I used Alice's cell phone to call Frankie to gloat and place a couple of new wagers. I bet half my winnings on the Philadelphia 76ers over the Boston Celtics and half on Phoenix Suns over the Golden State Warriors—two suicide bets but ones that gave me great odds. The Celtics and Warriors had been getting a little too cocky lately. I had the feeling they were both vulnerable. Their winning streaks had run just a little too long.

I arrived at Alice's at half past eight. Her car wasn't there. I went around back and found two freshly killed raccoons lying among the garbage scattered around her yard. I picked up a half dozen spent cartridge casings. I carried the dead raccoons by their tails to the edge of her yard and flung them as far as I could into the woods.

I popped the lock on her back door, hoping to find the gun in the house. I searched for ten minutes but came up empty. I reset the lock, and then drove to her theater in Niagara-on-the-Lake. She wasn't there. I cruised through the town and drove by her friend Loretta's place near the water, but no sign of Alice or Loretta.

I wondered if Alice might have gone to her audition in Toronto for the TV series. I tried to remember what she told me.

Next time, listen better, I scolded myself.

I arrived at the museum at a quarter to ten. The roofers were already working outside. All the traffic in the parking lot had obliterated any signs of Big Mo and Goose. I let the roofers inside to work on the walls.

I found a message from Pilot on my voice mail saying he'd be in later but not giving any indication when later was.

I was still wrestling with all the questions from the previous night.

I got busy online and found mentions of Billy McCasters right away. He was a footnote on a few websites devoted to conspiracy theories about JFK's assassination. McCasters had been born and raised in Buffalo. He had served in the US Marines during the Second World War in the North African and Italian campaigns. He was a decorated sharpshooter with fourteen confirmed kills to his credit. He had also been arrested six times for extortion and assault but had been convicted only once for breaking someone's legs with a baseball bat. He served a two-year sentence in Attica. He had been shot to death in the basement of his home in Buffalo on May 18, 1969. Entry to the home hadn't been forced. According to the article, the police assumed that either he had left a door open or McCasters knew his assailant. The only photo I could find was one of him in his Marine uniform taken a quarter of a century before he had been shot.

It wasn't much, but it suddenly triggered an idea.

I went to the basement to the original spot where I had found the .38. I hunted around for a few minutes until I found the old newspapers and tea towel that the gun had been wrapped in.

I took the yellowed newspaper wrappings upstairs to my office and spread each sheet out one at a time.

It was a long shot, but I had been hoping the gun might have been wrapped in an article about the murder.

I was sure I was out of luck when I saw that the pages had come from the sports section and were filled with nothing more dramatic than baseball news.

Then, I glanced at the date, and alarm bells immediately went off in my head.

Saturday, May 17, 1969.

The day before the murder.

I rechecked the date of McCasters' murder through every source I could find on the net.

The murder hadn't been discovered until late in the afternoon on Sunday. The story hadn't appeared in the papers until the next day, Monday, May 19.

Of course it made sense. Everything made perfect sense.

The answer had been hiding right in plain sight all the time.

I felt like a bomb had gone off inside my head.

I had to speak with Pilot.

Even the offhanded remark, which Carlene had made the previous week, made sense. She had suggested that my father had been thinking about getting rid of her. When I joked that maybe he was thinking about killing her, she said, "You don't believe he could do something like that, do you, you simpleton?"

How much more had she known about Dad than me?

CHAPTER 41

I TRIED REACHING PILOT, but he wasn't answering his phone.

I returned to the car and cruised along Victoria Avenue, hoping to spot him walking to work. I stopped at his building and buzzed his apartment, but no one answered.

An elderly woman arrived, dragging a white miniature poodle on a leash. She asked me who I was looking for. When I told her, she said she'd seen Pilot leave a half hour before, heading toward Victoria Avenue.

I cruised slowly toward MurderLand but didn't spot him.

At the office, I could do little but pace and pretend to keep myself busy by paying bills and filling out government forms. I also dodged two calls from Wally Lavaleer. When I checked my voice mail, both of his messages were the same—reminders that I was supposed to sign some papers the next day or his deal would be in jeopardy, and there would be hell to pay for me. In the second message, he also informed me that he was setting up a meeting for the two of us at three o'clock and that I should call his secretary to confirm.

He hadn't yet received my registered letter terminating his services, or he was ignoring it.

Either way, I had no intention of returning his calls.

By eleven thirty, I still hadn't heard from Alice or Pilot.

Relax, I told myself, but I couldn't relax. My mind was spinning out of control.

I picked up sandwiches for my father and Clive, and headed to the nursing home.

Clive showed up twenty minutes after I'd arrived. He reminded me of the party that night as I handed him the extra sandwich.

"Show up any time after six. These people are serious party pigs," he said, sitting in the chair next to the second bed and unwrapping his food.

"Thanks," I said. "I just might."

"Oh, and by the way, some elderly gentleman visited your father this morning. Cranky old fellow. He said his name was Pilot."

"When did he leave?"

"A half hour ago. Said he had to catch a bus to go to work. I couldn't imagine a place where someone that old would be working."

"Nothing is what it seems to be, Clive."

"What's that supposed to mean?" he shouted at me as I ran out the door.

I found Pilot on the first floor dusting some photos.

"That was nice of you to visit my father," I told him.

"I think he's improved a little since last night."

"Maybe he has. You mind coming to the office? I'd like to show you something."

He put down the dustcloth and walked with me to the office.

Once there, I showed him the newspaper sheets on my desk.

"What do you see?" I asked.

He studied the first page. "Dodgers beat the Giants. Yankees beat Boston. What's the big deal?"

"Take a look at the date."

He glanced at it quickly. "So? It's an old newspaper, Harry. I don't know what you're thinking, but it ain't worth nothing."

"It's dated the day before Billy McCasters was shot and two days before the story appeared in the newspapers. This is the newspaper that was used to wrap up the .38 that shot McCasters."

"Uh-oh." He looked at me, his expression suddenly frozen in stone.

"The only way this makes sense to me is if someone used the gun and wrapped it in a day-old newspaper."

He looked at the floor. "Sometimes people keep newspapers around a long time, Harry."

"Sometimes, Pilot. But that's not what I think happened here. I think either my father acquired the .38 the same day as McCasters was hit or someone here whacked McCasters. I need you to tell me the truth. Who shot McCasters? Was it you?"

He looked me right in the eyes. "It wasn't me, Harry. I swear."

"Then, it was my father."

He remained silent, staring at me.

"It was my father, wasn't it," I repeated. "That's what you meant when you said, 'Just like your father.' My old man screwed up, too, didn't he? He should have dumped the gun."

"You know how he could never throw anything away," he mumbled.

"Was McCasters involved in the Kennedy assassination?"

"You don't need to know."

"Was my father? Was my grandfather involved? Is that what you meant when you said you watched their backs?"

"Nobody needs to know anything. What's done is done? That's all I'm gonna say." He started to get up.

"Pilot. I have to know. You're the only one who can tell me what's going on here. Did Carlene know any of this?"

"Your old man should have gotten rid of that witch a long time ago."

"Gotten rid of her? How?"

"I've said enough. You can fire me if you want, but I've said all I'm gonna say. And even that's too much. Right now, I'm going home. All this talking is tiring the hell out of me."

I watched him shuffle out the door. Part of me wanted to run after him and shake his bony little body until he told me everything he knew. Part of me didn't want to know anything.

After he left, I tried to work, but my mind kept coming back to everything that had happened in the last twenty-four hours.

I started to compose a list of all the crazy things I had heard Pilot say over the years. At one time or another he had inserted himself into some of the highest profile, unsolved murders of the twentieth century. I flipped through the museum manual, checking them off.

Bugsy Siegel, crime lord and founder of modern-day Las Vegas, was shot by a sniper with a high-powered rifle in his girlfriend's living room because he allegedly was misappropriating money from his crime syndicate partners back east. Case officially unsolved. Pilot said he witnessed it.

Albert Anastasia, also known as the Mad Hatter and the High Executioner of Murder, Inc., was gunned down in the barber shop of the Park Sheraton Hotel in New York in 1957 because he allegedly was trying to muscle into Meyer Lansky's Cuban gambling operations. His two shooters were never identified. Case officially unsolved. Pilot said he saw the hit.

Sam "Momo" Giancana, Chicago crime boss, lover (with Sinatra and JFK) of Judith Campbell, was shot by persons unknown in his Oak Park basement while cooking spaghetti sauce in 1975, allegedly because his crime syndicate partners thought he might give evidence on them in an upcoming trial. Case officially unsolved. Pilot said he was there.

Defrocked Teamsters leader Jimmy Hoffa, who had been pardoned by President Nixon six months early from his prison sentence and fooled by Nixon's people into signing a document that banned him from running for the Teamsters presidency for the foreseeable future, mysteriously disappeared in 1975 while in a vicious court fight to have the ban overturned. Kidnappers unknown. Hoffa was later declared legally dead. His body was never found. Case officially unsolved. Pilot said he had been there.

And what about Abe "Kid Twist" Reles, the canary who could sing but couldn't fly, the guy who had coined the terms "hit" and "contract," and turned the ice pick into a tool of death? He had fallen out of the sixth story window of the Half Moon Hotel in Coney Island in 1941, while in police custody. He died under mysterious circumstances right before he could give testimony that might have sent more top syndicate bosses to the electric chair. Case officially unsolved. Pilot said he knew what happened. What did Pilot mean when he'd said, "Nothing is ever what it appears to be"?

Even the Jean Harlow charm bracelet had me thinking overtime. Was it possible New Jersey crime boss, Longy Zwillman, retrieved the bracelet he'd given Jean Harlow after her death? Did he carry it as a talisman in his pocket until he was found hanged in the basement of his New Jersey mansion? Had the rumors been true all these years that his suicide was a covered-up murder to keep him from testifying against his friends in the National Crime Syndicate?

Could the bracelet have been given to someone for safekeeping or been taken from Zwillman's pocket by someone before he killed himself or was murdered?

What about President Kennedy? How many times had I heard Pilot say he was on the grassy knoll when JFK was assassinated?

What should I make of the McCasters connection, I wondered. What am I not seeing? What don't I want to see?

One thing that I did see was that my father would have been too young for at least half of the killings. Did that mean my grandfather had been involved in these? Pilot said he had provided cover for both of them.

The ringing telephone woke me from my open-eyed nightmare.

I checked the caller ID. Wally Lavaleer. I let it go to voice mail. I played his message. "Call me, damn it, or you'll regret it."

Of course, I didn't call him. The idea that he might be under pressure from some Buffalo goons warmed my heart.

Not that I was all smiles.

I had solved nothing. Real answers were still as scarce as rocking horse shit.

And Alice still hadn't called.

I was beginning to wonder if she might be sitting in jail somewhere on gun charges.

The roofers were already gone, and until I was able to finesse something more out of Pilot, I wasn't about to get any farther than I already had. I locked up and decided to take another shot at Alice's place in Queenston.

Her car was still gone. I went around back and found three raccoons on her porch. They barely moved as I jimmied her door again and searched the house a second time hoping to find the gun or some indication of where Alice might be. I came up empty on both counts.

This is definitely not good, I told myself as I headed to my car.

I was just rounding the corner, still thinking about Alice when a blow to the side of my head knocked me to the ground.

CHAPTER 42

THE FIST BELONGED TO DUANE MORTHWELL, and he wasn't quite finished with me. He gave me a boot in my side, which I was able to partly block with my arm.

"What the hell is that for?" I asked, inwardly cursing Alice for taking my gun.

His voice was low, measured, and simmering with rage. "You fucking hung up on me. Don't ever, ever fucking hang up on me again."

He kicked my thigh.

"What the hell are you doing here?" I sat up, and at the same time glanced around for something to use as a weapon. The ache in my side and leg made it unlikely that I could outrun him.

"We need to talk." He backed away a few feet—a move I took as a signal for me to get up.

"I told you, Duane. You and I shouldn't be talking on the phone, and we definitely shouldn't be seen together. How'd you find me?"

"I've been following you, fuckhead."

"Well, stop following me. Get out of here. Leave me alone. I told you I'd get in touch when I have your money. You got my attention. Now, we need to go back to the original plan."

"That's not how it's going to work. You're going to get me my money, and you're going to get it for me right now."

"Wait a minute, Duane. If you'll recall, I came along and helped you out of your Johnny Johnson troubles. I'm trying to help you now. What is your problem?"

"You don't give a shit about me. Empty your goddamned pockets."

"Duane—"

He moved a step closer with raised fists.

"All right, all right." I emptied my pockets, handing him the last of the cash I had on me. "Are you satisfied? You have two grand there."

"This is just the beginning." He stuffed the money in his jeans. "You're going to get me the rest—thirty-eight thousand—within forty-eight hours, and then we'll talk about what happens after that."

Ten, I wanted to shout at him. I owe you only ten. You only did half the job. Wally Lavaleer is still alive. Instead I told him, "Let's not get ahead of ourselves here. First of all, you have all the money I have on me. I told you I'm having cash flow problems. Second of all, where'd you come up with the new number? That's nowhere near what we agreed on."

"The agreement's been changed." He took an audiocassette out of his pocket and smiled. "You know what this is?"

"An audiotape."

He tossed it to me. "It's a copy of the tape I made of you telling me to whack your stepmother and the shyster. All the parts of me talking are gone. What's left is your voice."

My mind froze for a couple of seconds as I tried to process what Duane had just told me.

Why hadn't I seen this coming, I asked myself. This is not good.

"We obviously have to talk about this." I tried to think through all the ramifications.

"*We* don't have to talk about anything, motherfucker. From now on, I talk. You listen. Because you're not running things now. I am. You're my new junior partner."

"Aren't we forgetting something, Duane?"

"And what would that be?"

"That I have you on video shooting Johnson?" I waved the cassette he'd just handed me casually in the air. "The tape you have of me could be construed as almost anything."

"Except you don't have the copies anymore. Because it wasn't hard to find out where you hid them. All I had to do was follow you and ask around. I broke into your lawyer's office. I stole the photos and memory stick and destroyed them. If you think I'm bluffing, give your lawyer a call." He handed me Melanie's card.

I used Alice's cell phone to dial Melanie's office. She picked up on the second ring.

"Harry, how are you? Listen, sorry I haven't gotten back to you, but I've been tied up with a number of things."

"No problem, Melanie. Could you do me a favor right now? Could you check to see if the package I left you the other day is still in your files?"

"Of course, it's there, Harry. Where else would it be?"

"Would you just check?"

"I'll do it later and get back to you."

"Melanie, I need to know right now. It's important."

"Harry—"

"Just do it, Melanie."

"Okay," she sighed. Duane grinned from ear to ear while I waited. The longer Melanie was gone, the more confidence I lost.

Finally, she came back on the line. "It's gone, Harry. I thought I might have misfiled it, but it's gone. Someone must have taken it. I need to notify the police."

"No. Don't do that."

"Harry, someone broke into my office. They removed something from a locked drawer. I have to call the police."

"No you don't, Melanie. If you call them, they'll drag me into it, and I'll have to tell them there never was an envelope. Now, how will that make you look?"

"This is crazy, Harry. What was in that envelope? Are you in trouble?"

"I can't talk about it now."

"Harry—"

"We'll talk later. Just don't call the police. Okay?"

"Okay."

As soon as I hung up, Morthwell told me, "If you're entertaining any ideas of knocking me off, think twice. A copy of the cassette I just gave you is on file with my new lawyer, Wally Lavaleer."

The hollowness in my stomach expanded into my throat.

His eyes narrowed. "If anything happens to me, Lavaleer will be the one going after you."

"You're smarter than I thought."

Without a word, he punched me hard enough in the chest to send me staggering backward a couple of steps.

"That's the trouble with all you people." He rubbed his fist like he was getting ready to hit me again. "You all thought I was stupid. I'm not stupid. I'm dyslexic. I didn't do well in school. That's a fact, but that don't make me stupid. Did you know Einstein was dyslexic?"

"No."

He swung at me again. I turned and blocked it with my arm.

I took a quick step back before he could throw another punch. "Hey, I get it. You're smart. You don't have to prove it. I'm impressed."

"That last punch isn't for now. That's for the lunch money thing."

"Wait a minute, Duane. You used to beat *me* up and steal *my* lunch money. Remember? Why should that be my fault?"

"Because you never cared why I did it. None of you did. You know why I used to beat you up and steal your lunch money? Because half the time my granny drank up the social assistance check by the middle of the month, and there wasn't any money for my lunch."

"So, why didn't you ask me for money?"

"Think about it, shithead. I didn't want anyone to know. I didn't want anyone laughing at me."

"Everyone knew your family was on social assistance."

"Yeah, but I had to pretend they didn't."

"I'm sorry."

"Like I care. All you need to know is that I want the thirty-eight thousand you owe me within forty-eight hours."

"We agreed on twenty."

"You put me through a lot of work. I figure you owe me twenty thousand for what I did. And twenty thousand more for the tapes of our phone conversation. I already took two from you. That leaves thirty-eight. I'm not a thief. I just want enough money to get to a quiet place, find work, live a quiet life, and stay out of prison. I've been there. I don't want to go back. And you don't want to go there either. Keep that in mind."

"I will. I'll do what I can, but can I ask you a question?"

"Okay."

"What happened at Carlene's?"

"What do you mean, what happened?"

"You only did half the job, Duane."

"Lavaleer never showed. I improvised. I thought dumping the gun in the dumpster and calling the police was a nice touch."

"It was, but what happened to the other gun? The Chinese knockoff of the Russian gun."

"You don't need to know. What you need to know is that you get me my money in two days. You meet me at Brock's Monument. Five o'clock. Friday. And no bullshit, man. Find a way."

He pointed a finger at me like a gun to make sure I got the point.

I waited until he drove off before heading to the Lexus. For all the pounding I'd taken, I was in surprisingly good shape—at least physically.

Mentally, my mind was spinning.

How had I not seen this coming? More to the point, what was I going to do about it?

For the moment, I really hadn't a clue.

CHAPTER 43

THE FIRST THING I HAD TO DO was figure out a way to keep Duane Morthwell from bushwhacking me again. He wasn't a natural killer, but he could hurt me or do something stupid that would bring us both down. I believed he just wanted to get out of town. The best thing to do was get him his money as fast as I could.

I drove to Pole Catz to see Frankie to try to cancel the bets I'd made earlier.

"Sorry, Harry, all the money's been placed. I can't call it back."

"Then, lend me thirty-eight thousand. You know I'm good for it."

"Harry, Harry, Harry. Nothing's changed since the last time I said *no*. Has it?"

"You lent me money last time."

"I lent you a couple of grand. You want that. You got it."

I took what he gave me for walking around money.

I still hadn't solved the immediate problem of finding the cash to pay Morthwell. I drove to the museum and spent an hour in the basement, sorting through boxes, looking for more things to sell. I was also hoping to find another gun until I could locate Alice.

I found nothing of value.

I even phoned Pilot on the pretense that I wanted to see how he was doing. I was hoping to get up the nerve to ask him if he had any ideas on handling Morthwell. It crossed my mind that I might find it necessary to make another trip to the toxic waste pond.

Pilot wasn't answering his phone.

I thought about Clive's party. While searching my pockets for the slip of paper with the address, I turned up my mother's watch.

Maybe it is lucky, I told myself. If I didn't have it, my situation might be worse.

The address I had written down was only a five-minute drive from the museum. It was way too early for any normal party, but Clive said it would start at six. It was already half past six.

On the way over to the party, a cop car with its siren blaring came at me from the rear.

I pulled to the side of the road expecting the cop car to slow and park behind me, but it flew by at full speed. Before I reached the party, two more squad cars with sirens wailing passed me.

I flipped on the radio, wondering if the cops might be heading to my party, but the newscaster said there'd been a shooting off Portage Road on the north end of town more than a mile from my destination.

The address Clive gave me was in a normally quiet, residential neighborhood filled with older homes. That evening, both sides of the street were filled with muscle cars and dragsters.

One thing was immediately obvious. No "big money" was at this party.

I might have kept driving if a parking space hadn't opened up in front just as I approached.

I kept wondering what the neighbors must be thinking as I parked and headed toward the house. I could hear and feel the music thumping through the night air. Despite the cold, a dozen people were milling around in front, talking and drinking. Most of the partygoers appeared to be barely over the legal drinking age.

As I made my way through the crowd on the front porch, stopping for a moment to take a toke off a joint that was making the rounds, I wondered how long it would be before the party was busted.

Stepping through the front door felt like stepping inside your own heart. The Afro-punk rock was blaring so loudly that I half expected to see the paint on the walls begin to peel off.

I glanced at the drunken, stoned, multi-pierced, and multi-tattooed freaks and wondered how many of them realized they were going to be deaf after a few more years of this.

I pushed my way through the throng, wandering from room to room, hunting for Clive, and stopping every so often to share a toke with someone.

I was surprised to see anyone I knew, let alone Reggie Baker. He was coming toward me with three beer bottles threaded between the fingers of each hand. Baker was at least forty years older than the next oldest person in sight, which was me.

"What are you doing here?" I asked.

"Covering a story." We both had to shout to be heard over the noise.

"What kind of story would you find here?" I could barely hear myself, let alone him.

"The police found a winning lottery at Johnny Johnson's apartment along with an old will that left everything to his two kids from a previous common-law marriage."

"You told me something about that." Two women, who looked barely past puberty and drunker than skunks, approached Baker from behind, took his arms, and began pulling him away from me.

He yelled at me, "The kids split one point six million. Eight hundred grand apiece. They haven't stopped partying since they found out."

"No shit. Who are they?"

His drunken escorts continued to pull him out of hearing range. "These two think I'm going to put them in the story," he yelled before he disappeared into the mob.

To follow would have meant fighting through too many bodies. I headed in the other direction toward a less populated and less noisy corner where I was able to rest my eardrums for a few minutes. A tall, hollow-cheeked dude, wearing a cape made of tinfoil and what looked like adult diapers for shoulder pads, tried to sell me some meth. I declined.

Clive appeared from the other direction just as the meth dealer wandered off.

"A pleasure to see you, my friend." He gave me one of his elaborate handshakes with one hand while holding a stogie-sized joint with the other.

We shared the joint. The marijuana floating around the party was exceptionally strong. The top of my head felt like it was becoming airborne. I was sure I was hallucinating when I saw a tattoo-covered man wearing

a loincloth walk through the room on his hands with a small boa constrictor entwined around his legs and feet.

As if reading my mind, Clive shouted in my ear, "You're not hallucinating, Harry. I thought the same thing."

"Strong stuff," I shouted back.

"Indeed. You want to meet the investors?"

"Maybe in a minute." My lips felt rubbery. What I really wanted to do
was sit down and hopefully stop the room from spinning.

"Come meet the money," Clive said with a broad grin. "Don't worry.
Everyone here is feeling the same love." He took my arm and half pushed,
half pulled me through the crowd toward the far end of the house.

"My new girlfriend and her brother were abused by this fellow Johnson when they were children. The mom and kids left and never saw him
again until the police showed up and told them they'd inherited a winning lottery ticket. They are already borrowing against it while the legal
shit's being worked out. Neither of them knows much about finance. I
told them I could put some of their money to work on the street and make
twice what they could from the bank. You're my big chance."

Clive steered me to a closed door that was guarded by a two-hundred-
and-fifty-pound bald guy wearing a black-and-white striped caftan.

The bald guy exchanged high fives with Clive and opened the door for
us.

Entering the inner sanctum took my breath away—literally. Incense
and candles were burning everywhere. A shirtless, skinny guy with arms
so tattooed they were blue and red from the wrists to the shoulders and
an equally skinny woman with jet black hair in a shiny, black rubber
jumpsuit were puffing dope through a double-hosed, three-foot-high
hookah. Others were smoking joints or vaping. The air was so thick with
smoke I could cut it with a wave of my hand.

The music was muted just enough for me to hear the grunts of a couple humping in the dark recesses at the edge of the room.

"The brother and his new woman," Clive said, nodding toward the for-
nicating twosome.

I followed Clive through the smog toward two figures in the far corner
sitting on a couch. One was a heavyset brunette in her early twenties with
her hair in long pigtails and wearing a floral Muumuu. The other was
Gina, dressed in a black open-weave fishnet body stocking with a

plunging neckline. Her pierced nipples poked through the mesh. The snake I had seen pass by earlier or its twin was wrapped around Gina's shoulders. The Muumuu lady was holding a mirror between them while Gina did lines of some kind of drug through a rolled bill.

"That's the new heiress," Clive shouted in my ear.

"The one in the Muumuu?" I asked hopefully.

"The other one. The one sniffing the coke. Gina." Clive introduced me to Gina. "Sweetheart, this is the business person I told you about."

Gina stared at me with big, glassy eyes and coke dust on her nose for fifteen seconds before a flicker of recognition kicked into her stoked gray matter.

If I had even the tiniest glimmer of hope that I might get my hands on any of Gina's new fortune, it vanished as soon as she started laughing so hard she had trouble catching her breath. The Muumuu lady snatched the mirror away so Gina wouldn't blow the dope off it.

"Oh, my God, not you," she said, between gulps of air. "Clive, honey, this guy's my ex-boss. Putting money in MurderLand would be like flushing it down the toilet."

"Just hear him out, sweetheart," Clive begged her.

"Sorry, hon. He's bumming me out just being here. There's no way I'm putting anything into that sewer. Be a sweetie and get him out of here."

Somewhere I'd read that the vast majority of lottery winners who score big go through all of their money within five years. I was willing to bet Gina and her brother would set a new record.

"Sorry, my man," Clive said, walking me to the front door. "I'll have a talk with her and make her reconsider."

"In the meantime, don't quit your day job."

He gave me a small, sad smile. I could see the disappointment in his eyes.

He led me through an elaborate goodbye handshake and hug. He also handed me a joint before I left.

"For the road," he insisted.

Two minutes later, I was back in my car and partially deaf in both ears. The party wasn't a total bust. I was pleasantly high.

Or at least I was until I turned on the radio. The newscaster said:

This just in, listeners. The two victims of the shooting in the north end earlier this evening have now been identified as attorney, Melanie Wickers, and her client, Nessa Wiley. The two victims have been taken to the Greater Niagara General Hospital. Their condition has not yet been released. The alleged shooter is Valerie Runge, a constable with the Niagara Regional Police, and spouse of Nessa Wiley. Runge is still at large. She is believed to be armed and dangerous, and is said to be driving a late-model, dark blue Honda Accord.

CHAPTER 44

ON THE DRIVE TO THE HOSPITAL, I couldn't help wondering whether the dark, midsized car I'd seen following me over the past few days belonged to Valerie Runge.

Melanie was in serious condition in the recovery room. A bullet had gone through her side, hit a lung, and ruptured her spleen. I wasn't able to see her.

Nessa was in better shape. Although she'd been shot twice, the first bullet had gone through fatty tissue on her side and the second through her shoulder. Neither bullet had touched any vital organs.

Nessa was in a private room by herself. A guard was posted at Nessa's door, but he let me in after Nessa okayed me.

"What the hell happened?" I asked as soon as we were alone in the room with the door closed.

"Oh, Harry, everything just came unraveled. It's so awful. Valerie and I went to see Melanie to get our wills redone. The next thing we knew we were arguing about problems in our relationship, mainly Valerie's insane possessiveness. Melanie tried to mediate. Before we knew it, Val and I were talking divorce."

"Nessa, did you and Melanie become involved?" I thought of Melanie's new secret lover.

"Look at me, Harry. Look me right in the eyes and listen to me. There is nothing between Melanie and me. She's my lawyer. Val was furious because Melanie was helping me start divorce proceedings."

"Okay. You don't have to get so pissed."

"I am pissed. The police asked me the same question for the better part of an hour."

"Did Valerie know about you and me?"

"What *you and me* are we talking about, Harry? She knew you owed me money and paid me back."

"Don't play stupid with me, Nessa. Someone's been following me around in a dark, midsized car."

"Oh shit, shit, shit." She breathed through clenched teeth.

"You told Valerie about us?"

"I might have said that we had dated in high school."

"Should I be keeping an eye out for her?"

"It wouldn't hurt, Harry. Sorry. I never meant any of this to happen. All I wanted was a no-fault divorce."

"Nessa, just remember, you're not the one who shot anybody."

"You're right. I hope Valerie has enough sense to turn herself in before anyone else gets hurt. If you see her, tell her I really care for her. Tell her the best thing she can do is turn herself in."

If I see her, I'm going to run like hell, I told myself.

I tried again to see Melanie, but they still weren't letting anyone visit her.

All the way home, I kept a keen eye out for Valerie Runge, Duane Morthwell, the skeleton-faced guy, and anyone else out there with a grudge. Driving around was getting much too complicated.

Alice's Jetta was parked in front of my place between a silver Porsche Targa coupe with vanity plates that said, "SPOYLT," and a purple Neon. I recognized the Porsche. It belonged to Alice's friend, Loretta. I couldn't recall seeing the Neon before.

Inside, I found three people naked on the bed in my bedroom. Alice and a dark-haired guy in his mid-twenties were sleeping soundly side by side with their heads toward the headboard. Loretta was turned the other way, lying on her stomach on top of the bed watching a foursome on the porn channel.

"Hi," she said, barely looking up. "You must be Harry. I'm Loretta, Alice's friend. We were going to wait for you and do a foursome, but then we did some Soma and things got a little hectic." She rolled on her side, revealing big breasts and a shaved crotch. "Alice said you liked unusual things. She really wants to please you. You want me to wake them?"

"I'll take a rain check. Who's the guy?"

"Norman, our Pilates instructor. Not much imagination but good staying power."

"Glad to hear that." I spied Alice's clothes and handbag on a chair in the corner and headed toward them.

"You have any dope?" Loretta asked.

"Some bud."

"No Soma?"

"No."

"Not interested." She rolled onto her belly again and watched TV while I rummaged through Alice's things looking for the High Standard .22.

"What are you looking for?" Loretta asked.

"Nothing."

"If you're looking for the gun, it's probably in Alice's coat in the hall closet."

"Thanks."

"Don't mention it. If you happen to find any Soma, come back."

I went to the closet and found the .22 with the silencer in Alice's coat pocket. The magazine had three shots left.

I retrieved the ammunition from my coat, went to the spare bedroom, closed the door, reloaded the gun, and read for several hours before finally falling asleep with the pistol under my pillow.

THURSDAY

The sound of someone entering my room woke me. Dawn had already broken. I was able to see fairly well in the dim light. Otherwise I might have shot Alice and asked questions later. I pretended to be asleep to see what she was up to. She went straight for my clothes and began rummaging through them.

"Is this what you're looking for?" I asked, holding up the gun.

"Actually, I was looking for my cell phone." She held it up along with the joint Clive had given me at Gina's party. Alice sat on the bed.

"Are your two friends still asleep?" I asked.

"They left. I have to be at rehearsal early this morning. You want to sleep with me or get some breakfast?" She lit the joint and took a hit, then handed it to me.

I took a toke. I could do breakfast alone. I opted for the quickie. For the first time I really started enjoying being in bed with Alice. She was— take your pick—very inventive and loved sex, or a great actress. I didn't care. We made love for an hour. We laughed a lot and finished with smiles on both of our faces.

I could get used to her, I told myself as we took a quick shower together.

Immediately afterward, I warned myself: Don't get addicted to her. Stay focused.

Over cups of instant coffee, I told her, "I tried to find you yesterday."

"You were trying to find your gun, Harry," she laughed. "To answer your question, I made a quick trip to Toronto to see the producer of the cable show."

"Did you get the part?"

"There were five or six better-known actors than me trying out for the part. We'll see." She finished her coffee, kissed me on the cheek, and headed to her car.

After she drove off, I drank another cup of instant coffee and checked the basketball scores. Boston had trounced Philly, but the Suns had beaten the Warriors. I was in the black but not by enough to solve my financial problems.

The shooting of Melanie and Nessa was still the top story on the car radio on the drive to work. Valerie Runge remained at large. I kept an eye out for her Honda and made sure I had easy access to my .22 at all times.

I arrived at the museum just after eight. Pilot had already let the construction guys in to work on the walls. I went to my office and phoned Frankie to see what looked good. The smart move would have been to take the money I had riding with Frankie and pay off Duane Morthwell, but with the pistol in my pocket again, I was feeling cocky. I decided to bet everything. I spread my bets over three NHL and two NBA games. Winning just three out of the five would pay for the roof and Morthwell with some room to spare.

Finally, I got out the list I had been toying with the day before. Something was nipping at the edge of my consciousness, just out of reach. I went over and over the notes, recounting the stories of Abe Reles, Bugsy Siegel, Albert Anastasia, Longy Zwillman, JFK, Sam Giancana, Jimmy Hoffa, Billy McCasters, and the others.

It took me a half hour before it finally jumped out at me.

I called Pilot into the office.

"I'm busy. I ain't got a lot of time for chitchat, sonny boy," he said, sitting down in the chair opposite me. I was glad to see he was back in his usual grumpy mood.

I waited until he had lit a new cigarette from the old butt, and then I said simply, "Jimmy."

"Jimmy?"

"Jimmy," I repeated. "Not Jenny. Not Ginnie. But *Okay, Jimmy. Not in the face.* That's what my father's been saying, isn't it?"

He puffed on his cigarette without answering.

Like a deer caught in the headlights, I thought.

"What does it mean, Pilot? Was my father involved with Jimmy Hoffa's disappearance? Did something go wrong? Is that what he keeps remembering?"

Pilot took the cigarette out of his mouth and looked at it as he rolled it between his yellowed fingers.

"Talk to me, Pilot. Were my father and grandfather hit men? Is MurderLand a front?"

"Your grandfather was a businessman. He owned a bar in New York. He came up here and opened the museum. When your father got old enough, he took over the museum."

"The bar belonged to Owney 'The Killer' Madden. Grandpa sold it and came here in 1942, shortly after Abe Reles flew out a Coney Island hotel window."

"What do you want me to say, sonny boy?"

"Just tell me the truth."

"And then what? Are you going to change the way you feel about your grandpa and your old man?"

"No."

"Then, why?"

"Closure."

"Let me ask you something, Harry. What if there is no heaven or hell, no afterlife, no reincarnation? What if everything you see right here is all there is, and if there is a God, he or she lets you and me do whatever we choose to do? If that's it, then maybe the only conclusion you can draw is that nothing you know really matters."

"I need to know, Pilot."

"Maybe you only think you need to know."

I started stabbing in the dark, trying to penetrate through his wall of obstinacy.

"What about the Jean Harlow charm bracelet, Pilot? Were my father and grandfather involved with Longy Zwillman's murder? Did they take the bracelet after Zwillman was hit?"

"Your father and grandfather never stole anything. Everything they ever had in the museum was bought or donated."

"But they killed people."

"Not my place to tell you that."

"What can you tell me? What did you mean the other day when we were talking about Abe 'Kid Twist' Reles, and you said, 'Nothing is ever what it appears to be'?"

"Now, *that* I can tell you," he said, taking the cigarette out of his mouth for a second to clear his throat. "How does a guy who's being guarded night and day by cops in a hotel room get hit?"

"Okay, how does he?"

He smiled just like he used to smile at me when he was telling me stories as a kid. "You get word to him through people he trusts that his boss, Anastasia, is about to hit him. Then you sneak in some wire to help him escape. He ties the sheets and the wire together to make a rope to climb down the wall of the hotel where he thinks people are waiting with a car to drive him away. Only, you see, Reles weighs at the time maybe a hundred and seventy or eighty pounds and the wire that's been smuggled in can only hold a hundred and thirty pounds."

"So it snaps, and he plunges five stories to the sub roof of the hotel and dies," I said.

"Lots of ways to skin a cat," he said, returning the cigarette to his lips.

"What about Anastasia? Crazy Joey Gallo claimed he and his brother shot him."

"You think anyone would give a contract like that to a big mouth like Crazy Joe?"

"What about Bugsy Siegel? Two or three people have come forward and claimed they were the shooters."

"Believe what you want."

"Do you know what really happened to Kennedy or Hoffa?"

"Listen, sonny boy, I told you enough. You're making me tired with all these questions and answers." He started to get to his feet. "Right now, I gotta go visit your father. I told him I'd come see him this morning."

"Better yet, I'll drive you." I started to get up.

"Down, boy. I don't need your help. I'm not that old. Besides, me and your father have things we need to talk about in private. Maybe if I'm still there when you arrive, I'll hitch a ride back, and we can talk some more."

"I'd like that."

He gave me a wave, a smile, and the thumbs-up sign and disappeared down the hallway.

Be patient, I told myself.

What other choice did I have? If I didn't find out the truth about the past from him, I'd never find out.

By ten thirty, I had let three calls from Wally Lavaleer go to voice mail. When I played back the messages, they were all reminding me that I needed to sign some papers regarding the building project. If I didn't sign, the project would be cancelled. I felt no sympathy for him.

I also called the hospital to check on Melanie. She was out of intensive care but still in serious condition. She was sleeping. I couldn't talk with her. I called the florist and had flowers sent to her and to Nessa.

Just before eleven, I went to the men's room before heading out to visit my father.

As soon as I entered the lavatory, I caught a whiff of something that didn't smell right. It made me think of burned flesh. There was no sign of anyone along the bank of sinks, but then I noticed Pilot's feet under the door of the middle stall. His pants were puddled around his ankles.

I had an instant creepy feeling.

"Hey, Pilot, I thought you left. Everything all right?"

No response.

"Pilot, you okay?" I tapped on the stall door.

Still no response.

I tried to see into the stall through the crack between the door and the frame, but all I could see was the far wall.

Shit, I thought.

I knew what to expect, but I still kept telling myself he must have fallen asleep as I opened the stall door beside him, climbed onto the toilet, and peered down.

CHAPTER 45

PILOT WAS SITTING ON THE TOILET SEAT with his back resting against the tank and his head back, staring at the ceiling with unblinking eyes.

I reached down and flicked open the latch to his stall. I ran around to the front of the stall and opened his door.

I felt for a pulse in his neck. There was none. There hadn't been a pulse for some time. He was cold.

The scorched flesh smell came from the burn marks on his mouth where the stub of his unfiltered cigarette had finally burned itself out. All that remained was a little nub of ash between his lips.

I walked to my office and called 9-1-1. Before the ambulance and cops arrived I hid my gun and returned to the restroom with a blanket, which I draped around him.

A couple of uniformed cops and two ambulance attendants showed up about five minutes later. They were followed by the coroner and my two favorite detectives, Sills and Mallard.

The coroner found an open envelope in the inside pocket of Pilot's MurderLand blazer. From the amount of wear on the envelope, he probably had been carrying it around for some time. The coroner opened the envelope and informed us it contained a copy of Pilot's will.

"Looks like you're the executor and beneficiary of Mr. Pringle's estate, Harry," Sills informed me after the coroner passed the will to him.

Pilot's will instructed me to contact the medical school where he planned to donate his body. I returned to my office and called the number in the will. I was connected immediately to the chief administrator of the program. She knew who Felix Pringle was even before I gave her the reference number in the will. "Mr. Pringle has been calling us regularly for the past six months, telling us he was going to die soon. Everyone in the department knew him. He was a charming man. He called at least once, sometimes twice a week to make sure we were still accepting the remains of our donors for use in our own teaching program. We needed to reassure him every time that we don't sell or donate body parts to other institutions or businesses. We'll miss his calls. I'm sorry for your loss."

Since Pilot indicated in his documents at the medical school and in his will that he wanted no ceremony or monument, the administrator said they would take care of everything.

By twelve thirty, the police, ambulance workers, coroner, and Pilot's body were gone.

I was less than numb. More like empty. After retrieving my gun, I stopped by Tony's to pick up the sandwiches for my father. I tried to act like nothing had happened. On the drive to the nursing home, Pilot's death finally caught up with me. My eyes suddenly and unexpectedly filled with tears. I felt like a giant fist was squeezing my throat. I pulled to the side of the road until the crying jag passed.

Clive was on duty when I arrived. The whites of his eyes were the color of tomato juice. He was so hungover he couldn't even look at his sandwich or talk much above a mumble.

I spent my time talking to Dad. I didn't have the heart to tell him Pilot was gone. So, I talked about how the ice was breaking up on the river and spring was coming. When I listened to him whispering back, I was certain he was saying, "Okay, Jimmy, not in the face."

"What could possibly be going through your mind?" I asked, running my hand gently over his head. Why had this particular event been the one that had stuck in his mind? Something must have gone terribly wrong.

Instead of returning straight to the museum, I stopped at Pilot's apartment.

I took the ancient elevator to the third floor. I used the keys the police had taken from Pilot's pocket to open his door, which, a little surprisingly, was protected with two heavy-duty security locks. *Surprisingly*—because I couldn't imagine he had anything worth stealing.

The apartment had a slightly musty smell. All the old stuffed furniture and hunting trophies I remembered from my childhood were still there.

On his desk was a letter addressed to me that said simply:

Dear Harry,

If you are reading this, then chances are I'm dead or incapacitated. Your grandfather and father were the only family I ever cared about. So I want you to have everything. Enjoy.

And remember, the secret of happiness is: Lower your expectations.

A rich man's someone who believes he has more than he needs no matter what he has.

A poor man's someone who believes he hasn't enough no matter how much he has.

Don't waste your life chasing other people's dreams.

Pilot

Unlike his will, which had been dated two years before, and signed with a firm signature, this note was in spidery handwriting and had been dated on the night he had helped me get rid of the bodies of Big Mo and Goose. The thought that he might have had a premonition of his own imminent death sent shivers down my spine.

In an accordion file folder inside his desk, I found an insurance policy made out to me for one hundred thousand dollars, a bank statement showing savings of fifty-six thousand dollars, and brokerage statements, the most recent of which showed he had a portfolio worth one million eight hundred and sixty-five thousand dollars. I was an instant millionaire.

In three other folders I found his brokerage receipts going back to the 1970s, showing how he had been investing small amounts at a time, presumably out of each paycheck, investing in winners and dumping the losers.

He had also saved the birthday cards, Christmas cards, and thank-you notes that my mother, and later, the more thoughtful housekeepers, had forced me to write for the presents he gave me. He even had a complete collection of my school photos.

He also had family photos of my grandfather, grandmother, my parents, and me as a kid, many of which I was seeing for the first time.

In a bottom drawer was a large collection of hammered and milled English gold coins—the oldest guineas were from the reign of Henry VII, the newest from William and Mary. The gold alone was worth a small fortune.

In a fireproof box under the desk, I found the original of his will as well as sixty-five thousand in Canadian cash.

I was awed not only by the amount of the money he had accumulated but by the sentiment and wisdom hidden behind his old crusty façade. I had to stop and wipe tears from my eyes more than once.

In the spare bedroom, Pilot had created a laboratory with a sink and water piped in from the bathroom on the other side of the wall. The room contained his taxidermy equipment. In one corner, I found an old oak cabinet with narrow drawers. In each drawer were glass eyeballs of different sizes for fish, game, and human mannequins. Along the inside wall was an oak and glass bookcase with books on taxidermy on the two top shelves. On the bottom shelves were two dozen carefully labeled bell jars of various sizes with various body parts and organs. I found six more shrunken heads. Three of the heads were labeled as actual Jivaro trophies. Three were his creations from cadaver parts he purchased. At the back, in another jar, floating in formaldehyde like a large white worm was the penis of John Dillinger, Public Enemy Number One, just as it had appeared in the photos that Pilot had shown me.

The first thing I noticed when I entered his bedroom was the view through the window. I could look over the rooftops and see straight to the front entrance to the convenience store where Johnny Johnson had been shot.

Had Pilot actually witnessed the comings and goings of Duane Morthwell and me that night?

It was another question that I couldn't help asking but would never be answered.

The second thing I noticed was a burgundy and blue pearl bowling ball sitting in an ashtray on top of an old oak highboy dresser like it was a piece of sculpture. The ball was a surprise because I had never heard Pilot mention an interest in bowling.

I picked up the ball out of curiosity. I tried to put my fingers into the holes but found something blocking one of them.

It was a piece of rolled-up paper. I used my little finger to grab it and coax it out.

It turned out to be a note written on a quarter of a page of the same manila notepaper and in the same spidery hand as the note Pilot had left me on his desk. It said simply:

The proof is _not_ in the pudding, sonny boy.

"The proof is in the eating of the pudding." Cervantes, Don Quixote.

No salutation or signature appeared on the note as if he knew I would find it.

What the hell kind of proof was a burgundy and blue pearl bowling ball anyway?

Or was the bowling ball just there to get my attention so I'd find the note?

I examined the ball, trying to glean some additional information. Pilot's name was imprinted where the manufacturer's name would normally appear, suggesting he had it custom made or somehow made it himself. Otherwise, it appeared to be just what it was—a bowling ball.

The bedroom was spartanly furnished. In addition to the dresser, it contained only a small bookcase, a wooden chair, a neatly made bed with a blue bedspread, a nightstand with an analog clock radio from the 1960s, and an ashtray with a single, stubbed out unfiltered butt.

The closet was half full of slacks, shirts, MurderLand blazers, and shoes. On the top shelf were three old Samsonite hard-shell suitcases. The dresser contained socks, hankies, underwear, and sweaters—all neatly folded. A wooden box sat under some socks in a corner of the top drawer. Inside the box were old gold signet rings, tie clips, cuff links, and a Hamilton wristwatch dating from the 1940s. Beside the box was a Kodak Duaflex IV medium format camera.

The bookcase contained some real surprises. Mixed in with old paperbacks of westerns and mysteries were several pristine hardcover first editions by Ernest Hemingway, Mark Twain, and F. Scott Fitzgerald. When I pulled the copy of *The Adventures of Huckleberry Finn* from the shelf, a large manila envelope sitting beside it slipped out and fell to the floor.

I picked up the envelope, opened it, and pulled out a large black-and-white photo.

I recognized the scene immediately. It was a crystal clear shot of the Kennedy motorcade with JFK and Jackie plainly visible and smiling. It was from an angle that I had never seen before—from the grassy knoll looking across Dealey Plaza.

On the other side of the car was a clear photo of the Babushka Lady. She was smiling and holding a camera chest high in one hand. I felt my head spin as I looked at her face and recognized her. At almost the same instant, I noticed something hanging from the collar of her coat. Even without a magnifying glass I could tell it was a hexagon pendant watch.

CHAPTER 46

I NEEDED ANSWERS, and only one person could give them to me.

I slipped the photo into the envelope, locked the apartment, and drove to Virgil.

Betsy Stein's Chrysler was parked in the driveway in front of the carport. I parked behind it, walked to the front door, and rang the bell.

"Oh, Harry, hello again," Betsy greeted me cautiously. "Is everything all right? Has something happened to your father? You don't look well."

"Pilot just died."

"Oh, I'm so sorry. Would you like to come in?"

I nodded and went through the door, catching a hint of her cheery bubble bath scent. I forced myself to fight back new tears.

"Can I get you a tea or coffee?" she asked.

"No, thank you. I just need to talk."

I followed her into the living room, carrying the envelope with the photo. We sat in the same seats as last time.

"What happened, Harry? On your last visit, you said Pilot was still working. It must have been very sudden."

I gave her a quick rundown of the day's events.

"It must have been a terrible shock for you," she said sympathetically.

"The strangest part was this," I said, taking the photo out of the envelope and handing it to her. "I found it at his apartment."

She held the photo carefully by the edges and looked down at it for what felt like an eternity.

"That's you, isn't it? You're the Babushka Lady. On your lapel, that's the pendant watch that you said was my mother's."

She looked up. "But I did give it to your mother years afterward. She always admired it. She wore it until she lost it. Just like I said."

I slipped the .22 out of my coat pocket and laid it carefully on the coffee table between us. "When I found the gun and the pendant together, I thought someone had accidentally placed them with each other by mistake. But it wasn't an accident. They belonged together."

Betsy sighed. Her eyebrows went up slightly as she looked down at the gun.

"Was the gun also my mother's? Was she involved in my father's *other* business?"

She gave me a small, sweet smile. "No, Harry. This was my weapon. As far as I know, your mother never knew anything about your father's other business."

"But you did."

"It was a long time ago," she said softly.

"I need to know."

"What exactly do you want to know, Harry?"

"Were you and my grandfather and my father involved in the Kennedy assassination? Was Billy McCasters? Was Pilot?"

She nodded. "But not in any way you could imagine."

"What's that supposed to mean?"

"Wait here a moment," she said as she got to her feet. "I want to show you something."

She disappeared down the hallway and returned two minutes later carrying a large manila envelope and a magnifying glass. She sat down and pulled her own black-and-white photo out of the envelope, turned Pilot's photo toward me, and placed the second photo beside it.

The second photo was another shot of the motorcade taken from about where I imagined the Babushka Lady to be standing. JFK and Jackie were both smiling.

"Did you take this?" I asked.

She nodded and handed me the magnifying glass. She pointed to the top of the photo on the other side of the president's car and said, "Look here."

Through the magnifier, I could see the four men on the grassy knoll on the other side of the motorcade.

On the right was a short, thin man with a camera in front of his face—presumably taking the photo of the Babushka Lady that I'd uncovered at Pilot's.

Next to him was a man in his forties with a medium build, dark hair, and arms folded over his chest. He looked a lot like Billy McCasters.

Next to him stood a third man with his right hand extended in front of him, giving a thumbs-up sign, and an older man on the far left with his hands in his pockets.

"My father and grandfather," I said in a low voice, pointing to the last two.

"Yes." She pointed to the man in the middle and then the one with the camera. "And Billy McCasters and Pilot."

"They were there. On the grassy knoll. Were they part of the assassination plot?"

"They went there to stop it."

"I don't understand."

"Do you know who Sam Giancana was?"

"Yes."

"And James Hoffa?"

"Yes."

"You know how much they hated Kennedy and why?"

"They both hated him because they'd helped get Kennedy elected, and they felt he'd double-crossed them by letting his brother, Bobby, the attorney general, prosecute them."

"Hoffa believed that if Kennedy was killed, Nixon could be drafted to run in '64. Hoffa's people were already deeply enmeshed with Nixon's people. Giancana wasn't satisfied just being the top dog of the Midwest. He wanted to be top dog of the National Crime Syndicate. The boss of bosses. It was a power play. He wanted Kennedy out. Hoffa convinced Giancana that Nixon would run, and Nixon could be bought and stay bought. Once the two of them set the ball in motion to eliminate Kennedy, they had no trouble recruiting willing participants."

"Such as?" I asked.

"Everyone, Harry. They recruited Florida mob boss, Santos Trafficante, who brought in his pal, Carlos Marcello, the head of the New

Orleans mob. They had an army of men to draw on—wise guys in the crime syndicates who wanted to become made men, angry Cubans and rogue CIA operatives who had lost relatives and friends in the Bay of Pigs fiasco, and assorted misfits like Lee Harvey Oswald who were trying to worm their way into the intelligence community, the mob, or both. Everyone wanted in on the action."

"Was Nixon involved?" I asked.

"I don't know. Nixon was in Dallas for a board meeting. I heard Giancana tried to keep Nixon there by arranging a lunch with one of his associates, but Nixon flew out at the last minute."

"Who tried to stop it?"

"Meyer Lansky. He was furious when he found out that Giancana had gone ahead on his own."

"Lansky called my father?"

"Lansky called Owney Madden."

"The guy my grandfather bought the bar from in New York. I thought he had retired."

"It's difficult to retire in this business. Owney was still involved. He was running casinos in Arkansas. Owney called your grandfather. Your father, Pilot, and I were part of your grandfather's crew. Lansky sent people in from all over the country to try to shut it down. We were sent to find McCasters on the grassy knoll and stop him. We were successful. Nicholas Delmore of Newark sent a crew to stop the Corsicans who were hiding in the sewers. Frank DeSimone sent guys from Los Angeles to stop the Cubans who were set up under the triple underpass. Gambino got to Marcello in New Orleans, and Marcello put in a call to Joe Civello, his underboss who ran the operations in Dallas. Civello sent out two crews to stop two of the renegade CIA guys from New Orleans who were supposed to take up positions in the Dal-Tex building across from the Texas Book Depository. Finally, there was Jack Ruby."

"So Ruby was involved."

"He was one of Civello's boys. Civello personally called Ruby, and Ruby sent his two best guys to stop the crazy kid Oswald in the depository building."

"But something went wrong."

"Ruby's boys got caught in traffic. They got there late. When they did arrive, Oswald wasn't where he was supposed to be."

"So my father was giving the thumbs-up sign because he thought everything was all right."

"We all did. No one ever thought Oswald, with that old Mannlicher-Carcano, could hit the broadside of a barn.

"But he did."

"Yes, he did."

"And he was the sole shooter?"

"Yes."

"And was Ruby ordered to kill him?"

"I don't know."

"But you do know that McCasters was taken out because he could have exposed what really happened."

She nodded.

"And my father did that?"

She sighed. "Everyone involved knew how it worked, Harry. After Kennedy was killed, anybody involved either kept their mouth shut or was silenced. It isn't difficult to understand. No one could change what had happened. Nobody wanted the story to come out. The best thing was to get on with other business. Most of the people connected to the fiasco understood."

"But not Hoffa and not Giancana."

"They thought they could play both sides against the middle. In 1975, the House Select Committee on Assassinations had its eye on both Giancana and Hoffa. They'd both been hinting to friends and acquaintances that they knew something about the Kennedy assassination and might want to trade it to the Feds in exchange for amnesty for any pending charges against them."

"Were my father and grandfather involved in taking out Sam Giancana?"

She nodded.

"And Hoffa?"

"Yes," she said softly.

"Were you there?"

"I was there when we picked up Hoffa. He thought he was meeting with people who were taking his contract to hit Frank Fitzsimmons, the president of the Teamsters and the man who he thought had helped Nixon deceive him."

"Something happened. Something that my father can't get out of his mind." I explained that he seemed to be repeating over and over, "Okay, Jimmy, not in the face."

"All I can tell you is that Hoffa took a swing at your father as we were driving away from the shopping center. Your father hit him back. Hoffa had a bloody nose. Your father calmed him down. Once Hoffa realized there was nothing he could do to escape his fate, he asked your father, 'Not in the face, okay?' He was probably already thinking about the viewing at the funeral hall. When we changed cars, he was still alive. I drove home with one of the other members of our crew. Your father, Pilot, and two others drove off toward the airport with Hoffa."

"Do you know what happened to Hoffa's body?"

"No."

"How did this all get started? How did my grandfather and father get into this business of contract killing? What happened?"

"How does anything get started? It's hard to say. Way back in the 1930s when Owney Madden still owned the bar in New York on Eighth Avenue along with the Cotton Club, and your grandfather was one of his bartenders, Owney asked your grandfather to help out his old friend, Longy Zwillman. Zwillman's girlfriend, Jean Harlow, was having trouble with husband number two, an older, well-connected gentleman named Paul Bern. Bern was impotent. He used to beat Harlow whenever he tried and failed to have sex. Harlow was afraid that Bern would keep his promise to ruin her career if she walked out. He couldn't have. She was already too famous to touch, but Bern was an important man with Irving Thalberg and pulled a lot of weight around Hollywood. She was a kid. She believed what he told her. Your grandfather was someone who was smart and resourceful. They sent him to Hollywood."

"And he made Bern's death look like a suicide."

"Your grandfather had a talent, Harry. He did what he did well. He left confusion. That's the key to a good hit. People are probably still talking about some of the hits he worked on."

"Like Reles, Siegel, and Anastasia?"

She nodded. "Reles had information that would put Anastasia in the electric chair. Benny Siegel was out of control. He was stealing from the syndicate. He had been warned several times to stop. Anastasia wanted to take over Meyer Lansky's Cuban operations and was about to start a war between the families."

"And Zwillman? Was he another alleged suicide that wasn't?"

"Zwillman was working on a deal with federal prosecutors. He was about to name names. He knew how the business worked."

I glanced down at the two photos.

"It's like playing God," I said.

"Doing what we did?"

"Yes, and having this information in your hands and not letting anyone know what really happened."

"Harry, we're all little gods in our own way. We redraw the lines in the sand that we will or won't step over. We follow the rules we choose to follow and break the ones that suit us—whether it's little things like driving too fast and endangering someone else's life, or cheating or deceiving another person, or when one nation eats itself into collective obesity while hundreds of millions in other countries go to sleep hungry. We all draw our own little lines in the sand, deciding where it's all right to step and not step."

"Do you ever feel guilty?"

"The only time anyone feels guilty is when they step over a line they've drawn for themselves. How else could we make sense of a world where a few hundred thousand people are killed by a tsunami or a few thousand are killed by an earthquake, and we flood them with aid, but many more are dying from wars, famine, and sickness all the time, every minute of the day, and we barely notice? How else can we worship books and movies filled with violence and frivolousness and all the rest that cross one person's line but not another's line? We justify. We offer our own interpretation of justice. We create our own reality."

"But you could change history," I said. Betsy had tied up the loose ends to just about every theory out there in the mother of all conspiracies. "You could set the record straight on the Kennedy assassination once and for all."

"No, Harry, even if I told my story, the water is too muddied now with lies and pseudo-facts for anyone to believe the truth. Besides, Americans love their myths and conspiracies. They need them. It's part of what makes them happy. In the end, there's nothing you can do to change the past, Harry. You can only go forward."

She picked up the gun by the barrel and handed it to me. "This belongs to you, now, Harry. I don't want anything to do with guns anymore."

For a second, I saw over those rosy apple cheeks, through the wire rim glasses, and into her pretty blue eyes. Underneath the sugar and spice was the steely look of a woman I would not want to meet in a dark alley with a gun in her hand.

And yet at the same time, I was strangely drawn to her.

CHAPTER 47

AFTER MY VISIT WITH BETSY, I returned to Pilot's and began moving the important papers and most valuable items to my car. I took the cash, gold coins, bank books, brokerage statements, insurance policy, the original will, Pilot's notes to me, his jewelry and watch, several books from his library, the Jivaro heads, the Dillinger trophy, and the bowling ball. I planned to send the movers in the next few days for the rest and store everything in the basement of MurderLand until I could figure out my next move.

By the time I reached the museum, the roofers were just finishing for the day. I checked my messages and found a half dozen from Wally. I ignored them and unloaded the car. I tucked all my booty away in the storage area in the gift shop but kept the bowling ball with me because its quirkiness made me think of Pilot. I emptied an ashtray and used it as a stand for the ball, giving it the most prominent spot on my desk.

I was just finishing when the front door buzzer sounded. I expected it to be Wally Lavaleer.

It turned out to be Reggie Baker.

"Hey, you hear the news?" he asked.

"What news?"

"You got any of that good scotch left?"

I thought about turning him away, but after all I'd been through, I decided I could use a stiff drink, too. I led him to my office, poured us both tumblers of my father's best, and clinked glasses with him.

"Did you hear that Pilot died this morning?" I asked.

"Yeah," he said before downing half his glass in one gulp. "He used to scare the crap out of me and my friends when we were kids. Said, if we tried to steal anything, he'd put an ice pick in our ears and scramble our brains."

I held up the ice pick that had belonged to my grandfather. "He meant it."

Baker nodded reverently. "Amen. May he rest in peace." He tossed back the rest of his liquor and poured himself a refill.

"What's the big news?"

"The police spotted Valerie Runge driving near the hospital. Police thought she was probably casing the joint, getting ready to go in and try to finish the job. They gave chase. They cornered her down by the falls. She emptied her gun at them. She didn't hit anyone, but she managed to reach the rail, climb over, and jump off the cliff before anyone could grab her. They're still hunting for her body." He took a gulp of scotch. "Unless of course, she made it over the falls alive."

"Even if she did, she'd die of hypothermia in this weather."

He smiled. "I'm counting on them not finding the body."

Through his glazed eyes, I could imagine the wheels turning in Baker's head as he contemplated milking this story for weeks, if not months.

"And that's not even the best part." He smiled so broadly I could see his receding gums.

"There's more?"

He drained his glass and filled it again, insisting on clinking it against mine, which was still half full from my first pour.

"Forensics did an analysis of the bullets they took out of Nessa Wiley and Melanie Wickers, and guess what? They matched the fatal bullets from the gun that killed your stepmother. Now, what do you make of that?"

CHAPTER 48

I DIDN'T KNOW WHAT TO THINK. I was shocked. How could the gun Valerie Runge used to shoot Melanie and Nessa be connected to the murder of my stepmother—a murder that I had so carefully planned? It made no sense. "Are you sure?"

"Yeah, I'm sure. And get this. They've recovered one of the bullets from the gun that Valerie Runge used this afternoon to fire at police. It's a 9 millimeter. The cops are sure it's from her service weapon—a Glock—which they believe she took with her over the falls. So, how does your stepmother hook up with Valerie Runge?"

"Wasn't one of the bullets that shot my stepmother from a 9 millimeter?" I asked.

"Yeah. But not a Glock. A different gun. Probably a Chinese knockoff of a Russian piece. They haven't found that weapon yet."

What was I missing, I wondered. Did Duane dump the Russian gun somewhere after he shot Carlene?

Think.

"Valerie Runge was one of the first officers on the scene when I found my stepmother's body. Maybe she found the murder weapon at the scene and pocketed it," I suggested.

He nodded. "That's one idea the police are kicking around. They figure she may have already been planning to shoot her wife and their lawyer."

"That must be it."

"Maybe it isn't that simple. I'm trying to find a connection between your stepmother and Valerie Runge."

Behind the bleary eyes, I could see the look of a predator. Baker was on a hunting trip. He just wanted a story. If he could tie me into it, then, so much the better.

"I haven't a clue how Constable Runge and Carlene could be acquainted."

"Hmmm," he said doubtfully.

Tiny bits of information were trying to hook up in my brain. Maybe I did know more than I thought. The really weird part was trying to imagine a connection between Valerie Runge and Duane Morthwell.

My head reeled. Something Pilot said came back to haunt me: "Nothing is ever what it appears to be."

"Have you spoken with either of Runge's two victims?" I asked.

"You mean your high school girlfriend and your lawyer? Call me naïve, Harry, but you seem to be one of the missing links in this story."

Baker had done his homework. I didn't bother to confirm or deny his assumptions. I waited for him to answer my original question.

We played the staring game for a minute before he answered. "I haven't spoken with either of them, but I heard from the police that neither of your two friends have any idea how Runge is connected to your stepmother." His voice oozed cynicism.

"If I hear more," I said, re-corking the bottle, "I'll be sure to let you know. I have to get to work. It's been a rough day losing Pilot."

"Yeah, sure. No problem. Thanks for the drink. Sorry about your friend." He finished what was left in his glass. I walked him to the front door and locked it behind him.

I tried to work, but my head kept returning to what Baker had just told me. How the hell had Valerie Runge ended up with the gun that shot Carlene?

As I expected, Sills and Mallard showed up late in the afternoon and asked me what I knew about the connections between Valerie, Nessa, Melanie, and Carlene. I told them I didn't know anything, and they left. I put in another hour, trying to catch up on paperwork, but I was way too distracted by the thoughts of a possible connection between Valerie and Carlene to get much done. I decided to pack it in for the day. I set the alarm and headed out the rear door into the dark parking lot.

I should have been paying more attention.

I was halfway to my car when I heard a familiar voice ask, "What's your hurry?"

I turned around to see Wally Lavaleer and another man standing in the mouth of the driveway no more than twenty feet away. A dark van had been backed into the driveway, blocking the view to the street.

The guy beside Lavaleer was holding a baseball bat in one hand.

I had only seen the second man once, and only for a moment, but I immediately recognized him.

He was the skeleton-faced asshole with the dark, scraggily hair in the dark Ford van, who had nearly run me off the road three nights before.

"I'm really busy right now, Wally. Maybe another time." I took a step toward my car. The skeleton-faced man took a couple of quick steps, positioning himself between me and my car.

"You really should hear what I have to say, Harry," Wally said.

"I don't think we have anything to talk about."

"Maybe not." His smile widened. "Then, again, maybe we should discuss your relationship with a certain Mr. Duane Morthwell."

Morthwell? *Shit.* Lavaleer definitely had my attention, though I tried not to show it. "Who?"

"Harry, don't play stupid with me." He gestured toward the skeleton-faced man. "Gunnar didn't try running you off the road the other night for the fun of it. If I could have gotten rid of you, it would have cleared the way for my hotel deal. But...well, mistakes do happen."

Gunnar nodded.

Lavaleer continued. "Since then, however, circumstances have changed, particularly after a visit from Mr. Morthwell, who you claim not to know. You still don't want to talk?"

"I'll listen, but it's just the two of us. Okay?"

"Okay. Gunnar, stand by the van. Keep an eye on things from there."

Gunnar nodded without expression.

I waited until Gunnar was out of hearing range. "So, tell me what's on your mind, Wally."

"I'll do better than that, Harry. I'll tell you a story. A few days ago, a guy called my office and said he wanted to make an appointment with me. He wouldn't tell me his problem over the phone. On a whim, I decided to see him. In walked this loser who told me he had a sealed package that he wanted me to hold onto. I should keep it sealed and only turn it over to the police if something happened to him. I asked him what was in it. He wouldn't say. All he wanted to know was how much it would cost him. I told him a price; he paid me and left."

"And you opened the envelope."

"Harry, Harry, Harry. A perfect stranger walks into my office, hands me a sealed package, and tells me not to open it. It could have been a disgruntled client dropping off a bomb. I *had* to open it."

No response from me.

"You know what was inside?" he asked.

Still no response from me.

"An audiocassette, Harry. I had a bitch of a time finding someone with an old audiotape machine that would play it, but I finally did. As soon as I played it and heard your sweet voice, I knew I had struck gold. I had proof you planned Carlene's murder. My problems with you were over, unless of course you'd rather let Gunnar finish what he started."

"So, what do you want?"

"I tried to explain to you, Harry. I have some papers for you to sign. My only interest is making sure the deal with the hotel goes through. And you know what? I'm going to make sure that you get Carlene's cut. No hard feelings, Harry. You'll walk me to Gunnar's van right now and sign the papers, and that's that."

"And if I don't?"

"I'll turn you over to Gunnar." He tilted his head toward his thug. Gunnar must have caught the sound of his name. He raised his chin and took a few steps in our direction. Wally held up his hand and Gunnar stopped.

I wanted Gunnar closer.

"I guess you got me, Wally." I started walking toward Gunnar.

"I guess I do."

"I can see where you're coming from. It makes sense," I said.

"Yes, it does."

I stopped only a few yards from Gunnar. If I kept my voice low, he was still just out of hearing range. "Now that we're going to be partners, do you mind answering a question?"

"If I can." Wally gave me one of his fake smiles.

"Did you have anything to do with the hit on my father?"

He thought about that for a few seconds, and then finally said, "That was Carlene's idea, Harry. Once she realized how she could cash in, she got creative."

"But you helped."

"I made the arrangements with Gunnar. I shouldn't be telling you this, but I want you to realize that I'm serious about the hotel deal. What happened with your father, and the arrangement I'm working out with you, is nothing personal. It's strictly business."

The image of my father lying helpless in his bed for the past six months smoldered in my brain.

I smiled. I didn't bother to reply. I slipped the .22 out of my pocket and pumped two shots into Gunnar's chest and two in his face, dropping him like a steer in a slaughterhouse.

CHAPTER 49

"WHAT HAVE YOU DONE? What have you done, what have you done?" Wally wailed. He fell backward trying to backpedal away from me. He landed in a sitting position and started to get up.

"Stop," I said, pointing the gun at him.

He stayed on the ground, holding his hands in front of him like he was hoping they could stop a bullet. "You're crazy, you're crazy, you're crazy. Don't hurt me, don't hurt me, don't hurt me," he moaned. "I'll do anything you say."

"Quiet, Wally, or I'll kill you."

"You don't have to do that. I'm in this as deep as you are. We can work something out. I can help you."

"Please be quiet."

"You're going to kill me, aren't you?"

"If you don't shut up, I will. I'd prefer that you just get up and help me move your friend."

I motioned with the gun for him to get up.

"You don't have to hold the gun on me."

I didn't answer.

Gunnar was lying on his back with his eyes open, staring at the sky. A trickle of blood ran from the two bullet holes in his face down the side of his cheek.

I was sure he was dead, but I put another bullet into his head to impress Wally.

"I think I'm going to be sick," Wally announced. He bent over and gagged, but nothing came out.

When he was finished, I told him, "Pick up your friend and stuff him in the back of the van."

He looked at me like I was crazy.

"Do it. Now."

He gagged twice more but managed to get his reflexes under control. He grabbed Gunnar under the arms and dragged him to the rear of the van. I opened the rear doors on the van and stood to one side as Wally dumped the body in back.

I picked up the baseball bat and tossed it on top of the body.

"You're going to kill me, aren't you?" Wally wanted an answer. I suspected he was trying to read me and decide whether to make a run for it, take a swing at me, or wait me out.

I tried calming him down so he wouldn't do anything stupid.

"Relax, Wally. What I need from you right now is a little cooperation."

"What do you want me to do?"

"I want the tape Duane Morthwell gave you and any copies you made."

"Once you get your hands on it, you'll kill me."

"If I kill you right now, what do you think the chances are that anyone would find the tape among all your files? If they found it, what are the odds they'd figure out what it is? And even if they figured out what's on the tape, you'd still be dead. Your best chance of coming out on the right side of this is to give me the tape. Where is the tape?"

"It's at my office."

"And the copies?"

"I didn't make any copies."

"We'll talk about that."

"I swear, Harry, I didn't make any copies. I did make a mistake. I underestimated you. All I want is to forget any of this ever happened. What do you want me to do?

"Get in the van. Drive."

I got in the jump seat in back where I could keep an eye on him and wouldn't be seen from the street. He drove to his office like he was taking his driver's exam. I made him park in the lane that ran behind his building.

At my insistence, he disabled the security system before we entered his building. We walked up the rear stairs.

Inside his office, I watched over his shoulder as he opened a safe and took out the envelope with the tape in it.

I made Wally play the tape. It lasted only a few minutes. It didn't show me in the best light, but without Morthwell's half of the conversation, it was pretty wobbly.

"Tell me, Wally, out of curiosity, what did you have planned for Morthwell? Was Gunnar going to get rid of him?"

He nodded. "Yes. Can I ask you a question?"

"Sure."

"Are you intending to kill Morthwell? If you are, maybe I could help as a gesture of loyalty."

"I'll deal with Morthwell. Right now, we need to take care of the van and Gunnar's body."

I took the tape recorder and the tape. On the way out, I repeated my immediate concern. "I'm thinking you must have made one copy."

"I didn't make any copies, Harry. I told you."

We returned to the van. I got in back. He drove.

I gave him directions while he worked at convincing me I shouldn't shoot him.

"I'm an accessory to a homicide," he told me. "Even if I made a deal with the police, I would be disbarred. My life would be ruined. I want what you want. I'll do anything you say. Name it. I'll break the deal with the hotel people and make sure you come out with a profit. You're a businessman, Harry. Think about it."

I pretended to think about it for a minute before telling him, "I imagine there are a lot of ways we could do business together."

"So, you and I are okay?" His eyes were bright with hope.

"We're okay, Wally. Unless of course I find out that you have a copy of the tape somewhere. I'm a businessman. I understand risk. But you need to understand that, too."

"Harry, don't even go there. That's the only copy."

I kept him heading north along streets with little traffic.

"Where are we taking Gunnar?" He sounded more relaxed. I liked that.

"I'll show you. We'll be there soon."

"I'm glad we're working together, Harry. I can be a real help to you. Business is business. Right, Harry."

"Whatever you say, Wally."

Close to the edge of town, I had him turn into the driveway of old industrial building that sat in a small field. The field backed onto thick woods. The property was for sale. The building was boarded up. I told Wally to drive to the back parking lot close to the woods.

He parked in the handicap spot near the rear entrance to the building, and said, "If you're thinking of burying him in these woods, I know a much better place."

At that moment I was thinking about my father lying helpless in his bed, an image that I could never forget. I was wondering whether I needed to explain that to Wally. It made me angry in a cool, detached way.

"Wally, I want you to know this isn't business. This is strictly personal."

I shot him three times in the head before he realized what was happening.

I recalled something Freud was supposed to have said: "There are no laws against touching fire because the burn is a sufficient deterrent. There are laws against murder because...well, it's pleasurable, at least to some killers."

It didn't feel pleasurable to me. It felt like nothing.

It's done, I thought as I checked to make sure Wally was dead.

After I retrieved the spent cartridges and the documents he had wanted me to sign, I headed toward the museum. It would have been nice to have someone like Pilot to drive me back, but he was gone, and I had no one else. I had to improvise and hope for the best. I walked back with the documents, the tape, and small recorder in my pocket. I stuck to streets where I would be least likely to be noticed. I kept out of the headlights of the few cars that passed by. It took me an hour to reach the museum, dispose of the tape and documents, retrieve my car, and head home.

CHAPTER 50

ALICE'S JETTA WAS PARKED IN FRONT OF MY PLACE.

Alice was in the bedroom. She was wearing a blanket and sitting cross-legged in the middle of my bed. In one hand, she was holding a script, and in the other, a glass of white wine. She looked up as soon as I entered the room, closed the script, and put it on the nightstand.

"Been here long?" I asked.

"Couple of hours. How was your day?"

"The usual. And yours?"

"All right." She smiled, holding up her wine glass. "You want me to get you a glass?"

"I can use yours." I hopped on the bed beside her. I took a drink from her glass. "Where are your friends?"

"Probably at home doing nothing. Want me to call them?"

"No."

"Would you like to see what I did?" she asked bright-eyed.

"Sure."

She opened the blanket, leaned back, and spread her legs like a frog. She had shaved off her pubic hair.

"Nice."

"I thought you'd like it. Loretta said you couldn't keep your eyes off hers. You want to touch it?"

I smiled.

She pulled my head between her legs.

An hour later, after we were finished making love, she raised herself on one elbow, and said, "There's something I should tell you."

"You're taking the job in Vancouver."

"Hmmm. How did you know?"

"You were reading a script. When do you leave?"

"Next week. But I have to go to Toronto tomorrow to take care of a few things."

"What did Derek say?"

She giggled. "He freaked. He never liked me. Now, he's acting like I'm ripping his heart out."

"He'll get over it."

"You can come visit me sometime if you want." She toyed under the blanket with what was left of my dick.

"Maybe."

"Think about it."

"Okay."

"Let's cuddle."

A very strange day, I thought as we snuggled under the covers. My oldest friend had died. I'd inherited a bundle. I'd found out I come from a long line of killers. I'd shot two people to death. I had avenged the hit on my father. I had been sober for most of the day. And the most beautiful young woman in the world was about to disappear from my life, and I knew in my heart I had to let her go. She was better off without me.

Was this what it felt like to grow up, I wondered.

CHAPTER 51

FRIDAY

ALICE HAD TO LEAVE EARLY, so we were up before dawn drinking instant coffee when Detectives Sills and Mallard arrived.

A dog walker had discovered the van and the two bodies hours after I left the scene. The police had been investigating all night.

Alice was shocked.

I pretended to be shocked.

The other body belonged to Gunnar T. Hyde, a mink farmer and owner of a body shop outside of town.

Alice had never heard of the other man.

I told them I had never heard of him either.

Alice and I gave alibis for each other.

They wanted to know what I knew about the hotel deal. I told them what Lavaleer told me. I explained that I had opposed the deal from the beginning. I never met any of the other people involved in the project. As soon as Carlene died and I regained control of my father's estate, I gave notice to Lavaleer that I was terminating his services and cancelling all agreements he or Carlene had made on behalf of my father. I explained I had stopped taking his calls.

Sills and Mallard kept their hunches close to their vests. After they left, I turned on the TV. The story of the two murders was just breaking. The newsroom broadcaster reported that Gunnar Hyde had previously been charged with several crimes, including assault causing bodily harm, burglary, and operating a meth lab. Lavaleer had been his attorney and had gotten him off each time. The reporter at the murder scene said knowledgeable sources were theorizing that Wally Lavaleer's death might be related to a hotel construction deal he had been working on. According to the news, the police were taking a closer look at the possibility that my stepmother's death was also related to the same deal. The murder of Carlene, Lavaleer, and Hyde were likely carried out by professionals. The unofficial source reported that the police were inclined to believe that Constable Valerie Runge had not been connected to Carlene's death. They were theorizing that she might have found the weapon used to kill Carlene at the crime scene. They thought Valerie might have simply pocketed it and later used it to shoot Nessa and Melanie.

I still had too many unanswered questions to know what to think.

The last thing Alice did before going out the door was take her black dress from the closet. "I'm going to save it for the next time we see each other," she said.

"Okay."

I walked her to her car. We embraced and mused for a second about whether we had time for one last quickie, but each of us had places to go and things to do.

I watched her drive off.

The sky overhead was a bright cerulean blue with little wisps of clouds. To the north, in the direction that Alice turned as she exited the driveway, I could see the plume of mist hovering over the falls like a volcano getting ready to blow.

I picked up the newspaper on the way inside. After the turn of events over the last few days, I wasn't at all surprised to find that I had won all five of the bets I had placed with Frankie the day before.

Sometimes life was like that. I was in the lucky zone again. I had been there before.

I felt omnipotent. I felt nothing could touch me, which was good because I had one more piece of business to take care of.

I reloaded the .22 and drove to the quiet street where Duane Morthwell lived.

As expected, his ancient, rusting Camaro sat in his driveway.

I parked a couple of doors away, walked across the lawn of the abandoned house, slipped the lock on the side door with my screwdriver, and pulled the door open slowly to keep the hinges from squeaking.

Once inside, I moved cautiously with the .22 in my hand. I crossed the kitchen to the hallway. I could hear Morthwell snoring in the bedroom.

Two more steps and I was standing in the doorway, watching him sleep. He was wearing a faded black T-shirt and briefs. He was lying on his stomach with his arms folded under his head. The blanket was twisted between his legs. The pillow was on the floor. There were no weapons anywhere in sight.

I picked the channel changer off the dresser and watched him stir when I clicked on the TV. As I cranked up the sound, he first adjusted his arms, rolled over, and then, sat straight up, startled.

"What the fuck?" he gasped, eyes raking across the room from the TV to the gun and me.

"Put both hands on top of your head and lock your fingers together."

He did as he was told.

"What do you want?"

I flipped channels until I found the local news. They were about to repeat the story of the murders of Lavaleer and Hyde.

"I want you to see something interesting."

He watched the news segment in silence.

When it was over, I switched off the TV and put down the remote. I kept the gun trained on him.

"You going to shoot me?" he asked without emotion.

"That depends on whether or not I get your copies of the tape."

"They're in the dresser. Top drawer. One's a copy of the edited version. The other's the original."

I opened the drawer and found two tapes and an old cassette player/recorder.

"That's all the copies?"

"Yeah, except for the one I gave the shyster. No reason to make more."

"How'd you make the duplicates?"

"Off the tape deck in the living room."

It made sense. "What did you do with the jewelry you stole from my stepmother?"

"It's in a plastic bag in the bottom drawer."

I opened the bottom drawer and found the jewelry. I pulled the bag out of the drawer and held it up.

"I thought I told you to dump this in the river."

"Haven't gotten around to it yet."

"You should learn to follow directions."

"I'll make a note of it. So, what happens now? Can I put my hands down? They're getting tired."

"Sure. Just leave them in your lap where I can see them."

He lowered his hands. "You gonna shoot me now?"

"Tell me what happened when you went to my stepmother's."

"What do you want to know?"

"About the other gun. The 9 millimeter. You don't have it, do you?"

"No."

"You never had it, did you?"

He shook his head.

"You didn't shoot Carlene."

"I shot her afterward."

"With the .38. The gun I gave you. After she was dead."

"Yeah."

"What happened?"

He scratched his tangled locks. "I did like you said. I got there around three. I parked in the driveway next door and walked over to her place. The shyster's Mercedes wasn't there, but your stepmother's Lexus was parked out front."

"Why didn't you abort like we agreed?"

"There was another car parked out front. A red Miata. I thought Lavalcer might have switched rides. I snuck up on the rear of the house and looked in to check things out. I could see across the kitchen into the dining room. I saw Nessa Wiley talking to a woman who looked like the woman you described as your stepmother."

"Nessa?"

"Yeah, Nessa Wiley. From high school. Thin chick with long legs, small tits. Screwed and gave head to anyone who asked. Not me, never asked, but I heard she made a porn film."

I forgot he would know her, too, from high school. "Who told you about the porn film?"

"Can't remember, but I definitely know it was her at the house."

"Go on."

"I was only there a couple of seconds when I heard another car drive up out front. Your stepmother left the dining room and came back a couple of seconds later with another woman. The other woman was yelling shit at your stepmother, calling her a whore. The next thing I knew the other woman pulled a gun and shot your stepmother in the chest. Nessa was freaking out. I was too stunned to leave. Nessa got the other woman calmed down and then marched her toward the front door, telling her, 'We'll just go home. No one will know it was you.'"

"What did this other woman look like?"

"Tall, husky, blond. I didn't know who she was at the time, but later, I recognized her face on TV. It was the constable, Nessa's partner, the one who shot Nessa and your lawyer."

"And they took the gun with them?"

"Yeah."

"So you went inside after they left, put another bullet in Carlene, and stole the money and jewelry from the bedroom upstairs?"

He shrugged. I could see a little smile forming on his lips. "I had a deal with you. I figured if I could implicate the shyster it would be just as good as killing him. What I really wanted to do was get the money you promised me and split. I ain't cut out for this James Bond shit."

"You got cute with the tapes."

"That was only for backup. If you brought me the money this afternoon like I asked, I'd be gone. I'm a lot of things, but I ain't stupid." He looked at his hands, then back at me. "And now, I'm probably dead."

"If you feel like dying, you'll have to do it on your own watch."

"What's that supposed to mean?"

I reached in my pocket, pulled out a packet of money and dropped it on the bed beside him. "This is your once-in-a-lifetime chance to prove what you've been telling yourself all your life."

"What's that?"

"That you're smart. There's eighteen thousand dollars in the packet. You took two from me the other night. This is the balance I said I'd pay you. Technically, I don't owe you anything because you didn't kill Carlene or Wally, but the fact is I want you out of here. I don't ever want to see you in this part of the country again. Understand?"

"I'll be gone by sundown," he said, without taking his eyes off me. "Count on it."

I wasn't worried. Morthwell had the raw, animal instincts to know when the deck was stacked against him. Could he make trouble for me down the road? Very unlikely. If he ever told anyone what really happened he would probably end up in a straitjacket. More to the point, he had no way of proving anything he said about me. And if he did talk, he'd end up implicating himself in the Johnson murder.

I stuffed the tapes and the jewelry into my coat pocket and left.

CHAPTER 52

STILL CHEWING ON WHAT MORTHWELL TOLD ME, I stopped by the nurse's station at the hospital. Melanie's condition had been upgraded to stable. She was sleeping.

The policeman guarding Nessa's door was gone. Nessa was awake. Her eyes were red. She said she'd been up most of the night crying over the loss of her partner.

"I'm sorry about Valerie," I told her.

"I am, too," she said. "She never should have hooked up with me. I guess I'm just not ready to settle down."

"You want to tell me what really happened?"

She pursed her lips. "I thought everyone knew. It's been in the papers and all over the TV. Like I told you, Valerie and I went to Melanie to get our wills redone. We ended up in an argument, and the next thing I knew, I'm hiring Melanie to represent me in a divorce."

"I'm talking about the night you showed up at my stepmother's house. The night I was supposed to meet you at the hotel. The night I stood you up."

"I don't know what you're talking about."

"The night that Valerie shot Carlene."

She froze.

"Nessa, believe me. It was the best thing that could have happened to Carlene. The last thing I want to do is make trouble for you. I just want to know. Valerie didn't find the pistol at the murder scene the next day. She brought it with her."

Nessa shook her head but it was the kind of shake that seemed to be saying: "Yes, yes, but it's too hard to discuss."

"You weren't just getting a divorce from Valerie, were you, Nessa? You were Melanie's secret lover."

Her eyes were teary. "What can I tell you, Harry? I'm a slut. I like to fuck. I met Melanie, and I couldn't help myself. She's the sexiest woman I've ever crossed paths with."

"And Valerie found out."

"She suspected something. She started to follow me."

"That day you came to see me and invited me to meet you at the hotel, you thought she was onto you?"

She nodded.

"And that's why I couldn't get a date with Melanie. You and Melanie already had one. But then you cancelled on her once you set up the date with me. That's why she called me back."

"I was protecting her. It was too dangerous for me to see her. Valerie had a gun that she'd picked up from one of her busts."

"The Chinese copy of the Russian 9 millimeter?"

"Yes, and she said if she ever caught me in bed with another lover, she'd kill her. She said she could get away with it because she was a cop and the gun was untraceable. I'm a law enforcement officer, too, Harry. I know how these things work."

"So, what was I? The decoy? If she had found us in bed that night at the hotel would she have shot me instead of Carlene?"

"No, Harry. She didn't take my screwing around with guys very seriously. I'm bisexual, but she was convinced that I was just confused. I was in need of a good lay, and you fit the bill because I couldn't risk seeing Melanie."

"You really are a slut."

"What can I say?"

"I don't mean that in a bad way, Nessa. I find it endearing. But what I don't quite get is where Carlene fit in."

"I'll tell you, Harry. I owe you that much, because in a way it was a little bit your fault. But I swear if anyone ever asks me about it, I'll deny it to my dying day."

"My fault?"

"You stood me up. I was horny. I was drinking too much. I was sitting in what was supposed to be our hotel room pissed out of my mind. I decided to go looking for you. I knew you lived at your father's place, but I didn't realize that you stayed in the guesthouse. Carlene was downstairs. She heard me drive up and opened the door just as I got out of the car."

"She let you in the house?"

"She recognized me from yoga classes. Carlene and I belonged to the same health club. Carlene wanted to know what I was doing there. I just told her the first thing that popped into my head. I told her I was looking for you because you owed me money. She found that interesting and invited me in. She told me she happened to be downstairs because her boyfriend had just left. They'd just had a fight. We started talking, and the next thing I knew the doorbell rang. Carlene went to answer it, and moments later, Valerie came barging into the dining room pushing Carlene and screaming she was going to kill her. Carlene was half hanging out of her bathrobe, which didn't help. I tried to reason with Valerie, but she was beyond reason."

"She took out the Russian knockoff and shot Carlene dead?"

Nessa nodded. "She was going to kill herself. I talked her out of it. It was my fault. All I could think of was getting Valerie and me out of there."

"But you had the presence of mind to pick up the spent shell casing."

She nodded. "You should have been a cop, Harry."

"Maybe in another life. Go on."

"I got Valerie to her car and told her to drive home. I followed behind in my car. That morning, she went into work early and made sure she was one of the first officers on the scene once Carlene's body had been discovered."

"Where's the gun she used to kill Carlene?"

"I guess it was on her when she went over the falls. I don't really know."

"Does Melanie know about this?"

"She doesn't know any of it. I just needed to get it off my chest."

"Thanks for telling me, Nessa."

"How'd you find out?"

"You don't need to know. Rest assured, your secret's safe with me."

"I owe you."

"Consider us even. What about you and Melanie? Are you two likely to stay together after this?"

"I don't know, Harry, but I'll tell you, she's the best sex I've ever had, and she's a lot of fun. So we'll just have to wait and see. The greatest thing about her besides the sex is that she isn't crazy jealous."

Nessa was fading rapidly by then. She was fighting to keep her eyes open. I was tempted to ask her about her rumored movie career but decided to leave it for another conversation.

She was asleep, snoring softly with her mouth slightly open a few seconds later.

I left. I tried Melanie's room again. She was awake but still pretty doped up. She had enough wires and tubes attached to her to launch her into space.

"Hey," I said, sitting beside her and taking hold of her hand. "I hear you're going to be all right."

Her fingers moved against the palm of my hand.

"We'll get together when this is all over. Maybe get married if you don't have anything better to do," I joked.

"Don't make me laugh," she whispered. "It hurts like hell."

Even hurting like hell, she could barely keep her eyes open.

"I should go. You need your sleep."

She nodded.

"You need anything from the outside world?"

"Bring me some you-know-what next time." She managed a tiny grin as her eyelids strained to stay open.

That's my girl, I thought. I leaned down and kissed her on the forehead. She was already asleep. I left feeling good, knowing she would recover.

CHAPTER 53

I PICKED UP A COUPLE OF SANDWICHES AT TONY'S.

On the way to the nursing home to visit my dad, I thought, holy shit. I set out to kill someone, and I believed I'd successfully done it. Then, I end up solving the murder that I thought I'd committed, and I discover I hadn't done it after all.

Clive was in a sour mood. He said Gina was sleeping with at least three other guys.

"We agreed not to see each other," he told me, "And this job's really beginning to suck. I'm getting tired of dead people." The bed beside my father's was vacant again.

I might have offered him a job on the spot if not for the fact that I wanted him to continue to look after my dad. Clive was the only one in the nursing home who seemed to give a genuine shit about him. On the other hand, I could use a good loyal man like Clive. I hedged my bets.

"If you end up quitting here, come see me. Once the museum is up and running again, I may have an opening. Right now, I want to make sure you give my father all the attention he needs." I took a roll of bills out of my pocket, counted off a thousand dollars, and insisted he take it.

"Your father is in good hands. I promise. Perhaps on my days off I could come by and learn more about your business. I've never been there, but I've looked it up. It's on all the tourist websites. I might have a few ideas. I don't know if you would be interested."

"Of course I'm interested, Clive."

He smiled shyly. "Can I tell you one of my ideas now?"

I could see the childlike hope in his eyes.

"Sure."

"Over the months we've been talking and from what I've been reading in the business magazines, it sounds to me like you need something to attract young people. Optimally, it should appeal to both sexes and parents, too."

"Exactly. You've identified the problem. Now, how do you fix it?" I turned to go.

"There's more. You want to hear it?"

"Go ahead."

"I would start by changing the name."

"MurderLand is what we're selling. It's the brand. Like Coke or Apple or—"

"PeaceLand."

"PeaceLand?" I was stunned. I didn't know what to say.

"Yes, PeaceLand—a museum dedicated to memorabilia and displays of famous martyrs for peace. Maybe you split it into two different floors or different corridors on each floor so people can pick and choose where to go. You get the thrill seekers who want to see gore in one place, and the others can go through, avoid the disturbing exhibits, and see mementoes of good deeds, personal artifacts, and relics of the martyrs. I'd exhibit the lives and deaths of universal martyrs like Mahatma Gandhi, President Kennedy, Martin Luther King, Jr., and John Lennon. I would recreate the terrifying moments of the anonymous student standing in front of a tank during the Tiananmen Square Massacre. I'd rent visual reality headsets to the clients to give them a perspective of what it must have felt like moments before the tank crushed the young man to death. I would have a room dedicated to the students killed in North American and Canadian schools by acts of violence. The last three exhibits before the exit would display stories about peace advocates Albert Einstein, Nelson Mandela, and Malala Yousafzai."

"But they're not martyrs for peace. They're survivors for peace."

"Exactly," he grinned. "The last three exhibits leave the customers with a good feeling, a feeling of hope. PeaceLand becomes part of the future. It fits right into the theme here in Niagara Falls. Danger. A natural wonder. A peaceful border. The Rainbow Bridge. The Peace Bridge. It all works together."

"Wow." My head was exploding by the time he finished. I could see the future. "You put a lot of thought into this. I think you're onto something."

His grin widened. "Thank you. But I also need your advice on another matter."

"Of course."

"How do I make a good idea like this pay off?"

My father let out what sounded like a little laugh at that moment. When I glanced over I could have sworn I saw the tiniest grin on his face.

"We'll talk," I promised Clive. I made an appointment with him to come by the museum on his next day off.

Before leaving the nursing home, I borrowed Clive's phone to call Frankie, reminding myself that I still hadn't replaced my old phone. I told Frankie I wanted to swing by to pick up my money. From the way Frankie tried to stall me, I knew he would have trouble putting such a large amount together on such short notice. I felt a sense of delight in making him squirm for a change. I finally told him, "Send Joey and Pinkie over tomorrow to deliver the money." The idea of turning Joey and Pinkie into my errand boys had a nice symmetry to it.

I knew it was going to be a great day when the radio newscaster broke the news of a gang war that been raging for the past twenty-four hours between Big Mo's gang and a rival gang. The war had been sparked by the mysterious disappearance of Big Mo and Goose. Members of Big Mo and Goose's gang believed Big Mo and Goose had been killed by a rival gang. They had attacked the clubhouse of the rival gang, killing three of its members. The other gang had retaliated and killed three from Big Mo's gang.

I felt a sense of civic pride in helping to reduce the gang population in the Niagara Peninsula.

Returning to my office, I sat down and started to scratch out a list of pros and cons for changing MurderLand into PeaceLand. As engaging as this was, I was also feeling a little down. I wished I had my dad beside me to talk about the future of MurderLand. I was also feeling more than a little lonely without Pilot hovering nearby. So, when the front door buzzer sounded, I welcomed the distraction.

I looked through the window in front. Outside on the steps was a guy about thirty and stocky with a tanned, square face, and thick black hair,

He was wearing an expensive camel hair coat. A black Jaguar with New York plates was parked at the curb in front of the no parking sign.

I opened the door and was pummeled by the smell of aftershave lotion.

"Mr. Holiday?" the man asked in a take-charge voice that reminded me of Lavaleer.

"Yes."

"My name's Victor Leo from Buffalo. My father is a major investor in New Heights Hotels. We were working with Mr. Lavaleer and your step-mother for six months on redeveloping this property. Can we talk?"

"Sure. Come in."

As we walked toward the office, he glanced around with a frown that suggested he was already envisioning the best way to tear the place down.

"Nice trophies," he said entering the office. He walked up to Old Smokey and patted his head. "I bagged a grizzly in British Columbia last year. It weighed almost eight hundred pounds, which is big for a female."

He threw his coat over the back of the couch and sat down in the chair on the other side of my desk like he already owned the place.

I sat opposite him.

"You bowl?" he asked, studying Pilot's bowling ball in the ashtray on my desk.

"It belonged to a friend who died recently."

"I'm sorry," he said, not sounding very sorry.

"What can I do for you? You said you wanted to talk."

He straightened his cherry, gray, and cream-colored tie. His suit looked custom-made.

"I know it's a little soon after the death of Mr. Lavaleer, but we wanted to touch base with you and let you know that we're fully committed to going ahead with the hotel project."

"That's nice, Mr. Leo, but didn't Mr. Lavaleer explain to you that I wasn't interested?"

"I don't see how you couldn't be." His eyelids dropped a notch. He went on for several minutes explaining the intricacies of the deal and how much money I would make compared to what I could make from the property as is. It was clear that he knew his stuff.

"Sometimes it isn't about money," I said. "You wouldn't happen to know the secret of happiness would you?"

"I know what would make my father and me really happy, Mr. Holiday. Your signature on the final agreement that I've been working on for months." No, he definitely doesn't know, I thought as he rattled on. "My family's invested a great amount of time and money in this deal. I'd like to remind you that your organization and my organization have an agreement in principle already."

I didn't like the threatening tone, but I remained dead calm. "You really want to go to court and fight about what my father's late ex-lawyer and my late stepmother may or may not have said to you? The bottom line is that the papers that needed to be signed haven't been signed. If you sue me, I'll counter sue, and we'll be doing it in my jurisdiction."

He drummed his thick, polished nails on the desktop. "I understand you're in no position to sue."

"You understand wrong, Mr. Leo."

He leaned forward with his fingers spread on the desktop like he was getting ready to pounce. His eyes had grown cold and malevolent.

"You don't know who you're dealing with, do you, Mr. Holiday?"

"Who would that be?"

"You really think the unfortunate deaths of your stepmother and Mr. Lavaleer were accidents?"

I wanted to laugh. This guy in his fancy suit actually thought he was going to scare me by pretending he'd had Carlene and Wally killed. The shit must be really hitting the fan for him back home, I reckoned. This was probably his deal—his and Wally Lavaleer's—and it was crashing and burning right before his eyes.

"You aren't threatening me, are you?"

"When I get done explaining what you need to know, I think you'll get the point. I have interests to look after, and they include this place, whether you like it or not. So here's how it's going to work. You—"

I could have let him go on. It might have been amusing, but I was finding him tiring. Before he could see it coming, I reached out, grabbed his tie halfway up, and yanked it down hard toward the desk. With my other hand, I slammed the ice pick down as hard as I could.

It went through the center of his tie and deep into the wood, pinning him to the top of the desk.

As I expected, Victor Leo immediately jerked his head back, tightening the tie like a noose around his neck, choking him.

I pressed my face close to his and said, "*No* means *no*, Mr. Leo."

"You're choking me to death." He spat out the words as his fingers clawed at his collar and tie.

I'd made my point. He was unlikely to come back any time soon. I yanked the ice pick out of the desk.

Arms flailing, he flew backward with such force that he knocked over his chair and landed on the floor.

Unfortunately, he also knocked over the bowling ball, which rolled off the desk before I could grab it.

Instead of bouncing as I expected, it shattered into several large chunks. I saw something roll out of the center and disappear under the liquor cabinet, but I had no time to look for it.

I stepped around the desk to the other side and pulled Mr. Leo to his feet. I grabbed his camel hair coat, escorted him to the front door, and threw him and his coat outside.

"Don't ever come back here," I said. He stood facing me, stroking his tie with one hand, too stunned to move until I started toward him. He scrambled into his car before I could reach him.

I waited until he drove off before I headed inside.

I'd called his bluff, and he'd folded. I had no worries about him returning.

I was enjoying being decisive. Money and my newfound killer genes were giving me extra confidence. I wondered if it might be an interesting idea to add a virtual reality experience at the museum where you time-traveled and tried to change history by preventing some of the crimes exhibited at PeaceLand. Clive's idea of changing the name to PeaceLand continued to intrigue me. The kid had a head for business.

Once in the office, I examined the pieces of the bowling ball and realized that it was hollow like a coconut but much less durable. It was made out of plaster, not resin, and weighted inside with lead to give it the feel of the real thing. I suspected the plaster was the same or similar to what Pilot used to firm up his taxidermy specimens.

But why would anyone—presumably Pilot—make a hollowed-out bowling ball, I wondered as I worked my hand beneath the liquor cabinet to retrieve what had rolled under there.

At first, when I grabbed it, I thought it must be a small stuffed animal of some sort.

Only when I pulled it all the way out did I realize what I had in my hand.

A shrunken head.

I didn't need to look that hard to know it wasn't a Jivaro head.

No. It was definitely one of Pilot's jobs. In my hands, I was holding the unmistakable little bulldog-faced head of James "Jimmy" R. Hoffa.

"Nothing is ever what it appears to be," I heard Pilot whispering in my ear even though I knew no one was there.

ACKNOWLEDGMENTS

I would like to acknowledge and thank the following people who spoke or corresponded with me, encouraged me, read early versions of *MurderLand*, offered suggestions, or helped in other ways:

Al Abramson, Salem Alaton, Rosemary Aubert, John Barr, John Beck, Bruce Beery, Susan Belany, Nathan Bress, Howard Brody, Richard Brownell, Cynthia Coulter, Andrew Covato, Dan Covato, Jon Covato, Larissa Covato, Michael Covato, Richard Covato, Barbara Dinger, James Dubro, Alex Dukay, Jill Fitzgerald, Joan Frantschuk, Alan Glazner, Linda Glazner, Raymond Glazner, Dwight Golan, Helaine Golan, Terry Guerin, Linda Hatch, William Hatch, Madeleine Harris-Callway, Phil Haynes, Uno Hoffmann, Robert Kerr, Dan Kramon, Kay Kramon, Bill Kurchak, Iris Leigh, Miriam Leigh, Nathan Leigh, William Leigh, Kiu Leung, Tom Levin, D. J. McIntosh, Erin McMullan, Earl Manners, Alex Markman, Paul D. Marks, Peter McGarvey, Christopher G. Moore, Jerry Pruitt, Mark Pultman, Garry Rusoff, Baiba St. John, Richard St. John, Alicia Scarth, Joanie Shirriff, Ross Skoggard, Eric Slone, Coleen Steele, Elizabeth Vihnanek, Diane Wanat, Cindy Weiss, Jeff Weiss, Jon Wolfe, and others who I unintentionally may have missed.

ABOUT JOSEPH MARK GLAZNER

MurderLand is Joseph Mark Glazner's eighth mystery novel. He has written seven others under his own name and his pen name, Joseph Louis, including the Shamus and Arthur Ellis nominated *Madelaine* (Bantam Books, NY, 1987).

Glazner's new thriller, *MurderLand*, marks his return to some of his favorite themes—revenge, greed, conspiracy theories, love, hate, and desperate characters willing to commit murder. This time, he writes from inside the head of Harry Holiday, his antihero and most irreverent character yet. Harry is an out-of-control, young businessman, gambler, and ladies' man, planning the perfect murder to save the family's business and himself. The family business—MurderLand—is a landmark but failing museum of murder and gangland exhibitions located in the heart of the old amusement and casino district of Niagara Falls, Canada.

The idea for a museum housing a world-class collection of shocking, murder-related objects grew out of memories of Glazner's mother, the beautiful, eldest child of immigrants, who supported her parents and siblings as a Seventh Avenue dress designer and sketcher during the Great Depression. In the late 1940s, after Glazner was born and the family had moved to rural Warrenville, New Jersey, his mother reinvented herself as a businesswoman, small-town politician, civic volunteer, and inveterate collector of antiques, vintage clothes, costume jewelry, art glass, and anything broken that she thought might one day be repaired but never was.

Following in his mother's footsteps, young Glazner collected old swords and guns to display on the walls in his basement. He also collected contemporary guns to shoot in the fields and woods around his family's home. Unlike Harry Holiday, he had no heart for hunting or killing. He ruled out the military, left home at eighteen for Los Angeles, and became a writer.

The struggles of the small business owner in *MurderLand* are a backhanded homage to Glazner's father, a charismatic, high-school dropout from the mean streets of Brooklyn, who became a manufacturer of gloves during the Great Depression in New York City. Glazner's father moved the shop to Plainfield, New Jersey when gangsters tried to extort money from the business in the early 1940s. As a teenager, young Glazner worked on the line in the New Jersey shop as a presser and cutter in the early 1960s. From that vantage point, he witnessed firsthand his father's valiant but doomed efforts to keep the business alive while battling early onset Parkinson's disease.

Glazner's interest in Niagaa Falls as a setting for *MurderLand* can be traced back to his first visit there when he was ten. On a family trip to the falls, Glazner crossed his first international border and was amazed and intrigued by the little bit of Canada he saw on the other side. Years later after moving to Toronto, he began to visit the Niagara region regularly as an escape from the big city and soon realized it was the perfect place to locate his fictional *MurderLand*. Niagara was a border region dividing America and Canada, each with its own subtly different but overlapping cultures. Its world-renowned natural wonder—the falls—was both exciting and dangerous. As a tourist region, it catered to the rich-and-famous and commoners alike. The old amusement district at the falls reminded Glazner of the amusement parks, country fairs, traveling carnivals, sideshows, and roadside museums of his youth in America.

The inspiration for using some of the Prohibition and Depression-era gangsters mentioned in *MurderLand* came from tenuous connections to Glazner's antecedents and stories he heard as a child. Owney "The Killer" Madden, the owner of the Cotton Club, helped finance the prototype of an invention patented by Glazner's Grandpa Ike. Glazner's Uncle Harry, the high-school, one-handed chin-up champion of Brooklyn, was a childhood friend of Abe "Kid Twist" Reles, the first field marshal of Murder Incorporated. Arnold Rothstein, the gambler who fixed the 1919 World Series, occasionally escorted Glazner's Great Aunt Fanny on visits to a Manhattan jail where Great Uncle Lew was serving a year for vehicular manslaughter during the Roaring Twenties. Great Uncle Lew, a slum kid who went to the prestigious Hotchkiss boarding school on an athletic scholarship, later had a line of credit from bootlegger Waxey Gordon to sell liquor during Prohibition to his old Park Avenue classmates. Great Uncle Harry (not to be confused with Uncle Harry) and Harry's stepfather, Ted Joffe, (Glazner's step-great grandfather) had a concession to sell liquor during Prohibition under the umbrella of Abner "Longy" Zwillman, the Al Capone of New Jersey.

Like his main character Harry Holiday, Glazner picked up street wisdom from older mentors. Great Uncle Murray, a battle-hardened rifleman in World War II, and Glazner's Uncle Sam, a combat GI who had been force-marched across Germany as a prisoner of war, both told him the way to survive the worst of times was to be able to laugh at yourself and make fun of the devil while the bullets were flying.

Glazner's father, a man who loved Edgar Allan Poe and hated guns, showed him how to act cool under fire when he swapped himself for three Boy Scouts being held hostage by a crazy, shotgun-wielding redneck during a camping trip gone wrong.

In addition to writing novels, Glazner has been a tabloid writer, journalist, screenwriter, and independent communications adviser, forecaster, and speechwriter for Canadian and US corporations and governments in banking, telecommunications, and many other fields.

Glazner is a graduate of the University of Southern California (BA, psychology, *magna cum laude*, 1967) and a member of the Phi Beta Kappa Society. He lives in Toronto, Canada where he continues to write crime novels and memoirs. A glimpse into the life Glazner led in his twenties during the early years of the sexual revolution, free love, and the Vietnam War is portrayed in his memoir, *Life After America*, which recounts his arrival and his first two years in Canada (1967-1969) as a war resister, FBI fugitive, new Canadian immigrant, and John Lennon's early collaborator on John and Yoko's "War Is Over" peace initiative.

www.ingramcontent.com/pod-product-compliance
Lightning Source LLC
Chambersburg PA
CBHW071204100726
47908CB00002B/502